ANGEL EYE

ANGEL EYE

a novel

Madeleine Nakamura

CANIS MAJOR BOOKS

Book design by Mark E. Cull

Library of Congress Cataloging-in-Publication Data

Names: Nakamura, Madeleine, author.
Title: Angel Eye: a novel / Madeleine Nakamura.
Description: First edition. | Pasadena, CA: Canis Major Books, 2025.
Identifiers: LCCN 2024033393 (print) | LCCN 2024033394 (ebook) | ISBN
   9781939096210 (paperback) | ISBN 9781939096227 (ebook)
Subjects: LCGFT: Fantasy fiction. | Novels.
Classification: LCC PS3614.A5737 A84 2025 (print) | LCC PS3614.A5737
   (ebook) | DDC 813/.6—dc23/eng/20240724
LC record available at https://lccn.loc.gov/2024033393
LC ebook record available at https://lccn.loc.gov/2024033394

The National Endowment for the Arts, the Los Angeles County Arts Commission, the Ahmanson Foundation, the Dwight Stuart Youth Fund, the Max Factor Family Foundation, the Pasadena Tournament of Roses Foundation, the Pasadena Arts & Culture Commission and the City of Pasadena Cultural Affairs Division, the City of Los Angeles Department of Cultural Affairs, the Audrey & Sydney Irmas Charitable Foundation, the Kinder Morgan Foundation, the Meta & George Rosenberg Foundation, the Albert and Elaine Borchard Foundation, the Adams Family Foundation, the Riordan Foundation, Amazon Literary Partnership, the Sam Francis Foundation, and the Mara W. Breech Foundation partially support Red Hen Press.

First Edition
Published by Canis Major Books
An imprint of Red Hen Press
Pasadena, CA
www.redhen.org

For a departed friend

ANGEL EYE

Chapter 1

I was eating breakfast with the other addicts and akratics in the Westbrook solarium when Dr. Thirkeld came to say good morning.

"You're looking so well today, Adrien," he said. He reached out to pat me on the shoulder.

I dropped my flimsy wooden spoon with a clatter and turned to face him. "If you touch me," I said, "I will be forced to bite you."

The paperwork for a biting incident would be extensive. We both knew this. He put his hand away; the patients within earshot of my threat looked pointedly in the other direction.

Thirkeld watched me with raised eyebrows. "Violent behavior isn't tolerated here, Adrien. Nor threats."

"Then let's all agree to keep our hands and teeth to ourselves," I suggested, and picked up my spoon again.

"Now, Adrien—"

"Stop using my name like that. At the very least, you may call me Desfourneaux." Family-name basis was a comfortable place to be with the solarium doctors. It helped give the illusion of an even playing field, something to cling to.

Thirkeld grimaced. I'd finally gotten through to him. "All right, Desfourneaux. A pleasure as always." With that, he was off to check on his other patients, weaving through the rows of simple, bare tables in the dining hall to seek out whomever else he wanted to speak with.

The problem with committing to a care program is that once the first grand gesture is made, once you've come crawling through the solarium doors on bloody knees, the time must actually be served. I'd done almost two months, and now that I was nearing the end of my stay, I was running short on politesse. I'd meant, at first, to be outpatient; I'd meant to be done within a few weeks. Unfortunately, sobriety and stability have their own dictates.

To my left, one of my fellow patients *tsk*ed at me, an older woman with iron-gray hair named Grette. I liked Grette; she was sharp, although her lucidity waned from time to time. "You shouldn't push him," she said.

I raised my glass of watered-down solarium orange juice to her. "He oversedates you, you know."

"And how can you tell?" she asked, brow furrowed.

My smile was not quite genuine. "I used to be a doctor, remember?"

Her expression cleared. She remembered again. "Well, good for you."

I'm afraid I've given the wrong impression of myself. I'm usually better-tempered, more even-tongued. The solarium was keeping me from my teaching job, however. The surveillance, the blank walls, the smell of sanative alcohol and aseptika, the hum of too many voices contained in the same space—I needed to get away.

I played with my spoon and watched my peers, trying to decide whom I would miss when I was out, and whom I would not. There were only a few of the first category. I didn't resent the others, but a solarium isn't the best place to make friends.

The low drone of conversation sent me into a reverie of distraction until Thirkeld was on his way out of the dining area. He passed me again and slowed. I closed my eyes for a moment, regretting my irritability. If he were inclined to be vindictive, he'd make the rest of my stay less tolerable. I enjoyed a lax standard of observation by this point, and he could change that if he wished.

He left me suspended in uncertainty for a few long moments. I suspected he was relishing it. Something in my expression displeased him; he sighed. "You know, you could stand to be more cooperative," he told me, brushing a piece of lint from the shoulder of his blue doctor's coat. "There are far worse places to be than Westbrook. I was trained at the Rheinhold solarium, and let me tell you, we didn't have to put up with *biting*."

"I thought threats weren't tolerated here," I said.

"It's not a threat. I'm asking you to appreciate your position. You could be chained to a wall in some Cambyssian madhouse, dying of sepsis. Have some perspective."

I could only be silent.

Thirkeld's jaw tightened, then relaxed; he gave me a conciliatory nod. He had made his point. He was satisfied. "I meant to tell you that your keeper and personal doctor are coming to see you later today. Around four."

My throat closed involuntarily, a quick gulp; I turned away. He strode off.

Grette propped her chin up on her hand and watched me, her cataracted eyes narrowed. "Were you like *that* when you were a doctor?"

"No," I said.

"Hmm." The intensity of her gaze had not lessened.

I couldn't quell the unaccountable need to defend myself. Thirkeld could consider me a rabid animal, and that was tolerable, but I couldn't stand to have another patient compare me to him. "I wasn't like that," I said.

My weary tone satisfied her. She moved on. "You still have your new keeper? The Vigil boy?"

I swallowed my remaining humiliation to answer. "Still Gennady, yes," I said.

She tapped her temple. "Something's not right with him."

Anyone who'd met Gennady Richter knew that. "Yes," I said mildly. "But look around. Remember what they say about glass houses." I nodded up at the expansive solarium windows.

After a moment of deliberation, Grette snagged a piece of burned toast off my plate and took a bite. I murmured a halfhearted rebuke. "You tell him hello for me," she said with her mouth full. "And Dr. Tyrrhena too."

"I'll tell them," I said. My appetite, always unreliable, was gone. I left Grette with the rest of my food and went to my room to while away the time until my visitors came.

My solarium room was small and bare but livable, painted powder blue. The windows were wide, if barred, and I had a door that closed. There were, as Thirkeld had reminded me, far worse places to be. It wasn't my house; it had no workshop and no bookshelves, no kitchen, but I had forfeited all that voluntarily in exchange for my reparation.

It had been worth it. The gears of my mind spun smoothly again. The nepenthe was out of my system; I no longer shook or lay awake at night craving, and I reminded myself of that grace as I sat motionless on the bed and waited for my friends. Voluntary, voluntary. It had all been voluntary, and I had only one more week before I was done and could go back to work. Before my place in the world was no longer that of a junkie daimoniac.

The less flattering words for the things I am circle, often, in silence.

A dull flare of pain traveled up my arms; I smoothed my hand gingerly up the intricate fractal scarring on my right wrist. The patterns ran up the inside of each arm, branching over my chest and back. The worst pain had eased by then, but I sensed there would be no further improvement.

The sting reached the end of its path and burned out, leaving only a vague tingle when I touched my wrist again. My mind turned relentlessly back to the limited dimensions of my room, the featurelessness, the time turning stale. Westbrook was overcrowded and lonely in equal measure, and I was more eager for my company than I cared to admit.

When they arrived, I didn't even need to get up and open the door. Gennady burst in without warning.

I startled; he didn't notice. His rache hound, Lady, padded inside and curled up on the floor at my feet. She was small as far as the creatures went, and sweeter than most. When she showed her teeth in a wide yawn, I was no longer unsettled as I had been when I'd first met her and Gennady. "We're here," Gennady announced, dark-eyed, dark-haired, and black-clad, his Vigil saber at his hip.

I looked at the open door and back to Gennady. "I see that. In our talks about manners, have we covered knocking yet?"

He squinted, thinking it over. "Maybe. I forget."

"Wonderful." Despite my admonition, I was smiling. Gennady's careless honesty endeared me to him more than I liked to admit.

Malise Tyrrhena squeezed her way past Gennady and sat next to me on the bed. The day had grown humid; her tightly curled brown hair floated around her like a halo. "Any change, my dear?"

"There's been nothing so far," I said to her. No akratic episodes, very few scattered symptoms. My time in the solarium had been largely free of them: my daimon had gone silent.

"Good." Malise looked me over, a professional's gaze, evaluating me. Once she had made her judgment, she smiled and relaxed. "Thirkeld claims you threatened to bite him," she said.

Of course he'd told them. I wasn't sure what I'd expected. "Thirkeld is an idiot and a quack," I said delicately.

"Is he a liar?"

"He is not."

Gennady made a biting motion in the air, gnashing teeth forming an unpleasant grin. "Good job, Professor. Show 'em." At my feet, Lady thumped her tail in amusement. Their approval embarrassed me more than Malise's mild censure; I looked away.

"I know you're frustrated," Malise told me. "It's just another week." She reached out and straightened my glasses.

"I want to work," I said. "I want to sleep in my own bed—I can't stand the noise here. I miss my atelier."

Malise nodded. "It'll be waiting for you." She and Gennady had been house-sitting for me, although I wasn't entirely certain I could trust Gennady not to steal anything. I'd have to chalk up any losses to a fee for the service of maintaining the place.

Since Malise seemed to have no new concerns about my condition, I turned to Gennady. "So, keeper," I said dryly. "The doctor has spoken. What about you?"

He shrugged. "You seem fine to me. Don't see any needles hidden around here. You got any needles?"

I'd often thought of it, and there were ways to get around Westbrook's system—but I'd behaved. "I don't."

"Then I think you're good," he said. Lady chuffed softly, an affirmative echo.

Part of me was never able to relax until I heard the all-clear from my keeper, even if that keeper was Gennady. The job entails, partially, seeing what the akratic can't. An unwell mind can't be trusted to monitor itself.

I needed to change the subject. "What about you all?" I asked Gennady and Malise, with a glance for Lady as well.

"I'm keeping busy," Malise said. "Halicar's is doing all right. The Chirurgeonate is muddling along."

Busy was good; Malise loved her work. Still, I pressed. "You're happy?"

"I am," she said with a small smile. I found, to my relief, that I believed her. At the beginning of my solarium stay, she had visited me with dark circles under her eyes, the evidence of too many nights lost to worry. Now the haunted aspect had left her.

Gennady, meanwhile, was devoting himself to avoiding my gaze. "Gennady?" I asked. "How are *you*?"

He cleared his throat, uneasy. No one before me had ever bothered to ask him how he was feeling, and it often showed. On the floor, Lady raised her head and meowed. As his bonded rache, she could feel his discomfort intimately. "I'm fine," Gennady said. "I went to see Captain Corvier this week."

"How is he faring?" I asked. Privately, I hoped the answer was *not very well.*

He'd tried to kill Gennady. I'd stopped short of killing him in return, but that didn't mean I needed to wish the man good health.

"He's okay," Gennady said, then made a face. "I mean, not really. He's in prison. You know."

I did know. The Penumbra would not be kind to Corvier. The Penumbra was not kind to anyone. That was that.

I reached down to scratch Lady briefly behind her pointed, vulpine ears. It had taken some time before she or Gennady would even dream of allowing that, but now it passed without comment. "In any case, I'm glad to see you all," I said.

An errant spark of lightning drifted from one of my hands as my attention slipped. I brushed it away, and it winked gently out of existence. "Your magic," Malise said, watching the spark die.

I drew a breath and held it for a strained moment. "It's still broken," I admitted. There were few opportunities in the solarium to practice magic, but whenever I conjured more than a tiny thread of lightning, the resulting headache was debilitating.

A pull of distraction tugged me aside, insistent, insidious. I could picture the moment of the initial damage perfectly, as if months had not elapsed: the Penumbra's dirt yard churned red with blood, illuminated in vivid detail by my lightning bolt. I could still recall the sensation of Captain Corvier's dwindling life, a single thread of silk threaded through the bolt. Breaking my own spell to spare him had torn something open inside my magic. At first, it had seemed a gift; I was stronger, unrestrained—and then, in the days after the battle, the wellspring slowed. My power withered.

Malise saw that I was drifting and returned me to the present. "You'll figure it out," she said softly. She knew what the damage meant. Without magic, all that's left of me is deficit.

The itch to try again presented itself, and I held out a hand, calling a flickering strain of lightning into my palm. *Beautiful,* I thought. Nature's greatest art. Then, viperlike, the pain struck, a shredding, shrieking sensation; the lightning guttered and died. I bit back a whine as my fractal scars sparked.

"Dumb," Gennady said, casting a doubtful eye on me. "Stop doing that. You know it'll hurt every time."

I caught my breath with some difficulty. "I can't *not* try," I said irritably. "I'm a magician."

Malise sighed. "Once you're out of here, you'll be able to work on it more reliably."

"I'm a professor of magic. How am I going to teach my students if I can't manage any practical demonstrations?"

"You're only teaching theory classes when you get back," she reminded me. "You have plenty of choices that won't require any actual magic."

"It's humiliating."

Unlike the nepenthe, I hadn't chosen the rift in my magic. I resented its presence more than anything else. It seemed overzealous that I be punished for sparing a life.

"For now," Malise said, "just take your treatments and focus on going back to work."

The university had promised me that my position would still be waiting for me, more grace than I could have ever thought to ask for, but returning would have its aches and pains.

"Treatments," I said, and coughed. "Yes. If you please."

Gennady had been watching Malise soothe me with an expression of hesitant curiosity, like a child observing animals in a menagerie. Now he motioned to Lady; she stood, stretched, and went to join him. "You want us to leave for this?" he asked.

I blinked in surprise—that he had any concern for my privacy was unusual. He was genuinely improving. "If you like," I said, and gave him a bright smile.

Without saying goodbye, he swept out the door as abruptly as he'd entered.

"Quite a protégé you have in him," Malise said to me, and turned to place her hands on my temples. "Quite a keeper."

"It's worth a try." Gennady had earned my consideration.

She hummed and began to cast.

I'd been receiving treatment from Malise for many years, but I never reconciled with the ache and chill of it, the feeling of my mind shifting—a labyrinth constantly transforming to keep the daimon trapped. The hurt was necessary, akin to the pain of an immunizing injection. I closed my eyes and let her do her work, waiting for the magic to drain away.

When Malise was done, she drew back and framed my face for a moment before letting me go. "There. That should hold you for the week."

There were unexpected times when Malise's kindness nearly undid me. I ducked my head.

"You're all right," she said.

"Thank you, my dear."

A flash of déjà vu struck. We had been here before, the two of us. We would be here again one day. "Do you really think the Pharmakeia will be happy to have me back?" I asked.

She considered, rather than answering immediately, and I was grateful for that. "Yes," she said eventually. "You belong there."

"I was tried for witchcraft. People might not trust me."

"You were acquitted." Malise shrugged. "You were protecting the Pharmakeia. Everyone reasonable will understand that."

I could only offer a weak smile. Not everyone is reasonable.

"Chin up," she said. "You'll be there soon, if you can only avoid biting Thirkeld for the next week."

I crossed my arms. "He makes it difficult."

"I know he does."

"I'm not a real person to him," I said, sobering. "None of the patients are. He looks right through us."

Malise knew exactly what I meant. She had no solutions for me. "You're real to me," she said, simply.

It was enough. Speaking to Malise always brought a kind of relief nothing else did—the relief of slipping back into a native language after weeks spent abroad. The tension left me; we talked for a while longer about how work was going for her at the Chirurgeonate and what I thought of my fellow patients at Westbrook, enjoying each other's company. But eventually, as always, it came time for her to leave.

She gave my arm a squeeze and stood. "I'll try to visit again before you get out," she said. "And Adrien?"

"Mm."

"I'm proud of you. You know that."

I dug my nails into the skin of my right wrist, an enduring habit. "I was sober for nearly ten years, and I threw it away."

She countered me with ease. "You came here right after the dust settled. That matters."

"Maybe."

"It does."

I tried to nod.

Malise reached to gently separate my nails from my skin. "I have a gift for you, actually, before I go." She dug inside her pocket and came up with a delicate bracelet strung with many blue stone beads, small and spherical. A prayer bracelet—an angel eye.

She handed it to me; I took it with some confusion. "I'm not an astrolater," I said. "It's beautiful, but—"

"You don't need to pray with it. Just count the beads when you get anxious. It'll give you something to do besides scratch yourself. I'm an alienist; trust me. It's worth a try."

I did trust her. I slipped the bracelet onto my right wrist and turned it, passing the beads through my fingers. They were cool to the touch, pleasantly so. I could hide the angel eye beneath my sleeve easily enough, I found. One, two, three . . .

She smiled. "If it doesn't work, throw it away. But give it a chance."

"I will."

"Excellent." With that, she turned toward the door.

When she was gone, I lay back on the bed and counted the motes of dust floating in the air, the cracks in the ceiling. Every so often I raised my hand and tried to conjure more lightning—never full bolts, just flickers. It hurt; I kept trying. By the time I'd had enough, I'd summoned a migraine fit to bring tears to my eyes.

So I scratched my wrist a little more, turning the angel eye's beads whenever I remembered myself, and I continued mentally composing syllabi for the Pharmakeia, and I dreaded dinner with a passion.

I never did bite Thirkeld. The week passed. I had no belongings to collect upon release; all I had to do was walk through the front gates into the sun, unfiltered by solarium glass. The light settled into the folds of my clothes immediately, feather-soft, fresh-smelling.

The first thing I did when I left Westbrook was go to the bank to reclaim control of my money. Gennady had been given control while I was indisposed, and I was afraid of what I'd come back to—but he hadn't spent much at all, aside from the solarium costs. He hadn't spent *nothing*, but I was still proud. Vigil lieutenant wages aren't generous. It was a feat of self-control for him.

The second thing I did was go to the market to get some food that didn't taste like captivity, and third, I went home and slept like the dead in the middle of the day. I had never loved my house more, never so loved the quiet presence of the Aqua Circadia's water near it or the dense crowding of my bookshelves. Before I stumbled into bed, the ambric lights strung from the ceiling flickered and glowed with my joy.

I was due back at the Pharmakeia the next week, and there was work to be done before that—but in the meantime, I set consciousness aside for a while. I didn't even try to make my magic work again; for once, I enjoyed a rest without a headache. There was a future to consider now, a life to go back to. I had survived Westbrook intact again, and now it was time to examine how the world had spun in my absence.

Chapter 2

My peace lasted until Primidy the next week, when I woke in a total panic and was dressed for work by six o'clock. I spent an hour, at least, looking at myself in the mirror—did I look sane? Did I look safe? Did I look healthy? I've been told, most often by Gennady, that I have a vaguely consumptive air about me, and that weighed on my mind as I stared. Which shirt to wear? Which jacket?

Then I realized that if anyone were inclined to hold my time away against me, my clothing would not convince them otherwise, and I forced myself to eat breakfast with grim determination. A little tea, a little bread, nothing much.

The Pharmakeia was only a short walk away in Deme Palenne, the same deme as my house. I went slowly, taking in the sights along the way. The Aqua Circadia moving along peacefully, the pleasant markets, everything down to the even-cobbled streets. Plenty of places in Astrum are *nice*, but Palenne appeals to me in a way few others do.

It didn't matter that I took my time and relished it; the journey was over before I blinked. I had no opportunity to truly prepare myself. When I stepped back on campus, everything fell into place. My second home was still waiting for me. The university still stood, after everything, and I belonged there.

I felt the ever-present hum of the magic inhabiting the Pharmakeia soak into me; I sunned in it like a cat as I walked to my first class. The Archmagister had promised me the use of my old favorite lecture hall when I returned. I was due to give my introductory lesson of Modern Mekhania that morning, and I headed to the hall of St. Osiander without delay.

The day passed in a hectic blur. I taught my classes without letting my nerves overpower me, although some of my students whispered through my lectures. That was only to be expected. It was impossible to keep the nature of my interruption from everyone, and word spread quickly. Some of the whispers were concerned, others malicious, and none of them ever quiet enough to escape me.

"He was in a solarium, you know," a girl in the back row of Modern Mekhania murmured to her friend.

"What for?"

"What do you think? He's an akratic."

"Oh," said her friend, with something like sadness.

I was seized by the ludicrous urge to correct her. *Well*, I'd call, *actually, it was mostly the drugs this time.* I wondered if it would feel nice to shock.

Thankfully, the urge went unanswered. I let her talk; the temptation came and went to address the issue at the beginning of every first class. It would do no good, I knew. All I could do was focus on the work and on reinhabiting my office.

Less easy to tackle were the reactions of my peers. For the most part, the other professors I happened to encounter were cordial, even solicitous—but every so often, I saw in one of their faces the briefest flashes of fear or disgust. The coworker to the left of my office welcomed me back enthusiastically; the one on the right locked her door when she saw me.

It'll be easy to guess which reactions had the greatest impact on me. When I had a break, I fled into my office and put my back against the door. I'd had to vacate it, and I hadn't managed to fill it with the usual towers of paper and books in only a day, but the space served as a comfort nevertheless. I turned Malise's angel eye around my wrist, counting the beads in the hope that they would somehow dull my nerves.

One, two, three . . . the bracelet didn't fix anything, but a small distraction helped. Malise had been right.

Things could be so much worse, I reminded myself. The Pharmakeia could still be in the state I'd last seen it—ravaged by Prefect Mulcaster's attempted coup, split down the middle. It had healed in the time I'd been away; the atmosphere was no longer one of deep paranoia and hostility. I'd heard that the faculty who'd supported Mulcaster had been dealt with, either by firing or by imprisonment in the Penumbra, depending on the severity of the offense. In a way, I was lucky—I'd escaped the responsibility of helping the Pharmakeia rebuild.

After the first day, things were easier. I've always liked a routine, and settling into one made all the bruises along the way far more tolerable. Once there was no crisis, the earnest work of reestablishing my life could begin.

There was still one professor I hadn't seen. Casmir Leynault. He'd visited me only twice during my stay at the solarium, by mutual agreement; despite everything, I wanted to see how he was doing now. He was with the Department of Light Studies, but I was shy of seeking him out in those offices. We'd have to stumble upon each other.

We *did* stumble upon each other, a few days after my return, in one of the hallways. I saw him reading a posted flyer, a little too pale and gawky as always—he'd cut his brown hair since I'd last seen him. I waited to be overcome by the adoration I'd once had for him, but it didn't happen. Above anything else, I felt ill at ease, as though I were about to introduce myself to a stranger.

"Casmir," I said.

He turned to me. After a moment's struggle, his face arranged itself into a hesitant smile. "You're back," he said.

"It wasn't much of a vacation," I said, in tones of contemplation. "Everyone in the resort cried constantly, and the food was terrible."

He stilled, eyes widening in abrupt horror.

Instantly, painfully, I felt myself flush. "It's a joke," I murmured. I buried a flash of resentment that he doubted my lucidity to *that* extent.

"Oh!"

"Yes."

"I just couldn't be sure."

I concluded that there was no use taking offense. "I have a moment," I said. "Should we get lunch?"

He paused before nodding; I wondered if he felt the same gulf between us. "I'll treat you. Let's go."

We went to one of my favorite places, Emeric's, a Camattran café not far outside the Pharmakeia. It was mostly frequented by students and faculty, and the tables were all topped with small potted plants.

"So," Casmir said, when we were seated with our drinks. He toyed with his cup, staring at his reflection in his coffee instead of me. "How are you settling in?"

"It's hectic, but I'm happy to be busy."

"You're healthy?"

I set my tea down with more force than was necessary. "My magic isn't fixed."

Finally, he made eye contact. "But everything else . . ."

He wasn't my keeper anymore. I didn't have to answer in detail. "I'm all right," I said, and nothing more.

"Good. I'm happy for you."

He was sincere. As if he'd spoken the command word to dispel some malediction, I felt an instant lightening, the sense of something drawing gently to a close. "Thank you, Casmir."

"I just wanted to say," he began, and then stopped.

I waited without helping.

"I hope you don't hold it against me that I didn't visit you much."

"We agreed that was best," I pointed out. The reason for that agreement lay heavy between us: we'd argued; he'd slapped me. Things were not the same.

Casmir nodded sheepishly. "In any case, I'm glad we could catch up now. I'll be leaving Astrum soon for research."

I smiled. As long as I'd known him, Casmir had wanted to research abroad. "For how long?"

"A year, at least. I'm going to Sere Saebat; there's an opening at the University of Liaohe."

"Liaohe," I said, trying to recall what they'd published.

"For their projection technology." He made a rectangle with his hands, imitating, I assumed, the body of some new instrument the Saebar mekhanics had constructed.

"You must be eager."

"Eager *and* terrified," he said.

As I studied Casmir, it occurred to me that something in him was changing. There was a thoughtfulness in his bearing now; an edge somewhere was beginning to round. I wasn't the only person who had been altered by the events of two months ago. I felt no particular gratitude for that, but I was glad. "I'm sure it'll be wonderful," I told him.

He raised his cup for me to clink; I obliged.

"My Saebar isn't fluent," he said ruefully after he'd sipped. "It's not *bad*, but it could be better."

"Let me hear your pronunciation."

Carefully, in Saebar, he recited, "Please help me. I'm lost. Which way is the university?"

I shrugged. "You sound fine to me. Are you planning on trotting that sequence out often?"

"Everyone says Liaohe's a labyrinth," he said. "I'm sure I'll get to use it more than once."

"Well, you're braver than I."

I hadn't meant anything by it, really, only that being lost in a strange city sounded miserable to me, but Casmir dropped my gaze and shrugged. "I'm not sure of that."

I could reassure him. I could say something tender, and it would feel natural—like reciting a long-memorized poem. But there was danger in that instinct. Although I could forgive him, I would not step closer. "There's no call for that. You're not built for self-deprecation," I said instead, wryly, and sewed another stitch in the healing wound.

He laughed, and that was all we spoke of it. I gave him pointers on his Saebar pronunciation as we finished our drinks, each of us taking great pains to be cheerful. When we parted, I didn't look back at him. He was welcome to his year away. I hoped Sere Saebat would hold all the secrets he desired.

~

Meanwhile, I had secrets of my own to unravel. My free time that first week was spent trying to figure out what, exactly, was wrong with my magic. I identified a handful of other professors who claimed to be experts in matters of magical anomaly, and with some effort, I convinced some of them to advise me. Each but one proved to be an utter waste of time.

Talmont's distracted ramblings were useless. Dizianne seemed, basically, a bit stupid. Whitson's theories were hundreds of years out of date. By the time I was finished meeting with them, I'd started to consider the real possibility that there was no hope for me, and I was going to spend the rest of my days as a broken magician. There were few worse fates.

But on my last inquiry, I found some hope. Janin Gailhardt told me that yes, she was actively treating a group of subjects for magical difficulties, and yes, I could be a part of the trial, and no, she wasn't afraid of me for the things I'd done two months ago.

Gailhardt was a few years older than I and tall, only just shy of my height, with a square jaw and high cheekbones—an odd combination that somehow made a trustworthy impression. "It's taken me a while to get this group together," she said as I stood in her office in the history department's building. "I've been trying to find people with some sort of problem casting—trying to figure out what causes it. You'll fit right in."

"Thank you," I said stiffly, feeling the shame of my plight. "I've been meaning to get around to fixing it, but I . . ."

She eyed me for a moment. "You were away from the Pharmakeia. Yes."

I was grateful enough for her tact that I decided to be straightforward in return. "The solarium doctors were ill-equipped to address it."

She sighed. "I have an akratic sister. She's been in and out of the solariums since we were children."

"I'm sorry."

"I just mean that it doesn't bother me."

Gailhardt had always been kind to me. She'd always been on the right side of whatever strife the Pharmakeia found itself embroiled in. When Prefect Mulcaster's people had made their bid for power, she'd resisted. We weren't close friends, but I trusted her.

And if she was going to perform experiments on my magic, she should probably know my medical history. I lifted my chin. "It was nepenthe this time."

She shrugged. Wry, good-natured. "For my sister, it's rosethorn."

"Stars," I said. "What a world."

"Come to the hall of St. Monnier on Oktidy," she told me. "At seven in the evening. I'll introduce you to my other subjects, and we can get started."

I gave her a blinding smile. "Thank you, Gailhardt."

"Of course," she said, as if it were only to be expected.

All at once, I found that I had reached my limit for socialization. I bowed goodbye and left her to her work.

When I went to see Gailhardt on Oktidy, I had no idea what to expect. Unreasonably, I worried the trial might resemble the awful experiments I'd witnessed before Mulcaster's attempted coup. What I found instead was an orderly lecture hall, a neat circle of ancient chairs, and a group of people who looked perfectly respectable. Gailhardt saw me walk in and motioned for me to join them.

Out of four people, I recognized two as Pharmakeia affiliates, one student and one professor. The others seemed to be magicians from different walks of life, stranger-brethren from outside the university. All of them seemed comfortable with each other; they had found solidarity in infirmity.

"We have a new member," Gailhardt said, nodding at me. Her voice carried well in the hall.

"Desfourneaux," I admitted, and bowed, avoiding their eyes.

The group chorused a series of *hello*s and introduced themselves one at a time. "Come sit," said an older man—the professor, Livios Alectus. I took a chair.

A woman in heavy, dramatic eyeshadow cocked her head at me. Mary Armand. "So what's wrong with you?"

Please, no, I thought; *we don't have the time.* I had to abridge. "My magic hurts me when I cast," I said. I couldn't stop myself from adding, "What's wrong with *you*?"

"Oh," she said blithely, "whatever spell I try always comes out the opposite of what I want."

"I fall asleep whenever I use mine," the Pharmakeia student announced, almost proud of himself. Alain Durrell. I wondered how on earth he took his practical exams.

One member of the group in particular caught my eye. Oliver Harcourt, a man in his late thirties. He had been listening to the others with amusement and now spoke up again as if reluctant to be left out. He wore bright colors, each piece of clothing a different shade. I would have called it all garish if he'd been even slightly less good-looking.

"My spells just don't work," he said. "I try to cast, and nothing happens. Nothing whatsoever." He had striking dark eyes and sandy hair, and his voice had a certain musicality to it. He was also smiling at me, and I began, preemptively and secretly, to panic.

He caught me staring, of course; I had to acknowledge his gaze somehow. I smiled back. He gave me a nod, and miraculously, my nerves quieted.

It was nice, truly, to know that I wasn't alone in my injury, that I was not, as I sometimes suspected, a unique disaster. Gailhardt saw my posture soften and immediately set to work. From a nearby table, she picked up an ether meter and brought it into the circle of chairs. "Let's take our measurements," she said.

She pointed the instrument at each of us in turn; the dial settled on various numbers and symbols, whirring and clicking. Without any context, I couldn't so much as guess what the readings meant. I had no access to Gailhardt's research, no knowledge of her calibrations. I was a subject, not a collaborator.

The same was true when she brought out a spectrometer and examined us all a second time. "Much better this week," she told Alain, and he grinned, gap-toothed.

I waited for the moment when Gailhardt would cast on us, use her magic to probe or somehow treat us. She wasn't a healer; she had only her considerable talent with stone and earth, but that wouldn't preclude her from reaching out with her magic to diagnose our anomalies. But instead, she asked us to cast for her observation.

I chose to go last. One by one, I watched the others fail to use their magic—it fizzled or backfired or roared out of control. Oliver's failed to present itself at all; he tried to move some water contained in a glass, but there was no change. In Alain's case, he simply toppled over, only to be caught by Mary. An air of well-worn disappointment suffused the room.

When I was up, I was seized by the need to show that I *was* a competent magician. An inconvenienced magician, granted, but skilled. With effort, I called a full bolt of lightning to my hand and twirled it lazily, enjoying the impressed murmurs from the others, the soothing of my ego—

Then I yelped like a kicked dog as the lightning flew to pieces and an ice pick headache came slamming in.

"A little over the top," Gailhardt said dryly, and jotted something down in a notebook.

I sat down and put my head in my hands, mortally embarrassed.

Livios whistled. "Nasty."

What a brilliant insight, I thought, biting my tongue hard to keep from being cruel. The ambric lights overhead pulsed in time with my headache.

Oliver leaned forward, watching me with a frown. I peeked up at him, trying to look a shade less wretched, and he mouthed, *All right?*

I nodded on pure instinct. He smiled uncertainly and turned his attention elsewhere, leaving me feeling somewhat bereft.

The rest of the meeting passed without incident. Gailhardt made her recommendations to everyone toward the end. Eat well; get some sleep. Try to avoid the sun, for Livios, and the opposite advice for Mary. The group dissolved into rueful but convivial conversation as everyone retrieved their coats.

For whatever absurd reason, I hoped Oliver would speak to me again. Even more absurdly, he *did*. He rose from his chair, stretched, stuck his hands in his pockets, and drifted toward me. "Desfourneaux, right?"

"Adrien Desfourneaux," I said. I wanted him to have my given name.

"Looks like a nasty headache."

"It's fine," I said, and wiped my watering eyes.

He grinned. "Liar."

I hadn't expected to be called on it. Before I could protest or attempt a joke, Mary beckoned him over to her to say something, and he slipped away. "Feel better," he said to me. I blinked after him.

Gailhardt found me where I was dithering near the doorway, unsure if I should speak to her again or not before I left. "So?" she asked. "What did you think?"

"Fabulous," I said.

She raised her eyebrows. "You're disappointed that I wasn't able to fix you within the first meeting."

There was no use denying it. "That, and I made a complete fool of myself."

She didn't even attempt to conceal her laugh, although I sensed it was a benevolent amusement. "Let's say you presented a clear example of your symptoms."

"Too clear, maybe."

"Maybe," she said, then sobered. "Will you be back next week?"

I already had weekly appointments with Malise. The thought of setting up more obligations didn't appeal—but I had no other good options. "Of course."

She nodded firmly. The other subjects were filing out of the lecture hall; Gailhardt and I headed through the door, and she flipped the ambric lights off as she went. "Maybe I'll see you tomorrow," she said.

I lifted a hand to bid her goodbye, took one last glance around for Oliver, and turned to make my way home—

Then, in the instant before I turned, I saw Gailhardt pause. She was looking over my shoulder into the empty lecture hall, her jaw set in fear, eyes wide. Abruptly, I realized that the other subjects stood in a cluster in the hallway as well, angled toward whatever she was staring at.

Something was still in the room. The lights flickered back on.

Chapter 3

In the classroom, where they couldn't possibly have gotten without any of us seeing, stood two black-clad strangers. A man and a woman. The swords on their hips shone; I felt my breath leave me.

For an instant, I imagined that one of them might draw their blade, charge, and impale me to the hilt—but the momentary fancy was for nothing. Their weapons stayed down.

"Sorry to intrude," said the leftmost figure, a man with unruly black hair and a noble's accent. He gave me a wide smile and stepped away from the ambric switch he'd just flipped.

"Ahh," I said thinly.

Gailhardt crept forward. "It's after hours," she said. "The Pharmakeia is closed to visitors. How did you get inside there? Were you watching us the entire time?"

The man fished through the pockets of his long black coat and showed her a badge adorned by the silver symbol of an archaic shield crossed by a sword. "We're inquisitors," he said reasonably. "We're here to inquisit you."

"That's not a word," Mary called from the back of the group.

He responded with a good-natured wink. "Maybe not! But the fact remains. You're being inspected. There are concerns about the nature of this gathering. After the incident with Prefect Mulcaster and the traitor magicians, you can understand why the Clementia would be interested in monitoring you."

"They're not threats," Gailhardt said quietly. "I'm just trying to help them get better."

The other stranger, the woman, stepped forward as well to glare at Gailhardt. I could see the tension in her, carefully coiled and well maintained within her various sharp angles. "They're magical aberrations. We need to confirm that they're no danger." Her voice was magnitudes harsher than her companion's, although she had a highborn accent as well.

They were both sword nobles, I guessed. They had the right leanness to them, a sense of self-possession and awareness. I took a shaky breath. "You're not witchfinders," I said.

The man wrinkled his nose and advanced upon me, stopping only a step away. "No, no. Nothing like that."

"Then why—"

He put a hand on my shoulder; I forced myself not to shy. "There's no need to be worried," he said. "Not if you're all good citizens."

It was such a peculiarly ominous thing to say that I laughed involuntarily.

"Why don't you introduce yourselves?" Gailhardt suggested.

"Theophile Wycliffe," said the man. "Please, call me Theo."

"Valary Silvestra," said the woman with considerably more resentment. "Call me Inquisitor Silvestra."

I eased back until I was no longer quite so close to Theo.

Disjointedly, in stages, all of us bowed to the inquisitors, and they bowed in return, Theo more graciously than Silvestra.

"We'd like to conduct some short, easy interviews," Theo said.

Gailhardt grimaced. "We were all about to leave. Did you not gather enough information while you were in there spying?"

The others in Gailhardt's group murmured in indignant agreement. "It's by order of the Clementia," Silvestra said. "The new Clementia. The purged Clementia. We're conducting an inquisition of the Pharmakeia *and* the Chirurgeonate to destroy any remaining treasonous or dangerous elements."

Her words cleared any chatter from the air. When we were all silent, she spoke again. "Magic is dangerous. Magic needs to be controlled."

"You need more original messaging," I said, before I could stop myself. "Don't you think this rhetoric is a *little* tired? Haven't we all heard this speech?"

I have trouble, sometimes, with keeping quiet. My self-inflicted headache sharpened. Silvestra bridled and took a step toward me, but Theo pulled her back.

"You want anyone who helped Prefect Mulcaster to be held accountable, don't you?" Theo asked me. "There may still be allies of his who remain here undetected. People died because of them. Don't you want justice? Don't you want us to make sure the Pharmakeia is a safe place for all your students, so nothing like that happens again?"

I provided no answer. It was a rhetorical question, and we both knew it.

The déjà vu of their arrival was nearly too much to take; it reminded me undeniably of the witchfinder occupation of the Pharmakeia in the early days of Mulcaster's conspiracy. I wasn't as afraid of the inquisitors as I was of the witchfinders, but they made the hair on the back of my neck stand up.

"Let's go back into the lecture hall," Theo said. "We'll just have a few chats."

What else could we do? We went inside and sat back down. I took a chair next to Oliver this time.

"I volunteer for the first interview," Gailhardt said, her arms crossed.

The inquisitors looked at each other.

Theo shrugged. "All right." He leaned forward in his seat, earnest. At least he didn't have the same predatory sharpness to him that many witchfinders have, the sharpness that was present in spades in Silvestra. "So—let's get to it. I don't want to waste your time. Have you ever hurt someone with your magic?"

"I have not," Gailhardt said.

"Are you planning any kind of rebellion?"

"No."

"Are you conducting these experiments on the people here for any sort of harmful purpose?"

She glared. "Of course not."

After a keen, studied silence, Theo sat back. To my immense relief, he seemed satisfied. It had been easier than I'd expected. "Well. That's all the questions, actually."

"Oh," Gailhardt said, blinking.

Theo sighed. "Listen. We don't really think you're doing anything illegal. It's just that we're bound to check it out. Yes, you're anomalies, but you all seem nice enough. We're not here to make you miserable."

I found myself tempted to believe him. Something about the easy tilt of his posture made him seem truthful. The temptation faded quickly, however.

He went through Alain, Mary, Livios, and Oliver next. Alain was nervous; Mary was obstinate. Livios answered calmly and Oliver with perfect cheer. I found myself admiring the way he let the questions roll off his back without any apparent discomfort.

When Theo came to me, I froze.

"Have you ever hurt someone with your magic?" he asked.

"Oh, yes," I said breathlessly. Beside me, Gailhardt winced in sympathy.

I readied myself to explain, but before I could, Theo stopped me. "The question was just a formality. I know about you—I know about your witch-craft trial."

There had been more than one trial at that point in my life, but I would not be the one to point that out. I couldn't assume which one he was referring to—regardless, my answer was the same.

"I was acquitted," I said.

"So you were." And he moved on to the next question without delay, a mercy I was unprepared for. I found myself grateful.

"Are you planning any kind of rebellion?"

"No."

"Do you harbor any ill intent toward your fellow citizens?"

"I don't."

He was about to move on when I found my voice again. "I'm curious," I said. "I need to know—you were inside the room while our meeting was going on? How did you stay hidden?"

"You don't need to know that," Silvestra said.

Theo ignored her. "It's just a bit of technology." He took out a small mekhania sphere, composed of intricate, spinning parts—he clicked a button on it and vanished. Everyone except Silvestra gasped.

After a moment, with the sound of the button clicking again, he reappeared, looking somewhat smug.

"That's incredible," I said, instantly obsessed. "How does it manage that? Some sort of manipulation of light?"

"Not at all. It's only canned mind magic."

My enthusiasm vanished. It was a far less impressive explanation, and I felt somewhat infringed upon. "That thing is casting mind magic on us."

"Ambiently. To block us out of your perception, yes," Theo agreed pleasantly.

"Is that legal?"

"We're the Clementia," Silvestra snapped. "It's legal."

Theo clapped his hands softly and nodded at her. "That's one way to put it. In any case, that's all of them interviewed, then. Do they seem like scheming masterminds?"

She growled something to him under her breath.

"Then let's get out of their way." He rose and bowed to all of us again.

Silvestra followed, impassive. "We'll be watching," she said.

Theo raised his eyebrows at us, as if to communicate fond exasperation with her, and then they took their leave.

Instantly, Gailhardt slumped farther down in her seat and put a hand over her eyes. "Saints. That was awful."

"It's not over," Oliver said mildly. "They'll be skulking around."

My headache pulsed. We stewed in uneasy silence for a few long moments before Livios broke the stasis and stood. "Let them skulk. I'm getting home to my family." He was gone without further delay.

With equal haste, Mary and Alain followed, bidding the rest of us good night and disappearing into the witchlight gloom of the Pharmakeia after dark. Oliver stayed where he was.

I helped Gailhardt up. "Are you all right?"

"I've been better," she said. "I wish you hadn't mouthed off to Inquisitor Silvestra."

"It was stupid," I admitted. The glint of the sword Silvestra had worn at her hip flashed through my mind. "I'm sorry."

Gailhardt shook her head. "I don't disagree with what you said, but . . ."

Finally, Oliver stood. "Sometimes you just have to say what you mean."

I wasn't sure he was right, but I smiled anyway. "Maybe."

"It's getting late," Gailhardt said. She took a quick, curious look at Oliver and me, and then she left the two of us alone.

"She's right," I said. "We should go." I found it difficult to talk to Oliver, even so briefly. He was both handsome and friendly, and the combination was vaguely painful to weather. I would have to be sure to keep my distance from him, I thought. I would have to be careful. There was so little room in my life I could cede to distractions.

That determination lasted for another second and a half, until he asked, "Do you live close enough for me to walk you home?"

"Yes," I said instantly, and then squeezed my eyes closed to scold myself. "Well—twenty minutes away, if you're willing to walk that far."

When I glanced up again, he was shepherding me into the hallway. "I'm willing. You look dizzy. Someone should make sure you don't fall into a canal."

I was startled enough that I nearly forgot to respond. When I had remembered my manners, I murmured, "Thank you. I appreciate it."

"Magical aberrations have to look out for each other, don't they?"

I laughed, mortified and delighted in equal measure. It jarred my headache, but I didn't mind. We set out for my home in Deme Palenne.

"So," Oliver began, as we left the building and set down a winding path leading out of the Pharmakeia. "You're a professor, right? What do you teach?"

"I'm with the Department of Mekhania Studies, officially, but that's not my only subject."

He tilted his head. "Is it common for professors to work without one focus like that?"

"Not very."

"Ah," he said with a smile. "So you're special."

I struggled to find the right reply. I consider myself special, of course; I always have. But it's never quite polite to admit it. "In some ways," I said uselessly, after failing to think of anything better.

Part of me wondered if the comment had been a jab, but he chattered on with complete openness. "You know, I always liked mekhania when I was at the Pharmakeia. I wasn't cut out for an academic career, but . . ."

"What *do* you do?" I asked. "If you aren't with the academy, I mean."

"I'm an actor."

"That's an interesting choice for a magician," I said.

He shrugged; I sense that he had retreated from me by a degree. "I know it's not very impressive."

I scrambled to clarify myself. "That isn't what I meant at all. *Interesting* is a good thing for me. I like theater."

When he brightened again, I felt it like a sunbeam. "Did you always know you wanted to teach? I always knew I wanted to act."

I hadn't. I had always wanted to be a doctor. In childhood, I'd healed bees with crumpled wings and operated on homemade dolls. Finding my second calling as a professor had come at too high a price. I thought of the Philidor solarium disaster and reached for Malise's angel eye bracelet on my wrist to count out a few beads.

"No," I said. "I didn't always know. But I'm happy I do now."

He watched me curiously; I thought he'd seen something of the regret on my face. "Do you mind if I ask something I have no business asking?"

I braced myself for the worst. "Go ahead."

"That inquisitor, Theo. He said something about a witchcraft trial, didn't he? Why were you tried?"

I found that I could not bring myself to explain Philidor. There was no earthly way. I would have to answer as though I were sure Oliver was referring to my *second* witchcraft trial, the trial of two months ago. With that in mind, how could I explain myself without frightening him? Then I wondered if I had a *responsibility* to frighten him—after all, what I had done was violent.

"You're aware of the bloodbath at the Penumbra a few months ago," I said.

He nodded.

"I was there, and I struck a man with lightning."

He glanced at me sidelong as we walked, trying to reinvent his impression of me to suit this new fact. "Why did you do it?"

"To keep him from murdering my friend."

"Did you kill him?"

I saw a chance to preserve myself and snatched at it hungrily, thoughtlessly. "No. I broke my spell to save him. That's why I'm in this group."

"Well," he said, at length. "It makes sense that you were acquitted, then."

The wave of relief reduced me to inanity. "Really? You think so?"

"If you'd done it with a blade, who would have cared?"

"He *was* a Vigil captain," I said weakly. "Someone might have cared still."

I hadn't meant it as a joke, but he laughed, and the melancholy tension broke. "I hope you don't think I'm rude for asking a thing like that when we've just met."

The reminder that Oliver was essentially a stranger jarred me. "No," I said haltingly. "Anyone would be curious."

He acknowledged that with a sanguine shrug; I searched his face for signs of fear. There were none, but nevertheless, I couldn't bring myself to speak again until we had reached my home. When we got to the door, I drew a breath—but he filled my silence for me.

"I'll see you next week," he said cheerfully, and left me standing outside my house. I went inside feeling lonelier than I had since my first week in the solarium.

The next day, I confirmed that there were more than just the two inquisitors around. They haunted the Pharmakeia, lying in wait to interrogate any magician unlucky enough to attract their attention. I told myself that we had survived the witchfinders' occupation months ago, and we would survive this as well. Still, it could only be a bad omen. It *meant* something.

Everyone else was thinking the same thing, and it set us all on edge. I encountered this first with Phaedra Keynes of the Department of Thanatology, who lacked any equanimity to spare in the first place. The discipline of death-lore sometimes attracts an unpleasant personality type, and Keynes was the best example. After my return, she'd begun to mutter about me whenever I was around, stage whispers meant for me to hear. We hadn't gotten along before my latest stay at Westbrook; it had only gotten worse since. I gathered quite clearly that she thought I was incompetent and insane. I ignored her, with effort, until she grew bold enough to needle me directly.

She latched onto me one day as I was passing one of the several ossuaries Thanatology keeps on campus. I quickened my steps as I went by—but they weren't quick enough. She'd caught me. "Desfourneaux," she said, drawing inexorably closer.

I whirled to face her. "This can't be happening. You can't really be this petty."

"What can't be happening? You're not feeling paranoid, are you?"

I bit my tongue until I could speak with relative calm. "There's no reason for us to have this conversation."

She widened her eyes. "Can't I talk with a coworker?"

"Please just get to the point."

"You should resign," she told me.

Although I had requested it, the brutality of her answer knocked me back a pace. "What?"

Evidently, the tension in the Pharmakeia's atmosphere had stoked Keynes's bloodlust. She was no longer playing with her food. "You're a danger to the students," she said.

I knew there was nothing I could say to convince her otherwise. No capitulation would satisfy. So, against my better instincts, I said, "If I'm so dangerous, are you sure you should be provoking me constantly?"

Her mouth pursed in fury. "I could report you to the Archmagister for that threat."

"Phaedra," I hissed. "Can we please, please just pretend to be adults? Just for thirty seconds, until I'm out of your sight? Could you possibly manage that?"

People around us were staring; a knot of students was crowded at a nearby corner, pretending not to watch, and a few more thanatology professors goggled at us nervously.

"I won't apologize for saying what everyone is thinking," Keynes said, and bared her teeth at me in a humorless grin. "You're a danger to *all* of us. You threatened Kirchoff *with magic* in front of half the faculty. You should never have worked again after the Philidor solarium."

It took nearly all my effort not to flee. Instead, I returned her smile. "Isn't Kirchoff in prison?" I asked delicately. "Isn't that Thanatology's claim to fame—that your department chair was a traitor? Who's to say the lot of you weren't in league with Kirchoff?"

I didn't really believe it. I said it just to throw Keynes off balance.

It worked; she narrowed her eyes at me. "How dare you?"

"Maybe the inquisitors should be looking at *you*," I said.

"Is that what you intend to tell them? You think they'll take the word of a mad witch over mine?"

I lost the remainder of my composure; in the corner of my vision, I saw a fleck of lightning dart from one eye. "We could always find out," I said. I found myself inexplicably thinking of Gennady, of what he would do.

Keynes said nothing. I saw genuine unease in her face, and it made me sick. Whatever momentary triumph I might have snatched from her silence was crushed by the realization that I had proven her right.

One of the other thanatology professors, a woman in her eighties, stepped forward to draw Keynes back from me.

"Please," I said. "Please leave me alone." I turned to brave my way through the small crowd that had gathered, and Keynes let me go without another word.

It was only right, given what I had said about the inquisitors, that I ran into Theo immediately thereafter. He was standing to the side, watching me; I'd been too distracted to notice him—that, or he had been using one of the inquisitors' invisibility spheres to observe unseen. As I drifted away, he caught up to my side and walked with me.

"You know you shouldn't engage with people like that," he said, as if we'd already been in conversation.

"I know." I could only be glad he didn't have Silvestra with him.

"Getting into these kinds of confrontations with other magicians doesn't look good."

"She's been goading me," I said. I knew it was a weak excuse.

"Oh, yes. That jab about the Philidor solarium was a nasty one."

I turned to look at him as we walked. "So you *are* familiar."

"I like to know who I'm investigating," he said. "I check their histories. Yes, I'm familiar, but only in the broadest strokes."

"It was a mistake," I said, numb. "I don't know what else to say."

Theo shrugged, as if it were nothing to him—as if my past didn't matter. I was relieved, until he spoke again. "Then let's talk about the other things she was saying."

"Remind me," I said.

"She called you mad."

"If you know my history, you know exactly why."

"You and the solariums," he said ruefully. "It is something of a theme."

"I'm not dangerous," I said, for lack of anything else.

"Probably not."

I knew I was indebted to him for that concession; I dipped my head.

"If you haven't caught anyone who needs prosecuting in Gailhardt's group," I said, "where will you look next? Elsewhere in the Pharmakeia?"

"The Chirurgeonate," he said. "We suspect there may still be healers there who assisted Mulcaster with murdering comatose patients. Plenty of them were weeded out, but you can never be sure."

I shuddered. A healer willing to use magic to harm is a dangerous thing: a scalpel cuts both ways. "Best of luck."

"Yes, well. I'm sure you'll be glad to get us out of your hair."

I couldn't pretend otherwise. "Rather. Don't take it personally."

"I'll try," he said wryly, and checked his pocket watch. "I need to be off. Try not to get into any more interesting fights while I'm not around."

I saw him off with a weak wave and silently wished the Chirurgeonate good luck.

If ever I had doubted that Gennady had changed since I'd first met him, that he'd developed some kind of affection for me, I was reassured when he and Lady showed up outside my lecture hall after class that same day.

"I saw the inquisitors sniffing around," he said immediately upon seeing me walk out, without introduction. "Like the witchfinders, back when everything else was happening."

I made a face. "They've been making themselves known, yes."

"So I wanted to check that everything's still good," he said.

It was easy to forget sometimes, given how he seemed to think of himself as invincible, that he was capable of being worried. I smiled. "Everything's still all right," I said. "So far, at least. I'm not convinced that'll remain the case, but for now . . ."

"Okay," he said. At his side, Lady huffed quietly, as if unconvinced.

I remembered everything that Gennady had been through recently and looked him in the eye, trying to reassure. He stared back, uneasy and bristling. "Whatever happens, we'll be fine."

His response came immediately. "That's not true. You could definitely get hurt."

"I think 'we'll be fine' is something people say to each other regardless," I said.

"That's stupid."

I had no easy reply. "Then we can try our best, at least."

He nodded curtly, then squinted at an inquisitor who happened to be passing by. The inquisitor slowed to look me over, and Gennady bared his teeth. "Keep walking," he said to the man.

I shook my head at him, but the inquisitor had already stopped. "I'm sorry?" he said.

Gennady smiled. "I said keep walking."

"Don't antagonize them," I muttered to him. "Please?"

He ignored me, although Lady seemed to shrug.

"What's a Vigil soldier doing here?" the inquisitor asked, not without some contempt. Not all branches of the Clementia are fond of each other.

It would be nice if for once, just for an instant, Gennady could soften that unmitigated hostility of his, but it wasn't to be. "None of your business," he said.

"Seeing as we've been assigned to investigate the Pharmakeia, it *is* our business. Now answer."

"He was just visiting me," I said quickly. "We're friends. That's all."

"Magicians and Vigil aren't *friends*," the inquisitor said.

I controlled my voice. "Not generally, no, but we are. Please excuse him."

I hoped that the inquisitor would think the confrontation was beneath him. In that, at least, I was rewarded. After a long, suspicious pause, he shook his head and kept walking.

I held my breath until he was out of sight, and then I turned to Gennady. "*Must* you?" I said.

He raised a defensive hand. "What? *Keep walking* is pretty friendly. I just didn't like the way he was eyeballing you."

"We're all used to that here," I said. "You should try to reconcile yourself to it as well."

"Whatever. It turned out fine," he said. Lady snorted.

I felt I had to impress my point. "You may not like them. I certainly don't. But I hope you won't go around picking fights with any inquisitors you see."

The grin he gave me was not entirely reassuring. "No promises."

I *tsk*ed. "Why no promises? What's so hard about that to promise?"

The question sounded far more curt than I had intended. His expression vanished into a peculiar flatness. I winced; I recognized it. He was retreating into an old carapace, a strange second skin. "That's what I'm like," he said inscrutably. "That's all. You know that."

I chose my words with care. "I just want you to be safe."

He was barely audible. "I'll try."

I couldn't ask for more than that. "All right," I said.

He bent down to give Lady an idle scratch behind the ears before straightening up and giving me a mocking half-salute. "Well, Professor, I'll see you around."

"Thank you for checking in on me," I said, feeling the nagging sensation that I had somehow failed.

He gave no reply and strolled away whistling, tuneless, with his rache beside him.

Chapter 4

The interaction with Gennady at the Pharmakeia began to eat at me. I could have been kinder, I thought; I could have acknowledged him better. After all, he'd come because he was worried, and I was not the only one still nursing recent scars. The failure couldn't rest—I decided, after some debate, to go and visit him. I'd see how he was doing. I'd make sure he was all right.

He'd told me where he lived only with great reluctance, although I'd never pressed him on it. He seemed to object to the basic principle of anyone knowing. Still, we'd become friends, so he'd given me an address one day.

His apartment was in Deme Nymphes, near the Vigil commissariat he served out of. The station wasn't particularly well maintained, I was given to understand. Still, he seemed proud of it in his own way. I went to his door one day in the evening when I knew he'd be home, hoping he'd still answer if I was unannounced.

He answered with Lady at his heels. The rache reared up and put her paws on me when he opened the door, far more effusive than he ever could be. They didn't hold my curtness against me. I staggered back a step or two; Lady disengaged and sat down nearby.

"What do you want?" Gennady said.

"Hello to you too," I said gently.

"Hello. What do you want?"

"I thought I'd come see how you were doing. I wanted to make sure you two were well." I took care to include Lady in the sentiment.

There was a look he got on his face whenever anyone extended any amount of concern to him: a pinched, muffled sort of bewilderment. It had gotten fainter as time went on, but he wasn't likely to be cured of it any time soon. "Um," he said.

The pause went on for long enough that I began to feel silly. "Well?"

"We're good," he said with a glance toward Lady.

"Good. We could go for a walk."

I saw him start to roll his eyes. "Or not. It's your choice," I added.

It's your choice was yet another thing he wasn't used to hearing. It stopped him short. Gennady needed to be socialized, not unlike a feral kitten. I wasn't the best choice for the job, but there was no one else.

Lady laid her head on her paws and looked up at him quizzically.

"God," he said under his breath. "Fine. Whatever."

Fifteen minutes along the main street, I decided. He'd be able to take fifteen minutes. "Thank you."

"Let me get my saber," he said. Of course. He was still dressed in full Vigil uniform—why *not* bring his weapon along with him on a simple walk? Soldiers are like that, I reminded myself, and waited as he disappeared back into the apartment, shortly to reappear with his weapon in tow.

We stepped out into the street. He shoved his hands deep into his pockets as Lady trotted at his side.

I knew better than to push him to talk after he'd already agreed to the outing. But, to my surprise, he remembered on his own. "So," he said after a few minutes, painfully awkward. "You're a professor again."

"I am."

"Is that fun?"

"It's not without its hiccups," I admitted, thinking of Keynes. "But I wouldn't have anything else."

"People don't fuck with you because of what happened? Because of Captain Corvier?"

"Naturally some of them do. But most are gracious."

He thought about it for a while. "Want me to beat anyone up?"

"I don't," I said, as archly as I could manage. "I really don't. You can't offer that to people."

"Why not?"

So many Vigil are unswervingly violent. The training they undergo as children does it to them. They're recruited; they bond with their rache; they transform. I sighed. "Do you really want to talk ethics?"

He wrinkled his nose. "No."

"Then just trust me."

Just as I was beginning to feel comfortable, something caught my eye. A group of five inquisitors, elegant but somber in dark cloaks, was strolling toward us on the street. Sword nobles like Theo and Silvestra, I could see. It seemed that was a constant amongst the inquisitors.

Of course, of course, of course. Although the street was plenty wide enough, Gennady clipped one of them on the shoulder as we passed, and she stumbled. I readied myself for disaster.

"Watch your step," she said to Gennady in a voice of silk. She spoke without introduction. Her hand rested comfortably on the hilt of her blade.

"What?" Gennady said.

"I said watch your step, boy."

I closed my eyes, sick with trepidation, before looking up again immediately—I couldn't be caught unawares. "You got too close to *me*," Gennady snarled, his voice twining with Lady's hisses.

Astrine nobles don't have the same sort of absolute authority they do in some other nations. That doesn't mean it's a good idea to antagonize them; there could absolutely be consequences. I grabbed Gennady by the sleeve. "Don't," I said.

He shook me off effortlessly and leaned in closer to the noble who'd spoken as the four others in her cohort began to close ranks.

"Gennady," I said thinly.

"You don't get to tell me where to walk," he said to the inquisitors.

"Do you see who you're talking to?" one of them asked.

"Doesn't matter a bit to me," he replied. "What do I care who the hell you are? My name's Gennady Richter—there, now you know who *I* am."

I said, again, "Gennady."

"Shut up, Professor." The inquisitors were still ignoring me. A few bystanders watching at a distance murmured uneasily.

"Come on," said the woman who'd spoken to Gennady first. "Give us some trouble."

He held fast, not taking the invitation yet.

"You shouldn't bait him," I said. "You really, really shouldn't."

Slowly, Gennady eased back, almost ready to turn away. We stood silent and motionless for a moment, all of us ready for further offense. I'd tell him how proud I was when we had escaped this, I resolved; I'd shower him with affirmations—

On cue, one of inquisitors said, "Ugh. Look at that rache. What an ugly creature." He moved to kick Lady, and everything devolved irretrievably.

Gennady punched the man in the face as hard as he could, which was, may I say, remarkably hard. Lady leapt upon him as he fell; everyone except for me descended into a flurry of violence.

I'd had only a few opportunities in my life to watch people fight in deadly earnest. Usually, Gennady had been involved. Still, I never got used to watching him fight, watching the terrible precision with which he moved and the arctic cold of his expression. In the past, I would have been afraid of him, but I now found myself afraid *for* him.

Some fighters are elegant; they make it an art. Not Gennady. As I watched him hack and slash with Lady frenzied at his side, there was nothing less like art in the world. He was very nearly unique in his unparalleled effectiveness—and he would have been able to take all five inquisitors, I thought, if it hadn't been for me.

I stood uselessly at a distance, calling for them all to stop, pulling my hair, at a loss. Finally, I managed to catch the attention of one of the inquisitors—and as I did, I realized that it had been the last thing I wanted. The instant she stopped ignoring me, she lunged for me. Before I had the time to be surprised, she snared me from behind, her blade to my throat. I could smell the leather of her gloves.

"Maybe you want to reconsider," she said to Gennady, panting. She was bleeding from a superficial cut on one cheek, inflicted by a glancing slash from Lady's claws.

Gennady hesitated. For half an instant, he let his grip on his saber falter. It was all his opponents needed; just as he met my eyes, one of them bore him to the ground. The inquisitor pinning me in place threw me forward, and I stumbled away. In a flash, Gennady lay there with five swords drawn on him, a halo of blades around his face.

Lady paced back and forth with her tail puffed and tucked between her legs, whining and keening. If Gennady died, she would die with him—such is the rache bond.

I imagined the sound she would make if the sword nobles executed Gennady then and there. I stepped forward, and despite myself, there was lightning at my fingertips. It hurt, but that was nothing to me then.

"Don't," I said. "Let us go. Forget about this."

They all looked at each other, communicating silently. "I see that lightning, magician," one of them said. "What are you going to do with it? Is that a threat?"

I could not bear another witchcraft trial; I put my hands behind my back. "It isn't," I said. "But let him up."

"He attacked us. By all rights, in self-defense, we could slaughter him right now."

Gennady spat invective, uncowed. He had the caution to stay still and leave his saber on the ground, but not much else.

I shook my head, trying to conceal my desperation, trying to seem like someone who knew how to bargain. "There must be a solution besides killing him right here."

Another inquisitor cocked his head to one side, looking down as if Gennady were a particularly disgusting insect. "The Penumbra," he suggested idly. "Prison should teach him a little respect. We outrank a Vigil lieutenant—look at his uniform."

"No," Gennady said.

I said, "Absolutely."

They all raised their eyebrows. "Gennady," I said carefully. "Would you like to live?"

He growled at me.

This was as far as the inquisitors would yield. I knew that without a doubt. "You should let them take you to the Penumbra."

I knew what Gennady had experienced inside the Penumbra before. I knew what *I* had experienced there, and that it was nothing half as bad as what had happened to him—yet I still woke from dreams convinced I was there. Going back would wound him, but there was no other choice. It was prison or death, and the inquisitors' swords were dipping closer by the moment.

"Say you yield," I said, nearly begging. Then, to the inquisitors, "Just take him to the Penumbra. Manufacture some little charge, worth a few days—you'll have your satisfaction."

"Professor," Gennady said. There was a tiny seed of hurt in his voice.

One of the nobles moved his blade more quickly toward Gennady's throat, and I gasped. "Yield, Gennady."

Lady howled mournfully. That, more than anything I'd said, seemed to break him. He said, with unfathomable loathing, "I yield."

Slowly, the blades around him withdrew, and he pulled himself to his feet. He didn't go for his saber where it lay on the ground. I'd take it after the nobles were done with him, I thought numbly. I'd keep it safe. A Vigil officer's saber is worth more to them than a simple piece of metal; it's a matter of spiritual security.

The woman who'd threatened me took Gennady roughly by the arm and dragged him forward a few paces. "Nicely negotiated," she said laughingly. "Don't try to come with us."

I stood still, although I wanted nothing more than to follow them. If I could only accompany them while they brought him to the Penumbra, I could monitor him, counsel him while he endured his return to prison. I could insulate him.

But all I could do, as they hauled him away with Lady dragging herself wretchedly behind him, was pick up his saber for him. The handful of by-standers who had remained to watch the scene eyed me nervously as I re-trieved the blade off the ground. Something overtook me for a moment when I picked it up. I'd never held one before—I'd never realized the feeling of danger that could accompany wielding a weapon. Using my lightning had never given me the same sensation.

The heady instant passed quickly, and I was only slightly nauseous again. I can't imagine what the people who saw me holding the unsheathed saber thought of me as I made my way back to Deme Palenne. There was no way on earth to mistake me for Vigil; perhaps they thought I'd stolen it.

When I was home again, I let myself in, set the saber down on my coffee table, and stared at it with my heart in my mouth. Gennady had been taken. I had no guarantee that he wouldn't be murdered before he reached the Pen-umbra, particularly if he resisted—and I feared he might.

Then there was the element of guilt. I had condemned him to a place I knew would bleed him. Even if it had been necessary to save him, the weight of my choice was palpable.

Finally, after I was done agonizing, I prepared to head to the Penumbra. The inquisitors hadn't told me not to *visit*. Deme Nymphes was closer to Deme Eudora than Palenne was; whenever I got there, he'd probably have already been booked.

I hired a caleche and rehearsed what I would say to Gennady as the streets flashed by. *I'm sorry. I had to. Are you all right? How long will you be here? Do you forgive me?* I knew him well enough to guess the answer to the last ques-tion, at least for the foreseeable future. He liked me better than most people. That wouldn't exempt me from his temper.

The Penumbra is one of my least favorite places in the entire city, and there are many to choose from. The overwhelming atmosphere of suffering that emanates from the prison was already sinking into my skin as I approached the dirt front yard. To my great surprise, I froze.

I could swear, as I looked out over the flat expanse toward the prison's gray stone front, that I still saw the bodies lying in front of me. I still saw the dirt churned red with soldiers' blood.

Gennady would have it worse. I set my jaw and went inside.

The Penumbra's ceilings are dark and low; the sound of the feral cats warring with the guards' raches is often unbearable. I went to the lonely outpost that served as the front desk. "My friend was recently brought here," I said to the guard staffing it as his rache eyed me suspiciously. "Gennady Richter. He fought with a group of inquisitors, and . . . well. He's Vigil, actually."

"Oh," the guard said. "Sure. Lieutenant Richter." He made a sympathetic face. Even if the inquisitors outranked most Vigil, the soldiers wouldn't admit it happily. "I'll show you over."

It was just as it had been the first time Gennady was imprisoned—but there would be no saving this time. There was no final battle to set him free soon, only an unknown sentence set out for him by the inquisitors. I followed the guard as he led me farther into the Penumbra.

It would have been difficult to ignore all the suffering faces I saw as I passed through the cell blocks, so I didn't try. Several pairs of haunted eyes caught mine; I forced myself not to linger on them. It seemed a sin, almost, that I was walking free when so many were not. The cells were cramped and very poorly lit, and I could hear resentful whispers echoing against the walls.

When we found Gennady, which wasn't quickly, I was taken with immediate relief. His cell was surrounded by other Vigil and their raches, and I could tell at a glance that they were comrades. He was sitting up against the wall facing the bars with Lady on his lap, conversing idly with the group of guards as though he were not in prison.

When I walked up, he refused to look at me. "Bastard," he said, as the other Vigil watched me with curiosity. "You did this. You put me here."

"But you're alive," I said softly, trying not to be angry. Of course he would blame me. He didn't know how not to. "You attacked the inquisitors, but you survived it."

He had the grace to nod, although he still wouldn't look at me.

"Are you hurt?" I asked.

"Nothing bad."

"Good. That's good."

"I hate this place," he said without taking a pause. "I used to like it. Now it gives me the creeps."

I rested one hand on the bars. There was no point in asking him why he'd once *enjoyed* the Penumbra. "You almost died here. It makes sense."

He seemed to have remembered something, the little fact of my having healed him on the brink of death, and he finally glanced over at me. "I can't help it, you know. The way I am."

To agree, to absolve him, would have been to give him up for damned. "I think you can," I said. "You already have. I've seen it."

"Maybe I'm just pretending."

"That's still an improvement. Everyone pretends sometimes."

He grinned unpleasantly at me. "You pretend more than most people."

He'd accused me of as much before, and there was an element of truth to it. I looked away.

He took my silence as wholehearted agreement. At least it seemed to cheer him up. "That's fine," he said. "No need to be embarrassed about it."

I felt supremely uncomfortable talking about this in front of the other Vigil, but they weren't leaving. I forged onward. "The point is—it's worth something to try."

"Yeah? And what makes *you* the expert on being good?"

I was ready for the question. "Nothing much, but I'm all you have right now. You could find better teachers, but would you listen to them?"

"Definitely not."

"Then there you have it."

He subsided morosely. Lady pawed at the bars, listless. "You really think I've gotten better?"

"Much better," I said.

After an unreadable pause, Gennady dismissed it all with a sigh. "Listen, they said since I hit a noble, I'll be in here for three months."

I passed a hand over my eyes. Three months would be too much for Gennady to bear. I didn't *want* him to bear it; he had been ready to walk away before the threat to Lady. I wasn't sure what Vigil soldier alive could have declined that fight. "No," I said. "No, I'll figure something out."

"You're not Clementia."

"I'll beg Theo and Silvestra," I said. "The other inquisitors—the ones from Gailhardt's meeting."

He tipped his head to one side, stroking Lady's fur idly. "Why would they do anything for you?"

"I don't know, but I'll try."

There was a long, suspended silence. The other Vigil with us watched me keenly.

"Go do that now," Gennady said. "I'm bored in here. It's cold."

I nodded and hurried off to the Chirurgeonate to try and find the inquisitors.

Chapter 5

The Chirurgeonate is huge, and I set out to find Theo and Silvestra with the knowledge that it might take me some time—if they were even there in the first place. They might have continued lurking around the Pharmakeia, or they might be anywhere in the entire city. Still, I had nowhere else to look.

After some time spent asking every passing face if they'd seen anyone matching the inquisitors' descriptions, I finally got somewhere. Yes, one of the orderlies said, they were in the Caserio building, bothering the doctors there and making their traditional inquiries.

I tracked them down and found them hounding a grim-mouthed healer as she walked down the hall to her next appointment. "We hate to interrupt," Theo was saying to her gaily, "but we really do need you to answer the questions by order of the Clementia."

"I can't stop you," the healer said coldly.

"Have you ever killed a patient?"

"No," she said. "I haven't. Now get away from me."

Silvestra took up the attack, determined. "Were you ever allied with Prefect Mulcaster? Did you ever follow his orders?"

The healer whirled on her. "I never did," she said, words clipped. "Never once. Leave me alone."

"We'll just be in touch, then," Theo said, and drew Silvestra back so the healer could pass by them.

The two of them saw me hovering nearby and glanced at each other before approaching—a wordless communication I couldn't interpret. "Desfourneaux," Theo said. "Don't tell me you've come all this way to make a surprise confession."

Silvestra watched me with narrowed eyes. I ignored her. "No. I need a favor, actually," I said, without any attempt to cushion the request. The longer I waited, the longer Gennady would be in the Penumbra.

Theo adjusted his cloak idly. "Surprising. What is it?"

"I have a friend," I said. "A Vigil officer. He got into a fight with a group of your fellows, and they threw him in the Penumbra."

"Goodness," Theo said. "And?"

"You want us to do something about it," Silvestra said. To my surprise, she sounded as if she were considering it. I'd expected an immediate rejection, but she looked interested.

"If there's any way you could intervene, I'd be grateful," I said.

"On what basis?" Theo asked. "Our beautiful budding friendship?" His words were playful, but for the first time, I could spot his steel. He wasn't pleased.

"I have no other recourse," I said. "I'm grasping at straws. Gennady is important to me." I couldn't make the argument that he was too good for prison or that he was an upstanding citizen. Neither was remotely true. My objection to his sentence was entirely personal, and I was willing to admit that. No one should have to suffer just because the inquisitors had provoked them, but I cared because it was Gennady.

"Say *please*," Silvestra said abruptly.

"I'm sorry?"

"Say *please*. You're asking a favor. It's polite."

I thought of Lady's howls as the inquisitors had dragged Gennady away; I counted out ten beads on Malise's angel eye bracelet.

"Please."

"Now," Theo said, "Valary, don't be cruel."

"I'm not. I'm just setting the tone." She smiled flatly at me. "How about this? You owe us a favor. You owe us a little service."

"By all means," I said, "find a way to phrase that more unpleasantly." I regretted my tone immediately, but she didn't react except to shrug.

"You can help us monitor the magicians around the Pharmakeia and the Chirurgeonate. You'll inform us how things are going. It'll be easier for you to tell; no one around here will even consider letting us in."

"I'm not a doctor," I said. "Your focus right now is the Chirurgeonate. I can't help you with that."

"The two institutions are closely tied," Theo said thoughtfully. "Most of you went to school with each other up to a certain point. And it's better than nothing. Always good to build a network."

It seemed as though they were seriously considering my proposal. I didn't argue any further. It stung to imagine myself as an instrument in their machinations, but I was going to need to bow.

"Service, then," I said, through gritted teeth. "Yes, I'll owe you a favor. Just tell the Penumbra that Gennady's charges have been dropped on behalf of the inquisitors."

"The others will be put out about it if they find out," Theo said.

Silvestra scoffed. "They're always put out."

Theo nodded at me. "We'll spring your Vigil friend by the end of the day."

With that weight lifted, I was able to manage a single deep breath. I had the distinct sense of exchanging one peril for another, but I hoped I had traded well. "Thank you," I said.

"Just give us some time to finish up a round of questioning here, and then we'll get to it," Theo said.

I drew a breath to protest the delay, and Silvestra blinked hawkishly at me. The protest died on my lips; I stepped back. Best not to push my luck.

Theo's smile was sublimely unconcerned. "We'll be seeing you."

I murmured a weak acquiescence and left them to their duties, shedding the Caserio building as quickly as I could. I wouldn't go back to the Penumbra right away, I decided. Gennady would be out soon enough, and I doubted he wanted to see me again before then. His ire needed time to cool. If I couldn't promise him an exact hour that he'd be freed, his anticipation would only worsen.

Then, selfishly, there was the fact that another task had been added to my ever-precarious stack of obligations, because I was now without a keeper. No one who has spent time in the Penumbra, no matter how brief, can retain the Chirurgeonate's blessing to be a keeper. Gennady's previous stay had been wiped from his record by virtue of Mulcaster's defeat, but this altercation would not be. Now that Gennady was marked, it would be nigh impossible to keep him on in a capacity any official solarium would recognize, should I need it again.

The pang of loss I felt was undefinable and bizarre. No, he had never been a gifted keeper, but I was comfortable with him. There was no need to pretend. He was like a student to me; between the two roles, we had an equal balance of power. I could keep him in check just as he kept me. It was equitable in a way my place as the akratic had never been.

And now that was over, all because of a single, stupid fight. I hadn't drawn him away from the inquisitors quickly enough, and in return for that failing, I would need to find someone else.

Lucky, then, that I was already at the Chirurgeonate, and that I knew Malise might be in her office at that hour. I trusted her to make some decent recommendations. It was something to do with myself for the moment, something to keep me from succumbing to anxiety on the spot.

I took my time as I walked to her office, not eager to impose my demands on her. When I got there, her door was propped open by a stone weight in the shape of a snake. I'd gotten used to seeing that snake; it comforted me.

I knocked on the doorframe, and after a pause, Malise called, "Come in."

Sheepishly, I presented myself. At the sight of me, she straightened up in her chair, taut with alarm. "Saints. You look pale. Is everything all right?"

"Oh," I said, "Gennady was thrown in prison. He fought a group of inquisitors right in front of me. He'll be out soon, but I need a new keeper now, and I was hoping you might make some recommendations."

She digested.

"That boy is a lot of trouble," she said eventually. I knew she would pick the details from me later, but for now, she had mercy. I admired her restraint.

I nodded. "It could have been so much worse."

Malise got up from behind her desk and came to take me by the arm, leading me to the blue settee. "So. A new keeper."

"He really wasn't doing an awful job. Even if it was early days yet."

"I'm sorry," she said, squeezing my hand.

I knew Malise had been doubtful at times of Gennady's suitability. I rubbed my eyes and looked away.

"What kind of person are you thinking of hiring next?" she asked.

Not another soldier, certainly. I had room enough for only one of those. "I'm not sure," I said.

"Well, which of your keepers in the past did you like?"

I searched my memory and found, to my total perplexity, that I could only think of Casmir. I opened my mouth.

"Not him," she said patiently.

I tried again, and the fog cleared. "Ezra," I said.

She frowned. "Blond Ezra? Ezra from Deme Drusilla?"

"He was fine," I said. I remembered that he'd never raised his voice.

"You told me once that he used to increase his fees every time you cried," she said. "You said he kept a ledger."

"Only by a fixed amount. It wasn't a percentage increase. It didn't stack—"

Looking pained, she hurried to stop me. "Besides Ezra."

"Heloise, then. She was—"

"Heloise the cultist?"

"That's not fair. Every fifth person in this city is a cultist of some sort."

"She tried to have you exorcised."

"It was well meant," I said.

"What about Thomasin?" Malise asked. "The attorney? That was Thomasin, wasn't it? You liked her."

"Thomasin was very kind," I said. "Very kind. Very professional."

"But?"

"Too easy to lie to," I said faintly.

For every keeper who had failed me, there was someone I'd proven myself unworthy of, and for every keeper who'd misused me, there was an unremarkable name I'd simply forgotten.

Malise and I subsided into silence. I found my thoughts drifting toward the shadowed past; when I forced myself to reanchor, the image of Gennady's cell in the Penumbra imposed itself instead. "Maybe I'll hire a doctor this time," I said. "Someone I won't have to explain anything to."

"Someone with more training," she said.

"It's worth trying."

"There aren't many doctors who double as keepers," she said doubtfully.

"I know that," I said, sharp with momentary annoyance. Nothing needles me more than the assumption that I don't know something when I do.

She quieted, and I hated myself. Malise rarely rose to meet me when I was irritable. She had perfected the use of a brief silence and a questioning look. That was always sufficient.

"I'm sorry, my dear. I'm frazzled. Forgive me," I said.

She eased me off the hook with a faint smile and continued. "I can see about getting you some interviews soon."

Although this had been my idea, I balked. "I haven't even seen Gennady again—"

"I know you," she said gently. "If you let yourself avoid this, you'll do it indefinitely, and that could go wrong."

She was right. I had no retort.

"Give me a day or two to pull together some ideas, and we can interview them together," she said.

I swallowed my pride. "Thank you."

Her smile brightened; I felt the tiniest bit better. I could trust her with this. If it had to be done, at least I could do it with her help.

"We could have dinner tonight," I added. I needed to tell her about the halo of blades wreathing Gennady's face, the chill of the Penumbra, the inquisitors' strange bargain.

"Seven at your place?"

I almost always hosted. Malise was not a good cook. "Seven," I said. I could only hope that Theo and Silvestra had been truthful, that Gennady would be free by then.

As it turned out, none of Malise's recommendations appealed to me in the slightest until the very last interview, which was held in an empty examination room in the Hessalon building. The doctor's name was Florian Albrecht, and he caught my attention immediately.

Florian was in his forties, with sleek black hair and unusually pale gray eyes. His blue doctor's coat suited him well. He was waiting for us when we entered the room, seated with his hands neatly folded in his lap. "Dr. Tyrrhena," he said to Malise as I closed the door behind us. Then, startling me, he added, "And Adrien Desfourneaux." He had a fine voice, sharp and carrying.

I stared. Malise had promised she'd let me introduce myself to any potential keepers. "Have we met?"

"You reputation precedes you."

"Which reputation?" I asked. It was no great pleasure of mine that there were several to choose from.

"Your involvement against Prefect Mulcaster," he said, and I nodded, hopeful. "But I've heard about . . . everything else." I cursed myself for believing it would be that easy.

"This is Dr. Florian Albrecht," Malise said, only for the sake of politeness. Florian stood, and he and I bowed shallowly to each other.

He had a set of silver rings on his hands, one on each index and ring finger. He caught me looking at them and held them up to the light.

"They say silver enhances the power of healing magic," he said.

I eyed him nervously. "They" were not a reliable source, if so.

"Just a superstition, of course," he said. "They're really only for show."

I relaxed.

"I'm told you're looking for a keeper," he said, when I failed to make the leap myself. He turned his gaze on me, curious and intense, and I shifted beneath it, unsure what to make of him.

"I am," I said faintly. "Malise found your name. If you're free for the job, we might discuss it."

He looked me over for a long, long moment, and I was abruptly very aware of how I must appear: neat, but always tired, never quite healthy. He nodded. Evidently, I'd passed whatever silent test he had administered. "Let's talk."

I glanced to Malise for support; she smiled at me, but suddenly I found myself wondering if I was asking too much of her. Our previous interviews had taken some time, and I knew she'd had a long day already. It might be best to show initiative.

"I can finish up alone," I told her.

She replied only hesitantly. "You're sure?"

I nodded. "I'll let you know tomorrow."

"I don't mind staying."

"Go on, my dear."

"I do need to be getting along to Halicar's," she admitted, checking her watch. "The church birds need feeding." She touched my shoulder, encouraging, before turning to Florian and inclining her head to him. "The hospice staff speak highly of you."

"That's wonderful to hear," he replied. "I'll try to live up to it."

"Trying is all we can do," she said wryly, before leaving me alone with Florian.

I returned my full attention to Florian. Now that Malise was gone, he seemed more intent. When he sat down once again, I stayed standing, ignoring the second free chair near the empty bed. It felt as though I were being given a job interview—although by all measures, the situation was the opposite.

"So," Florian said. "I'm sorry to be indelicate, but we won't make much progress otherwise. What's your condition?"

"Dithymic akrasia," I said, in the same exacting tones as I always made the declaration. No room for misinterpretation, no room to hide.

He nodded. "I have experience with that. How severe?"

"Moderately," I said stiffly. I've never enjoyed comparing myself to other akratics.

"I'll need more detail," he said.

I knew what sort of detail he needed, and the discomfort of providing it tied my tongue for a moment. When I was sure I wouldn't stutter, I answered. "I need a solarium occasionally."

"Any psychosis?"

Somehow, I induced myself to make a vague sound, meaningless but impossible to mistake as a denial.

Another nod. Florian seemed to make the determination that my exact clinical details could be pried from me later. "All right. Tell me about yourself, then."

I found that I couldn't even provide that much. Not on command, in this sterile room, with no time to think. "Would you go first?" I asked, hating how timid I sounded.

He crossed his arms. "I think that's only fair. I specialize in end-of-life care, I live in Deme Molosa, and I often spend time at the museums. I've received a number of distinctions from the Chirurgeonate over the years. I like Eloran food." He paused and ensured that I was holding his gaze directly. "And I'm a good keeper. Effective, or so I'm told."

I decided that I believed him. There was little to judge by, but he had an effective air about him.

"What sort of magic do you have, besides your healing?" I asked. I was curious; Astrine healers almost always possess a second elemental talent, but I couldn't sense what his might be.

"I only have the healing," he said. "It's an abnormality, but not a deficit." He smiled. "It makes me quite the doctor. We all have a purpose we're born to; I'm lucky to have found mine."

I nodded, keenly interested, and opened my mouth to pester him with questions.

"Your turn to talk," he said patiently.

All the inanities I'd been preparing disappeared without warning, and I was left only with uncomfortable truths. "I'm vain," I said, "arrogant, capricious, irritable, quick to judge, quick to bruise, difficult to manage, frequently unreasonable."

He leaned in by an inch. "Is that all?"

I shook my head. "We'll get to everything else eventually. Let's just start with all of that."

"None of it is anything I haven't seen before." He tilted his head at me. "Besides, you interest me."

It's a mortal flaw of mine that I love, above almost anything else, to be found interesting. "Is that so?" I asked, trying not to smile.

"Let's not pretend that your career has been uneventful," he said dryly.

My smile faltered.

"You also strike me as a bit odd, frankly," he continued.

"Odd," I echoed. I braced myself.

"It's a sense you give off," he said, making a reserved gesture with one hand, rings flashing. "You have an aura of a sort."

I knew what he meant. All my life, there had been something not quite right about me, an undefinable fault situated perfectly in my blind spot: I was aware of it only because others reacted to it. I had no way of identifying it; all I knew was that people could feel my deficit like a static current in the air around me. Crucially, now, although Florian had clearly noticed it, he didn't seem put off.

"I hope you won't take offense. I'm not saying it's a problem," he added, once I had failed to respond for long enough. His fine, sharp voice had acquired an unreadable edge. I took it to be the edge of questions left unanswered.

"You don't mind strangeness," I said, feeling as though I were already indebted to him.

"No. I have a curious mind, and you're something of a puzzle."

I've always approved of curiosity. I've always approved of being noticed, even with the agonies it entails. I couldn't help myself. "Well," I said, "I don't object."

"Does that mean you'll hire me as your keeper?"

I had exhausted all the other interviews. I wanted the whole thing done with. Forcing myself not to overthink, I took the plunge, hoping Malise would be proud. "I can't pay you exorbitantly. I'm on a professor's salary."

The satisfied smile he gave me settled my decision. "That isn't a problem. Well, then, Adrien, it's a partnership."

"A few other things you might want to know," I said. "I should state them."

"Such as?"

I tried to breeze past the declaration, but my tongue stuck. "Nepenthe. I was addicted to nepenthe."

"Not uncommon," he said gracefully. "I'm used to keeping addicts. Would you like me to go over my policies for doing so?"

I felt mysteriously bereft that my offering had provoked no particular response; I shook my head. "I'm sure I can guess most of them."

"Very well. Knowing can help, but . . ."

"No need."

He shrugged. "So be it."

"I also have a problem with my magic," I continued. "A break in it, a tear—I injured myself a few months ago. I'm participating in a study to try to heal it."

Florian's interest sharpened yet further; I could tell by the furrow in his brow. He tapped his fingers thoughtfully against the arm of his chair. "That shouldn't change anything for us."

I had no more will to enumerate the things that were wrong with me. "What do you expect of me?" I asked. Keepers always have expectations that must be met if the partnership is to succeed.

There was no hesitation before he answered. "Punctuality when we're due to meet, respect when we interact, and obedience when it's necessary."

"Obedience," I murmured. It's a common requirement, but I've never liked it.

"I know that's hard to swallow, but it's a necessary part of the arrangement."

I didn't answer. My obedience to keepers had not always come cheap.

"There will be times when you want to do something stupid or dangerous," he said, "or when you won't want to do what's necessary. I need to be able to counter that." He struck the perfect tone: simple and open.

The loss of self-determination never ceases to burn, no matter how many times we prove ourselves incapable. I knew better than to go it all alone. I only nodded.

"Good," he said. "Thank you. This will work nicely."

Somewhere between Florian's straightforward assessments and the way he smoothed his hair back when it fell too far into his face, I began to feel a certain sort of guilty attraction. I'd slept with keepers before, always to my extreme regret—and I'd been in love with Casmir, of course. The closeness of the bond can lend itself to those mistakes.

But before the feeling could make itself known beyond a faint shadow, out of nowhere, I found myself retreating, thinking—inexplicably—of Oliver. That meant nothing, I told myself, but it *was* time to excuse myself from the Chirurgeonate. "It's been a pleasure to meet you, but we'll have to speak more later," I told Florian.

"Likewise," he said. "Before you go, may I have permission to pull your solarium records?"

He asked so casually that I wondered if I was in the wrong for being taken aback. A new alienist might understandably need records, but a keeper? "Do you really need those?"

"To help you better, yes."

He provided no other justification. None was needed. I wanted to be helped. "All right. I'll send Westbrook the form."

"Perfect." He nodded pleasantly and gestured toward the door.

I left him alone in the examination room and made my exit, wondering apprehensively over the hint of attraction I'd felt. Oliver and I had barely spoken, but something about our briefest of interactions had a tighter hold on me than the magnetism of Florian's interest.

It wasn't worth thinking about, I told myself. There was no use.

I stepped outside the complex into the streets of Deme Palenne, listening to the sounds of the growing night. Worry for Gennady resurfaced violently, warring with my other preoccupations as I walked back to the Pharmakeia. I needed to pick up some work from my office to take home with me, or I'd spend my sleepless night uselessly. I couldn't allow wasted time.

Adrift as I was, I hope you'll forgive me for taking it as a sign when I ran into Oliver on my way up to my office.

He was leaving the hall of St. Monnier, where Gailhardt's meetings usually were. I had to look twice when I saw him, just to make sure I hadn't somehow conjured his shade while I was thinking about him.

He raised a hand to me when he noticed me walking toward him. "Adrien."

"Oliver," I said, pleased that he'd remembered my name. "What are you doing here? I didn't know there was a meeting."

He put his hands in the pockets of his profoundly orange jacket. "There isn't, but sometimes I stop by to see Gailhardt just to chat. Get a little more individual time, see how she's doing—you know. She just left. I was on my way out after her."

"I'm glad someone's checking in on her," I said.

He nodded. "Where are you going?" he asked, with the perfect level of casual intent. "I'll walk with you."

I told myself that he was only being friendly—it was a normal offer to make to an acquaintance. "My office is just nearby. I need to pick up some work," I said.

"It's dark. You're still working?"

"I need something to keep me busy tonight. I'm not anticipating any sleep."

"An insomniac," he said, eyebrows lifting in sympathy.

"If we really need to diagnose the problem," I said archly.

He put his hands up and grinned. "No, no. No need at all."

We walked together up to my office; I hesitated a moment before I opened the door, not wanting him to see how untidy the room had gotten. Finally, I'd had the time to fill it with the usual stacks of books and paper and miscellanea—but I had to get my work, so I let myself in and tried to act as though I hadn't noticed just how disorganized the space was.

Oliver gave a short chirp of a whistle like a startled bird. "That's a lot of stuff."

"Is it?" I said vaguely.

"Sure. If one of those book towers falls over on you, you're done. Crushed."

"How macabre."

"I'm an actor," he said. "Prone to morbid fascinations, you know."

"I'll take your word for it."

I was enjoying the back-and-forth, I realized, as I picked up the paperwork I was looking for and closed the office door again. I wasn't feeling the same kind of drawn, awkward obligation that conversations often produce in me. I was *comfortable* with Oliver as I was with very few people—and there was no sign that he sensed the alienness in me that Florian had remarked upon.

The realization left me staring at him in consternation for a moment too long, clutching the papers to my chest.

He blinked back at me. "What?"

I whirled away and set off down the hallway, back toward the front of the building. "Nothing at all."

"You're sort of a nervous type," he said. It was noted with absolute tolerance.

"So I'm often told."

"That's all right. I have a lot of nervous friends."

I could see why that might be. He had a soothing temperament. I declined to tell him so, not wanting to give up the very last shreds of my pride. Instead, I asked, "What sort of magic do you have? I never quite caught it during Gailhardt's meeting." I had, in fact, caught it clearly—but I wanted to hear him talk.

"Mine works with water. Oh, I used to be good enough at it. I could make water out of nothing."

"Poiesis," I said, impressed, and resisting the urge to quibble about the technical accuracy of *out of nothing*. "That's not common at all."

He preened a little as he walked. "I know." And the preen faltered. "But I've lost it now. Nothing works."

I knew his ache intimately; I rushed to soothe him. "Gailhardt seems to be an excellent teacher," I said. "You're bound to improve."

"I have, some, but it's still broken." He paused. "It started with an accident, actually."

He seemed to want to continue, having now opened this door; I made an encouraging noise.

With practiced ease, he took on a light, conversational tone. "I fell from a height during a play. I was the great chevalier Vaeryn, calling my love to Lady Callista from the balcony—it was right before the end of the second act, and the damn ladder slipped underneath me. The whole audience heard my spine break."

"Stars," I murmured, for want of anything else.

"The Chirurgeonate fixed my back. Nerve by nerve. I know not everyone is that lucky. I was in a chair for two years, but my magic never worked again."

I'd noticed a peculiar sort of delicateness to Oliver's gait, but I had chalked it up to an affect of his, a performer's walk. Now I realized that it was the careful movement of someone who had been forced to relearn how to stand. I wondered if his back still pained him as my fractal scars pained me.

He seemed to know what I was thinking. "It's difficult to run. Not a good idea. Sometimes it twinges."

"How awful," I said. That he was confiding this to me so freely felt like a gift.

"It was," he said quietly, sobered for a moment.

"The magic will come back to you, at least. I believe that. Just give it some time." I hoped that my utter sincerity would help make up for any potential condescension. I knew how he felt, and I hoped that counted for something.

His smile reappeared. "I'll do that. Besides, I've recently discovered more reasons to go to the meetings."

I wasn't confident I'd heard him right; I muttered indistinctly, and he laughed. We kept walking.

When we got to the exit of the building, I stopped short. "It was nice running into you," I said.

"Sure," he said. "I'll see you around, Adrien."

I needed to get over myself. Even if Oliver was interested in men, there was little guarantee that he was also interested in men like me. Still, something possessed me to be bolder than I thought possible. "You do know where I live," I said. "You could always drop by."

It paid off. He brightened almost hopefully. "I always could, couldn't I? I'll keep it in mind."

My moment of courage was short-lived, and I turned to escape—but just before we parted ways, he paused. "Listen," he said, "this is going to sound strange."

I listened, not without some apprehension.

He reached into his pocket and pulled out a pack of cards. Not playing cards—tarot cards, pale blue with gold accents spidering in the corners, each overlaid with a constellation map. "Do you know what these are?" he said.

"The Astragestum tarot," I said. "I learned how to read those when I was a student, just for fun. I'd forgotten that until now. May I see?"

He handed them over for me to shuffle through. The deck was old, but perfectly intact.

"I go to the pawnshops sometimes, and I found these," he said. "I picked them up on a whim, since they were pretty. They seemed like the sort of thing an academy magician would know about. I was just curious."

I drew a card idly. Lucrece's Temple in the Court of Rulers, upright. Devotion, loyalty. Immediately, as if bitten, I replaced it. "They don't mean anything, but they're interesting."

He watched me for a long moment, thinking. "Well, do you want them? If you know how to read them."

I had no idea what possible use I might have for tarot cards. "I don't see why not," I said immediately. The thought of a present from Oliver was abruptly precious.

"Then they're yours." He held up a finger. "But you'll have to read my fortune someday."

"It's a deal." I slipped the cards into my jacket pocket.

"I'll hold you to it." He waved easily at me, turned, and melted into the evening, leaving me standing alone until I remembered that I had somewhere to be. The walk back home was over in a single instant: I replayed our conversation in my head the entire way there.

Chapter 6

The next morning, I saw the inquisitors. They were at the Pharmakeia, not the Chirurgeonate as they'd said they would be—and immediately, I knew that something was wrong. They traded looks when they saw me and headed over, cutting their way through the crowds of students and faculty like sharks.

The only possibility I could imagine was that something had gone awry with Gennady. Of course—of course I'd been wrong to think I should wait before visiting again. How could I have been so callous? I met them halfway and was speaking before they could begin. "Gennady?"

Theo blinked in confusion and then shook his head. "No. He was released just fine. Made a hell of a lot of noise about it, but he's all right."

The panic subsided slightly. "Then what?"

They both paused, evaluating me, and the atmosphere dropped a few degrees. I couldn't have expected what Silvestra said next. "How common are heart attacks, Professor Desfourneaux? Do you know?"

"They're about to be ever so slightly more common if you don't tell me why you're asking right now," I said.

Theo snorted, but it was humorless. "It's happening again," he said. "Patients at the Chirurgeonate are dying. Ones who should have been stable. There's a rash of heart attacks going around, several times the normal incidence."

My vision began to tunnel. There could not be a repetition of Mulcaster. I wasn't sure the Pharmakeia or the Chirurgeonate could survive it. "Ah," I said, and went to go sit down on a nearby bench.

The inquisitors followed me inexorably and stood looking down on me. "It isn't connected to Mulcaster," Theo said. "At least, we don't think so. Whatever it is, the motive seems to be different."

That was precious little comfort.

"Tell us," Silvestra said. "What do you know about healing?"

I dropped my face into my hands. "What do you want to hear about? I haven't been a part of that world in years and years."

"That isn't quite true," Theo said. "You visit the Chirurgeonate at least weekly."

Startled, I looked up. "As a *patient*. As a friend to one of the doctors." Then I realized what was already manifestly obvious, and all of a sudden, I couldn't see for rage. "Stars and saints," I said. "You suspect me. That's why you're here. What do I need to do to prove myself? How many years must pass? Should I nearly die in service of the Clementia again? Would that suffice?"

But Silvestra was ready for me. "Do you think years can erase the Philidor solarium?" she asked, and I despised myself for how I'd protested. Of course they'd suspect me. Of course that was only natural. What right had I to blame them?

"No," I said thickly, "but I would never do that. I wouldn't."

"The other doctors, then," Theo said. "Have you ever noticed any who seemed suspicious in any way? Were there ever any you suspected of some sort of bad intent toward their patients?"

"I've never looked at one and thought they seemed like a serial killer."

Silvestra narrowed her eyes. "So you think this is a serial killer. When did we say that?"

The scars on my wrists sparked. "A singular moment ago," I snapped. "If someone is going around killing patients with heart attacks, I fail to see what other label we can put to it."

Theo stepped in before Silvestra could bridle. "You'd tell us if you knew anything, wouldn't you? It would be your duty to your city. An angel of death—and that's what this is, an angel—is no joke. Not to mention the favor you owe us."

In truth, "healing magic" is a misnomer. It's more the ability to manipulate the body as the caster wishes. For the most part, it's used for good, and so we've named it optimistically—but that's all it is. Optimism. I fought back a shiver.

"I would tell you," I said to Theo. "And I *will* tell you, if I happen to find anything out."

They both sighed. "We'll be keeping a wary eye out," Silvestra said mulishly. "Expect to see us around."

"You should concentrate on the Chirurgeonate," I said. "I hope you aren't planning to haunt the Pharmakeia just because you still suspect me while the angel wreaks havoc there."

"And *you* should avoid telling us what to do," Silvestra said.

I resolved to count to ten on my angel eye bracelet and got to four before I couldn't help but respond. "God forbid you actually catch the murderer instead of focusing on me for spite."

Her hand strayed to the hilt of her sword, and I felt myself pale humiliatingly.

"And with that," Theo said, "I think we should go." He tugged at her elbow.

I watched them leave, barely breathing, while my mind raced. Something was coming. Something was already here. I took a moment, then, to consider the specifics of the word *angel*. A dread creature, unknowable, many-eyed and terrible. I could only hope the Chirurgeonate's angel was nothing so grim.

The news hadn't hit the Pharmakeia at large yet; there was about a day's delay between the atmosphere of the two campuses. I kept it all to myself until classes were over, absolutely unwilling to be the messenger. I wasn't sure what it would do to me to find out that anyone else shared the inquisitors' suspicions.

As soon as the workday was over, I sprinted to the north exit of the campus and then stood frozen, caught between obligations. On one hand, I needed to check on Gennady after his release—he'd be in bad shape. On the other hand, I needed to find Malise and see how she was doing, considering the new developments.

I flipped a draca for it, finally. The coin picked Gennady. I promised Malise silently, fervently, to be as quick as I could, and then I rushed home—I had to pick up Gennady's saber before I went to him.

∼

It took some time before Gennady answered the door with Lady trailing unhappily behind him. He looked as though he hadn't combed his hair in some time, and the dark circles under his eyes betrayed his usual affectation of invincibility.

"Oh," he said to me. "It's you." The resentment in his voice was palpable.

"How are you?" I asked.

"You got me thrown in the Penumbra and then you left me there," he said. "So—not great."

"Actually," I said tiredly, "you got yourself thrown in the Penumbra, and I got you out. I assume the inquisitors told you I indebted myself to them for you." I felt guilty, but I wasn't delusional. I knew the sequence of events.

Several months back, he might have denied it all. For all I knew, he might have turned on me. But we'd made progress; for now, he looked away. "I guess."

He stood aside to let me inside the apartment, and I entered. It was largely bare, utilitarian, but there was an honesty in it. Still, he had no talent for making a home look like a home. Everything was clean, but not sparkling—neat only by virtue of its emptiness. It was a nothing-place. Gennady lived in his head, not in the world.

I held out his saber to him and waited.

"Thanks for asking the inquisitors," he said, and took the blade reverently. He held himself stiffly, like a mekhanical doll in need of winding. He was trying.

I managed a smile. "You're welcome. And really, how are you? How were you treated?"

"Everyone was fine about it. Just . . ."

"It's still a cage," I provided.

"Yeah."

I wondered if the experience would make him doubt the Clementia at all. Would it occur to him that the rest of the prisoners had it so much worse? But there was no way I could risk asking. "I'm sorry," I said.

Lady rested her chin on the floor and looked up at me, her expressive face mournful. Without her viciously serrated teeth visible, she looked sweeter than usual. I bent to give her a quick scratch behind the ears. Gennady would never accept a hug to welcome him back into the free world, so that would have to do.

"You didn't have to come," he said.

"I did."

"Why?"

"For one, I had to return your saber."

He shrugged. I realized that I couldn't leave it there. "I care about you," I added. "I have a responsibility toward you."

He parried my sincerity effortlessly. "Like hell you're responsible for me. Aren't I the keeper?"

I winced. "No. Not anymore. With the offense on your record, the Chirurgeonate won't recognize you officially in that position anymore. It'll be too difficult to work around."

A strange shadow of hurt flitted across his face. He'd never been naturally suited to the job, never made it much of a priority, but I knew that he valued my trust.

"They dropped the charges," he said.

"I know."

"Guess you need a new keeper, then," he said with brittle cheer, banishing the shadow.

"I'm sorry," I said. I didn't mention that I'd already found a replacement. It felt distinctly like a betrayal.

"What a shitshow," he said. "Wish you hadn't made me go on that walk." Lady gave a small meow, almost a rebuke, and he looked down. "Wish I were smarter."

"With time," I said gently.

"How much time?"

"I can't be sure."

"I hate waiting," he said.

"We all do."

I watched him battle the instinct to snap at me. Somehow, he succeeded. The result was a morose, pointed silence.

"Do you need company, or do you need to be alone?" I asked.

Gennady looked at Lady. She seemed to shrug; he glanced back at me helplessly. "I can't tell. I don't know."

"Then I'll stay a little while."

The extent of Gennady's hosting abilities was to lead me into his bare kitchen and sit me down at the scarred wooden table while he made himself a sandwich. It would be too much to ask him to talk; I watched him assemble and eat the entire sandwich without comment while Lady thumped her tail mournfully against the leg of my chair. I didn't want to stare at Gennady, so I made eye contact with Lady instead—her expressive eyebrows quirked occasionally, as if she were saying, *Don't mind him.*

"Great," Gennady said eventually, having not quite swallowed his last bite. "Now I want to be alone."

I had no idea what he had gotten out of having me sit there, but he seemed infinitesimally more settled. "All right," I said, standing and checking my watch.

"You got somewhere to be?" he asked.

"I do need to go see Malise soon." I wondered if the new angel had taken any more victims while I'd been watching Gennady eat lunch.

He squinted at me hard, the gears in his brain turning, trying his best to interpret my expression. It was difficult for him at the best of times, but he was determined. "There's something wrong."

"Yes," I said with a despairing laugh. "Now that you mention it. There's an angel of death loose in the Chirurgeonate, killing people with heart attacks, and I'm under suspicion for it, so I need to go see if Malise is all right. She almost certainly won't be."

He blinked and tilted his head as Lady did the same. His reaction came gradually. "Man," he said blankly. "Things are warming up again already."

I drew a deep breath, feeling the *unfairness* of the thing like a frustrated child. "Already."

"We beat the last one," he said with a shrug. Naturally, he was taking it all in stride. What did innocent deaths mean to him if they were strangers? He lived in a small world.

"We did, and we came out scarred for life," I said. It was difficult to moderate the acid in my voice. "Let's not dive toward the arena again yet."

"I won't hurry. Not unless there are Vigil getting killed."

I found myself indignant at his selfishness, and then I realized that he was only agreeing with what I had suggested. I had no direct stake in the matter this time either. I wasn't going to be leaping into the fray myself.

"Then let's hope they catch the killer soon," I said, in lieu of anything else.

"Go tell the healer hello for me," he said, dismissing me.

"Her name is Malise," I reminded him, and headed off for the Chirurgeonate.

Malise was still in her office, working late as always. When she called to welcome me and I slipped inside the room, I found her seated at her desk with her hand over her eyes.

She glanced up, and I hated to see the way she looked—the light that had always shone from her was pale and guttering. "You're here because you heard?" she asked.

"The inquisitors asked me about it," I said. I went over to help her to her feet and into a hug.

She sniffled. "They don't think you're involved?"

"Of course they do. But I sent them away without them making any direct accusations."

"How dare they," she said quietly.

"Have you lost any patients to this?" I asked.

Her face crumpled. "A few, yes. They were all in poor condition, but they shouldn't have died."

The blue ambric fairy lights she kept in her office flickered gently as my lightning reached out for them, beyond my control. "Heart attacks," I said.

"Heart attacks," she confirmed. "I thought we were done with this after they chased Mulcaster's people out."

I rocked her slightly. "I thought so too."

"I can't take it again," she said flatly. "I can't. Do you remember the last time we had this conversation? This same room, this same shadow."

"I remember."

"The Chirurgeonate doesn't feel safe anymore."

Malise was the consummate healer. She had dedicated her entire life to the betterment of the Chirurgeonate, and as I stood there holding her, I hated the angel for making a mockery of that.

"Will you at least promise me to stay away from it?" she said. "Let the inquisitors deal with it?"

"I promise," I said. I meant it. Her approval made it far easier for me to accept being a coward.

"Good."

"What about you?" I asked. "Can I expect the same of you? You're closer to it than I am." If she was hurt, I decided, I would be burning something down.

"I'll try, but if learn anything, I'll have to act." Malise was smart, but she was also good. I inclined my head to show her that I'd accepted it.

We stood in a miserable reverie for a minute or so longer before she extricated herself reluctantly from my hug and took half a step back, shaking herself off, pulling herself back together. "Is everything else all right? Have you seen Gennady? Did the inquisitors help him?"

It was no wonder she wanted to talk about something other than the murders. "He's fine," I said. "He told me to say hello, actually."

Her expression relaxed by a fraction. "Good."

"He'll mend, at least," I murmured.

"What did you decide about Florian Albrecht? You never told me."

In fact, I'd been avoiding the discussion. I looked away. "I hired him. He seems intelligent enough, effective enough. Why not?"

She straightened my glasses for me. "I'll hope for the best. I've never spoken much with him, but there weren't many options. Let me know if you want me to coordinate with him."

I didn't. Asking more of her was out of the question. "It's humiliating," I said quietly.

She and I both knew that there was no other choice. Yes, I could hold my job, so long as the Pharmakeia would allow me some leave. Yes, at the very best of times, I could live briefly as though nothing were wrong with me. But I'd proven more than once that going without a keeper was asking for calamity.

"It's only a little help, my dear," she said. "You're just paying for help. Everyone does it. If someone can't write, they go to a scrivener. If they can't take up a hem, they go to a tailor."

Personally, I'd never had a tailor hide all the sharp objects in my house for me, but then again, I'd never asked. I didn't want to be contrary with Malise; I nodded and forged onward. "I'm sure Florian is worth a try."

"If he doesn't work out, we'll find someone else."

"He says he finds me interesting," I said, showcasing my vanity, trying to cajole her into a smile. She wanted to move away from the angel—I could give her that.

It worked. She snorted and shook her head. "Oh, *interesting*. Well, that settles it."

"I didn't have a chance."

The momentary distraction lost its power. I watched Malise start to weaken again in the soft glow of her fairy lights and put out an arm for her. "Let's go someplace. You need to be away from the Chirurgeonate for a while."

"And if there are more heart attacks while I'm gone?"

"You know better than to think like that."

Silently, she took my arm, conceding.

I took her to a teahouse in Palenne, the Void and Plenum. We had now made a two-time pattern out of going for tea after her patients began to die; I could feel the grooves worn by repetition. I hoped by all the saints that there wouldn't be a third time, if we could manage to somehow get through the second.

The Void and Plenum wasn't busy that day. Malise's sniffles attracted a few uncomfortable glances, but no one questioned us. Everything was pleasantly neat and clean in the teahouse, and the smell of the teas in their glass display globes enveloped us. We found a table in a corner and sat.

"I don't know what to do," Malise said.

"I wish I had the answer. But it isn't your fault."

"Oathbreaker," she said bitterly. "We all swore. We swore we'd never . . ."

"You don't understand because you're not a killer," I said. "There's no point in trying."

She closed her eyes and leaned back in her chair. "No, I shouldn't have brought it up. Let's talk about something else."

I struggled to find anything decent to talk about whatsoever. "I've met a man," I said finally. "This lovely magician from Gailhardt's trial group."

"Oh, a man." Her voice picked up the slightest teasing lilt—it was strained, somewhat manufactured, but we were both trying. "What's his name?"

"Oliver," I said, playing with the beads on the angel eye bracelet she'd given me. "He's an actor."

"An actor. How glamorous. Is he nice?"

"I think so. Although he dresses like a maniac." I retrieved the pack of Astragestum cards from my jacket and put them on the table to show her. "He gave me these as a gift."

"It would be good for you to date outside the academy," she said, examining the cards. I knew we were both thinking of what a disaster my affection for Casmir had been.

I shook my head. "There's no *dating.* I've just . . . it's as I said. I've met him."

"Maybe I'll meet him too, someday," she said.

"I hope so. You'd get along. I'm certain of it."

A wizened server approached the table; Malise and I pulled ourselves out of our slouches and made our tea selections. A light green tea for me, blackberry for her, and some sweet bread for the table. I didn't think either of us was very hungry, but it wouldn't do to starve.

"You like this man," Malise said after we were alone again.

"Yes," I said tiredly.

"Do you think he likes you too?" she asked.

I had to cut past several layers of scar tissue to find my answer. "I think he may." Then, so as not to curse myself, I added, "As an acquaintance, at least."

She was too kind to say the obvious: *That must be a nice change.* My inclination toward men who did not want me back was well established. "Then let's hope you make a friend," she said instead.

I looked away. Suddenly, giving too much attention to the topic seemed almost inappropriate. Malise had been single for years, and I knew she wished for more. "What about you? Have *you* met anyone?"

"Not yet," she said gently. "You know I'm very busy."

"She'll be perfect when you find her," I said.

She rested her chin on her hand, watching me with wry disapproval. "Don't tell me you feel guilty."

"You deserve some luck," I said.

"I absolutely do. But I can be patient."

"You'll have to show me how you do it someday," I said, a weak joke. Patience has never been a virtue of mine.

She shook her head. "And give away my secret? What knowledge would I have left to hold over you, my dear?"

"You know there would be quite a lot."

We both sat back in our chairs and sighed.

"You could try meeting women at the Pharmakeia," I suggested.

"Oh?" She smiled. "I don't suppose you've noticed any particular beauties?"

"It's not my area of expertise," I said primly.

That drew a snort of acknowledgment from her. "Good personalities, then."

"Some, I think. You'll have to meet Gailhardt sometime."

We both knew it was all hypothetical. The conversation was improving her mood, I could see, and I allowed myself a little pride in that.

"Do you actually know how to read tarot?" she asked, shuffling the Astragestum cards I had forgotten about by then.

I picked a card at random: a set of three feathers, Adelai's Falcon, in the Court of Martyrs. Upright, not chimeric. "Mercy, patience, and forgiveness," I said, and returned the card to the deck.

She shook her head. "What nonsense."

"Of course. They're charming, at least."

The server came back with our tea; Malise put a great deal of cassonade in hers, and I took some bread to eat. We were quiet for a time, each of us looking at the cards with something like trepidation. There's no such thing as true fortune-telling, but we had entered dangerous territory regardless.

"Read for me," she said eventually, bravely.

"Pick three cards."

She picked. Adelai's Falcon again, upright. The Demi-Lune, in the Court of Monsters, upright. The Vidame of Swords, chimeric. "What do they mean?" she said.

I shuffled them all back in. "Nothing," I muttered. "Nothing at all."

"Nothing good, you mean."

"It's nonsense, remember?"

And we left it at that.

When I walked her home, neither of us said a word about the newborn peril. We kept the angel off our lips. By the time I was alone at home, however, my preoccupation grew.

I was afraid once more. I was afraid for Malise, yes, and afraid for the angel's victims, but my concerns were not all unselfish. A new upheaval meant stress, and that had particular implications for me. Only recently, the Mulcaster affair had accompanied an akratic episode; I regretted the things I'd done, and I regretted the things that had been done to me. When I considered that there might be more to come, I felt small.

Akratic dread is best described indirectly. Imagine, if you'll indulge me, that you've been blindfolded and trapped in a house of mirrors. You suspect something is there with you, hunting you; you can't be sure, but sometimes you think you hear it moving. To know the danger, to find your way out, you'll have to remove the blindfold—but you don't. You choose to stay sightless, because above all else, you know one thing:

You must not see your own reflection. Never that.

That's what it's like. I tried to reach inside to seek the daimon, to know if it was sleeping, to feel if its breath was hot—but there was nothing. I couldn't tell.

Please, I said to it. *Sleep awhile longer.*

That terror rested high in my throat, but it didn't choke me. Not yet. Not until I went to see Florian.

Chapter 7

I was afraid of the daimon, but I wasn't ready to ask Malise to check for me when she was already so preoccupied. Perfectly reasonable, then, that I might look to my new keeper. He might be able to see something I couldn't.

I went to find Florian a few days later after my classes were over; he was in his office in a corridor of the Hessalon building I'd never visited. When he answered my knock and I entered, the first thing I noticed was how pristine the room was. Not a thing was out of place—the one bookshelf he had was tidy, with all the books presented in precise rows. His papers were organized perfectly. Even the small potted plant on his desk looked exactly placed.

"I wasn't expecting to see you so soon," he said, eyebrows raised. He'd been writing something—I noticed that his handwriting was mechanically precise—but now he set his pen down.

I winced, contrite. "I know. I'm sorry."

"Don't be. What is it?"

"The heart attacks," I said.

He stilled very slightly. "Yes. There have been heart attacks. They're getting more frequent."

I hadn't heard that, but I was hardly surprised. "The last time something like this happened, it was at the same time as an episode for me." I spoke awkwardly, never fond of explaining myself.

Florian voiced the connection after I had failed to do so for long enough. "And you're worried the two will coincide again."

"I may not be involved this time," I said, "but I can't shake this . . . superstition."

He watched me narrowly, assessing me. I felt the unique, familiar burn of a keeper's gaze; he certainly had the job down well. "Go on."

"That's it. I'm just worried."

"Have you talked to Dr. Tyrrhena about this? Has she checked?"

"She has enough on her mind. I didn't want to bother her—maybe it's nothing."

He was still watching me with the same keen evaluation. After a pause, during which he seemed to come to some opaque, definite conclusion, he said, "If your instincts tell you that something is wrong, it's perfectly reasonable to honor the feeling."

I blinked at him, adrift, caught off guard by the understanding. "Ah."

I thought he'd tell me to monitor myself, to be vigilant, to come to him if I suspected anything. Instead, he said, "Should I move in?"

Bewildered, I froze. "What? Now?"

He leaned back in his chair. "It hasn't been long since your relapse," he said bluntly. He'd already read my solarium records. "Not long at all. And you're aware that it takes very little to trigger another one, so soon after."

I bit my tongue hard and fought the urge to cover the long-faded track marks on my right arm. "I'm *perfectly* aware, yes."

"Then it might be best to be proactive. Also consider the issue of your broken magic. You're off balance; until that's resolved, you might want someone around."

I wanted my independence. I wanted to pretend, at least for a while after leaving Westbrook, that I had any pride. But I wanted, above all, to be sober, and now that felt precarious.

So I bent. I bent without a second thought. I'd only just gotten my space back, only just made my house my own again, but I nodded at Florian without a trace of hesitation. There could be no more nepenthe.

"I'll give you my address," I said, pulling my hair. "Come whenever's most convenient for you."

He smiled faintly; I scraped a measure of satisfaction from his approval. "Better safe than sorry. Write it down for me, and I'll bring what I need tomorrow."

Even if I had agreed, tomorrow felt too soon. I didn't say so. Instead, I took the expensive pen he handed me and scribbled my address on the scrap of notepaper he provided. He squinted at my terrible handwriting, so unlike his own, but he didn't ask me to clarify. "Around when tomorrow?" I asked.

"Eight at night or so. That should give us both plenty of time."

I stood back, wondering what I'd agreed to, and he sighed. "Until you're more stable, it's sensible to have someone watching you. You're making a good decision."

"No one's ever accused me of being sensible before," I said.

"Maybe you should try changing that," he said mildly.

Immediately, I felt ashamed of myself. "Maybe." I *would* try, I told myself. I would try, and this time I would change, and if there was truly an episode waiting for me, I'd weather it with as much grace as I could.

"You'll be all right," he said. "With a little supervision. There's nothing to worry about."

"I know, but . . ."

"Trust me. Can you do that?"

I could at least imagine it, I discovered. He seemed so genuinely concerned for my well-being. I nodded.

"Very good."

"Thank you," I said quietly. Despite the praise, I found myself eager to be alone.

He noticed me angling toward the door and nodded at me. "If you need to go, I won't stop you."

I muttered an excuse about needing to pick something up for dinner and fled.

I spent that night and a considerable number of the early morning hours feverishly cleaning my house. It wasn't in bad condition, but something about Florian's combined charitableness and clear expectations encouraged me to make the place as presentable as possible. I cleared the books from off my bed and sorted them on the shelves where they belonged; I stocked the kitchen, too, for his possible convenience.

The day until his arrival passed slowly, slowly. Classes seemed interminable, and the time between was spent hiding in my office. I went home late and sat in my living room until eight o'clock, trying and failing to grade assignments. When Florian knocked on the door, I waited fifteen seconds to make it seem as though I hadn't been sitting there already.

"Good evening," he said, when I answered. He'd brought only a few bags with him. From what I could see, they were mostly clothes.

"Is it?" I said weakly.

I'd meant little by it, but he paused noticeably before shrugging. "It can be if you put in the effort."

A last flicker of doubt went through me; I extinguished it. *I'm going to get better if it kills me,* I thought, and showed him inside to the spare room I kept.

I called it a guest room, but apart from Malise on the odd occasion, there had never been any guests there. Only keepers.

He took his time walking through the house once he'd put his bags down. I held my breath, hoping he'd find it all acceptable—but he gave me very few clues as I followed him around like a hopeful cat. "Everything's so pristine," he said eventually, in neutral tones. "Is it always like this?"

"Not in the slightest."

"Then it was good of you to clean."

"I couldn't *not*."

He gave me a smile, and suddenly the hours of tidying were worth it. Someone approved of me; I was approved of—the relief had an almost physical warmth to it.

"There's plenty of space in the spare room," he said. "I'm sure I'll be comfortable."

I felt myself more a host than an akratic, for the moment. "I can make something for dinner," I said. "If you haven't already eaten." I'd only just started cooking again after not feeling up to it for quite some time.

"Would you like me to help?" Florian asked.

He didn't seem enthusiastic, and I don't usually enjoy other people in my kitchen. I shook my head. "That isn't necessary. Just get yourself comfortable, and I'll make chicken and pilaf."

It felt nice to be able to provide something, no matter how small or how briefly. If I was going to be kept already, at least I could make my own small contributions. I cooked while Florian unpacked; when he was done with that, he went into the living room to read, and neither of us spoke until it was time to eat.

I found myself mysteriously preoccupied with whether or not he liked the food. Although I watched him as he ate, he made no indication either way. It shouldn't matter, I told myself, but it *did* matter. It mattered especially in the absence of conversation. I couldn't kill the feeling that we should be talking, getting to know each other better.

He paused when he saw me watching, his clean, precise movements slowing to a halt. "Is something wrong?"

I shook my head. "Not at all."

"You're staring."

"I was just wondering if you were happy with the food," I said lamely.

He squinted in surprise and then nodded, as if the idea were a novel one. His smile came on again. "It's good," he said. "Of course."

I relaxed a little. Then, immediately, as if to punish myself for having arrived at a comfortable juncture in the conversation, I said, "What are your hobbies?"

He put his fork down. "Ah."

I froze in the middle of a bite.

"You're laboring under a misconception here," he said patiently.

"And what is that?"

"We don't need to be friends."

I straightened up, recoiling from a sharp pang of hurt. "I'm sorry?"

He shook his head. "It's best that we get along well, but you shouldn't preoccupy yourself with making sure that we're *friends*. I'm your keeper; it's much the same as why you don't need to be friends with your doctor."

"I'm actually very good friends with my doctor."

He gave me a look. It wasn't a particularly severe look, but I felt it. "You know what I mean."

"Shouldn't I at least *try*? What could be the harm in that? If we do end up being friends, all the better. It may not be necessary, but—"

"There's no use giving yourself another thing to worry over. My presence here is supposed to reduce your stress, not increase it."

There seemed to be something to that line of logic, but I still wasn't convinced. "It can't hurt—"

"Don't be difficult," he said. It was said with an absolute lack of rancor. I shut up.

As I was wishing for the earth to open up and swallow me, there came a knock at the door. I sprang up instantly, unthinkingly—I had no idea who it might be, but a buffer between Florian and me could only be welcome.

Once I was up, I looked back at him. I still wanted to make sure he didn't object.

He motioned me toward the door, and I went.

It was Oliver. Somehow, he looked perfectly at home standing outside my door. An alien flood of hope swelled in me; he was holding a small glass container of baklava, and I found myself smiling.

"I mentioned I might drop by," he said.

"You did." I'd invite him in for dinner; I'd made enough food; I wouldn't have to navigate my conversational failures with Florian alone—

"It smells nice," he commented, looking past me into the house. When he saw Florian, he nodded and waved, a graceful motion.

"Will you come in?"

He beamed; I showed him in, doubly glad that I'd cleaned for Florian.

"Oh," he said. "Cute little place." He bowed to Florian.

I murmured my thanks, watching Florian. He was looking at Oliver thoughtfully, but with neither curiosity nor concern.

"I'm Oliver Harcourt. We're friends," Oliver said, smiling at me. "Through Professor Gailhardt—do you know her?"

Florian shook his head. "I'm with the Chirurgeonate. We don't know each other."

"A doctor," Oliver said. "Now that's something."

I had prepared to be jealous of Florian, but Oliver's easy demeanor made it impossible. It was just another kind thing to say from a man with plenty of kindness to spare—and, inexplicably, I had somehow already qualified as *friend*. I couldn't resent it.

"Will you stay for dinner?" I said.

He didn't hesitate. "I don't see why not."

I was turning to go into the kitchen and get Oliver a plate when Florian said, "I don't think that's a good idea."

My stomach dropped; I wheeled back on him to protest. Oliver tilted his head in confusion, so endearing a gesture that I found myself furious with Florian. "Why?" I asked.

Florian pursed his lips, and I could read his meaning immediately: *Do you really want me to say it out loud in front of him?* Whatever his reasoning was, it wasn't something I wanted shared with Oliver.

But I needed an explanation. I didn't budge.

"Err," Oliver said.

Florian turned to him apologetically. "Adrien is feeling a little under the weather," he said, with admirable concession toward discretion.

Not yet, I wanted to hiss. *Not right now.* If that changed soon, I might not get any more chances to have dinner with Oliver.

Florian seemed to take no pleasure in it; he gave me a sympathetic shrug. I remembered, with a thrill of regret, that I'd offered him my obedience. I'd offered not to be difficult.

"Under the weather? Is that so?" Oliver asked slowly.

"Just a little," I muttered. "Maybe."

"You're *his* doctor?" he asked Florian.

"No," Florian said.

"Then what?"

The instinct to lie seized me mercilessly and refused to let go. I was ashamed, but I said it anyway. "A friend. Another friend."

Oliver's gaze pierced me; I saw at once that he knew I was lying about something. He couldn't know what, but I hadn't fooled him—I hadn't even expected to.

He didn't call me on it. He didn't call me on *any* of the bizarre situation. Instead, he smiled. It was muted, but it seemed genuine. "Well," he said, and backed away toward the door. "Another time, Adrien?"

"I hope so," I said fervently.

He set his dish of baklava down on my coffee table on his way out.

When he was gone, I sat in frozen silence, watching Florian chew as he resumed his meal.

"He seems pleasant," he said finally.

"He is."

"I'm sorry," he said, "but—"

"I wanted him to stay," I said.

The interruption did not go unnoticed, but he decided not to chide me. "I can see that you're invested in him."

My utter transparency made me flush. "Is there anything wrong with that?"

"Not in and of itself," he said, "but keep in mind that you're in a vulnerable place right now."

"You think—"

"I do think." He examined his glass idly as if checking for water spots, his silver rings glinting in the ambric light. "Becoming too attached to anyone right now might be a mistake. Mistakes might cost you. Think of *his* well-being, too."

"It would only have been dinner," I said. The instinct toward anger was draining away; instead, I was merely tired.

He stood, pushing his chair back into place. "You wanted a keeper." There was a gentleness in his words that made me look up. "I'm sorry it isn't always easy, but I'm looking out for you. This is my job."

If he and I were not going to be friends, I wanted to ask, what was wrong with seeking it elsewhere? But I didn't want to frustrate him. "All right," I said.

"You may not want to see him alone," he said. "If something goes wrong, it'll destabilize you."

So that was that. Here was the advice and care I was paying him for, and if I didn't like it, that was far beside the point. I nodded.

He went into the spare room, apparently finished with dinner and all its trappings, and I picked up our dishes. I wanted nothing more than to leave them in the sink and slink off to bed, but I made myself wash everything and tidy the kitchen. All the better for appearances. I retrieved Oliver's baklava and stuck it in a cabinet somewhere.

Before I could go to bed, Florian called me into the spare room. I was fading hard by then, and I went only reluctantly.

"I think we should spend some time most days addressing the break in your magic," he said.

"I already have someone I'm looking into that with. Gailhardt."

He made a small sound of disagreement, as carefully controlled as the rest of him. "The matter is best left to a doctor. It's an issue of health, isn't it?"

"It's a matter of magic, and Gailhardt is an excellent magician—"

"Your best bet is to get treatment that takes into account the interplay of your magic and your body. A holistic approach."

He seemed to know what he was talking about so unflinchingly that I began to doubt myself.

"Has this Gailhardt made any progress over your meetings?" he said.

"Well, no," I said, "but it's early days. She needs to take her measurements."

"That isn't a good sign."

"You think she's incompetent?"

"I haven't said that. I'm not suggesting you stop seeing her altogether."

I hovered in the doorway, unmoored and useless. "It's going to take time."

"It doesn't have to," he said deliberately. "Not as much time as she might have you believe. If there's a possibility that I can help fix it sooner, why not take that chance?"

I was silent.

He surveyed me with understated frustration. "Or don't you want to get better?" he said.

Immediately, I flared. I had never wanted anything more in my life. "I do."

"Then you might agree to let me help you. You're paying for my assistance anyway—what's the difference?"

A terrible hope overtook me then, the hope that he was right, the hope that there was some easy, quick solution to the tear in my magic that I could reach out and touch then and there. "Very well," I said.

His gaze softened; I felt myself relax. "Come sit on the bed," he said.

Although we were in a room in my own house, it felt invasive to do so. Still, I sat as he asked.

He stood in front of me and put his hands out. I was about to ask what to expect when he pressed his palms to my temples and began to cast.

I panicked for an instant; I wanted, briefly, to force his hands away and spring up. He'd given me no warning. But as soon as his magic sank in, the feeling vanished. His power was warm and anesthetic, drifting through me like silver sunlight. I believed in him.

"I feel the rift," he said, from very far away. "Shall I?"

I made a small sound of assent, happy that he'd asked.

Not even his anesthetic was enough to dull the pain that followed. He was in me, abruptly, inside me, his magic suffusing me—and it burned. It burned as though I were wreathed in flame.

But before I could scream, it stopped, and I felt only the knife's edge of adrenaline and the gratitude of relief. Even the adrenaline faded quickly, leaving me nothing so much as exhausted. My vision blurred.

"That was awful," I breathed. "What did you do?"

"I helped seal the rift a little," he said. "That should help, with repeated exposure. Don't you feel different?"

I did feel different. I couldn't identify how, but he was far from wrong on that count. And I felt, somewhat paradoxically, much more at ease with him than I had before. It remained to be seen whether he could cure me, but the hurt had been only momentary. It had been necessary—like setting a broken bone.

I raised a hand to try to call a spark of lightning, just to test, and he warned me off with a disapproving sound. "I wouldn't suggest it. You need to let your magic rest."

The itch to try anyway persisted, but I let the matter lie.

"I'm tired," I said absently.

He smiled. "That'll happen. It's a natural effect of that kind of healing magic."

During my own time as a healer, I'd never noticed any such thing, barring the most extreme injuries—and never while Malise was healing me, either. Not to such a great degree. Then again, who was I to make judgments about the art? I shrugged.

"That's all I wanted to try for tonight," he said. "Best that you get some rest."

He helped me up. I stumbled out of his room to brush my teeth. It would have been polite to thank him, but the thought never occurred.

Nothing else happened that night; Florian's presence in the keeper's room was quiet. I barely felt him there at all. I couldn't hope to sleep, no matter how tired the procedure had made me. When I finally went to bed, I lay there in ceaseless thought, trying to monitor myself, trying to feel if Florian's precautions against Oliver were justified or not. There was never any answer.

I discovered, in missing Oliver, that it was possible to miss someone you hardly knew.

Chapter 8

The next thing I knew, it was time for me to go to Malise to be healed again. The endless task of maintaining my personal upkeep refused to stay done, no matter the inconvenience.

She wasn't crying when I went to her office, but I could tell that it was a near thing. "The inquisitors are still sniffing around," she said as she sat me down. "Accusing everyone of things. They haven't gotten anywhere."

"You have the best reputation of any healer at the Chirurgeonate. There's no way they're going to think you're the angel."

She twisted her hands together. "Some of the heart attacks have been patients I've treated. Four names so far, names I knew—"

"That doesn't mean anything. That doesn't prove anything." No one who spent more than five minutes with Malise would suspect her.

"Not to *you*, my dear."

"Not to anyone with an iota of sense."

"Are you willing to say that the inquisitors all fit that description?" she said lowly.

I was forced to shake my head.

"There's nothing to do but see how things progress. And—and try never to be alone with a patient for too long." I saw her remember that I was here for an appointment; she rallied herself forcibly and focused. "Forgive me. How have you been feeling?"

I thought about hiding it from her for her own good, her own peace of mind—but I knew she wouldn't want to be patronized. "I've been worried something is coming, actually."

"An episode."

I grimaced. "Why not?"

"You change rapidly sometimes," she murmured. "I'll take a look around when I treat you." I wondered at her phrasing. *Take a look around*, as if my mind were a dark room that needed scouting.

I glanced down at the edges of the fractal scars just visible under my sleeve. "And my magic is still damaged."

She put her arm around me. No false reassurances, no ignorant insistence that it would be just fine.

"Do you think it's a good idea to have the problem treated by a healer rather than having a Pharmakeia magician poke at it?" I asked cautiously.

She paused to consider. "You know I'm biased," she said. "I'm always going to think a healer's touch is the best solution."

"So that's a *yes*."

"A *yes* tempered by some self-awareness. I never tried to treat you for it because I don't have the right expertise; if you've found a healer who does, it may be worth a try."

I wasn't sure that Florian had ever claimed any expertise, but whatever he'd done, I'd felt safe afterward—I'd been impressed. I couldn't remember exactly why, but the feeling remained.

"It probably couldn't hurt," I said. Even as I said it, I knew it was untrue. Of course it *could* hurt. I just didn't think it would.

Malise was smart. "This is about Florian?"

"He already tried something on me, in fact."

"And do you think it worked?"

"That remains to be seen, but I'm hopeful."

"Hope is worth something," she said. "It's at a high premium these days."

Her endorsement lulled me. "Then I suppose I'll keep at it."

She patted my arm to draw my attention, then put her palms to my temples just as Florian had, although her touch was lighter and far more familiar. "We'll see," she said gently. "May I?"

I nodded. She treated me, and I was struck by how different her magic felt from Florian's. The coldness, the liquid soothing, it was all very unlike his. I felt a bit dizzy afterward, but it was nothing like the wholesale exhaustion that had accompanied his working.

The traditional relief Malise's healing brought faded when I noticed the furrow in her brow. Her gaze had taken on a studied, cautious character.

"Something's wrong," I breathed.

She put up a hand. "I don't know. Not *wrong*, exactly. But I felt something."

"The daimon," I said. I'd been right. Florian had been right. It was waking, and I was poised on the edge of some precipice again—there was nowhere left to hide in the house of mirrors. "What kind of episode?"

"I don't *know*. The feeling has changed over the years; it isn't static. I'm just not sure."

"Then what did it feel like?"

"Something different from you. I'm sorry. I can't be more specific."

An akratic is best served by pessimism. Prepare yourself for the worst. If it doesn't come, you'll have a pleasant surprise. I resigned myself. "It never ends," I said, with bone-deep resentment.

She took my hand and squeezed. "Whatever it is, you'll get through it."

I took a deep breath and stood up, offering her a brittle smile. "I should find Florian and tell him. He's already living with me. How convenient."

She'd been reaching for her pen; now she paused. "What, already?"

"Good instincts, it seems. He didn't want me to relapse. Thank you, Malise. I'm grateful." I gave myself the satisfaction of a whirling exit, turning and sweeping out the door without another word.

I found Florian in the aftermath of one of the heart attacks. He was in the Pavesse building, surrounded by a small team of other healers as they stood empty-eyed and afraid outside the room of a dead patient, speaking to each other in shocked half-sentences. I hung back, hesitant to intrude.

"The angel must have just been here," one doctor said finally, clutching the serpent's tooth locket around her neck.

"Or maybe they're *still* here," said another, staring around at her fellows.

"No need for baseless speculation," Florian said. "This one may have even been natural. We won't know until the examiners give their report." He caught sight of me and lifted a hand.

All of a sudden, my petty troubles and I seemed magnitudes less important. People were dying. What sort of candle could my little illness hold to that? But I was already standing in front of him. I could hardly tell him *never mind* and go away again. "Florian," I said, a placeholder while I figured out what else to say.

"Adrien," Florian replied patiently.

"Are you needed any longer here?"

He shook his head with a look inside the room at the dead patient. Following his gaze, I caught a brief glimpse of the corpse—an old man—before I made myself turn away. "There's nothing else I can do," he said.

"Then would you mind walking with me?"

He left his group colleagues and came to walk beside me as we left the scene.

"Did you see what happened?" I asked as we wound our way out of the Pavesse building into the sun. I wanted some fresh air.

For a moment, he was inscrutable—the pain of the matter, I assumed. Soon enough, his expression resolved itself into one of tired resignation. "I saw him just after the heart attack began. I didn't see who was with him before that. A near miss."

"Was he one of your patients?"

"He was. He was Tyrrhena's previously."

Another loss for Malise—I flinched. "I'm sorry," I said to Florian.

"So am I." He spoke with an edge. I resisted the instinct to apologize again. "Why have you come?"

"Malise found something while she was healing me," I said.

He looked over at me sharply. "What?"

"She doesn't know. She only says that it feels different. Wrong. Obviously, I was right—you were right. Something's coming."

He sighed. "That's unfortunate. At least it's not a surprise."

"What should I do?" I asked. I had never really expected any of my keepers to have the answer to that question before. They could help me through it all, but I didn't think they could fix anything. Florian felt different. Florian felt as though he would know.

But I was to be disappointed. "Just try to live as normal until the symptoms set in fully," he said. "Conduct your affairs as usual. We'll address the problems as they come." Much the same as Malise.

He noticed me looking ever so slightly put out and leveled a direct stare at me. "There are no easy solutions."

"I know. Of course."

He glanced over his shoulder, back to where the latest heart attack victim lay. "I need to get back to work," he said thoughtfully, as if mulling over an internal dilemma. "Thank you for telling me, but I can't do much about it now. I'll see you later today."

"Of course," I repeated. Mortified by my presumption, I left with haste.

I went home to read and cook and pretend that I was doing anything but counting the hours until Florian came home. Already, he felt like a part of my routine. He was late; it was long past dark by the time he arrived. When he did, I tried to act as though I hadn't been waiting, but I don't think I had him fooled.

"Did you learn anything else about the heart attack?" I asked him as he came in the door.

"Just that it was the angel, as we suspected. Nothing else." His tone forbade me from digging any further.

"I made soup," I said weakly.

He ate without evident relish again. A brush with the angel would ruin any appetite. I cleared away our dishes without his help, trying to take one more tiny thing off his mind. And then, of course, I undid that work tenfold after dinner; I subjected him to a long bout of whining in the living room.

"I'm not ready for it," I told him. "I'm not sure I can take it. I don't want it. I can't do it." I continued on in the same vein, without much new to say—repeating myself uselessly, hearing how irritating I was being without being able to stop it.

Then I complained about *everything*. I complained about my classes. I complained about Phaedra Keynes for nearly twenty minutes, making sure Florian knew exactly how much I hated her, exactly how publicly she had humiliated me. I complained about the new rip in my favorite jacket.

He withstood it all with admirable restraint, his unusual gray gaze never wavering. I fiddled with my angel eye bracelet as I ranted. He didn't say much, but he never interrupted me.

By the time I was finished, I was drained and ashamed of myself. The ambrics in my house flickered lowly with my temper, and my fractal scars sparked occasionally, drawing small hisses of pain from me.

"You seem to truly dislike this woman," Florian said neutrally.

"If I could snap my fingers and make her disappear, I'd do it."

He tilted his head. "Is that so?"

It had been hyperbole, but I was instantly ashamed. A much brighter mote of electricity floated from one of scars, and I winced.

Florian came up to me and grabbed my sleeve, pulling it up to better see the scars. When another mote jumped into the air, he shook his head. "Is it getting worse?"

"I don't know. I'll need to ask Gailhardt at the meeting tomorrow."

He didn't seem best pleased by the answer, but he didn't protest. "Tell me what she says."

I tugged my sleeve away, and he let me go. "I will," I said.

I wanted him to reply somehow to the torrent of complaints I'd unleashed, but I realized that he had little reason to. What could anyone say? "Excuse me," I murmured, to indicate that I was finally done, and looked away.

He made a brief, neutral sound of agreement.

Getting ready for bed that night was an absent affair; I was too distracted by what was coming and the mistakes I'd already made to give my evening rituals much of my attention. By the time Florian had retired to his own room and I was sitting up at my desk to read before bed, I had only the barest shreds of an attention span left.

No matter how long I stared at the book I was trying to get through, nothing made sense. Paragraphs slipped by, squirming under my gaze, refusing to be examined. I gave up, finally, after too long spent trying to battle it out. Lying in bed provided no relief.

Sleep came in the end, but only uneasily. I woke occasionally to the phantom pangs of an imagined heart attack.

Gailhardt's next meeting was, principally, awkward. I knew that I needed to make some sort of explanation to Oliver about what he'd heard at my house, and I failed utterly to do so, instead choosing to pretend it hadn't happened. He let me avoid him, blinking uncertainly after me from across the circle of chairs. I kept my gaze fixed at an empty spot on the opposite wall.

Beyond that, the meeting was also useless. What Gailhardt said when she took her measurements of my magic with her various instruments was, "I really can't tell. I can't tell if you're improving with time."

I tried hard not to descend into immediate judgment. "You can't tell? Why not?"

"Something's obscuring the readings."

It hadn't crossed my mind before that maybe an oncoming episode could interfere with my energic qualities enough to throw an ether meter or a spectrometer. I covered my face, feeling stupid. "I think I know what."

The rest of the group, Oliver included, watched me curiously. I couldn't go on.

Luckily, Gailhardt's intuition was sound. She deduced, from my shame, exactly what I wasn't saying. It required a moment of observation, but she drew her conclusion with a nod. "That's unfortunate," she said. "And interesting. That could very well explain it."

And briskly, mercifully, she moved on to Alain, taking his measurements instead without a word more. I found myself doubting Florian's assertion that she was ineffective, purely because I was starting to like her so much—not a rational progression of thought, necessarily, but I couldn't help it.

The others pretended not to be curious, and all of them even managed to keep any questions to themselves until the end of the meeting.

"So," said Livios, when Gailhardt had done all she could. "What were you talking about? What's interfering with your readings?"

"That's my business," I said gently.

"You won't tell us?" said Mary, as Alain watched.

"I won't."

"Aren't we friends?"

Not really, I thought. We might share a similar misfortune, but I wasn't sure the bond extended much further with her. "It's just a private matter," I said.

I couldn't be sure that either Livios or Alain wouldn't put it together on their own; my akrasia was known within the academy. I'd been obliged to explain myself several times over my career. With that in mind, I wasn't eager to do the work for them.

"It must be something embarrassing," Mary said. I thought she was trying to be playful, but the effect was irritating.

"Absolutely," I said. "Please stop."

She had the grace to look awkward. The others shrugged. "Well, then. Good night," she said.

While everyone got their coats on and began to head for the door, I found Gailhardt and pulled her into the corner. "I'm sorry for the timing of the . . . problem," I said. "I know it's inconvenient for your study."

She shook her head. "You don't need to stop coming. If you're still able, of course we'll have you."

I could make no promises.

"My keeper is trying a few things, at least," I said. "So even if I'm *not* able to come, at least I'll have someone doing *something*."

Her expression clouded. "Trying a few things?"

"He's a healer," I said. "He's been trying to approach the problem from that perspective." I was apologetic; I knew how it might sound.

"Your keeper doesn't think what we're doing here will work."

I looked away.

"Did you tell him it's a delicate process that'll take time, and that gathering data is a necessary foundation?" she asked.

"I did," I said. "I really did. And I don't intend to stop coming here; I trust you. But I'll take help from any quarter I can get it."

Gailhardt couldn't object to that, not when I phrased it that way. "All right," she said. "But keep me up to date on what he does—if he manages any results. I want to know that."

"I swear I will."

"Chin up," she said with a nod. "Is that reasonable to say?"

I made a gesture with one hand: so-so. "Easier said than done."

"But well meant," she said tartly.

"Thank you."

She smiled and finished packing up her equipment before leaving the room.

Oliver had stayed behind. This time his coat was peacock blue. I avoided looking directly at him even more assiduously, blocking him out of my vision like a hallucination, until he spoke to me. "I just wanted to say that I hope everything's all right," he said. There was a hesitance in his voice that endeared rather than annoyed me.

I should simply shut the conversation down. No good could come of it, I thought. I could only scare him off or disgust him. But two warring instincts steered me elsewhere: on one hand, I wanted to trust him, and on the other hand, I wanted to see if I could ruin it. Together, they brought out the truth.

"I'm a dithymic akratic," I said, as if talking about the weather.

He considered me with the tilt of his head that was slowly becoming familiar. "I've never met one."

"You almost certainly have," I said. "You just didn't realize it."

He winced, seeming to think that he'd offended me. Instinctively, wanting to reassure him, I moved a little closer. To my surprise, he didn't question me any further about the akrasia. I'd grown used to being picked apart whenever someone learned of it, but he filed away the information without a fuss.

"And you think that has something to do with your broken magic?" he asked.

"Not exactly. It might have something to do with why Gailhardt couldn't get a clear reading."

He didn't understand.

"Magic and the mind are closely intertwined," I said tiredly. "I may soon have an episode. That's all."

"Episode." Of course I hadn't avoided *all* inquiry. The question was implicit: *What does it look like?*

I had to claw the words out syllable by syllable. "You recognized the term," I muttered. "I'm sure you know the generalities."

"Sort of."

It occurred to me that clinging to the thread of connection I felt with Oliver was a form of self-torture. I saw the path forward clearly, and it was the same path as always. I knew that when I reached the end, I would be left right where I'd begun, with nothing to show for it but another black mark on my name.

But in the instant before I could turn away from him, he spoke again. "Listen, do you want to take a walk? Do you have time?"

Florian had warned me about this. I *knew* that I should refuse.

"All right," I said. I could sever the thread later, I thought. It didn't have to be tonight.

We walked through the halls silently until we'd made our way outdoors, and Oliver began to wander the campus. I could tell he had no specific course in mind. I stayed at his side, mute until addressed again.

"Do I make you uncomfortable?" he asked.

"No," I said, horrified. "Saints. No."

"It's just that you always seem a bit tense around me. Me specifically. I know I come on strongly—I can lay off if you like."

If I had already decided my interest in him was useless, there was no reason anymore to conceal my faults. "It's nothing you've done wrong. It's me. I'm—" I made a wild, sweeping gesture. "I'm not suited for any of this."

He stopped walking for a moment, gazing up at the stars instead of me, before resuming. "Huh."

A flare of petty drama possessed me. *I'm made of poison. I'm a black hole. I'm a parasite that always kills its host.* I could say those things and drive Oliver off with total efficacy.

I reminded myself that I was an adult. "I just have a busy mind," I said instead.

"The gears never stop turning?"

"They catch and rust."

He nodded. "Can I ask you more about the, ah . . ."

"Derangement," I provided.

His brow furrowed. "Now, I'm not a doctor, but I'm almost certain that's not a medical term."

Despite it all, I laughed. "Ask."

"Your friend with the gray eyes. He's your keeper, isn't he?"

To be *seen* is not always comfortable. I resisted the urge to pull my hair and lifted my chin. "Yes."

"Now I understand."

"I'm sorry."

"No, don't apologize."

I treasured that extension of grace while he thought of his next question. "Did you always have the—the problem?" he asked.

We had started to walk in a circle, rounding on our second lap. "No. It just happened one day."

"Like falling off a ladder," he said.

"Maybe."

"Could it ever go away?"

"Some people can get close." I had abandoned any hope that I would be so lucky.

"Some people."

"And others deteriorate forever."

"I'm prying too much," he said, after a dreadful pause.

"Tell me about your work instead," I said softly. Our last conversation shouldn't be all about me. I wanted to hear him speak about something he liked.

The transition was ungainly, but he nodded. "What do you want to know?"

"Do you ever get stage fright?"

He shook himself slightly, as if exorcising a shiver—a dramatic gesture, but uncalculated. "I had it bad after the accident, once I could act again. It lasted months."

"How did you fix it?"

"Just time," he said, shrugging. "They say time heals all wounds."

I remembered that some people saw time as a flat line rather than a circle and allowed myself to envy him for a moment. "Does it?" I said vaguely.

"Maybe not. It healed that one, at least."

The concession warmed me. "It must be hard work to memorize your lines."

"It's easier when the words follow a meter."

So that was the source of his pleasing, distinct cadence. He must hear meter in everything. Without warning, a sweep of loneliness took me, exquisite enough that my breath caught. I stood still and covered my eyes.

"Oh. I suppose I shouldn't keep you any longer," Oliver said. The uncertainty I heard made me look up again; he was watching me with pure concern.

I couldn't do it. He was *friendly*. Denying myself this was too much to ask, and that was that. "Walk me home again," I said.

He bloomed into a grin. "Absolutely."

We broke out of the circle we'd been treading and made for the Pharmakeia's nearest exit. Once I'd gathered the courage, I cleared my throat. "I like seeing you," I said. I meant *seeing you* only in the most literal sense of the word, but the intimacy of the phrasing struck me, and I felt myself flush.

He seemed to sense the same thing, but it amused him instead. "You know, Adrien, you're a very attractive man."

It was so outrageous that I nearly fled on principle.

He saw my expression even in the gloom of the evening and held up his hands. "I'm sorry. That was too much."

"You're actually *interested*," I said accusatorily, overcome with bewilderment. "You've—you've overplayed your hand now."

"You're interesting," he said. "So of course I am."

Saints, my fatal flaw.

"Dear God," I mumbled.

"I can't tell if that's a good reaction."

"I might not be fit for company soon," I said. "Any kind of company at all."

"We'll see. I don't see why I shouldn't keep talking to you."

For a moment, I could see that he was vulnerable. He raked through his hair, pace quickening for a few steps. "You haven't really mentioned if you feel the same," he said.

"Yes," I said softly. "From the moment I heard you speak."

He clapped his hands together. "Excellent. That's a load off my mind."

I found myself smiling. "You couldn't tell?"

"I thought so, but I don't like to make that kind of assumption."

It was far too early in our acquaintance to consider holding hands on the rest of the walk, which I regretted sorely. It wasn't too early to laugh, however, and he made me do plenty of that as we drew closer to my house. Acting benefits from a certain skill with comic timing; he had that well taken care of. Every motion of his seemed graceful in the dark, and I was grateful for the moments when his face caught the witchlight streetlamps.

It's not a point of pride for me that I'm hopeless against a man I want. I pine; I fixate. I'd done the same with Casmir, and it had very nearly killed me. I wanted it all to be over with for good, one way or another.

Imagine my dismay, then, when I realized that I couldn't even say good-bye to Oliver at the door for fear of Florian seeing and disapproving. I had to stop him just out of sight of the house to bid him good night, like a teenager with a secret.

"Here is good," I said under my breath.

He reached into one of the pockets of his blindingly colored jacket and produced a small, folded paper sheet: an advertisement for a play, garish and uniformly uppercased. "HARUSPEX AMBROSE AND THE CHILD EM-PRESS," it read, and underneath an illustration of an evil-looking little girl, the showing times for the upcoming play were listed. They were all in the following weeks.

"I'm Haruspex Ambrose," he said, with some amount of pride. "Come see it someday, won't you? We're at the Copper Arch Theater."

"I will," I promised. "When I can." Even if I had to drag myself to the theater, I would.

He held his hand out, and I gave it a brief squeeze before he took it back. "Then I'll see you later."

I hurried into the house, doing my best to conceal my awe, to partition away the abject confusion the night had left me in.

Florian received me with his usual measured cordiality, and if he noticed anything amiss, he gave no sign. "How was the meeting?" he asked when I passed him on my way into my atelier. He'd been examining a bookshelf in the hallway.

I tried to sound neutral. "Gailhardt didn't manage much."

He nodded without surprise and turned away. For the rest of the evening, he made no attempt to speak with me otherwise; I told myself that it was idiotic to expect him to. I could feel his attention on me, on my location in the house; that was enough—that was all his keeper's duties required of him.

He called for me finally just before I went to bed, to both my apprehension and relief.

"We'll try some healing again," he said once I had answered, and motioned me toward the guest room. As before, he sat me down on his bed and put his hands on my temples, and his magic came flooding into me, silver and warm. I was half afraid he'd somehow see in my mind that I'd deceived him, but he never said a thing.

"I don't suppose you'd like me to try addressing your akrasia as well?" he asked me as he was finishing up.

My answer came without thought. "I see Malise for that."

He stepped back and dusted his hands together. "Very well."

He drew a breath as if to add something, but the second sentence never came. After he nodded at me, I realized that I was being invited to leave and forced myself to stand, dizzy and longing to close my eyes.

"Good night," I said.

Florian made no reply.

Guiltily pleased that I hadn't needed to confess to my walk with Oliver, I crawled into bed and drifted in and out of wakefulness until sunrise, indulging in smudged, watercolored fantasies that I forgot in the morning.

Chapter 9

Although it felt as though Oliver's admission of interest had been a momentous event, my schedule remained the same. There were still things to do, and I couldn't spend all my time ruminating—neither my unsteady hope nor my dread of an oncoming episode were good excuses to slack.

If nothing else, at least the worry I'd felt for Gennady after his brush with the Penumbra was eased slightly by his continued presence at the Pharmakeia in the next week. He still stopped by, idling outside my office occasionally or catching me before class, adding the academy to a "patrol route" I wasn't sure actually existed. My impression of Gennady's place in the Vigil was that his superiors were content to keep him out of the way, and if he reported his time loitering in the Pharmakeia as a patrol, that was good enough.

The first time he intercepted me before my office hours were due to start, I opened the door and nodded him inside. "You look better than before," I said, by way of greeting.

Lady dipped her muzzle in acknowledgment. Gennady only squinted. "What?" He seemed to have no idea what I meant. If nothing else, he'd gotten better at lying. Either way, it meant he was at ease with me again.

"I just mean you seem well," I said.

"Sure. Whatever."

It became clear that he was not going to follow me inside the office, so I stepped back out and let the door close with a sigh. I wanted nothing more than to sit down; the tension of spending my days trying to analyze myself for more akratic warning signs had begun to induce something of a backache.

"You're all peaky," Gennady said.

I grimaced. "Only tired."

"Comes of being eighty years old."

"Gennady."

"Sorry. Seventy years old."

I was only lucky he hadn't gone to ninety. "I've been a little off balance," I murmured.

Lady's ears perked subtly. "That new keeper of yours is doing a good job?" Gennady asked after an uncomfortable pause.

I studied him, trying to tell if the question had been a veiled barb, if he resented me having replaced him—but the question seemed to have been made in the spirit of an offering.

"He's fine," I said.

"So he's not a piece of trash like the last one?"

"Casmir *tried*."

"Not that hard," Gennady said. Lady made a derisive chattering sound.

"In any case. Florian's fine, as I said."

I wasn't sure if Gennady would be able to perceive exactly how worried I was about Malise's intuition that something was wrong. Somewhat absurdly, I felt the urge to throw him off the scent. I had to offer him something that would shift his focus.

So I added, "Actually, he's not the only new person I've met lately."

"Yeah? What's that mean?"

I allowed a note of the wretched hopefulness I felt whenever I thought about Oliver to shine through my voice. "Well, there's this man from Gailhardt's trial group—she's the professor who's been looking at my magic—and he's quite nice, really—"

Gennady pulled a face and stepped away, already angling for an exit. "Never mind. Don't want to hear about it. Shouldn't have stopped by."

Perfectly executed. I could insulate him a while longer. "Another day, then," I said, and waved him off as Lady ambled behind him.

Alone with my dread once more, I went inside my office to finally, gratefully sit down.

As a small mercy, I had something to distract me in the near future: a field trip was scheduled for later that week.

The Gallery of Mekhania and the Palenne Natural Philosophy Museum are situated side by side on the same street, with a few hallways connecting the two complexes from within. I had always enjoyed going to both, and I thought my Modern Mekhania class might benefit from a visit to the gallery. Smaller examples of mekhania are easy to bring into the classroom, but there's nothing like seeing some more impressive specimens to instill a respect for the art.

Field trips were rare; my students were all eager to get out of the Pharmakeia for any amount of time. The gallery and the museum were close enough to walk to, and the interlude into the sunshine seemed to do them some good.

I planned to take them through the museum on the way to the gallery, admittedly less for their education than because of my own fondness for the place. It didn't quite fit the subject of the class, but it certainly couldn't hurt.

The ceilings of the Palenne Natural Philosophy Museum are magnificently high and made of fine glass, as is common with most of the grand architecture in Deme Palenne. Each room is vast; the hallways are wide and sprawling. Footsteps echo on the floor. I led my students past the exhibits of glittering rare minerals, past the wall of exotic fish preserved in oil with their scales shining. I could have spent hours on each, but we didn't have much time to linger, even if I could have justified it with the curriculum.

When we passed the centerpiece of the museum, though, I had to pause. The crown jewel of the complex is a double fossil—two tyrant drakes engaged in battle, one much larger than the other. They'd been found interlocked, sporting obvious skeletal damage, and were painstakingly articulated to simulate the encounter. The pedestals and supports that served as their perennial arena were several times taller than a human.

I was impelled to stop and stare, and my students followed suit. There's something about the sheer size of the animals that demands one's undivided attention. Although there's no danger from the dead, a part of us can never fully accept that. The rest of the hall of bones and fossils, lined with species both extant and extinct, faded into the backdrop.

One of my favorite students, a long-faced blonde girl named Xantha, appeared at my elbow. She squinted up at the drakes. "Professor?" she said.

I turned, sheepish, expecting to be scolded for the detour. "Hmm?"

"How can we be sure that they died fighting each other?"

"I wouldn't know," I admitted. "The damage to the bones builds some of the case, and I'm sure there are other signs, but I'm not an expert."

She seemed disappointed by the answer, but it was better than pretending knowledge where there was none. "It's interesting to believe, at least," she said.

"Absolutely. They usually aren't found so intact, even leaving aside the fact that there are two. It's a fantastic discovery." I noticed my tone rising, too quick and animated, and suppressed myself—but not before I heard one of the students in the back snicker.

I looked toward the sound. "Don't you think so?" I said gently. "I think so."

There was no answer; I shrugged. It was time to move along. I turned away from the fossils reluctantly and started off toward the gallery again, imagining that I could feel the creatures' hollow gazes on my back. The students followed. We left the drakes to their eternal battle.

I couldn't help but feel my mood lift when we finally got to the Gallery of Mekhania. Once we passed through the gate of delicate, elegantly wrought metal, we entered an area that was one of my specialties. I felt at home surrounded by the bizarre contraptions of the gallery; whether powered by pure magic or pure ambric energy or some combination of both, they were subject to my will.

"What do we most want to see first?" I asked the class. "The automatons or the vehicles?"

"Do they have witchfinder eyes here?" one of the students asked.

I shook my head. "The Watchtower keeps its secrets very well. No outsiders have access to that technology." Any replicas of the witchfinders' mekhania eyes are unauthorized, and possession of them comes with a prison sentence.

"Automatons," the group suggested as a whole, instead. I set our course for the wing of the gallery devoted to such things, the world of false life.

Upon entering, we were faced with a wall of glass cases filled with mekhanical humanoids, each perhaps seven feet tall. These were the combat models. From left to right, they grew infinitesimally more advanced as the versions passed by. Complex sets of gears served as their joints. Their features were articulated only crudely; there were no eyes, only the faintest indentations where eyes might be. They stood stiffly, giving the impression of staring straight ahead. With their bladed arms crossed over their chests, they seemed to be ready for battle at any moment.

Whenever I came to the gallery, I always entertained the briefest, uneasy fantasy of the automatons breaking their glass cages and turning on their onlookers. It was absolutely impossible—they had no source of power, external or internal—but something in the set of their metal shoulders brought the fear to mind, just as with the tyrant drakes.

"These are Aicorine designs," I told the class. "Inside the chest is a hollow compartment made of electrum magicum designed to hold a small animal. See the hinge in front? The animal's energy feeds into the mekhania, amplified many times by the electrum; the automaton moves only so long as the animal lives."

"Isn't that cruel?" a young man asked doubtfully.

"Of course. Aicor's magical laws are far laxer than ours. It would be illegal to operate these here. They're only for display and education."

I heard a murmur from the small crowd. Confused about what I'd said wrong, I opened my mouth to speak again, to clarify that I didn't approve of the Aicorine method—

"That's right," said Theo, as he sidled up beside me and slung an arm around me. "Extremely illegal."

I bit back a very genuine squeak of surprise and carefully removed his arm. Silvestra came up on my other side.

"Inquisitors," I said. I continued on sheer instinct: "You didn't strike me as the types to enjoy a museum."

"We aren't," Silvestra said. "We needed to talk to you."

I shook my head. "How did you know we'd be here?"

"We pressed the academy about your lesson plan for the day," she said. "The head of the mekhania studies department was able to tell us."

Their weapons weren't pointed at me yet, but I knew better than to take that for granted. My students murmured louder. Theo didn't seem quite as jovial anymore.

I looked the inquisitors over. "Are we going somewhere?" I said quietly.

"Well, yes. We have a little headquarters in Deme Alidor," Theo said. "Near the Watchtower, actually. It's an old witchfinder building, just repurposed. We thought we could spend some time there with you, Professor."

I struggled to speak. "I don't suppose you'd let me finish my tour of the museum first. These students have an exam coming up. Some of my comments on the exhibits here might be helpful to them."

"No," Silvestra said.

But Theo shrugged. "I don't see why not."

"Then try not to interrupt," I said, more strongly: suddenly, by some miracle, anger had overridden fear. They were disrupting my lesson. I turned to the class. "Any questions about the Aicorine automatons?"

No one said a word. We moved on to the far more impressive Saebar examples.

The inquisitors did not have the grace to linger in the back of the crowd as they accompanied us through the rest of the gallery. They stayed near me, one on either side. Once, Silvestra drew a breath to interrupt me, and I wheeled on her immediately. "They have an *exam*," I told her. "On Trimidy."

She stared in bewilderment. Theo laughed, impressed more than amused. I would succumb to anxiety once I was out of sight of my students, I decided. Until then, I had a responsibility to model something like courage for them—and to avoid any signs of a guilty conscience.

We finished with the automatons and moved onto the smaller inventions, the various measuring instruments and household conveniences. Vehicles were next: "The energy needed to power something of this size is too much to make regular use for the average citizen a reasonable possibility," I said flatly as Silvestra breathed down my neck. "As impressive as the invention is, they're unlikely to become widespread until technology improves."

My students watched silent and wide-eyed as I marched us through the whole of the gallery. Finally, when we'd come to the last exhibit—automated abacuses—Theo tapped me gently on the shoulder.

"Time to go," he said.

"I need to take the students back to the academy. It isn't responsible to leave them here."

"You're under arrest," Silvestra said.

I allowed myself a moment to adjust to that reality.

"Professor Desfourneaux," Xantha said bravely. "I can make sure everyone gets back."

I found it in me, somehow, to force an anemic smile. "That would be good of you." And I turned to address the rest of the students. "Don't count on getting out of your exam."

Xantha wrung her hands as the inquisitors guided me away.

The caleche ride to Deme Alidor was uncomfortable. Theo tried to make small talk on the way, but neither Silvestra nor I were having it. She answered him in monosyllables, and I answered him somewhat unkindly, and between the two of us we had him silent by the end.

The inquisitors' base had the same feel I had come to expect from Clementia buildings: a gray, uncompromising functionality. The architecture was blocky, and any decoration was spare. I hated it, and as they brought me inside, I let them know so.

"It's ugly here," I muttered.

"Good thing this place wasn't built to impress magicians," Theo said lightly.

"What *was* it built for?" I asked.

"The security of this city," Silvestra said. I fought the urge to roll my eyes.

They took me into a small room with no windows, a single table, and three chairs. The two of them sat. I elected to pace, finally allowing myself the luxury of anxiety. The smell of dust made me want to sneeze.

"I thought we were done with this," I said.

"We never said that," Theo said. "We never promised anything of the sort."

"So have you found some kind of evidence against me? Something that justifies taking me away from my work in the middle of the day?"

"Well," said Theo, "we certainly haven't brought you here for *no* reason."

"Then you have?"

Neither replied, which told me the answer. "Not at all," I said.

"We have reason to believe you know something about the angel," Silvestra said shortly. "That you're closer to the situation than you've let on."

"Should I take that to mean you still suspect me?"

"Not exactly," Silvestra said, before Theo could stop her. He gave her an exasperated look—she hadn't been meant to give that away yet.

"Then it's someone I know."

There was no explicit confirmation, but Theo said, "You keep some interesting company. That's for sure."

"Tell me who you're talking about. Definitively."

"We can't do that," he said. "We can't bias your answer; you'll have to give us the details without suggestion."

"Then I can hardly help you. How do you intend to interrogate me if you won't tell me who you're interrogating me about? Do you think I have the secret of who it is hidden away somewhere, and I'll confess it if you just ask me enough times?"

They looked at me with complete bleakness, and it was then that I realized they were going to do me violence.

"I'm a citizen," I hissed. "You have no right. I'm a licensed magician."

"That may be so, but this is an inquisition," Theo said.

I'd let them lull me into the belief that the Clementia was anything less than the sword of the city, ready to turn on anyone it deemed fit. Theo's easy charm, Silvestra's sullenness, they'd both concealed from me the hard fact of their occupation.

"Sit down," Theo suggested. "You'll want to." I sat. The two of them got up.

Sparks of lightning drifted around me, from my eyes, from my scars. I felt the rift inside me pulsing. "Control it," Silvestra said.

"They're harmless."

"Control it."

I closed my eyes and shut my magic deep inside. For a moment, I had a wild thought that I might call it all to the surface and summon it for a fight, but I realized that it would be nothing less than suicide to try. When I looked up, it was only reluctantly.

"Tell us about the people you know," Theo said, almost kindly. He came to stand in front of me.

"The doctors? I only really know a few."

There was an unreadable silence before Theo shook his head. "We can't specify further."

"It only makes sense for you to be looking at the doctors."

He shrugged. "Anyone could have information. Just talk."

"Malise," I said. "A healer. The finest person I've ever known. Beyond reproach."

Nothing.

"Gennady," I said. "Vigil. He has no possible connection to this."

Nothing.

"Florian. Another healer. My keeper. I don't know him well."

Nothing.

"Casmir. He's with Light Studies—he's left the city now."

Nothing.

There was no chance they could be talking about Oliver; I didn't dare to speak his name for fear of somehow turning their suspicion on him. I fell silent, and the inquisitors stared, their eyes identically blank.

I went through Gailhardt and her other test subjects. I went through the other professors I knew and what doctors at the Chirurgeonate I had any direct knowledge of. In abject desperation, I brought up my parents, long estranged, and any childhood friends I could remember. All throughout, they said nothing.

"Professor," Theo said unhappily. "Look. I'm not going to enjoy this."

A wave of fury swept through me. "I should hope not," I breathed, and took off my glasses to set them on the table. I didn't have a spare pair handy. "But spare me the reassurance."

He drew nearer and closed his gloved hands around my throat, applying only the barest pressure. "Go through the list again. Start with the healers."

"I can't tell you any more."

He squeezed.

Common sense told me not to bother trying to pry him off, that surely I'd only be punished even if I managed to get away. My body didn't listen. As soon as I was starving for air, I scrabbled uselessly at his hands until my vision started to fade.

I'd had this done to me before. My familiarity with the sensation didn't help. The burn of asphyxiation, the red-hot desperation, they don't get easier with time.

Once I was listing in my chair, Theo stepped away.

I could strike them both with lightning and simply walk out, I thought hazily. It would be easy if I could get past the break in my magic. *If*.

But the consequences would be too great, and I couldn't kill. I kept my magic quiet.

"Repeat the list," Silvestra said.

My voice hurt, but I tried again. I'd known Malise in school, I told them. I'd met Gennady more recently. Florian was new, and Casmir was not, and no, no, no, I knew nothing about any angels.

Theo stepped forward. I flinched hard. "I don't know anything."

"We won't be able to confirm that until we break you," he said. I will allow him this much: he looked genuinely upset, genuinely reluctant. It could hardly matter to me in the moment. I looked past him to Silvestra, but she wasn't watching me at all. She had one of the invisibility spheres I'd seen them use during our first encounter; she was tossing it up in the air and catching it again. The little game had the air of a distraction to it. She didn't want to watch.

"Don't touch me," I told Theo.

Again, he choked me. Again, when my vision was a star field, he let me go.

I wiped my watering eyes with a shaking hand. "I don't know anything."

I refused to cry in earnest. I have an easy instinct toward tears, but I wouldn't be showing them that. I tried to sit up straight again, tried to even my breathing, and waited.

"We can do this forever," Theo said gently. "I would rather not, but . . ."

Silvestra shifted uneasily. "We could break fingers."

He considered.

"Clementia," I snarled, my voice a withered thing.

Theo said, "Desfourneaux, work with us. We don't think it's you. We really don't. But there's no way you know nothing. You're *close* to this."

"I don't know how," I said. "You won't tell me who." He reached out again, and I jerked back with a whine. I couldn't escape Silvestra, however, when she grabbed my left wrist.

Almost tenderly, she separated my index finger from the others.

I felt myself perfectly balanced on the edge between terror and hatred. The knife spun, and finally, it landed on one side: I despised them. "Animals," I said.

"I'm sorry," Silvestra said; the apology sat poorly on her. I knew she could see how revolting I found it—I felt an involuntary sneer twist my face. As if to prevent me from commenting, she broke my index finger. The sound was somehow even worse than the pain, and I felt more than saw the lightning strike that left scars in the table in front of me.

"No lightning," Theo reminded me. "We'll use the antimagic cuffs if we need to."

"I don't know anything!"

Silvestra moved on to the next finger. I may have fainted, or it might have only been close, a moment crystallized out of time. Either way, the next thing I registered was Silvestra and Theo exchanging drawn looks as they moved back from me.

"I don't know," I said, the sawing pain in my hand closing my voice down to a whisper.

"We could keep you in the Penumbra until you tell us," Silvestra said. "Maybe the Umbra. You are a magician, after all."

The underground cells of the Umbra, situated beneath the Penumbra, are lined with hundreds of wards to keep their magical prisoners helpless. Every magician in Astrum has had nightmares about being held captive there. "No," I said. I was overcome with the urge to spit at the inquisitors. Thank the stars, it went unsatisfied.

"The Umbra, then," Silvestra said. She pulled me to my feet, refusing to let me buckle to the ground. Theo raised a hand sharply; I choked on my breath, an ugly sound.

"No—"

Without relish, he backhanded me.

I doubted. I could make something up, and maybe they'd let me go. I could throw some random doctor to the wolves, if only so they'd let me catch my breath again. Just for a few seconds.

They saw some of the hesitation in me as I reeled; they both paused.

But I rallied. "I don't know anything." It was the last time I could say it.

Silvestra sighed and let me collapse into my chair again. Theo shook his head ruefully. "Well, that's that," he said to her. "We could really hurt the man, but . . . this is past the point most citizens break at."

Silvestra seemed to be marveling at me. "Incredible. He doesn't know. We'll have to get other corroboration. How do secrets like this get kept?"

"Tell me who you're talking about," I rasped, as the cheerless gray room spun before me.

Theo patted me on the back. I nearly toppled over. "We still can't do that. Information security."

I swore.

The two of them watched me for a while, grim. My fear ebbed to a dull shriek.

"Well," Theo said eventually, "we can call you a caleche home. Or back to the Pharmakeia, if you want to get back to teaching."

I gave him a look of deep loathing.

"Home, then."

"You tortured me for nothing."

"We had to make sure—"

"For nothing. You tortured me for nothing."

"We tortured you in the service of Astrum and all of Martyr's Reach," Silvestra said, "and there will be no apologies for that." She retrieved my glasses from the table and set them on my face, adjusting them to be even, which I hated, hated, hated. That was Malise's gesture to make.

My throat hurt too much for me to retort. I let them put me in a caleche bound for my house in Deme Palenne without saying another word. Theo wished me well as I was getting inside, very sincerely, and I tried to laugh—but a coughing fit overtook me. I cradled my maimed left hand to my chest.

Chapter 10

By the time I was home, my shaking had subsided. I opened the door clumsily with my intact right hand and stumbled to the couch, and as soon as I had the option to collapse, I couldn't stand. Florian was sitting at the dining room table with a handwritten patient roster I'd occasionally seen him contemplating before; it was one of his few days off.

"You're early," he said. He hadn't looked up.

A few tears welled. I swiped them away with a raw noise of disgust, and instantly, he was at my side.

"Adrien?"

"The inquisitors," I murmured. "They took me to Deme Alidor."

Now the red marks around my neck and on my face were easy to see. He reached to touch one, and instantly I was scrambling away in a blind panic—he stopped moving. "I can heal that," he said.

He coaxed me forward; slowly, I edged toward him. When he put his hands around my throat, I thought I'd faint again, but his healing magic flowed fast and warm and wonderful. The pain wasn't gone—I'd still bruise—but he'd taken away the worst of it all. I gasped in relief. Immediately, the enervation that had come after he'd last cast on me set in.

"Let me see your hand."

Reluctantly, I showed it to him.

"This is going to be unpleasant," he said. Before I could brace, he pulled the broken bones back into position. I inhaled to shriek, and then I felt the cracks fuse as he healed me—a dissonant, nauseating jolt. An ache remained, deep, but the agony was gone.

Mending bones is no small task for a healer. Florian hadn't understated his talent. After a moment's pause, he hugged me to him. I melted into it, helpless against the offer of safety. "I couldn't tell them anything," I said.

For the briefest instant, I thought I saw him smile.

Then the wash of his magic shivered through me again, and the moment dissolved into silver bubbles. He brushed the now-faded bruise on my cheek; although it was a purely diagnostic touch, I leaned into it.

"They wouldn't believe me. That I don't know who the angel is. They think it's someone I'm involved with somehow."

He said nothing for a long time.

"Florian?"

"Strange," he said. "I can't account for that."

"I'm so tired."

He helped me to my feet and guided me into my bedroom.

"It's the middle of the day," I said fuzzily. "The Pharmakeia . . ."

"I'll tell them you're indisposed."

I tried to get up again, but he pressed me back.

I forced myself to speak. "I should go—"

"As your keeper," he said, "I'm telling you to take a break. Let me make your excuses to the Pharmakeia for you. They'll understand."

I'd promised him not to be difficult. I subsided.

From where I lay, his expression was strangely shadowed. "Do you want to sleep?" he asked.

I didn't; I shook my head.

A flicker of frustration marred his face; I felt it like a sudden impalement— but I didn't tell him to go ahead. Not yet. "No," I said.

"Adrien."

"No."

"It'll be good for you." He put a hand over mine, and I saw silver in his eyes.

I looked away, silently deferring. He might know best.

"Sleep," he said. The power behind his words was undeniable; it dripped from them, lined them like black velvet. My consciousness fled.

Healer's sleep has always left me with a headache. I've never taken to it. When I woke the next morning after hours and hours of thick oblivion, I wished I'd stayed unconscious.

Florian was gone from the house when I dragged myself up to check. I was hurt, for a moment, until I realized that I could hardly expect him to take another day off work just to stay with me. He'd already healed me. I showered and changed my clothes, and then, operating on habit alone, I walked to work without eating. What else could I do?

I caught a glimpse of myself in a bakery window as I walked, and the sight made me stop for a moment. I'd forgotten to comb my hair; the shadows under my eyes were deep. The bruises on my neck and face weren't gone, nor the ache in my fingers. Behind the window, a woman holding a tray of phyllo stared at me with alarm; I flinched from her gaze and moved on. I was already late.

I passed a few students from Modern Mekhania on the walk to my lecture hall. When they saw the state I was in, they understood very well what had happened. I could see the news spreading throughout the Pharmakeia like a contagion, but I was too tired to care.

Xantha appeared at my side to carry my books for me, which I allowed with a nod. I took them back from her once we were near the hall of St. Osiander. "Thank you," I said distantly. "Thank you very much."

"Are you going to be all right, Professor?"

"Not for some time."

"We should have stopped them," she said. "We should have done something."

I made myself look at her. "Don't say that."

She opened her mouth. I shook my head.

"I would go with them a thousand times before I would choose one of you to go instead," I said, as deliberately as I could. "There was nothing to be done."

She gave me a jerky nod; I dredged up a smile and rounded the last corner to my lecture hall without her. The instinct was there to comfort her for longer, but I wasn't sure I was capable of it.

Gennady was waiting near the door, leaning against a nearby wall with Lady at his feet. When he saw me, he waved briskly—then he really took me in, and he was striding toward me. Lady gave a sharp yip of alarm.

"What the hell happened to you?"

"Inquisitors happened to me. Please, Gennady. I'm late for class."

Something in my voice prevented him from following. Confounded, he let me past him into the room. He stood at the door and watched me as I walked to the front of the classroom; I didn't look up at any of the filled seats, and I didn't look back. *Clementia,* I thought.

I taught without directly acknowledging any student, although they were all rapt with bewildered attention, none of them even daring to whisper to each other. Absently, I reflected that I wished Silvestra had injured my right hand instead—at least it wouldn't hurt so much to write on the board. Within thirty minutes, my voice had started to go again, and I used the last of it to tell the students that they were free to leave.

They trickled out past Gennady as he stared in at me. Once they were all gone, he bounded inside like a restless puppy, skidding to a stop in front of me. Lady reared up to put her paws on me, and I gently dislodged her. *Clementia.*

"The inquisitors took you?"

"The inquisitors took me."

"What'd they do?"

"Torture."

"Okay," he said. "Which inquisitors? I'll go kill them."

"Why," I said, "why, why, *why* is the instinct of the Curia Clementia always toward violence?"

He took a step back, uncertain.

"You can't solve this by killing them. In fact, Gennady, very few things can be solved by killing people."

I was hissing at him now, hurting my throat—and I hated myself for it. He was only protective of me, only trying to show concern. He was doing the best that he could, and I was berating him for it. But I couldn't stop. "They think someone I know is the angel," I said lowly. "I couldn't tell them who, and they tortured me for it. It's over now. There's nothing to be done. Let it go."

"I have to kill them," he said, and pulled his hair just as I did sometimes. "Come on. I'll be sneaky. No one will know it was me."

"You couldn't be *sneaky* if your life depended on it," I said, largely without malice. It was simple fact.

Lady meowed softly. "They hurt you," Gennady said. He couldn't comprehend what I was saying. "Someone's got to die." It was in such moments that I was most angry at the Clementia—when I saw what they'd done to Gennady, what their machine had made him into.

"I beg of you," I said, "by all the saints, be sensible for once."

That *for once* stung him. I saw it, and I regretted it, and I dug my nails into my wrist, although my fingers throbbed.

"Okay," he said rustily.

"It's going to be all right," I said, once I'd recovered my wits. "I promise. It'll be all right."

"What about everything else?"

"Everything else?"

"You've seemed bad lately."

The daimon's shadow had been visible to him after all.

"It's another episode," I admitted. "Probably."

He fidgeted in place. "I hate it. I hate this."

I couldn't control myself. "Gennady, let me assure you, you probably don't hate it quite as much as I do."

Lady rumbled quietly. I took off my glasses and covered my eyes, blocking them both out of my sight until I could try again.

"Thank you," I said eventually, looking back up. "That's good of you. It really is."

He was silent.

"But I'm not fit for conversation right now."

He replaced the step he'd taken away from me earlier. "I want to meet that new keeper," he said inscrutably. "Don't you owe me that, at least? I want to see him."

Of course Gennady would fixate on my keeper as an object of suspicion. "Fine," I said, just to escape. "Come on Tetrady at seven in the evening. You can talk to him."

He nodded.

"Briefly," I said.

"Whatever."

For a moment, he seemed as though he might say something else, something scathing—but the moment passed, and he turned sharply away from me and marched away without another word.

I set myself down in one of the seats and put my head in my hands.

Later that night, after I had survived my workday by the skin of my teeth, I found that I couldn't resist the urge to go to the Chirurgeonate. Not to see Malise, no; I couldn't bear her horror yet—I wasn't going there for her.

I hadn't been to see my surviving patients from the Philidor solarium in some time. Normally, I tried to go once a week, but I'd been minimizing my time at the Chirurgeonate. The desire to check on them had grown steadily; the longer I went, the stronger my abiding guilt became. Although they would surely never wake, and it could make no difference to them, I liked to pay my respects in person every now and again.

Several had passed away since the incident, but ten remained. They were interred in rooms forty-three to fifty-three of the Chirurgeonate's Hessalon building. Once I'd slunk inside Hessalon, hoping I wouldn't run into Malise, I started on my way to room forty-three.

Even before I got there, I noticed a commotion emanating from the room. My stomach dropped—I rushed to see what was happening. It was Willette's room, an older woman who had been stable in her coma for years.

There was a team of doctors in the room with Willette—

With her corpse.

The doctors faded into an indistinct mass of Chirurgeonate blue as I carefully picked my way inside the room, heedless of the fact that I no longer belonged there.

Someone took me by the shoulder. I flinched before I realized that it was Florian—he was one of the doctors. "You shouldn't be here," he said. There was a strangeness in his voice, something lurking under the surface. Concern? Annoyance? I couldn't tell.

"She was my patient once," I said quietly. I didn't care that the others were staring at me. "What happened?"

"An orderly found her," he said. "We can't be sure if it was the angel yet, but . . ."

But it was a good enough guess. I stared at Willette's face—I had already memorized it over the years, of course, but I wanted to crystallize this moment as well. I wanted it preserved in glacial ice in my mind. She'd had brown eyes, I remembered, but I could no longer say with certainty what shade, and this forgetfulness felt tantamount to sin.

Florian began to steer me out of the room. "You shouldn't be here," he said again. I let him take me into the hallway, and then around the corner, until I couldn't see into Willette's room any longer. The faint bubble of disbelief I'd managed to maintain until then broke; I began to shake. The angel had reached me.

"I'm sorry we couldn't save her," Florian said.

"She wouldn't have been here if not for Philidor," I said. "I may as well have killed her myself." I hadn't administered our final treatment to every Philidor victim, but Willette had asked for me specifically.

Florian shook his head. "Listen to me. Those patients are never going to wake up anyway," he said, quite reasonably. "They're already dead, breathing or not. Nothing has changed, Adrien."

I knew that was true. I'd always known it. My chest hurt anyway.

He sighed. "I know that sounds harsh, but all I mean is that there's no use blaming yourself."

"I understand," I said with difficulty.

"She's through suffering, at least." He said it with the bone-deep conviction that must only come of working mostly with terminal patients.

"I hope so," I said. It felt insufficient, as though I should have more to say, but there was nothing. I had only that: a little hope that Willette was now comfortable in the dark.

Florian's odd gray gaze flickered between my hand and neck, cataloging my leftover bruises. "We can talk about this more tonight, if you like. If that would help you."

I wasn't sure that anything would *help*, but it seemed churlish to refuse the offer. "Maybe," I said.

He stepped back from me. "Then I'll see you at home. For now, it might be best for you to leave the Chirurgeonate. I need to find one of the inquisitors here and let them know there may have been a new attack."

"I still need to see my other patients," I said. I had come for only one reason. I couldn't abandon it.

He looked past me for a moment, distracted. "Not today," he said. "Another time. When you've let me know you'll be coming so I can anticipate that it may upset you."

A silver haze of doubt softened my resolve. He was right. "I suppose."

And he guided me toward the Chirurgeonate's nearest exit without any more protests from me. I silently vowed that I would visit again soon, as soon as it was safe—as soon as Florian approved.

I couldn't avoid seeing Malise any longer than my detour had allowed. It wasn't responsible. Still, when I went to find her the next day, it was with great trepidation. I knew that I was going to need to tell her about what the inquisitors had done, and about Willette, and I knew equally well that her reaction was going to be ghastly.

By that time, she was scheduled to be hedge healing at her church, Halicar's, instead of at the Chirurgeonate. I went to Deme Cherice where it was located, hoping that the place's curate—a surly little man named Ellis—wouldn't be there. I'd only interacted with him a few times, but I'd never enjoyed it.

Halicar's, so named simply because it was located on Via Halicar, had a dirt floor; it was full of flowerbeds and birds. Many churches keep sacred animals, but Halicar's dedication to the birds was legendary. The jet statue of St. Adelai by the altar watched over the creatures day and night. They were small songbirds, mostly, nesting in the trees that lined the spacious atrium.

The sound of the birds mingled with the sound of the central fountain as I stepped inside the church. Truth be told, although Halicar's was beautiful, I never saw what Malise saw in it. I felt no holy presence there. I believed that it was special, purely because she believed that it was special, but the details of *why* mystified me.

Malise worked out of a laboratory in the basement when she was hedge healing; I headed for the stairs. The priest and curate were nowhere around for the moment, thankfully. One of them was bound to be back at any moment. I needed to be quick.

When I found Malise standing at the top of the stairs with Theo and Silvestra, my resolve to see her took a significant hit—until it occurred to me that they might do something to her, and then I was striding over with lightning in my eyes.

I wanted to say something fearsome, something that would make them think twice or at least preserve my dignity, but it wasn't to be. I said only, "Don't hurt her." At least I managed to keep it from sounding like a plea.

"Adrien," Malise said cautiously. "We were just talking." Then she saw my bruises and put a hand out to steady me.

The two inquisitors had begun to look somewhat uncomfortable. I hated them; my scars sparked. "They're abducting people," I said. "They're taking people to Deme Alidor and torturing them."

"You're looking well, Professor," Theo said, with tired cheer.

Malise put the pieces together quickly. She stepped back. "No," she said.

"Standard procedure," Silvestra said.

I put myself between Malise and them. A feral certainty overtook me, the caliber of which I had never felt before: I would kill, I would die, before I saw Malise go to Deme Alidor. "You have no questions to ask her," I said. "You have nothing to say to her."

"That's for us to decide, with all due respect," Theo said.

I shook my head. "No. Go away."

"Professor," Silvestra began.

I moved toward her. "Go."

I saw Silvestra's first instinct rise sharply in her: her hand went to the hilt of her blade. But she hesitated, either out of guilt or out of caution, and the sword stayed down. Theo took her by the sleeve, pulling her back an inch with him as he retreated. "No need for things to become unfriendly. We'll be on our way for now," he said.

"I hope you won't be waiting to grab me later," Malise said, a quaver in her voice. A light frost had begun to show on the nearby surfaces; her distress was triggering her magic.

"No," Theo said unreadably, eyeing me. "No, we wouldn't dare."

As soon as he and Silvestra began to walk away, I hurried Malise down the stairs into her laboratory. It was messy; she hadn't organized the supplies in her cabinets or her various machines and instruments in some time. It bothered me—she was usually neat. Even once we were sure the inquisitors were gone, we didn't speak for a long while, letting the closeness of the basement walls silence us.

"I'm all right," I said, once I could manage it. "Are you?"

"I'm fine. You sound horrible."

I cleared my throat experimentally. "Thank you."

She brought one hand to my cheek, not quite making contact. "You've already been healed?"

"Florian helped it along most of the way. I think the rest can mend on its own."

Her brow furrowed. "When did this happen?"

"Two days ago."

An open flash of distress showed on her face; her next exhale was clouded with frost. I had kept it from her. I'd avoided her.

"I didn't want to worry you," I said, despite knowing I had no excuse.

"It worries me more to hear that," she said gently. She folded her hands in her lap, too tight and still.

She wasn't chastising me. An apology wouldn't fit. I nodded instead, the best that I could do.

That was enough. Her clasped hands loosened a bit, though her expression remained drawn. "The inquisitors really thought you could be a suspect?" she asked.

I shook my head. "They thought it was someone I know." And now I had a much narrower idea of whom. "What questions were they asking you?"

She shuddered. "They hadn't asked me anything yet. They'd just come up to me when you rushed in. But they've been talking to everyone lately; I'm sure it was just going to be a routine interview."

I willed myself to believe her, despite the fact that she clearly didn't believe herself. "Of course," I said. "A routine interview."

We sat inside the dreadfully cold laboratory together as I told her the general details of what they'd done to me, piecemeal, and she grew steadily more furious until I thought she'd burst out of the room to go find them.

"Someone ought to stop them," she said.

"They're the Clementia. No one can." I imagined Malise sitting in that windowless room and scratched at my wrist, pulled my hair, before turning to the angel eye bracelet instead. The blue beads slipped by one at a time as I counted.

"They won't come for me," she said. "There's no *evidence*. There can't be evidence."

"That's what *I* thought, too."

She had no answer for that.

I realized that I had yet to tell her about what had happened at the Chirurgeonate. "The angel," I said, but my voice failed. I tried again. "The angel killed Willette. Florian said we can't be sure it was them yet, but it had to be. What are the chances?"

Malise took my aching left hand to separate my nails from my right wrist again—I'd returned to scratching without noticing. "I'm sorry, my dear."

"This has to end."

We could think of nothing more to say after that. The twin specters of the inquisitors and the angel hung too nearly over our heads.

Malise would not be tortured. Malise could not be tortured. No one sane would believe she had the slightest thing to do with the angel. Her reputation would protect her. I told myself these things over and over again until we'd sat listening to the birdsong upstairs for another half an hour.

"I think I'd better get home," I said finally. "I need to make something for Florian to have for dinner."

"Florian," she said. "How is he working out? Have you started feeling any worse?"

And I realized that I couldn't quite remember. When I tried to wrap my mind around the question, all I could focus on was what his magic felt like, its anesthetic glow.

"He's fine," I said absently. "Everything's just fine. Be well, Malise."

I gave her a parting hug and made my way home. The angel eye bracelet weighed heavily on me as I walked.

～

"I don't think you should go to see Gailhardt this week," Florian said that night at the dinner table. I had indeed cooked for us, although it had taken everything I had in me.

I fought through my exhaustion to look up at him. "Why not?"

He folded the newspaper he'd been leafing through. "You're still recovering from your injury. You're unstable, vulnerable. It might not be helpful to have her go poking around."

I wanted to go to Gailhardt's meeting; I wanted to make progress—I wanted *desperately* to talk to Oliver again. The exhilaration of what he'd said to me now seemed bizarrely far away, but I'd still been counting the days until the next meeting.

"The trial's not far into its data collection. If I'm spotty, it may throw off Gailhardt's analysis somehow. I'm sure I'll be fine," I said to Florian.

He looked at me. "Oh?" he said. "You're sure?"

His voice carried no bite, but I felt instantly absurd.

"You need to give yourself space to breathe," he said. I couldn't deny that having someone experiment on me didn't sound appealing. I wanted to rest—and whatever Florian had been doing with his healing, at least he was convenient to me. I could let him try without going anywhere.

"She'll be disappointed," I said.

He nodded. "My opinion as your keeper is that you should avoid the stress."

I couldn't tell him that I missed Oliver, not when he'd told me to stay away. "I'll skip this week," I said. I thought of the paper advertisement still in one of my jackets with the showing times for Oliver's play—I'd see him soon enough anyway.

"Some downtime should help you settle faster," Florian said. "I don't want you to spiral."

It was a kind thing to say, of course, but the stab of humiliation it produced in me was acute. I got up from the table and cleared our dishes. Accepting that we had nothing more to discuss, Florian returned to his gazette. I hadn't read a single paper since the inquisitors had tersely acknowledged the possibility of an angel to the public—the indirect glimpses I caught already of the hysteria surrounding the topic were enough for me. I didn't need to keep atop the rumor mill.

After the kitchen was clean, I hurried to retreat to my bedroom, but I passed the atelier on my way. After a moment, I went back. The door was open.

"Florian," I called. "Were you inside the atelier?" I hovered at the dining room threshold to look at him.

He blinked. "No."

"The door is open. I always keep it closed."

"I haven't been in," he said cautiously, "but *you* have. Earlier today. You were working on something."

"I wasn't." How could I, with my aching fingers? When would I have had the opportunity?

"I don't know what to tell you," he said. "You were."

I couldn't remember anything of the sort. I hadn't been inside my atelier in nearly two weeks. "You're mistaken."

He paused, visibly committing himself to the maintenance of his practiced, moderated tone. "Adrien, you were the one who left the door open. Maybe you've just forgotten."

I bit my tongue nearly to bleeding and shut myself in the bedroom to sit down at my desk. Forgetting one thing does not a breakdown make, I told myself. *Everyone* forgets things. Everyone does.

But not like that. I rifled through the desk drawers to find some paper. I'd clear my thoughts—I'd work on one of the manuscripts I'd abandoned lately. I had monographs that needed attention. If I could only fix my mind on any subject long enough to *make* something, I could reassure myself that I wasn't much farther gone than I'd realized.

My favorite pens were missing. I always kept them on the desk. I would never have moved them.

I got up and wandered the house. "Florian, have you seen my favorite pens?"

He watched me again from the dining room table, newspaper forgotten to the side, cloaked lightly in shadow. I fancied that his eyes glowed slightly from within, giving the impression of a nocturnal animal gazing at me from a distance. "No," he said, head tilting a bare degree. The imagined shine disappeared. "I didn't know you had any favorite pens."

Methodically, slowly, I searched each room one by one until I found the set near a drafting table in the atelier, one pen uncapped. I picked them up slowly, as if afraid they would bite, and brought them back to my desk.

"They were in the atelier," I told Florian, reemerging into the dining room.

He raised his eyebrows. "I told you. You were working on something."

"I think I'm forgetting things," I said. I caught sight of myself in the mirror I kept above the hearth—deathly pale.

"It's normal to be absentminded sometimes," he said, but he stood up and crossed the room to me.

"This feels different," I said faintly. "It's just blank."

That brought him a step closer. I had the sensation of being looked *into*, as though the individual workings of my nerves were visible to him. "That's concerning," he said, with an air of understatement.

He led me back into my bedroom and sat me down on the bed. This arrangement, him standing before me, was beginning to feel familiar. "Do you want me to see what I can feel? I'll take a look around while we do the usual procedure."

Healing magic. That's what I needed. A little healing magic. If Malise wasn't around to treat me, to stave off whatever was happening, Florian would have to do. I nodded.

As usual, he dove for the break in my magic—I felt his warmth, his comfort, his skill and craft. The pain came, as it always did, but a silver rush smoothed it over. And I felt him go deeper, searching, illuminating my mind and seeking out the cracks.

Eventually, he withdrew, grim-faced.

"There's something wrong," he said. "Yes. I can feel you coming apart. It's not a standard episode; I don't know how treatable it may be. And your magic has improved since we started working on it together, but it isn't mending as quickly as I'd like."

"Well," I said distantly. "I'll ask Malise. If she can't do anything either—if it lasts, if it's permanent . . ."

"Then what?"

Then I would find enough nepenthe to comfortably put myself down. I could not tolerate the loss of my magic and my faculties at the same time. Together, they made up the sum total of what I had to offer the world. Every drop of usefulness. I'd long worried that one of these days I'd begin an irreparable descent; this might be it.

"Then we'll see," I said.

He seemed to hesitate before replying, as if wary of upsetting me. "I wouldn't count on her being able to do anything."

"We'll see," I said once again.

He put me to sleep again that night, and this time I had no feeble objections. If I didn't accept his spell, I wouldn't be sleeping at all.

I went to work the next morning—Tetrady, finally—almost looking forward to Gennady's scheduled visit. Despite the guaranteed awkwardness, I was keen to talk to someone else who knew me, ask him if I seemed as though I was completely losing my mind.

But the issue didn't sleep until seven o'clock when Gennady was supposed to arrive. Florian came to my office around the time I was supposed to be eating lunch. His knock was sharp; he looked displeased.

"What?" I asked, fighting a subtle panic.

His lips thinned in response to the bark, and I rephrased. "What is it, Florian?"

"Where were you?"

"Here," I said, bewildered. "I was here. Why?"

"When I set down my conditions for being your keeper, we agreed that you'd be punctual when we're due to meet."

"We weren't due to meet," I said, although I no longer believed myself. The ever-familiar nausea of dread, my constant companion lately, grew heavier.

"I told you to come find me at the Chirurgeonate at twelve. You never did. I thought something might have happened to you—I took time out of my schedule to come find you."

"I forgot," I said quietly.

His expression softened slightly, but it retained some steel. "If you knew you were forgetting things lately, why didn't you write it down?"

His disapproval seared me like a brand. I wrapped my arms around myself. "I just forgot."

He shook his head.

"I'm sorry, Florian."

"You've been a little difficult to keep lately," he said, his disappointment mild but genuine.

I pulled my hair, trying to repeat my apology. The words fizzled.

He let it go. "It's all right."

A rush of sick relief left me lightheaded. He wasn't holding it against me; the terrible pressure was no longer quite as close. "I'll do better."

"I know you will," he said, which I felt was generous. "I'll see you tonight." An addition hung unspoken in the air: *Hopefully.*

Of course. Tonight. "I forgot to tell you we'll have company, too," I said stupidly.

"Company."

"My friend—he's a friend. Gennady. He wanted to meet you—he's Vigil, he's a soldier—he was my previous keeper—"

Florian lifted a hand to stop me with an almost imperceptible sigh. "I would have liked to have known."

Some part of me buried far below thought, *It's my own house, for God's sake.*

I shook myself. "He won't stay for dinner. He never does."

"You said he's Vigil."

"Very much so."

"Your previous keeper."

"Not for long."

He was waiting for more details from me. I didn't provide them: explaining Gennady to *anyone* was a notable task, and explaining Gennady to Florian in particular was beyond my ability.

After another moment of pointed consideration, during which I sat uselessly like a mannequin, Florian tired of waiting. "Very well."

"He's coming at seven," I said.

He nodded briefly and turned away, and with that, he was gone, hurrying back—I had no doubt I'd made him late for something. I sat and stared at the closed door, my paperwork abandoned. I taught my next class in an ecstasy of paranoia, convinced that at any second I'd realize I'd forgotten to administer a test, or forgotten the material altogether. I never did, although that provided little comfort. Maybe I just hadn't realized it *yet.*

Chapter 11

When Gennady knocked, I almost turned him away. Florian's visit had gutted me of any energy. But I'd told him to come, and he had; it would be unforgivable to betray him.

From the moment he walked in the door, he was peering around for Florian, who sat at the coffee table waiting. Lady sniffed the air keenly, zeroing in on the unfamiliar smell as if memorizing it. "So you're the guy," Gennady said when he saw Florian.

"I suppose," Florian said.

"Are you, you know, *the guy*?"

I covered my eyes. "No," I muttered.

Florian hesitated before shaking his head. That hesitation struck me; I had never before imagined that he might have any sort of interest in me—why would the answer not come instantly?

I put it out of my mind. I had no space for the question at all.

Gennady seemed reassured. He wasn't *jealous* of the idea; I knew that—but he clearly didn't like Florian at all. "Great," he said. He stared blankly for a few moments, struggling to formulate his next move.

"So this is Gennady," I said weakly to Florian. "My friend. My protégé of sorts."

"You don't teach him magic," Florian said without any doubt. A Vigil soldier would have no magic.

"No," I said, and then realized that I hadn't the faintest idea how to explain the matter. "I suppose we talk ethics."

"I see," Florian said, and this time there was a great deal of doubt.

"He teaches me people stuff," Gennady said blithely. "Not so often anymore, because he's always busy."

Guilt overtook me. I'd had less room for Gennady, it was true. I'd been too caught up in everything. "I'm sorry," I told Gennady, trying to make it understood that I was sincere. "If I can," I said, "I'll make more time." The *if* might save me from being a liar.

"Sure," he said, and turned to address Florian. "Hey. You want to know something?"

"I'm hesitant to say yes," Florian said mildly. Unlike most magicians, he didn't seem intimidated by Gennady at all—not even by Lady, who was lurking around his ankles, tasting the air with her mouth open and her fangs gleaming.

"I'll tell you anyway." Gennady lifted his chin, fixing Florian with the bizarre stare I'd become familiar with over time. It was a cold thing, fathoms deep.

"Gennady," I said.

He ignored me. "I don't like you," he said to Florian. "I don't think you're doing a good job."

Florian blinked. "You have no possible way of knowing that."

"I can *feel* it."

"Gennady," I said.

"And I'll tell you another thing," Gennady said. "If you hurt Desfourneaux, I'm going to come find you in the night. I'm going to break each of your bones one at a time."

He never used my name. He rarely used anyone's name except for Lady's. I recoiled in horror. "*Gennady!*"

Florian dispensed a very thin smile. "It's nice to know that he has someone who's so protective of him," he said. "But you don't need to worry. I'm good at what I do, and you're no longer his keeper."

"Gennady didn't mean that," I said.

For half a second, Gennady glared at me before returning his gaze to Florian as if reluctant to look away for too long. "I mean it. I mean every word. He's bad news. I feel it, like I said. Like you feel a storm."

Like you feel a storm. I felt something too—a pull, a tug, some call to attention deep within myself. Some instant of recognition. Then it disappeared into silver motes, dissolved into warmth; the curtain slid back into place, and whatever was behind it ceased to exist once more.

I scratched at my wrist, mortally embarrassed. "I'm sorry," I told Florian. "I didn't know this was what he wanted."

"I didn't *want* this," Gennady said. "I was going to play nice, except then—" he jabbed a finger toward Florian—"I saw him. And I know what he is."

"What I am," Florian repeated.

"Hungry," Gennady said with a cutting smile. "Aren't you? That's it, right?

You're hungry all the time, and you're too weak to just learn how to starve like the rest of us."

Although I had no idea what he meant, my heart ached. "Stop," I whispered.

His fixated staring grew ever more intense. "I know the professor won't let me gut you right here, but I'm telling you now that I'm waiting."

Florian gave no answer, dismissing the threat as beneath him. He turned to me expectantly, and that elusive distraction returned. An itch, a faraway pain. I shook my head to try to dislodge it.

He rose and stepped toward me.

"Stay still," Gennady said tonelessly.

I understood that Florian could not reach me without taking the very genuine risk that Lady would bite him. He motioned; I went to him, and although Lady tried to nudge me away, I stepped around her.

Florian touched me on the shoulder. The feeling of distraction fled. "You're exhausted," he said. "Go wait for me."

Without looking, I could tell that I had only a moment to convince Gennady not to use his saber. "Please," I said, begging without reservation. "Please, listen to me. Listen to what I'm asking. I don't want you to be here. Just leave."

Lady barked sharply; the spike of noise made me flinch.

"I'm too tired for this," I told Gennady.

"Either he goes, or I take you with me," he said.

I was no longer sure of what exactly was happening, of how we had gotten here, of what had been said. I knew only that I had to get rid of him. Pure frustration introduced a tremor into my voice. "You're making it worse. You're making *everything* worse. What else can I do, Gennady—can't you *listen*?"

There was hope. At that, I saw him waver.

"I'd like to suggest that you no longer contact Adrien," Florian said evenly.

Gennady gave no acknowledgment. He and Lady listened for my reply, a single force of attention.

I had not the slightest idea what I would say until I heard my own voice: "Go away."

Lady was the first to retreat, slinking toward the door with her ears pinned and her tail lashing. Gennady didn't follow her, not yet. The hand hovering at his saber's hilt trembled finely. "Come get me when you regrow your fucking backbone," he said.

He growled deep in his chest as I turned away from him, unable to bear it any longer.

I didn't see them leave, but I heard the door slam, and the relief of it was profound and overwhelming. A wave of affection for Gennady rose—he had listened to me. No matter how wrong he was, no matter how inexplicable I found his reaction, he'd listened. I staggered blindly to the bedroom, knowing that Florian would be behind me.

I meant to sit on the side of the bed as I usually did for Florian's treatments, but I found myself lying down instead. Abruptly, I was too tired to sit up. A shining warmth lulled me, muffling everything as if I were underwater.

When Florian's shadow rose in the doorway, I fought to stay clear. He drew closer, standing over me. "Well," he said. "Quite a student you have."

I couldn't read his tone. I couldn't see his face properly. "I'm sorry about him. He means well."

"It'll be best to keep some distance from him until you've recovered. He's clearly a disruptive influence."

I said nothing. I could try to convince Florian otherwise later; I could get Gennady to understand later. I could sort it all out. Just not now.

He passed a hand over my forehead. His rings were cool against my skin. "Sleep," he said.

A shiver ran through me, purely physical; I couldn't identify what had caused it. "It's only seven-something," I murmured, struggling up.

He looked so put-upon, so long-suffering, that I was shocked into greater alertness. The fuzzy shapes of the room slid back into focus.

"You are so difficult," he said. "I've been more than understanding, but you're just so difficult."

Lady's bark sounded in my mind. *Look! Listen!* I shook my head at him, saying no—no to *what*, I wasn't sure, but I knew that I meant it.

Inexorably, he pressed me back onto the bed. A spark of lightning drifted from one of my hands, a last gasp of distress, and he watched it for a moment before shaking his head. "Really, Adrien."

"I don't want you to cast on me," I said with difficulty.

"You don't know what you're saying. Your mind is going," he said. The infinite sympathy in his voice made me ache with longing. "Just close your eyes, and maybe you'll be sharper in the morning."

"No," I said.

It was as if every time I'd let him put me to sleep before had combined into one hit; he covered my eyes and brought the world to a dead halt. I slept. When I woke the next morning, the only thing left of that moment was a wide, empty gulf. I would recall only later what he had done.

I moved through the two days in a silver daze, thinking occasionally of Gennady—I remembered that he'd visited, and that it hadn't gone well, but whenever I tried to retrieve any specifics, I found my concentration failing. It was a problem for another time. It had to be: the disorientation I felt every time I wondered about it verged on painful.

The only thing that brought me out of my mindlessness was the rediscovery of Oliver's advertisement amongst the papers in my office one afternoon. I'd missed all the showing times, I realized—all but one that very night. If I didn't go then, I would have misled him by saying I'd come. I *needed* to see him again, even if only on stage. Florian had told me not to talk to Oliver, but surely this didn't count.

I knew, of course, that it counted, but I put it out of my mind.

Florian was working late; at least I wouldn't need to explain to him where I was going, or why I'd put on nicer clothing. I spent an inordinate amount of time that evening staring into the mirror before I went to the theater, regretting how gaunt I looked, although I knew there was no way Oliver was going to see me in the audience. I wasn't even sure I felt well enough to try to talk to him afterward. Still, I wanted to look presentable. It was the principle of the thing.

The Copper Arch Theater was in Deme Lettia, not far from Deme Palenne at all, and it was as beautiful as I'd expected. It wasn't an upper-class establishment, more gilt than gold, but it was charming in the extreme. Each corner of the building on every one of its various levels was decorated with grotesques contorted into various dramatic affects—one singing, one crying, one clearly giving a speech, and so on.

The crowd that had gathered to see *Haruspex Ambrose and the Child Empress* was mixed. There were some baseborn patrons and some aristocrats, with a large majority being common citizens. A wide cross section of the city had come together to see Oliver and his fellow actors play.

I paid for my ticket and melted into the throng. I wasn't quick enough to get a good place, but I could still see, and I settled into the somewhat tattered velvet seat to watch.

The set dressing was minimal, and the lighting was spare. The music was, frankly, not very good. But the players were excellent. The child empress Elysia was portrayed by a diminutive teenage girl with an uncanny knack for the malicious pout of an evil ruler. The weak and foolish Prefect of the Curia Divae, Tasca Vinnatieri, was a frail, middle-aged woman with a remarkably strong voice. And Oliver, Haruspex Ambrose, was so transformed that I barely recognized him. He'd been made up in dark eyeshadow and golden clothes, and as he and the other actors spun out the tale in front of us all, I could only call him beautiful.

I knew already that the play ends, as an astonishing portion of Astrine performances do, in tragedy. Haruspex Ambrose kills himself at the climax of the play; he spills his blood to provide the child empress with all the drink she needs. Oliver's rendition of it was more unsettling than I could have ever imagined. His version of death was spellbinding. The theater held its breath to watch him, silent as a mausoleum.

When the curtain closed, the applause was thunderous, and I joined in after I'd weathered the surge of headache it brought. There was an encore; the cheers for Oliver were among the loudest. I found myself proud, although of course I had nothing to do with it at all. I thought once more about staying behind, trying to talk to him, but then I remembered Florian. If I was out for too long, he'd wonder where I'd been—and, I realized with a horrible lurch, the answer was that I'd been ignoring his instructions.

I promised myself that I would tell Oliver all about what I'd thought of his performance another time. Soon, soon. I didn't have to let go of the gleaming thread between us yet. Still, I felt its pull like a physical obstacle as I left the theater with the rest of the crowd and went into the street to wave down a ride home.

I was there for a while; it was a busy night. Soon enough, most of the crowd had dispersed on their way home, but I was still waiting—and I felt someone touch my arm.

For a ludicrous moment, before I spun around, I was expecting it to be Florian. I thought he might somehow have supernaturally known where I'd be. But it was Oliver, of course, and when I saw him, the relief and joy nearly knocked me down.

"You should have come to find me," he said, grinning. His makeup had been wiped off only imperfectly; he still wore a golden drape.

The misery that had accumulated since I'd last seen him coalesced into a single, burning point until I couldn't help myself. I threw my arms around him. "You were wonderful," I declared, and then set him back to look at him. He stared, his lips parted in surprise.

"Was I really *that* good?"

I swallowed. "You really were."

He recovered a small amount of his crooked grin. "Why, thank you." And he softened. "Are you all right, Adrien? I haven't seen you in a while. You look tired."

I was glad the mark on my face had almost entirely faded by then. *Yes,* I thought I'd say, *absolutely. I'm perfectly fine.* But I couldn't force the words out. "It's been difficult lately," I admitted, my throat tight. I let go of his shoulders quickly, mortified. It couldn't matter how at home with Oliver I felt; I needed to remember that I had no right to touch him.

But as if to compensate for me letting go, he reached out and brushed my hair back. "Come back into the theater," he said. "We don't have any more performances tonight. We can sit and talk. It'll be warm inside, at least."

Florian would be angry.

"Yes, please," I said.

He guided me inside to sit down in one of the boxes; we looked down on the stage together from our great height. A few of the troupe were on stage clearing props away, but other than them, all was still and silent. I marveled that Oliver could be so high up with no apparent discomfort, that his awful fall hadn't instilled a permanent phobia in him. It must have taken such work to achieve.

After a moment of extremely academic consideration, he put an arm around me. I leaned into him. "How do you manage it?" I asked. "Acting so convincingly."

"You need to believe it," he said. "In that moment, it's all true for you, so you barely even need to act. The character possesses you."

"Possesses," I said dazedly.

"Why has it been difficult lately?" he said. "Why haven't you been at Gailhardt's meetings? I've been missing you. I thought you might not even come to see the play for a while, but . . ."

"It's hard to explain. It's hard to believe."

"I'll believe you." It was said with such blithe confidence that I had to bite my tongue before I could respond.

"Have you heard anything of what's going on at the Chirurgeonate?" I said.

"Sure. Gailhardt told me before it was in the papers. They have an angel." He made a face. "Nasty stuff."

"Those inquisitors who interrupted the meeting a while ago," I said. "They've moved on to investigating the Chirurgeonate. They wanted to ask me some questions."

"What about? You're not even a doctor."

A wave of nausea swept through me as I remembered the sound of my fingers breaking. "They thought it was someone I know, and they thought I'd be able to give them the name."

"But you cleared it up?"

I nodded, and then on second thought, I shook my head. "They tortured me until they realized I don't know anything."

He went still. "They tortured you."

I needed to brush past the details. "I was healed, but—"

Subconsciously, I had put my left hand to my throat, giving myself away. He finally saw the bruises on both. Carefully, so carefully, he examined my fingers, then tipped my head back for a better look.

"I couldn't do anything," I said.

He swore viciously; when I drew back in startlement, he reached out to soothe me. "No, no. Forgive me. Steady."

I nodded blindly and prayed that he would kiss me. It was impossible that he might; we hadn't known each other for long enough; I was hardly looking my best; he must be feeling uneasy—

He did. He folded my aching hand into his and brought me close to kiss me very briefly. It was enough. "I'm sorry," he murmured. "Stars and saints, I'm sorry."

I wanted him, yes. That was all very standard. But he wanted *me*, which I had no way of explaining. In that instant, as could never have been avoided, an urge stronger than all others made itself known:

Ruin it.

"There was something else that happened," I breathed.

He must have heard the sickness in my voice; he tensed. "Hmm?"

"One of my patients died. Killed by the angel."

He shook his head. "Your patients? But—"

"I used to be a healer," I said conversationally.

"I don't understand."

"Oliver," I said, letting go of him, "have you heard of the Philidor solarium?"

The resulting pause was long and ghastly. "Yes," he said finally, the word dropping like a stone, tumbling all the way down from the box onto the bare wooden stage.

He waited for me to say something else, holding out hope that I didn't mean what he suspected. I was glad there was no need to elaborate; all I had to do now was stay silent.

My chance to take it back passed soon enough. Oliver shifted minutely in his seat, eyes widening. He would get up shortly, I knew, and he would ask me to leave, and I would never see him again. I resigned myself to it: in a twisted way, I was satisfied. It was exactly what I had expected and what I had set myself up for.

"I'm so sorry," Oliver said.

I had misheard him, certainly. "Pardon?"

"I'm sorry that all happened."

So I needed to find something else. The catalog of my life's disgraces was incomplete; I had yet more things to confess, yet more knives to use. I drew a breath and selected one: I would tell him about the nepenthe. That would do it.

He spoke before I could. "You must have really suffered."

"What?"

"Well, with the guilt. I can tell you regret it," he said cautiously. "You have this look in your eyes . . ."

It was so stunning that my temporary derangement snapped, leaving me with ringing ears. I was back again. "I would do anything," I choked. "Anything."

He nodded.

"Oliver, you don't hate me?"

Looking almost injured by the question, he exhaled slowly. "It's quite a thing," he said. "Quite a thing to know. But why would I hate you?"

I wanted to press him on it, interrogate his position. *Why not? Are you sure you understand? Really consider it.* But I didn't have the strength. I simply settled into the silence we held between us, enervated beyond words.

I was so sure that he would want to keep his distance now, that he would shy from my poisoned touch. Instead, he took my hand again. "Is there more?" he asked.

"Yes."

"You don't have to say it all now."

"I'm not a good person," I said.

"You might think that, but I have an eye for quality," he said. "I told you I spend time at the pawnshops, didn't I? When I'm looking through the shelves, I always find the best thing to take home with me. It's a sixth sense."

Beyond my control, I laughed horribly.

"I don't mean you're a stringless violin or a tattered dress," he said. "I mean you stand out to me like that. You glow."

Although he spoke with mild embarrassment, there was no evidence of real difficulty. This sincerity was natural for him. I had no idea how he managed it.

Oliver pointed toward my heart and tapped my chest. "When I saw you outside the theater tonight, I thought, *It's got to be that one.*"

I deserved none of this. I deserved to be struck dead where I sat. I didn't care. My balance left me, and I leaned against Oliver's shoulder gracelessly. It was all the reply I could muster.

To break the spell, a woman clearing the stage down below called up at us, "Oliver! You'd better not be making any more messes up there to clean!"

"Don't be nosy!" he called back down. The sudden noise shattered my reverie. "Mind your own business!"

The implication that we were doing anything more than talking made me cringe, but Oliver was there to coax me out of it. "Don't mind her," he said.

"Should I leave?"

He looked so disappointed that I regretted asking immediately. "Stay just a while longer."

I nodded in response, but my thoughts had scattered. "I think I'm losing my mind lately," I said. "Nothing's right. I'm always tired—I'm always confused. I forget things."

The twilight world we had constructed for ourselves was fading; Oliver's brow furrowed. "I don't know what to say."

"You don't have to say anything."

"It'll pass, won't it?"

"Maybe not this time," I said. "This isn't like what usually happens. Not at all. Maybe it's over."

"What are you going to do?"

"Wait," I said numbly.

Tentatively, he said, "I wouldn't mind waiting with you."

That offer struck me as far more valuable than any declaration of passion, which made my next words all the more bitter. "My keeper doesn't approve of me seeing you."

He made an expressive motion, an actor's gesture. "Damn your keeper. You're not a child. He can't control you."

"No, I suppose not," I lied. "Still, I don't want him to find out yet."

"So we'll sneak around." He gave me a weak smile. "How thrilling. Like a game."

I laughed, a little watery. "Like a game. And I probably won't be at any more of Gailhardt's meetings. He doesn't want me to go, and I don't have the energy anymore." I hated to portray Florian as some sort of tyrant when he'd been so understanding of my flaws, so permissive of me, so helpful, but I couldn't explain his complications well enough to avoid it.

"Then come to my apartment sometimes," Oliver said. "I'll give you the address right now."

"Please." I hurried to produce the small notebook and pen I kept on me at all times.

He snorted, clearly finding it a quaint habit, but it was fond. "All right," he said, scribbling the address on a blank page and handing me the notebook back. "There. Now you can drop by. I'm usually home in the late evenings."

I had no idea how I'd be able to get away from Florian at night, but I nodded regardless. I'd find a way. "Thank you," I said. Then, because once didn't seem to suffice, "Thank you. Really."

He nudged me gently. "You know, I honestly was worried you might not come."

"I almost forgot," I confessed, unable to keep the guilt of that oversight to myself. "But I found the paper you gave me."

"That's serendipity right there."

I'd never believed in serendipity. Not until then, and not for any reason other than the pleasure the idea seemed to bring him.

We sat awhile longer, watching the last stages of the cleanup. I thought about kissing him again, but the initiative deserted me. I could ask him to bring me home with him, risk Florian's disappointment in exchange for a

night with a man who wanted me—but I had no idea if Oliver would be willing to go that far. If the answer was *no*, I'd humiliate myself beyond compare.

"I do need to get back," I said. "I probably needed to get back a while ago."

"I'll see you to your ride," he said unhappily. I realized with a sharp thrill
that he was going to miss me when I was gone.

He helped me stand, and we descended from the box back down into the
street. It was chilly out now, and my best clothes weren't warm; I shivered.
"I'd give you my coat," Oliver said, "but . . ."

Best not to have any evidence. "But there's no guarantee when you'd get it
back," I said, in lieu of acknowledging that. "Don't worry about it."

No sooner had I raised my arm than a caleche came to a stop in front of us,
the horse's breath steaming gently in the night air. "I'll see you," Oliver said,
and patted me on the shoulder, an absent, unaffected gesture. My resolve to
leave nearly broke.

But I had to go home. "Please wait for me," I said quietly. I got in the caleche.

Oliver's warmth was slow to fade from me, but when it did, it left me freezing.
Once I was dropped off at home, I paced outside the house for nearly ten
minutes, steeling myself to go inside. Once the night's chill started to bite in
earnest, I swallowed my trepidation and let myself in.

Florian was sitting on the couch waiting for me. "Where have you been?"
he asked very casually.

I opened my mouth to lie to him and immediately discovered that I could
not. A silver pressure was present in the back of my mind, forcing the truth
out. "I went to see a play," I said.

"You didn't tell me you'd be out. I was worried."

"I'm sorry."

And he held up the paper advertisement with Oliver's name on it. I'd left
it out in my bedroom. "This play?"

I nodded dumbly.

"I seem to recall telling you not to risk anything with that man."

"It was just one outing," I murmured. "I haven't seen him at all lately."

He stood. "That doesn't change the fact that you disobeyed me."

Twin urges dueled within me: firstly, to throw myself into his arms and beg forgiveness, and secondly, to tell him that he wasn't my master, that I wore no collar, that if he wished to make me obey, he was welcome to try.

Silver pressure.

"I'm sorry," I said again. "I wasn't thinking."

"No. You weren't." He walked over to me. "Adrien, I can't convey how disappointed I am. First you spend all your time wandering the Chirurgeonate, never explaining why, and now you're disappearing at night. I can't keep track of you. I can't do my job."

I stared.

"Do you intend to do better in the future?"

"The Chirurgeonate," I said faintly. "What are you talking about?"

"Do you think I haven't noticed that you're constantly at the hospital?"

"Constantly? I visit, but—"

"I see you at the Chirurgeonate all the time," he said, his disapproval giving way to consternation. "Don't you remember the conversation we had before that Philidor patient died—?"

"After," I interrupted. "After she died."

He looked at me expressionlessly.

"Willette was already gone," I said.

"You were in the hospital that day *before* she died. We spoke. I told you to go home; that's why I was surprised to see you again later."

"No," I said, with no particular conviction.

"There have been a dozen other times. I'm usually too busy to speak, but I see you there over and over again, even when you're supposed to be teaching. You drift around the wards without saying anything to anyone. I'm sure it's you."

"That can't be."

He softened. "Because you don't remember."

"I can't tell you what I'm doing there," I said, and sat down where he had been. "I don't remember. I don't remember."

"What sort of business could you have there?" he asked. "We'll figure it out together."

"My solarium patients," I said. "Visiting them?"

"You're not always in the Hessalon building."

I had nothing else to offer.

"Have you considered the possibility," he said, "that your memory problems have been going on for longer than you realize?"

I shook my head. "Why . . ."

"If it's this bad already, that's a distinct possibility. I don't know what good it does you now to be aware, but it's better than not knowing." The implications of the discovery boiled underneath his voice. I turned away from them.

"I'm not sure," I said, my voice grating. "How on earth would I know that?"

"Don't snap at me."

I faltered and looked down. "I'm sorry, Florian."

"Stop telling me you're sorry," he said wearily.

I dug my nails into my wrist and waited. I couldn't even find the presence of mind to count the beads on the angel eye bracelet.

He sighed. "I don't know what you're doing at the Chirurgeonate. If you can't remember, then maybe I can try to follow you next time I see you there. For now, just try to monitor yourself. Be careful. And stay close to home."

I thought of Oliver's kiss. I thought of my notebook with his address hidden inside. Soon I would need to decide what to do about that, but not yet. Not when I was so tired. "I understand," I said.

"Thank you," he said. The controlled hint of approval in his voice soothed me. When I didn't move, he went on. "You know I have your best interests in mind."

"I know," I said softly. And I did know.

He sighed. "There's one more thing, I'm afraid."

I waited.

"Dr. Tyrrhena has asked me to take over a larger portion of your care. Your weekly healings, at the very least. She's struggling to keep up with her workload."

A modicum of clarity returned to me. "She didn't ask you that," I said.

It was a mistake. I felt the air change.

"I'd like to explain this to you without being interrupted," he said, and the insistent silver weight upon my chest grew heavier. My clarity faded. "Dr. Tyrrhena is not currently able to keep up with the level of attention you require, especially in light of your deterioration. We both think it would be a good idea for me to help with day-to-day maintenance."

I shook my head, willing myself not to panic. "She hasn't said anything to me."

"No doubt she was concerned about how you'd react."

I reached to touch the angel eye bracelet on my wrist. "She doesn't want to see me?"

"If it's *very important*, of course she'll still see you. But she needs some breathing room."

"Malise would tell me," I said. "She wouldn't have someone else—"

"I think you may be underestimating the effort it takes to monitor you," Florian said, "and I think you're not considering the stress she's under already."

The clear fact of the matter—that Malise would *tell me herself*, would never leave me to hear it secondhand—slipped away from me. I could only think of how to make it better. I could offer her something, surely, something to make her life easier instead of harder, for once, to apologize—

"The best thing you can do now is respect her wishes," Florian said.

I had to leave the room before I embarrassed myself. I stood and fled.

"Try to sleep well tonight," Florian said after me. "I'll be in the other room if you need to wake me."

For nearly an hour, I stood frozen in the center of my bedroom, trying to survive the sheer grief of what he'd told me, working desperately to examine the doubt that I was sure I'd felt. I couldn't catch hold of it long enough to think.

Finally, an abrupt pain like a needle stick inside my head made me gasp, and the will to stay awake deserted me in one fell swoop. I had to get ready for bed. I would give Malise her space; I'd put her wishes first. No matter how agonizing, I owed her that. I'd talk to Gennady again when I could. I'd figure out why Florian had been seeing me at the Chirurgeonate soon enough. That was that. In time. Later. Later.

When I managed to sleep, I dreamed of Haruspex Ambrose, pooled in his own blood. I dreamed of Oliver's hand in mine. I dreamed that I was wandering through the Chirurgeonate alone, and I couldn't remember why.

Chapter 12

St. Damien's Burial is one of Martyr's Reach's more peculiar holidays. St. Damien was martyred for Kephis—Kephis drove him to suicide in some spectacular manner, although no church of the saint can agree on what the method was. All agree that it was flashy and horrific, however.

I woke on the morning in question without remembering that it had come, thinking I still needed to go to work. Only when I left the house and noticed that certain shops and houses had been garlanded with white mourning flowers did I remember.

The relief of not having to teach was intense. Normally, teaching would have been a respite from the troubles of the time, but not now that I might be losing my mind. The possible meaning of my unremembered visits to the Chirurgeonate continued to needle me, but I refused to acknowledge it.

I couldn't go to work. I went to church.

I never saw a reason to adopt astrolatry, even when I took my oaths as a doctor. Oaths come cheap in Astrum. On that day, however, I thought a change of scenery might do me some good. I didn't need to pledge my faith to simply visit; I knew that St. Damien's church on Via Martinea in Deme Gilleray would be both quiet and largely deserted, and this was reason enough to go. Anywhere else I went, I might be expected to talk.

St. Damien's was an average church, possessed of its requisite share of indoor plants and votives. It had one defining feature: a set of bells, melted together during a long-ago plaguefire, that had never been repaired. The bells hung silently in their tower in remembrance of those lost to fever and flame—and, presumably, to suicide.

When I came to the church, I sat down in one of the pews without stopping to roam the area. There was no service taking place, and I saw no worshipers: St. Damien's devotees aren't the sort to gather joyously for a holy day. I was willing to bet most of them were home brooding.

I didn't attempt to pray; it would have felt both pointless and disingenuous. The respite from noise and other people was transcendent enough. As grateful as I was to Florian, having him in my house was undeniably taking its toll. It was necessary, of course—he was my keeper, and these were not the best of times—but I still longed to be alone in my house sometimes. For now, St. Damien's would have to do.

It was difficult not to close my eyes and rest, but I had a feeling that if I did, I wouldn't be able to resist falling asleep in the pew. I let my gaze drift instead, over the climbing vines and hanging potted plants, the light streaming in through the windows, kaleidoscoped by colored glass.

My thoughts strayed back to the saint and his unfortunate end. Several times in my life, I'd meant to die—but the similarities ended there. I shook myself to prevent any vainglorious thoughts of comparison.

If I really was unraveling permanently, the justification for killing myself had suddenly become much stronger. Before, I'd always been able to tell myself that at least I could be *useful*. Now, if I was finally to lose even that comfort, I no longer had any excuse. Malise would be unhappy, yes. Gennady would be set even further adrift. But they would eventually come to prefer it to dealing with an incomplete version of me.

A good day for it, I thought. Good enough. If I was going to try, now would be a sensible time. St. Damien's worshipers customarily paid for the burials of suicides on his holy day.

I had brought the Astragestum tarot deck with me, just to have something of Oliver's on my person. I took it out and drew a card: the Haruspex's Chalice in the Court of Martyrs, referring to the legend of Oliver's own haruspex. Drawn chimeric, not upright. Possible meanings:

Magician.

Penance.

Death.

I replaced the card and put away the deck, feeling foolish. Ending my life was a premature thought. If I didn't have hard proof that I was finally slipping beyond repair, it was irresponsible to act. I let any half-formed plans drift away, silenced like the church's melted bells.

"Professor Desfourneaux?" someone said.

I startled and looked up. It was Xantha, my student, squinting at me with concern. My mind took a moment to place her; I'd never seen her out of the Pharmakeia. "Xantha," I said, a little bewildered. She hadn't seemed like a follower of St. Damien.

"I didn't think you were an astrolater," she said, hovering awkwardly above the pew. I moved over for her, and she sat.

"I'm not. I just needed somewhere quiet. There aren't any bells to interrupt here."

"I'm not very devoted myself," she said, gesturing out to the church at large, seeming embarrassed by her presence. "I used to come once a sennight, but now it's more like once every few weeks. It's my family's church. I thought I'd drop by, just in case."

"Just in case what?"

Her brow furrowed. "In case St. Damien gets lonely having so few people visit him today. I don't know. It's a silly thought, isn't it?"

I shook my head. "Not at all."

That seemed to brighten her. "Anyway," she said. "I don't want to bother you if you came here for peace and quiet." She clearly had something else to say.

"I think I've already gotten all the quiet I need."

"Then—could I ask you about the inquisitors?"

I winced, but I waved her on. The matter had clearly been eating at her.

"Do you think they're making any progress on finding out who the angel is?"

"They seemed to think they were," I said. "But they wouldn't tell me."

She sighed. "That's too bad. I have a sister in the Chirurgeonate. She's terrified. I was hoping I could give her some news."

"I'm sorry," I said quietly, rubbing my formerly broken fingers.

A sudden fit of remorse seemed to take her. "I've reminded you. I probably shouldn't have asked."

I smiled, although the awkwardness I always felt when seeing a student outside of classes intensified ever so slightly. "When have I ever discouraged curiosity?"

"Never," she admitted.

"Then there you go."

I counted out a few beads on my angel eye bracelet to resist the urge to scratch.

"I'm scared," she said, after a significant pause.

"Of the inquisitors?"

"It just seems like something is always going wrong. None of us are really over what happened to the Pharmakeia before."

Sometimes, to my shame, I forgot that I was not the only one who had been marked by Mulcaster. I was grateful to be reminded. "I understand," I said. I knew without asking that we shared the fear particular to magicians in the midst of a witch hunt.

"Do you think they *will* catch the angel?" she asked.

"They have to. It's just a matter of time." I was reluctant to ascribe the inquisitors such competence, but the alternative was too terrible to consider—and surely, even without them, the Chirurgeonate itself would solve the problem soon.

"I hope you're right."

She seemed to have another question. I waited.

"I was just wondering, also . . ."

"Yes?"

"Do you know when you'll have our exams graded?" she said timidly.

I had to laugh. I'd been exactly the sort of student who would have asked such a thing in similarly dark times. "Soon."

She nodded. "Thank you. I don't mean to hurry you. I just get anxious about it—I'm sorry."

"Don't apologize. I'm sorry I haven't been quicker. It's just been . . ."

I lost the will to finish the sentence.

"Yes," she agreed. "It has."

She seemed to sense that I was nearing the end of my capacity for socialization; sheepishly, she got up.

Once she was about to leave, I was seized by a sudden fear—I'd come to St. Damien's to contemplate my own end. Was it possible that she had too? I'd never gotten into the subject with her, but she seemed prone to melancholy at times.

I had only a few moments to find a natural way to address the subject. There was no way I could. I'd just have to say whatever came to mind, no matter how peculiar it would seem to the conversation.

"You mentioned you're not devout," I said abruptly.

She blinked. "Not really."

"I think that's for the best. This idolization of death can never end well."

She was silent.

"It isn't a good solution to anything." In my own thoughts, I wouldn't make such a categorical statement, but she didn't need to know that.

"I'll keep that in mind," she said. Something about her tone made me glad that I'd said something.

I gave her a strong smile. "I don't mean to keep you if you need to get going. The thought just crossed my mind."

"Thank you."

"Any time." I tried to make it clear that I meant it. "We can talk any time."

"Well, goodbye, then," she said awkwardly, clearing her throat.

I nodded. "I'll see you tomorrow," I said.

"Tomorrow." And she hurried away.

Although my concentration was in tatters, I continued to work. Work, unfortunately, involved Phaedra Keynes. I'd forgotten about her with everything going on. When I next ran into her, she was in fine form and eager to remind me. As soon as I made eye contact with her, I could see that she was out for blood; I tried to duck past her, but she shouldered in front of me. I resigned myself to the interaction.

"Hello," I said flatly. "Let's get this over with."

"I hear you've been talking to those inquisitors," she said loudly to draw the attention of everyone else in front of the library.

"I wouldn't call it *talking*," I said. "They tortured me."

"So you admit you're a suspect. Enough of a suspect for them to actually do something about it." She stepped forward into my space; unwilling to play, I took an equal step back.

"They verified that I don't know anything," I said. "Trust me. They verified it thoroughly. We're all suspects to them, every magician—the only difference is that they've finally given up on me, whereas *you* probably haven't been ruled out yet."

She paled in fury and opened her mouth again, but I cut her off before she could speak. "Do you honestly believe I have anything to do with the angel?" I said. "Truly, honestly? Or are you only hassling me because you don't like me?" She was entitled to the latter option, I supposed—I just wanted to know.

I could see the answer as soon as I asked. Of course she didn't really think it was me, but she was scared of the inquisitors, and she wanted someone to blame.

"It *could* be you," she said. "Plenty of people think so."

Gailhardt's voice startled me. We were starting to gather a crowd; apparently, she was part of it. "Is it plenty of people?" she said to Keynes from somewhere to my left. "Is it really? Or is it just you, Phaedra, you heinous little frog?"

"I didn't realize you were so invested in Desfourneaux's good name," Keynes hissed. "Very sweet."

"It's less about anyone's good name and more about common sense," Gailhardt said. "He's not even with the Chirurgeonate."

"The inquisitors—I mean, think of Philidor—"

"It's very freeing to be capable of basic logic," Gailhardt said. "You should give it a try one day."

Keynes scowled, her face warping.

"Unless you want to go find an inquisitor to bother about this right now," I said, "can we cut this short?" I could only hope she wouldn't call my bluff and suggest that yes, we should find an inquisitor.

Luckily, she didn't. "Witch," she said, and stalked off into the crowd that had gathered. I watched her go without pleasure. By some metrics, I'd won the interaction, but it didn't feel like it at all.

Gailhardt began to shoo people out of the way. "Go on," she said to the crowd. "Go be useful somewhere." Slowly, everyone dispersed, murmuring amongst each other. She stayed standing with me until we were alone. I was grateful that she gave me some time to collect myself before starting her interrogation.

"So," she said. "That was unpleasant."

"I've never known why Keynes hates me the way she does."

"There's no accounting for that kind of person," she said.

I hummed in agreement.

"No one really believes what she's saying, you know."

"I hope not." My eyes prickled with exhaustion. "I really do hope not."

"You earned the academy's trust with Mulcaster."

"She isn't wrong about the Philidor solarium."

"No," she said levelly. "But she's wrong about everything else."

"Thank you."

"Where are you going?" she asked.

"Nowhere, really."

"Good. We can have lunch."

I couldn't think of a good reason to refuse; I nodded. She started off toward the nearest exit to the Pharmakeia, and I followed.

"By the way," she said. She wasn't going to let me off the hook. We'd crossed paths; we were coming to this subject whether I liked it or not: "Why haven't you been coming to the meetings?"

"Just what I said before. My keeper is trying to treat me for the problem, and he doesn't think it's the best idea to mix courses, so to speak."

She eyed me doubtfully. "You never gave me a proper try, you know. If you'd have been a little more patient, I think I really could have helped you."

The guilt forced me to look away. "I'm sorry. I wanted to, but—he was insistent."

"Oliver's been missing you."

"I saw him just the other day," I said softly.

She nodded. "Good. And this other treatment, does it seem to be working?"

"I don't know. Florian told me I shouldn't try using my magic until he's certain it's all fixed. I think it's doing something, though."

After a moment of thought, she sighed. "That's not bad advice. I can see why he might tell you that. No use testing unrepaired muscles. It's possible that I shouldn't have had you casting so much before, either."

"I'm sure you would have succeeded eventually," I said. "If he hadn't gotten to me first. I'm sorry, Gailhardt."

"You've seemed unhappy lately. I've noticed that. Whenever I see you around, you're . . ."

"It's a long story," I said weakly.

She considered me for a long moment. "You can tell me."

I made a noncommittal noise. "Over our food, maybe."

We went to the Camattran café just off campus. I couldn't make myself eat anything, but I had a little water. She ordered a sandwich, and we sat looking awkwardly over each other's shoulders for a while before she finally spoke.

"What's wrong, Desfourneaux?"

"It doesn't seem right to burden you with it."

She fixed me with a severe gaze. "I'm *asking*."

Her insistence broke my will to conceal, already wearing thin. I told her about the fine specifics of what the inquisitors had done, and I told her about how no matter what I tried to do, I was never able to be good for Florian. I told her that I was afraid I was losing my mind.

"It's driving me mad," I said after I'd explained myself. "Seeing the inquisitors around."

Gailhardt had begun to look somewhat nauseous. "As soon as they catch the angel, they'll be gone." She gave me a drawn smile. "With any luck."

"I don't think I believe in luck right now."

To my dismay, she winced as if afraid she'd offended me. "No, of course. Why would you?"

"I just mean I'll rest easy once they're gone, yes, but not before."

"I'm sorry for what they did to you," she said stiffly.

"They've undoubtedly done worse to others."

"You said they were sniffing around Tyrrhena?"

I twisted my hands. "If they were to take her . . ."

Gailhardt shook her head. "I'll pray against it. In any case, go see her. You really ought to talk to your doctor about your memory problems, anyway," she said, poking at a slice of bread. She hadn't been able to finish her food once I'd detailed my torture.

"I don't want to bother her," I said, unwilling to explain directly that Malise had asked Florian to shoulder more of her burden. It hurt too much to acknowledge. "Florian can help."

Gailhardt clicked her tongue in disagreement. "Nonsense. He hasn't known you as long as Tyrrhena. Haven't you two been friends since medical school?"

"Since undergraduate."

"You should ask *her.*"

"If it's not important—"

She blinked. "What could be more important?"

I had no answer. "Maybe I'll go later today," I said. "Our appointment would usually be today in any case."

"And for what it's worth," she said, "I've never noticed you gone from the Pharmakeia during teaching hours. No matter what that keeper of yours says."

"We don't cross paths that often," I said, exasperated. "You might very well not."

She shrugged. "Maybe I don't know what I'm talking about. If he says it's true, maybe it's true. But I have my doubts."

I wished dearly that I could take any sort of solace from that. "We'll see."

"Just keep it in mind, all right?"

"It's been lovely eating with you," I told her. "Thank you for checking on me." I was well aware that she had no obligation whatsoever to bother herself with my predicament.

"You're welcome."

I hesitated. "You really think I should ask Malise for help?"

She pursed her lips, debating how to answer. "People talked," she said eventually. "After Mulcaster, after the Penumbra, when the thought was that you'd died. Word got around about the way she took it in those hours before you showed up again. Howling like one of the wounded."

"Saints," I said.

"So without knowing the woman whatsoever, yes, I think you should."

Wordlessly, I nodded.

"I'm rooting for you," she said, without sentimentality. "I really am."

It occurred to me only after I left the café that we might be friends.

I went to see Malise as Gailhardt had suggested. I'd ask her what she thought about my declining faculties, my spotty memory, and if she gave any sign whatsoever that she needed time away from me, I'd wait as long as she needed.

While the atmosphere of the Chirurgeonate was grim and subdued, the wave of relief that washed over me when Malise answered my knock was incalculable.

"Adrien," she said, waving me inside. "Thank goodness."

"I promise it's important," I said, trying to read her expression, her posture, trying to see if she seemed too tired to treat me.

She sobered immediately and got up to shepherd me to the settee. "Tell me, my dear."

"I need you to look for something," I said. "Florian says I've been wandering around the Chirurgeonate at all hours of the day without ever realizing it. Without ever remembering."

She cocked her head. "I so rarely see you here without you talking to me."

"You could be missing me when you're at Halicar's. Or just in your office, or another building, or—"

"Every single time?"

"But it's possible," I said. "Malise, if my keeper says I've behaving strangely . . ."

She sighed. "Yes. It's possible."

"So you'll look?"

"Of course I'll look," she said softly. "Ready?"

"Ready."

She placed her hands on my temples as she always did.

When she began her healing, I allowed myself to hope that maybe she would find the problem and be able to fix it. Maybe, miracle worker that she was, she'd freeze it away for me. I felt the coldness seep in and waited.

It took longer than it had ever taken before. Nearly half an hour.

When she finally drew back from me, she shook her head. "I don't think you're sick," she said cautiously. "At least," she qualified, "not in the usual way. There's something there, but . . ."

"I don't understand. If there's something there, I'm sick."

"That isn't it," she said. "I don't know what I felt, but that isn't it."

"How do you *know?* It's—" I swallowed hard. "The akrasia is degenerative. It can be. Maybe I'm just getting worse."

"Do you trust me as a healer?" she asked.

"Yes."

"As an alienist?"

"Yes."

"Then listen to me. I think this is something new."

I squeezed my eyes shut.

"I'm glad you didn't reschedule," I heard Malise say, although a steady rushing noise in my head muffled her.

"I'm sorry?"

"Dr. Albrecht stopped by the other day to tell me you wouldn't be able to make this appointment. He said you'd reschedule later."

"You *asked* Florian to take over some of my treatment," I choked, looking back up.

I saw the realization crystallize in her gaze. My stomach dropped. "I didn't," she said slowly. "I never would."

Of course not, I thought for the briefest instant, before a wash of silver light swept away the thought. "He said . . ."

Malise's jaw tightened. When she spoke, although her voice was carefully controlled, a tremor thrummed below her words. "It's interesting to me that Florian would be telling you these things. They're not true."

"Stop," I said.

She framed my face, studying my eyes. "Has Florian been casting on you? I think you need to let me talk to him."

I eased away from her and stood. "You don't know him. I'm not sure what you're implying, but you're wrong." The words came out without my bidding, as if spoken by someone else.

"Adrien—"

"You recommended him to me," I said. "That was you."

For an instant, her calm slipped, and a deep flash of pain shone through. "I could have been wrong. I could have made a terrible mistake."

The silver haze had grown blinding. "I shouldn't have brought it up. Let's just forget it."

"He could be—"

The pain in my head urged me to flee before she could complete her sentence and bring everything crashing down. I went for the door.

But the instant I stepped outside, it became clear that something was very wrong at the Chirurgeonate.

An invasion had begun. The place was swarming with inquisitors, many of them dragging handcuffed doctors behind them. The handcuffs glowed evilly, even in the daylight—antimagic.

I stood transfixed for an awful moment, and then I went back inside Malise's office.

She'd stood to chase after me; now she stared at me with hungry hope. "Have you—"

"The inquisitors," I breathed.

Her expression closed. "No."

"They're dragging people away." We stared at each other, poised to run.

"Why?" she asked. "I thought there was only one angel."

"I don't know, but—are they looking for you?"

"I have no idea," she said.

"We should move you somewhere else. Hide. This is the first place they'll look for you if they want you."

"Not beyond the Chirurgeonate," she said. "I don't want them to be able to accuse me of fleeing if they catch us."

"One of your patients' rooms, then, so you'll have an excuse for being there."

"If we go outside, we're sure to be spotted."

"If we stay here, it's only a matter of time."

She drew a shuddering breath and nodded. "Then let's go."

We stared at the door, silently steeling ourselves, and gathered our courage at the same time. I opened the door for her, and we stepped outside. We needed to go slowly, avoid drawing suspicion—we could not give even the slightest impression of guilt. The surreal scene of Malise's coworkers being taken all around us could not faze us one bit.

We held it together, somehow, and we had almost reached the building we were heading for when an inquisitor walked by, dragging a dark-haired older woman behind him, and Malise suppressed a shriek of horror, and I knew that we were sunk.

"Chandra," Malise said. "Stars and saints."

Chandra caught sight of us and twisted against her handcuffs. "I'm innocent," she said. Her voice was raspy—from screaming in protest, I realized with distant horror. "I'm innocent."

Malise started forward. I took her by the hand and kept her where she was. "It won't do any good," I said as the arresting inquisitor watched us, devoid of all expression.

Chandra locked eyes with Malise pleadingly. "I'm *innocent.*"

Malise squeezed my hand hard enough to hurt. "I know."

We'd attracted their attention already; it was too late. I might as well ask questions. "If I may," I said, "what exactly is going on here?"

The inquisitor shrugged. "We've been gathering a list of doctors who bent to Mulcaster during that whole debacle. It's time to sweep them up. Hopefully one of them is the angel. Two birds, one stone, you know."

"There's no way," Malise said to him, letting my hand go. "There's just no way. I know Chandra. I know her character—I've worked alongside her for a decade."

I believed her. Malise reserved her full confidence for very few people, and I trusted it implicitly. If she said Chandra was innocent, I could only conclude that the inquisitors were now arresting innocent people. Of course I knew that *I* had been innocent when they had taken *me,* but this was different. These people would not be released with only a few broken fingers.

The inquisitor looked at Malise sidelong. "I wonder if *you're* on the list."

We could run, but they'd catch us.

Chandra made a horrified sound; the inquisitor jolted her into silence. He looked around and said, "For God's sake, Curtis. Show yourself and be useful. We're not even supposed to be using those things anymore."

Out of thin air, another inquisitor appeared near us, idly consulting a piece of paper as he pocketed one of the mekhania invisibility spheres. "What do you want?"

"Check these two against the list, would you?"

Curtis approached us, one hand on the hilt of his sword. "Names," he said.

I neglected to explain that I wasn't a doctor. "Adrien Desfourneaux."

He checked his list. "No."

"Malise Tyrrhena," Malise said. Her voice cracked, and I was gripped by the overwhelming urge to strike the man with lightning and run. The power sparked at my fingertips, and I flinched; I barely managed to resist. It would only ensure both of our deaths. There were too many inquisitors around to survive.

This time, Curtis paused as he looked at the paper. A sob rose in my throat.

"Yes," he said. "Yes, we've been looking for *you*."

Malise was utterly silent.

He produced a set of handcuffs from one pocket.

"This is a mistake," I whispered.

"Step aside," he said to me.

I stood statue-still, rooted to the ground.

He drew his weapon. "Step aside."

But I couldn't. I knew that I had no power to stop him from taking Malise, but I couldn't make myself move.

So he shoved me away. I stumbled and caught myself.

If I wanted Malise to live, I had to control myself. "It's going to be fine," I said to her. "Listen to me. It will be fine."

"Adrien," she said, as Curtis pinned her hands together behind her back and shackled her.

Lightning surged from me, striking the ground nearby, and he turned to me with his blade up. "None of that," he said warningly.

The metal of his sword had frosted from Malise's power, but now the frost faded away as the antimagic cuffs did their job. My head hurt. "You have to be careful with her," I said. "She's innocent. You'll see that soon enough."

"I think that's for us to decide," Curtis said, with a nod to the first inquisitor. I glanced over at Chandra again. She was ashen and silent.

"Please," I said.

"Shut up," Curtis said, obviously tired of me. But he didn't jolt Malise too much as he started walking her forward.

"Adrien?" she said to me again, her voice rising to a frenzied pitch.

"You'll be out before you know it." What else could I say?

I wanted to say far more; I wanted to talk to her for longer, offer more reassurances, exhort Curtis to behave himself, for God's sake—but he was marching her off, and I knew better than to try to follow them. The first inquisitor took Chandra along as well, and then I was alone.

I stood with my heart pounding and waited until they were out of sight before I let the panic take me and knelt there on the ground in the middle of the remaining chaos.

Chapter 13

I recovered myself and fled the Chirurgeonate before any other inquisitors could interrogate me again. As a cosmic joke, just as I was about to make clear of the complex, I ran into Dr. Henri Thirkeld.

He was walking free, a fact my lesser nature resented. He must have just been visiting the Chirurgeonate, a little break away from Westbrook. When he saw me, his eyebrows went up. "Desfourneaux," he said. "What are you doing here?"

"Visiting Malise," I said distantly.

"Oh. She was on the list, I hear."

"Yes," I snarled. Suddenly, I was right up in his face without meaning to be. "She was on the list."

He stepped back from me with a delicate sniff. "I didn't mean anything by it."

"She's innocent, and they're going to torture her."

"Now," he said, "I'm sure it's not so bad as all that—and I don't think they'd be arresting innocents."

"They tortured *me*," I said, "and I did nothing. I knew nothing. They admitted it afterward."

"I'm sure that was different."

"I've always genuinely hated you," I said with bitter calm.

He bridled. "There's no need for that."

"If you think for an instant that Malise Tyrrhena is guilty, you're even more of an idiot than I ever imagined."

"You really do make interacting with you the most unpleasant experience."

"It's in the hopes that you'll stop interacting with me."

He opened his mouth; I prepared the most venomous tirade I could muster and poised myself to deliver. Before I could, however, I felt a hand on my shoulder.

I staggered back to face the threat—another inquisitor? But it was Florian.

For half a second, I saw him clearly; I felt the sickness of his presence like an open wound. But he tightened his grip on my shoulder, and I weakened.

I shook my head, unbalanced. "You're all right," I said.

He nodded. "I'm all right. They weren't interested in me."

Thirkeld looked back and forth between us. "My keeper," I said tightly.

"Ah. So sorry," he said to Florian. Such condescension dripped from his smile that my vision darkened with rage.

And nothing could compare to the humiliation I felt when Florian laughed. "It's a unique job," he said. I eased away from his touch.

"You don't need to be picking fights with everyone you run across," he told me.

I swallowed my words and stared at the ground. We had to leave. There were more important things to deal with.

Thirkeld laced his hands behind his back. He had the power now; he understood that. "Do you want to say anything, Adrien?"

I gave him a killing look. "I don't."

Florian simply watched me. The sunlight around us turned silver.

"I'm sorry to have been rude," I said. The words were forced out of me.

"And?" Thirkeld said.

No power in the universe could have compelled me to go further. "And nothing," I said. "You'll have nothing more from me."

Florian shook his head. "If you'll excuse us." The disappointment in his voice cut deeply.

I closed my eyes as he took my arm and steered me away from Thirkeld toward the Chirurgeonate's exit.

"Florian," I began, once we were out of earshot.

He cut me off. "I wasn't aware you knew Dr. Thirkeld," he said.

"My least favorite solarium alienist," I said. "I hate him. Everyone knows I hate him."

"Why?"

"He's a bad doctor, and he's an idiot," I said under my breath as we cleared the Chirurgeonate and stepped into the open street. I was aware I sounded like an unreasonable patient.

"Strong words," Florian said thoughtfully, as though he were filing the information away.

Thirkeld didn't matter. I felt my preoccupation rising in a grand wave, until I could think of nothing but the look of terror on Malise's face. "Malise was arrested—"

"I know she was," he said. I stopped short.

"How did you know?"

He waved a hand. "I heard from one of the inquisitors that they were looking for her. While they were checking me against the list."

"I need to figure out a way to help her," I said. "She's innocent."

"Maybe."

"She *is*."

"Maybe," he said again.

I shook my head. "You need to believe me. This is important. Malise hasn't done anything wrong."

"You can't know that," he said gently. "You know, a suspiciously large number of the angel victims have been her patients."

"That's a coincidence."

"Or maybe not. I've been hearing whispers. There were people before today who suspected Dr. Tyrrhena. It wasn't the inquisitors alone."

"That doesn't make any sense," I breathed.

He brushed my cheek with one hand. I felt something shudder in my mind. "Your judgment hasn't exactly been the most secure lately," he said. "Is it possible that you've missed something? Is it possible that people change?"

"We're not talking about this," I said. "I refuse. We're going home."

For a moment, I feared that I'd miscalculated very badly indeed. But the look on his face, one of supreme danger, passed before I could even be certain I'd seen it. "If you like," he said.

We were both silent on the way home; he didn't try to touch me again. Even so, I could feel his presence like an accusation. I withered next to him, and by the time we were through the door, I was trying to think of ways to appease him. I couldn't compromise on defending Malise, but there might be something else.

I was still trying to think when he said, "Did you ever figure out why you've been roaming the Chirurgeonate?"

I shook my head wordlessly.

"Come here," he said.

I came without a second thought.

He put his hands in my hair, comforting me, soothing me. "I know it's been a difficult day," he said. "I know you're on edge. But you have to listen to me now. You're not going to want to, but it's important."

"I'll listen," I said faintly, my eyes nearly closed. I could feel a strange warmth pouring from him.

"I think she's been enchanting you," he said. "You go to her so often for treatment—it would be easy for her to lay some sort of magical working on your mind. Make you forget things. Make you pliable for her."

"That isn't possible."

"Anything's possible," he said, honeyed worry coating his words. "I think that's what's happening. It only makes sense, especially since I believe your memory problems started long before you began to notice them."

My dizziness worsened dramatically. "Malise is my best friend."

"Making it all the easier for her to take advantage of you."

Silver light pressed in on me, flashing through each individual nerve, snaking through the ventricles of my heart. He pulled me close to him, one arm pressing me against his side.

"Don't," I said, trying to break away from him—but he held me fast, raising a hand gently to my throat.

"I care about you," he said. "Come here."

I had wanted so badly for us to be friends. When he'd been cold to me, distant, I'd wanted his warmth so desperately. Now that I had it, it was nearly impossible to resist. In a sudden flood, like an arterial spray, the vague attraction I'd always had toward him unfolded. He wore perfume; I'd always known that, but in that moment it was overpowering. He trailed up my throat, cupping my cheek.

I made a sound. He drew back a few inches and smiled.

"Florian," I said, bewildered. He'd been so remote before, so reserved. This new affection was intoxicating.

"There you go. There you are. Trust me. You need to break free of her. What use do you think she has for you? What do you really think she's been making you do?"

I shook my head.

"She's been using you for the heart attacks," he said gently. "Making you kill. You've been her cat's paw. Why do you think she tried to transfer so much of your care to me? She was distancing herself from you in case you were caught."

I confess that I wavered then. With his magic soaking me through, his heat warming me—I wavered. I closed my eyes finally.

"But you're safe from her now," he said. "You're safe with me, and I'll keep your secret."

Then, finally, his magic reached the deepest cut in me, the lightning fracture, and I screamed. The agony of it took me by the spine and squeezed. I went to the floor.

I understood without question that if I believed Florian, the pain would stop. If I stopped challenging him and let him have me, it would be over. I would lose Malise, but I'd have *him*, and he would take care of me.

"I'm sorry I thought it was the akrasia until now," he said, kneeling and putting his hands at my waist. "I should have known it was her. Now look what she's done to you; you can't even stand."

He helped me up; I staggered and leaned against him heavily. "Come on. Come to bed. You need to lie down." We weaved our way toward the bedroom. Once we were there, he guided me onto the bed.

I sat. He pressed me back to lie down—and then he was on top of me. "I'm sorry I told you once that we didn't need to be friends. I'd very much like to change that now."

The pain turned sweet. It hurt, but I didn't mind any longer. He kissed me; I have no idea if I kissed back.

Oliver drifted into my mind. Oliver in his golden robe, Oliver with smudged eyeshadow and a smile. I turned my head away.

"So let's be friends," Florian said.

"Don't." I stuttered terribly trying to get the word out. Some integral structure inside me, a mental scaffolding, was starting to give.

"What's wrong?" Florian asked, helping me out of my jacket. "You're not still thinking of Tyrrhena?"

The thing within me struggling against his magic—my soul, perhaps—redoubled its efforts. I stopped his hand as it strayed toward the top button of my shirt.

He held my chin to make me look at him. His rings flashed. "She isn't your friend. Make your choice. It's me or her."

It had all been happening too fast for me to keep track of; I'd been too disoriented to think. Now it all ground to a halt.

Finally, he'd erred. His confidence had brought him too far. *Make your choice.* In that moment, I was helpless against his command: I would do exactly what he asked. I would grant him my absolute obedience. I would choose.

Florian or Malise. The superstitious say only love can break an enchantment so strong, and just this once, I'll bend to superstition.

I loved Malise. I would love her until one of us died, and after we were both gone, I supposed our ghosts would still walk the same paths, me haunting the Pharmakeia's library, her haunting Halicar's flowerbeds, our two specters meeting somewhere in the middle for tea until the sun collapsed. An instant of primal, uncompromising agony overcame me, and I feared an aneurysm—

The silver chains began to crack.

"It's you," I said. "It's been you." I remembered the deathlike sleep he'd brought upon me more than once—it wouldn't take much more than a push to make such a spell stop hearts. The curtain had fallen, and I saw now how easily his magic had weakened me. How I'd let him ensnare me without even a whisper of protest, too desperate for warmth to see clearly. I'd never been sick. The daimon was sleeping now; this was all angel.

Luckily, Florian heard what he wanted to hear. He nodded in satisfaction. "Of course it's me. You can trust me. I'll protect you from the inquisitors for what you've done."

Slowly, I said, "I believe you." I couldn't know the consequences of telling him otherwise. Would he break my mind by force? Would he simply murder me?

"Good." He went for my shirt again, and the wave of revulsion was too great to conceal entirely. I struggled up and cringed away before realizing my mistake.

"What's wrong?" he said.

A seduction was clearly his last resort, the last thing he could try to keep me in line. Physical connection can strengthen a witch's enchantment. If I refused, would he know that I didn't believe him at all? I had to assume that his plan was to keep me around for as long as possible so he'd have another decoy to give the inquisitors if he were close to being caught. That didn't make me *completely* indispensable.

I looked up at him from beneath my lashes, feigning shyness and a promise of desire and hoping I could make it at all convincing. "It's nothing."

"You don't need to be nervous."

I was breathing too quickly. I could see it in his eyes—the calculation, the analysis of my every move.

"Calm down," he said. "It's all right."

Numbly, I let him take off my shirt, my mind racing. I knew without a doubt that I could not endure sleeping with Florian, but the only other option was to risk revealing my realization. I might not survive that either.

The contempt in his gaze was well hidden, but not well enough. I burned under it.

He placed his palm against my skin, against the fractal scars marring my chest. They stung, sparked; I flinched. "Florian—"

"Go on," he said, with such patience and understanding in his voice that I almost wanted to believe him again. "Undress."

There was no longer any room to maneuver. I could submit to the strengthening of Florian's enchantment, or I could risk Florian murdering me in my own bed.

Oliver would understand, I assured myself. I would let him know when this was all over. I'd tell him that I had to do what Florian said, and he wouldn't hold it against me; he'd *understand*.

But my resolve failed. I couldn't do it; I looked up at Florian in a panic.

He frowned faintly, leaning in to examine me. I snatched my shirt back and put it on again, buttoning it unevenly in my haste. Without thinking, I got up off the bed to retreat from him.

I had a few instants to say something to maintain the ruse. "I'm not ready yet," I panted. "I need more time."

His frown vanished, replaced by a look of long-suffering patience. He believed me. He believed he had all the time in the world to break me. "All right," he said.

"Soon. I promise." I swallowed. "I'm just not sure I deserve you."

"Oh, Adrien." He got up off my bed and made to leave the room; he ruffled my hair as he went by. "Maybe you don't, but that doesn't matter to me."

I nearly laughed. It could have been a sob of despair. Either way, Florian heard the aborted sound and sighed. "Why don't you spend some time in your atelier tonight? You can work on something. That'll make you feel better. You'll calm down."

"I'll calm down," I echoed. I knew already that if I went into the atelier, I would find it unrecognizable. Florian would have been moving things around.

"Then, tomorrow, maybe we can do something nice together. You could take a day off, and we could go on an outing. What would you say to that? We could go to the Gardens."

He was confident enough in his enchantment to keep letting me outside the house. That was a good sign. I nodded. "I'd like that," I said.

The suggestion of a date made me sick; it confirmed that Florian liked to play with his food. Equally, there was no way of getting out of it. I couldn't refuse him any further without raising suspicion.

Florian moved deeper into the shadows of the house, leaving me alone. I lost sight of him and was immediately struck by the sensation of treading in black water, heavy with the knowledge that something massive lurked close by. I had escaped for tonight, but tomorrow held no guarantees.

As he'd suggested, I went to the atelier. Sure enough, everything had been moved around; my projects were no longer where I'd left them, and I couldn't recall what I'd been doing before. I busied myself trying to rearrange the gears and wires in a way that pleased me. *Calm down. Calm down.* The enormity of what Florian had done began to settle in. He was the angel; there was no other possibility. I was trapped in my own house with a killer, and if I didn't play my cards perfectly, there was no telling what he might do to me.

Could I kill him as he slept tonight? No, he'd hear me, he'd wake, he'd know. I knew I couldn't do it with a knife, and I could tell my magic wouldn't be up to the task. Unless I was healed of his enchantment, I couldn't face him directly.

I could tell someone. I had to tell someone. As soon as I was away from him, after tomorrow, I could turn him in. Who would believe me? How could I get Malise to safety?

Hours passed. I was so lost in thought and the process of organizing my atelier that I didn't notice Florian standing in the doorway until he cleared his throat. My heart lurched.

"It's late. It's time for you to sleep," he said.

I put down the collection of small glass discs I was sorting and stood. I worried he might hover over me as I got ready for bed, but he left me alone. He was biding his time, I reflected. Until he was ready to try again to cement his enchantment, his pretended investment in me had waned. He couldn't keep it up when it wasn't necessary. How bizarre, how pathetic and deplorable, that a part of me mourned its absence.

All I had to do was survive my outing with Florian tomorrow and fool him well enough that he wouldn't confine me to the house. That was all I had to do, and then I could tell someone. Then it would be over.

Chapter 14

Florian had me prepare some food for us to take to the Gardens. More and more, I noticed, he was relying on me to cook. "We can have a picnic," he suggested offhandedly as he skimmed through another newspaper, looking for word of the raid on the Chirurgeonate. I hid a grimace: the thought of forcing myself to eat in his presence was now profoundly unpleasant. Still, I put together a basket for us, and I made myself relax as I sat next to him in the caleche on the ride there. He touched me a few times, calculated caresses I endured without complaint.

Once there, we wandered through the mazy hedge corridors in search of a nice place to sit. The air smelled sweet; the sun was bright against the leaves rustling in the slight wind. It would have been beautiful if I had been in any other company. As it was, I found myself wondering if it would be possible to flee. Could I run fast enough? Where would I go? What would he do if he caught me?

I knew exactly what he'd do if he caught me. It kept me from trying.

When Florian finally picked a hollow filled with bamboo and koi ponds for us, he sat me down with him on a bench at the edge of one of the ponds. "Isn't this nice?" he said.

"It's lovely." That, at least, was no lie. The parts of the Vesperide Gardens with koi ponds in them had always been my favorite. There was something meditative about watching the fish swim in their endless circles.

Florian changed before my eyes. I saw him don the mask; I saw him make the conscious decision that it was time to work on me again. His features shifted, crafting a perfect facsimile of affection. "I'm glad you've decided to listen to me about what's been going on."

"I can't believe Malise would hurt me like that," I murmured. "I can't even imagine."

He tsked in solicitous agreement. "Sometimes we can't trust anyone. I wouldn't be surprised if that Vigil boy is in on it too."

Gennady, dear God, Gennady. He'd known. He'd warned me. I'd sent him away.

"I can trust *you*, can't I?" I asked Florian.

"Of course."

I could feel the veneer of my believability wearing thin; I needed to say something that would convince him completely. I remembered what Oliver had said about acting. *You need to believe it. In that moment, it's all true for you.*

"It's been such a long time since anyone has wanted me," I said, pretending I was speaking to Oliver. "I barely know what to do with myself when I'm around you."

"I suppose you haven't had many successful relationships, given your akrasia." His stunningly clinical tone irritated me a little.

But he was right. I'd had more than my fair share of disastrous affairs. "I haven't."

"It's for the best that you haven't dated recently."

"For my health?" I guessed.

Just as I had seen him make his decision to be sweet, I saw him now make the decision to try breaking me from another angle. "For everyone else's sake, really." So kind, his voice. So caring. Only saying what I knew to be true. Only saying it for my own good.

I shook my head to clear some of the rising silver from my eyes. I might have broken past the core of his enchantment, but it was far from gone. "What do you mean?"

He pursed his lips sympathetically. "An akratic of your type, especially with your personality, isn't suited to relationships."

"My personality?"

"You have to admit that you're quite manipulative—masterfully so. Besides that, you obviously struggle with violent desires. It's a poisonous combination, Adrien. The fact that it's common with your illness doesn't reduce your responsibility."

I found myself distracted from the main issue of my ruse. He was trying to crush me, and it was working. "I don't know what you mean," I said.

"I mean that you shouldn't be trying to involve unwary people in your problems," he replied patiently. "You should focus on surrounding yourself with people who are properly equipped to deal with you. People who understand what they've signed up for."

I couldn't help it: "I don't want to hurt anyone."

"But you do. Look at everything you've done. Look at the Philidor solarium and all the people you've killed at the Chirurgeonate."

"I didn't mean to."

"Yet it still happened. Listen—if I were to ask the men you've loved about you, what do you think they would say?"

I was scratching at my wrist again. I would draw blood soon.

"They'd say they were lucky to survive you," he told me.

It didn't matter that I knew exactly what he was doing, exactly his goal. The creeping vine of frantic misery continued to spread.

Florian regarded me with concern. "You're not a very self-aware person, Adrien. You shy away from the consequences of your actions; you don't accept culpability. But I can help you address that. I can help you get better."

"Culpability."

"To be perfectly frank, your career choices show me that you're not mindful of your impact on others."

"I don't—"

"You chose to pursue healing, even knowing your condition. Your patients at Philidor paid the price."

"I wasn't sick when the solarium disaster happened," I said. "It was a mistake. We all missed it."

Florian rifled through the picnic basket, idly looking for something to eat. Even as he was reducing me to my base components, his attention wasn't fully on me. "There you go again. Deflecting blame. You really believe that your illness played no part?"

I had believed that before. Now I doubted.

"Granted, those patients may have been better off in the end, but it was still shoddy medicine."

I thought of Willette, the Philidor patient Florian had murdered, of how she'd been before I'd destroyed her. The one thing she enjoyed doing was reading pennyblood novels; I'd brought them to her every week. The very last time I treated her, she told me she'd almost reached the final chapter of her latest one.

Florian seemed unsatisfied with my silence. He could go deeper. "And you chose, after that, to take up with the Pharmakeia. Another position of power. Working with vulnerable young magicians, students you could so easily harm."

"I would never hurt them," I said, my voice hitching peculiarly. I wasn't crying yet; it was more animal panic. I couldn't bear to hear any more, but there was nowhere else to go.

"You would."

"I've never wanted—"

"It's not always about what you want," he said. "This is something you need to work on. You only ever seem to consider yourself."

I fought to even my breathing.

He shook his head, affecting a troubled frown. "What about everyone else, Adrien? What about those you choose to bear your burdens?"

"I—"

He cut me off again with surgical precision. "Do they deserve to suffer?"

"I'm not—"

"No, they don't. But that doesn't seem to matter to you."

A part of me began to detach from Florian's voice, fleeing. I found myself thinking about Oliver. I imagined what it might be like to kiss him in the shade of the bamboo in the Gardens; I wondered what sorts of things he might like me to cook for special occasions. I tried to conjure his voice instead, speaking to me, telling me he'd stay. Telling me he forgave me.

But Florian was louder still. "You want victims and caretakers."

"No."

"I know it doesn't feel that way to you," he said, "but it's true. Now, I can help you be a better man, but first you must be willing to change."

Predictably, like an actor on cue, I burst into tears.

There was no anger or passion in his response. "Crying isn't going to solve this. *Hard work* is what it takes."

"Please." I didn't know what I was pleading for.

"Pull yourself together," he said. He took a piece of bread from our picnic basket and ate it neatly.

"I can't."

"You can. You chose to begin these theatrics, and you can choose to end them."

"I'm trying."

"Stop crying," he repeated, more slowly this time. "I'm not going to give you the reaction you're looking for. You may be used to getting your way like this, but it ends now."

I had always harbored a suspicion that my easy inclination toward tears disgusted others, that it appeared a cheap manipulation. Now, with Florian's help, I understood why. It *was* a cheap manipulation, and I had no excuse for not realizing so earlier.

All the more damning, then, that I could not stop.

Florian watched me with weary disappointment as I resorted, finally, to covering my mouth with one hand and squeezing my throat with the other until I was able to quiet myself.

"Thank you," he said, once I had recovered a little composure. "I'm not going to leave you, but first, you need to let me in."

"I'll do anything." I was no longer acting. The enchantment had begun to overcome me.

"Good. I'm proud of you. As long as you're committed to improving yourself, I'll keep you safe from Tyrrhena and the inquisitors."

I anchored myself to Malise's name as if it were a talisman. I needed to survive this for her. The inquisitors would still have her. Some of the silver cleared away again—I had avoided losing myself completely.

Florian was finished with his attack, and he said nothing else, seeming quietly self-satisfied. I watched the koi swim, trying to go numb; the lazy afternoon heat had a sedative quality. Around and around the fish went, trapped in their own tiny world. I felt myself nearing tears again once or twice in my contemplation, but I quelled the urge viciously.

"I'm tired," I said, after I could speak again.

"You're going to take what I've said into consideration," he said. It was not a question.

"Yes."

"We all have a purpose we're born to, Adrien," he told me, and although it was the second time I'd heard him say it, I understood it no more clearly.

He took me home again, and I barely registered the journey back. I spent it all revisiting events that proved, without a doubt, that Florian was right. Failed relationships, mostly, testaments to everything Florian had laid out so precisely about me. I thought the longest of one in particular, an old memory I often resurrected.

I was twenty-four years old, and there were things my boyfriend Danilo and I did not like about each other. He didn't like that I left my books all over our apartment; I wished he would do the laundry more often. He found me dramatic, and I thought he could be insensitive. The list was long.

We were also happy together, as happy as I had ever been with anyone. He was a poet in his spare time away from his work at an apothecary, which I found absolutely delightful, if inconvenient when I found myself paying most of our rent. I had moved in with him after three months of seeing each other.

After six months with Danilo, I graduated from medical school and began my career as a full-fledged doctor very promisingly with a manic episode. The daimon was still newborn, stretching its wings. I went along; I could barely sleep or eat, but my grip on reality was passable, and so I had far more time for my work.

The other benefit of my episode was that Danilo loved me more. When I first realized what was happening, I let him know in advance that I was sorry. At first, he seemed to find the apology perplexing; I knew he'd always wished that I would come dancing with him and his friends sometimes, clean up the apartment better, want to sleep with him more frequently. I did these things with enthusiasm now.

He especially liked the sex. Normally I was indecisive, a little shy and squeamish. I almost always let him be the one to start us off, and even then, I didn't indulge him often enough. Now, I told him that I would do whatever he wanted, whenever he pleased, provided I didn't have pressing work. He took me up on it; I exhausted him every night, which was almost enough for me.

So things were good for us, wonderful even, and I was feeling like the most intelligent and attractive man in the world until Danilo began to notice that I was insane.

When we'd started seeing each other, I told him that I was ill and gave him some idea of what to expect on the occasion of my episodes. He said he didn't mind—*Shouldn't a poet be open to a little madness?* he asked me, and to this day it galls me that I found it unspeakably romantic.

"I don't see what the fuss is," he said one night as I lay panting after he was done with me. "You're more fun this way."

And I was, until I wasn't. I began to glimpse shadows that weren't there, hear fragments of noise with no source. Never anything unbearable, never anything that overcame me, just enough to confirm that this would not be easy. Soon, the anger came. Anger, poor decisions—and the talking. I was furious with my coworkers, often with Danilo; I was spending too much of our money; I could not shut up. Of all these, the talking bothered him the most.

At first, he patiently listened to me ramble, at top speed, about no discernible topic. I went for hours into the night. "It's nice to see you interested in things," he said initially. And then he began to catch on to the fact that I was making very little sense, and soon enough he wanted me to stop.

Day by day, he grew more and more annoyed with me; I grew worse and worse to live with. We fought with increasing venom. Finally, he explained himself in unequivocal terms, and then I became a monster.

We were sitting at the kitchen table in the evening. I watched him eat his dinner, trying as hard as I could to be quiet. The pressure built. Finally, I drew a breath—to tell him that I was sorry, truly sorry, about how I had been lately, about the too-expensive clothes I'd bought and the way I'd snapped at him yesterday, and that I was trying, and would he please not leave me?

He jerked his head toward me. "Shut up," he said.

I did.

"Just shut up. I don't want to hear you talk."

I could have stayed silent. I chose not to. "I'm sorry—"

He pushed away his food. "Adrien, if you were sorry, you'd stop."

"I can't help it," I said. I said it not with contrition, but with petty irritation, and this damned us.

"I've been understanding," he muttered. "I've been patient. It's too much." He stood and pushed past me, going into the cramped living room.

Danilo needed a break from me. The man I loved needed silence, peace, space. Naturally, I followed him.

I'd made him hate me without even noticing it; he must have reached the tipping point long before now. He stared at me with fascinated revulsion, and I racked my seething mind to find something that he'd once liked about me. I could only think of one item. I looked up at him shyly, a look I knew to be effective from past experience, and took a step toward him with calculated meekness.

His face didn't change. I came closer. "I can make it up to you."

"Really," he said. "You really think I want to touch you now."

I'm sorry, I wanted to say again, and didn't. Instead, I put on a very small smile. "I thought it was certainly worth a try."

Through some superhuman act of will, he didn't hit me. "Look at yourself."

Without warning, I was breathless with fury. "You *like* me this way," I hissed. "You like that I'm *fun*. You like me better now than before. You said so."

He held up a hand. "Not anymore."

"I warned you," I said. It was difficult not to raise my voice. "At the beginning. I warned you very explicitly, in detail."

A moment of regret flickered across his face. "I didn't think it would be this bad," he said.

I struggled past my wrath. "I'll try harder," I said. "I promise."

He thinned his lips. "My friends warned me too, you know," he said. "They told me daimoniacs always turn."

I fought. I fought for my life, wavered, and fell. I didn't recognize the laugh I gave. "Well," I said to Danilo, quite sweetly. "That sounds like a personal problem for you. You were too stupid to understand what you were told."

There was still a chance, if slim, to at least part on good terms. I declined it. He hated the thing I was, and I hated him back: "Is it difficult being that impaired? Or is it blissful in its way?"

He recoiled as if bitten by a viper.

"You've always had some trouble keeping up with me," I continued. For the best effect, I injected my voice with exasperated sympathy. "This is partially my fault, I suppose, for expecting you to actually process words and ideas."

Danilo snarled and lunged for me; I skipped out of his reach with a startled giggle. *Well, this is it*, I thought. *I've gotten myself murdered.*

He tried again and caught my arm, and I raised my eyebrows at him. "Go on. Don't leave me hanging."

But he let go and pushed me away. Without looking at me, he pulled himself together. "You should leave," he said. "You should stay somewhere else tonight. I don't care where. And if you decide to come back, I can't promise I'll let you in."

"I don't suppose you'd let me go put on some nicer clothes?" I said, for no reason other than to hurt him. "And I could use a bit of makeup."

He watched me with total incredulity. I assumed the answer was *no* and went out into the city.

There was a bar close to Danilo's apartment. I had never visited it; I decided that now was as good a time as any. My plan required no thought from me. It had always existed in my mind, just waiting for me to discover it. I bought a single drink with my pocket change to justify my presence and set out to make eye contact with someone.

My attention span was short, but I didn't need much. I decided on the very first man who looked my way. He had red hair, and was older than me by perhaps twenty years, and I recall nothing else of his appearance. Not a single thing. I put down my drink—alcohol was not what I wanted—and went straight to him. I didn't take a seat next to him; we wouldn't be staying long.

He evaluated me from his barstool and nodded. "Looking for something?"

I opened my mouth to flirt and lost patience before I could get the first words out. "I need somewhere to stay tonight, actually," I said. "You look like you might help me with that."

He snorted with amusement and took his time answering. "You're not dressed much like a temple boy, and this is hardly a temple. Do you have a license?"

"You've misunderstood," I said, a touch impatiently. "You won't be paying me."

He now seemed to enjoy the game we were playing. "Then what's the scam? Are your friends waiting for us around the corner outside to hit me over the head and search my pockets?"

I hid my face, as if shy, to conceal my fury, the narrowing of my eyes. When I'd recovered, I put my hand on his thigh. "No. I'm a perfectly upright citizen," I said. "I'm a doctor, actually." My pride was still intact somewhere below the surface.

The man made a thoughtful sound. I smiled and leaned close to murmur, "The thing is that I'm also out of my mind, which is a wonderful opportunity for you."

He swept his gaze over me, more intently than before. "That's an awful line."

I wanted to be honest. I could tell him that I needed attention, warmth, pleasure. I could tell him that I *needed* someone.

"You know, you can do just about anything to a daimoniac," I said instead, cruelly. "You'll see. Then in the morning, I'll show myself out, and you'll have had an extremely nice night for free."

I watched him wonder what I meant by *anything*. I watched him decide that if I was trouble, I would be easy to get rid of. We left the bar shortly. He hailed a caleche; I got in without question. After a quick ride, he led me up the steps of a lovely white house, then into his bedroom. The walls were white; the sheets were white. I could only see white.

Before I undressed, he offered me a drop from a vial of rosethorn, which I declined. "Are you sure you don't want any?" he said. "It'll help you relax."

Rosethorn has an amnesic effect. I wanted to remember this. I capped the vial for him and handed it back. "No, thank you."

"Suit yourself."

Beyond that, we didn't converse. I got what I wanted.

∼

When it was finally over, I made a show of bliss to conceal my relief and curled up close to the man to cuddle his arm. "So was it a nice night?" I asked. "*Extremely* nice?"

He paused, and I had never felt such dread before. The thought that he might now send me stumbling out the door was unfathomable. I would kill him, I decided, or myself.

"Extremely nice," he agreed.

"I can stay here?"

That seemed to throw him. "You could have stayed regardless," he said curiously. "I wasn't going to toss you out in the middle of the night."

I refused to process his words, on the grounds that if I did, I would immediately begin to scream. "Oh."

He brushed my tangled hair back. "You had fun."

He wasn't asking; I had no obligation to reply. The temptation was there to simply lose consciousness, but I wasn't so far gone. My predominant desire, above love, above forgiveness, was to be less sticky. "I need to shower."

He let me clean myself first and was kind enough not to comment on the amount of time I spent or the hot water I wasted. He showered next, much more efficiently. I went to the bed to move the top sheet onto the floor and curled up.

I hadn't slept for more than a few hours at a time in several days, but physical exhaustion got me past the daimon almost instantly. I woke during the night only once or twice. The man never touched me, except on accident when turning over. I almost wished he would; I missed the way Danilo held me in bed.

When I heard the first birdsong outside, I realized in full exactly what I had done.

∼

The man wanted more at sunrise. I declined politely, thanked him, and dressed. I barely remembered to retrieve my glasses. He showed me to the door, and I realized that I had no money for a caleche to get myself home. He gifted me the fare and said he hoped he'd see me at the bar sometime; I told him—quite accurately—that I would soon be moving away.

The moment I was out of his sight, the tears came. I was quiet, but not perfectly, and the caleche driver said nothing to me about the display when she dropped me off. It was still early in the morning; Danilo would be home. I knocked.

He opened the door with an expression of weary contempt. I stopped crying immediately—out of fear, and out of respect for what I had put him through.

"I cheated on you," I said. "To find somewhere to stay."

He let me inside. Every question he could ever have about me was answered. "I'm going to work now. You should probably get to the Chirurge-onate. We'll settle it when we both get back."

Because, of course, the world existed outside of my personal dramas. I had things to do. I changed into my blue doctor's clothing and left.

The day passed slowly and surreally, without much word from the daimon. My tribute the night before had satisfied it for now. Every so often, I would think of the thing I had done and entertain the thinnest thread of fantasy that I might somehow escape unpunished. Even then, I had the nerve to hope.

I came home to the apartment a bit late. Danilo was at the kitchen table.

"Go ahead and pack your things," he said. I turned and went to find something to use as luggage.

It took me some time, although I couldn't carry much with me. He watched me incuriously all throughout. Like an automaton, I went through the necessary motions of packing up, until I was suddenly standing outside with my bags. It was long past dark by then.

Time and space realigned themselves properly; I realized that I was not going to get a proper goodbye. We were not parting as friends, and there would be no gentle end to the story. It was that, more than anything else, that stung me. I saw his face clearly, as I'd never seen it before—then I loved him, wished only that I could bandage the wounds I'd given him.

He told me, "Never let me see you again." I had to smile: that was something like a definite goodbye after all.

～

I wandered the city for a while, taking in the night air, until I decided that I was tired of carrying my bags and that I might be murdered after all if I stayed out any longer. Without thinking, I knew perfectly well how to find myself shelter again. I couldn't bring myself to try.

The thought occurred, wildly, to go to my parents. They lived in Deme Aufford, not too far away; I could try to visit. I had no illusions that they would let me inside the house, but maybe they would let me speak with them. We'd been estranged for over a year, but I still wrote letters, and the letters were never returned. Maybe they read what I wrote them—maybe my mother, at least, would talk to me for a few minutes.

Then I remembered myself. They would have denied me even our family name if they could have: all my life, they had grimly tolerated that I was a magician, that I was weak, that I was timid, but the final insult of my complete defectiveness had tipped the scales forever. There was no reason to try again.

No. I had only one real other option as to where to go, one option that was safe.

I showed up at Malise's apartment door somewhere around one in the morning and steeled myself enough to knock. I knew she'd be awake. But it was some time before she answered; she'd clearly been working.

She saw that I had my luggage with me and let me inside. It didn't take her long to grasp the situation, which was yet another blow to my ego. "Again?" she said. For one reason or another, I'd had the opportunity to call on her like this twice before. It was already familiar to me, which I enjoyed not at all.

I smiled. "Again." There were a thousand other things I wanted to say, all pressing insistently against the walls of my skull, but I smothered them. I left my bags at the door.

We walked past her little desk, stacked with papers, to sit on the couch. "What happened?" she asked.

And immediately I brightened with the pleasure of having something to talk about, a story to tell. There were lurid details. I could be clever about it; I could make her laugh. I straightened up and opened my mouth.

The look she gave me was tired. Even the daimon lost its appetite. Slowly, painstakingly, I cut the facts down to their essences. "I was doing well," I said.

Malise shrugged, a polite disagreement. I had been on my best behavior with her, but even she had seen some ugliness.

"Danilo was enjoying it. But he stopped. I got worse. And then yesterday..."

"Yesterday."

"I picked a fight."

She waited.

I was not a gifted storyteller after all. "I got angry," I forced myself to say. "I was angry with him, and I said terrible things to him, so he said I needed to sleep somewhere else that night."

She took my hand. Her questions continued inexorably. "Where did you go?"

"There's a bar near his apartment."

I didn't need to elaborate; she looked away.

Everything ached. "Then today he gave me the rest of the evening to pack up my things."

I had to catch my breath.

She squeezed my hand and let it go. "This was not your finest moment, my dear."

It was the mildest, kindest condemnation I could have ever asked for, and from her, it hit me like a sledgehammer nevertheless. "I know," I said.

"Were you hurt?" she asked. "Danilo, or—"

"No," I said desperately. "No, Danilo never hurt me."

"I can heal you of—of anything."

But I deserved my damage. I had worked hard to get it, and no one was going to take it away from me. I felt a mark beneath my collar; it was proof that for a moment, someone had wanted me. "No need," I said.

Malise shook her head.

My mind raced; I could almost hear the rush, the sound of a flooding river. The thought that finally made it through was a crippled thing. "I didn't even have to," I said in tones of injury. "The man I met, he was going to let me stay there anyway."

Malise made a sound of real unhappiness.

I remembered abruptly why I had come and took off my glasses to cover my face. "If I could stay with you for just a couple weeks. A week and a half. I just need to find somewhere else. I'll be quick."

But her first word to me when she'd opened the door burned like a brand. *Again?* The probability dawned on me that I was not as wonderful to be around as I liked to believe, and I was not quite as witty as I thought, and that living with me right now was perhaps too much to ask of any human being.

"Or I can stay at the Chirurgeonate," I said hastily, replacing my glasses. "Sometimes there are empty rooms. That wouldn't be so bad." There were other options too, which I fought not to remember.

A silence followed, during which I couldn't move. "Adrien," Malise said eventually. "I keep a set of blankets in the closet just for you."

Nothing in my life had hurt in exactly that way before.

I survived the moment. "We're going to have some rules, though," she said, with an element of dryness.

The daimon growled that rules are not for people like me. I let the flare run its course and shut it away. I would control myself for a few weeks, or I'd die trying. "Of course," I said—or tried to say. My voice failed.

Malise understood. "Well. Just give me a moment." With that, she disappeared into her bedroom, rifling through the closet. She came back with a pile of folded bedding, and I helped her spread it out on the couch before I sat back down.

"There's probably no use," I said. I tried to sound arch. "It isn't as though I sleep much."

She was unamused, but she humored me with a smile. "I'm going to make some tea for both of us. Uncaffeinated."

She left for the kitchen, and I devoted myself to shutting up.

In minutes, she returned with two mugs; we leaned against each other and nursed our tea for a long time in silence. Finally, the pressure in my head forced my mouth open. "I really was fond of Danilo," I said. I'd forfeited the right to say I'd *loved* him. "And he wrote me the sweetest little couplets sometimes." I left it at that.

She made a quiet decision. "The fight must have been terrible."

"It was my fault."

"What started it?"

"I couldn't stop talking," I whispered.

Malise rubbed her eyes. "Do we need to go to the Chirurgeonate?"

I shook my head blindly.

"All right."

"I'm sorry," I said, unable to think of anything else, unable to imagine what I could possibly offer. My body wanted to pace. I refused it.

She knew she couldn't let me fixate; she glanced at the bags I'd left near the door. "You don't have many things with you."

I hissed with frustration and leaned back to look at the ceiling instead of her. "My books," I said. "Nearly all of my books. And some of my projects, and some good pens, and one of my favorite jackets. That potted anthurium. Just . . . things. I left most of it."

She wrinkled her nose. "He isn't going to let you come get anything else when you're settled somewhere again?"

I remembered Danilo's stunningly neutral tone when he'd dismissed me and startled myself with a laugh. "No, I don't believe he is."

"Ah."

"Even though I warned him," I said with tattered self-righteousness. "I have no idea what he'll do with everything I left. Pawn it, I hope, and not burn it."

Malise drained her tea. The motion had the distinct air of someone tossing back a shot of alcohol. I left mine half empty, profoundly relieved that she hadn't yet said *I told you so.* It was against her advice that I'd moved in with Danilo.

"This should be over soon," she said.

"Probably." I sighed. "I'll miss it."

She took the comment with the amount of respect it deserved, which was none. "You won't."

I guarded the daimon jealously. "It helps me work."

"Of course. You're homeless and single now, but thank God you can work."

"It feels good." That was basic and childish and not even half of the truth, but I had no other real argument.

She turned me forcibly to face her. I remembered the man from the bar and shuddered; she saw it and let me go. "Please, Adrien. Don't tell me you're happy."

It would be satisfying to be angry with her. I could say things to rip her to shreds, just like Danilo.

"When it's over," I said, "I'll bring you breakfast every morning. I'll bake you whatever you want. I'll do your paperwork. I'll get a keeper."

I'd achieved some shred of victory. "Let's look forward to it," she said, her expression finally relaxing. "I'm going back to work now, my dear. I need to have this done by tomorrow. Borrow what you want from the bookshelves."

I sat and read the same page of an anatomy textbook over and over again, feeling Malise's presence like a lifeline, biting my tongue hard whenever I thought of something I needed to say. I was quiet, sensible, until she finally turned off the desk lamp and stood. "Good night," she said, waiting for my response before she turned away.

"I love you," I said to her.

"Try to sleep," she replied, which had always meant much the same thing in different terms.

I sat and fidgeted until morning, ignoring the occasional darting shadow in the corner of my vision. There was a small mirror on one of Malise's walls, visible in the moonlight; I turned away.

In the caleche with Florian, making our way home, I remembered Danilo— but I could so easily have remembered ten other things. It didn't matter. Florian had been completely correct about me, yes, true. There were now more pressing issues to deal with. I felt mostly a sense of bruised shock, and under that, foreboding: Florian thought he had broken me down enough now. He would try to finalize his control soon.

I thought I'd survived the day, at least. I thought I had a little more time, that I could escape tomorrow and make everything right. I was wrong. He tried again that same night.

Impatient, I thought distantly as he sat next to me on my bed once more. I'd barely moved since we'd returned from the Gardens.

He put his hand on my waist, fingers creeping over my side. Here I was at the cardinal moment; it was time to decide which fate I preferred.

In the end, I couldn't do it. All my efforts to pretend were for nothing. I threw my only shield away in a single instant; I shied violently and stood up to retreat across the room.

That was it. He changed. "By all the saints," he snarled, "for the love of the stars, what will it take?"

"I'm just not feeling well," I said tightly. "I'm sorry. I want to, but I can't right now—"

He strode over to me, backing me up until my spine hit the nearby bookcase. My nerve broke; I tried to summon some lighting to put between us—

But nothing came. My magic was dull and dead inside me, still weighed down by silver. I'd been letting him cast on me for too long. My fingers sparked, but that was all.

"That's not going to work," he said.

"I don't—"

"Stop pretending."

There was no use. I stopped.

I looked at him, beholding the revealed monster. He looked at me, gradually discarding the remnants of his mask. We came to an understanding. "You set the inquisitors on Malise," I said breathlessly. "You're the angel."

He shrugged. His wild frustration with my defiance had faded with unnatural speed: he was realizing that he still had every ounce of control he needed. The lifeless contempt replacing it was far worse.

"Why do you do it?" I asked. "Mercy? To ease their suffering? It's for their own good?"

Something about the hysterical upward pitch of my voice let him know that I wasn't the audience for those lines.

Instead, he said, "We all have a purpose we're born to."

I meticulously excised the urge to scream. "Why start now? Were you with Mulcaster?"

He seemed affronted; he pushed me harder against the bookcase. "As if I would be interested in a Clementia Prefect's machinations. As if I were a *novice* in need of direction."

My great insult had been implying that he hadn't already been killing for years. "Then why change?"

"I wasn't fulfilled," he said.

For only a moment, it struck me as ludicrous that he was answering my questions. Why bother? What did he gain? But behind the dull, alien malice of his gaze, I recognized a facet of my own heart. Florian must spend every day, every waking moment, needled by the knowledge that he was unsuited to the world at large. Walking alongside the living, hearing their beating hearts, feeling the warmth of their blood—it had to be agony for him.

I'd always imagined that I knew what it was to be other, to feel myself untranslatable. I didn't. Not compared to an angel. Of course he was eager to speak honestly; the only people who would ever see his true face were his victims.

"You're staring," Florian said flatly, and stepped back enough that he was no longer pinning me.

The absurdity of what he'd told me finally hit me as I searched the room for possible exit routes. "You weren't *fulfilled*?" I said. "You find this *fulfilling*?"

"Practicing in the solariums was a worthy enough endeavor," he said. "The average solarium healer has far too light a touch. They're too squeamish to make the hard judgment calls. It was useful work."

I would have killed Florian by tooth and nail, in that moment, if it would restore my memory of the exact shade of Willette's eyes. I would have eaten his heart if it meant she'd get to finish reading her last book. *I* had taken that from her, not he, but I knew no other victim's name. "How many?" I choked.

"Enough to see improvements."

"Why leave, then?" I asked him once my nausea had waned enough to speak again. "Why move to the Chirurgeonate?" I needed to keep him talking. I could think while he talked.

"It can be taxing to work with akratics. Eventually one tires of trying to help people who simply don't *want* to be helped."

He was using his human voice again. Taunting me. My intention to think of a plan while he talked shattered. "That's not the answer," I hissed.

His features stilled. He could have been carved from stone. "It wasn't enough anymore," he said eventually.

Of course. Solariums are small; even a few "accidental" deaths would have drawn notice. For Florian to remain uncaught there, his benevolence would need to go uncredited. Unclaimed. Not mercy at all, but chance. Not enough death, not enough attention—once his hunger outpaced his hunting grounds, he'd have to go somewhere bigger.

I spoke before I realized what I was saying. "You're an addict."

It was a mistake. I had finally provoked Florian in earnest. Oathbreaker, monster, murderer—I doubted he would shy from any of those, but *addict* was intolerable. "You know," he said, "you've pressed me to the limit. I've been patient with you so far, but I've never dealt with someone so ungrateful."

I had been in mortal danger before; I had looked death in the face. Never had I been so frightened as I was then, standing in my own bedroom. The details of the situation blurred, and for an instant, I remembered only all the other times I had infuriated caretakers. "Keeper," I said involuntarily.

"This is in direct response to the things you do," he told me, utterly flat. "This is a matter of proportionate reward. Because you won't let me do what's best for you. I want you to understand that."

I took a step away from him.

"Don't run," he said softly.

It was the little noise I made, a ragged gasp, that set him off.

He beat me. *Effectively,* but not savagely. Not for long, just for long enough.

More than anything else, it was disciplinary. I had never imagined Florian as a physical man, but he seemed perfectly at ease with it.

By the end, he was standing over me. In the fractured blur of it all, Malise's angel eye bracelet had come undone from my wrist; the tie was broken, and a cascade of blue beads had spilled across the floor.

"This can go one of two ways for you, Adrien," Florian said, only very slightly out of breath.

I waited, shielding my face. My glasses lay nearby, but I didn't dare retrieve them.

"We can let the inquisitors keep believing that Tyrrhena is the angel, or we can tell them *you* are the angel. We both know they won't believe you if you speak against me. I have a sterling reputation, and you have Philidor and Westbrook."

"We don't need to change anything," I panted. "If you stop killing for a while, they'll move on. You were going to keep me around just in case you needed another misdirection, weren't you?"

He tilted his head. "I'm not going to stop."

"Just for a little while. Just long enough to throw them off. Then when you do start again, you'll have me as your next decoy."

"You're saying you won't be any trouble."

"I'll never breathe a word against you."

"You haven't been particularly honest with me," he said patiently. "Why should I believe you?"

He was right in his suspicions, of course; I was lying. I tried harder to look pathetic. "You'll hurt me otherwise, won't you?"

To get a good look at my eyes, he reached down and tipped my head up. I shuddered, dizzied by the urge to bite. "That's right," he said. "I will, and I'll do more than that. Akrasia can always be worse. There is always an available room in a worse solarium. Don't forget that."

A last temptation toward obedience came; I banished it. "Then I'll do what you say."

"Get up."

I got up.

"Go away. Give me some time to think about what to do with you."

I picked up my glasses and went.

Chapter 15

I rinsed my mouth until the bleeding stopped, neatened my clothes, and crept back into my bedroom to hide once Florian had gone from it.

The only thing to do was wait until he'd made his choice about how to handle me. I couldn't hope to be allowed to leave the house until then; my future depended on his inclinations. If he was capable of learning caution, of believing that I might be a threat, there was no hope. Experimentally, I prayed. *Now, listen,* I thought, addressing each of the constellations in turn. *If ever there was a devotee worthy of your grace, surely it's Malise.*

As ever, nothing answered.

I sat down at my desk and picked up a pen, hoping I could soothe myself by writing something—but I could only stare blankly at the paper. As long as I was still trapped in the house with Florian, there was nothing. He might decide to put me under close observation somehow, and I'd have to be creative with how I worked against him. Or he might simply decide to kill me, and that would be unfortunate.

I stayed motionless at the desk for some time, willing myself to at least get up and pace, aching too much to do so. When Florian finally called for me to present myself to him again, it was a relief.

I came out into the dining room where he was waiting for me. "As long as you agree to be cooperative, I don't see why I shouldn't keep you around," he said without preamble. Even now that we were beyond his lies, he still maintained the same tone of careful patience. It made my skin crawl.

"You don't intend to stop killing?" I said.

"There's still work to be done."

"You really are something," I murmured.

He looked at me sharply. "I beg your pardon?"

Despite myself, against the desire of every nerve, I quailed. I wanted to be brave; I wanted to stand up to him. Instead, I said, "Nothing. I'm sorry."

He let it go. "In the meantime, all you need to do is behave. Keep the details of this to yourself."

"I will," I said, pondering what the best way to tell Gennady would be.

"I'll know if you don't." He tapped his forehead. "Don't think I won't be looking around inside that mind of yours from time to time."

There's no such thing as true mind reading. No spell can reveal another's thoughts completely. He was bluffing. Still, I hesitated. He was more powerful than most other magicians I'd encountered; who was to say what was beyond him?

"I won't cross you," I said softly. "Please don't hurt me again." It was easier than I care to admit to play the part.

He was satisfied. His arrogance, his confidence in his domination of me, was absolute. I vowed to make him regret it. "Stay away from anyone who might ask questions," he said. "Your Vigil friend. The actor. The inquisitors. You go to teach, and then you come home. That's it."

Home, he said, as if my house belonged to both of us. I swallowed hard, but I nodded.

"This will be the start of a partnership, then," he said. "Make something to eat, Adrien, would you please?"

So I cooked for him and daydreamed of poison.

I wasn't sure yet how to tell Gennady. I couldn't risk him charging in at full speed to murder Florian—he'd get himself killed without a doubt, and the thought of facing that guilt was more than I could bear. I needed some semblance of a plan first.

Instead, as soon I was allowed out of the house, I went to the inquisitors' headquarters in Deme Alidor. If I was to find out what had become of Malise, checking there seemed like a decent idea. True, if Florian learned that I'd gone anywhere near an inquisitor, he'd make me regret it. True, I was afraid. And true, I still felt the pull of his magic telling me to obey. None of that mattered.

I dithered outside the front door of the headquarters for a long while before I could muster the grit to go inside. Technically, citizens are allowed to enter most Clementia facilities, but it isn't really *done*. There were no guards outside as there might have been for a Vigil or witchfinder facility, which I took as yet another sign of incompetence.

When I did go in, the ache in my fingers, much receded, came back in full force. I could feel hands around my throat again. I could hear Theo and Silvestra's voices.

I wouldn't let it distract me from my purpose. I went inside and latched onto the first inquisitor I came across, a doughy, dour-looking man. "Excuse me," I said.

He turned and looked down his nose at me. "You're not really supposed to be in here," he said.

I gave him a thin smile. "I'd tend to agree, but I have questions to ask, and there's no law against it."

"Questions."

"About the arrests made at the Chirurgeonate."

"You're a doctor?"

"I have a friend I'm asking about."

"I can't promise to help you," he said.

I steeled myself to receive the worst of answers. "Malise Tyrrhena. She has dark hair, brown skin—she's very short. I was hoping you'd know something of what happened to her after she was arrested."

He gave me an inscrutable look. "What *happened*?"

"Was she tortured? Was she charged and convicted? Was she sent to the Umbra or—"

Or executed, I meant to say, and could not.

The inquisitor sighed. "You realize that we arrested dozens of Chirurgeonate people. Aside from the inquisitor who actually took her, it's not likely that any of us will remember one doctor."

Naturally. The average citizen was faceless and nameless to the Clementia. "Then how do I find out where the arresting inquisitor is? His name was Curtis, I think."

"We don't keep records of the assignments everyone is on."

"The witchfinders keep records," I retorted, for the pure frustration of it. "And I'm given to understand that you highborn newcomers consider yourselves superior to the Watchtower."

He growled. "I don't know what to tell you. If you want to spend your time wandering this place, you're welcome to it, but I can't guarantee that no one will lose their temper with you."

All I heard was *you're welcome to it*. "Perfect," I said.

"We're busy here," he said. "I have an interrogation to get to."

"Worst of luck," I said without really meaning to, and turned on my heel to wander.

Not every other inquisitor I encountered was so reserved with their irritation. A few of them touched the hilts of their swords or tried to crowd me, stepping too close and implying with various degrees of subtlety that they could arrest me for my presence. I ignored it all, going through the same course of questions with each person I saw. *Malise Tyrrhena, she looks like this, what's happened to her, and where's Curtis?*

Nearly all of them brushed me off immediately, telling me that they had other places in the city to be, or suspects to question. On my eighth try, I got lucky. I found the inquisitor who had arrested Malise's friend Chandra. He blinked curiously in vague recognition when I approached.

I didn't take the time to introduce myself again or make any pleasantries, too excited to have made some progress. I said, "The woman I was with, the one Curtis arrested. What did he do with her?"

He thought for a while. It felt like an eternity. I held myself very still.

"Oh," he said. "We convicted her. Immensely convincing eyewitness for those charges. Curtis took her to the Umbra. Why?"

"Because she's my friend," I said numbly.

"Tough luck. Choose your friends better."

"She's innocent," I said.

"Not according to the Curia."

I blinked away stray sparks of lightning. "There must be something I can do," I said thickly, a plea more than an assertion.

He shrugged. "Go home and forget her. She's a witch now. You're not going to see her again." The perfect equanimity with which he said it stung more than any hostility could.

"Do you know if she was tortured before she was taken there?"

"I'm not sure," he said, and for a moment, I thought I heard something like the faintest hint of sympathy in his voice. "But Curtis is pretty thorough."

I turned and made my way out of the building, walking as though through a fog.

It had been a mistake to come. I'd only been distracting myself from the obvious reality: there was only one thing for it. I'd need to convince the inquisitors that Florian was their real culprit, show them that his word was worth nothing against Malise. Only then was there any chance of delivering her from them.

I went to a market to buy an assortment of random items to bring home; I'd told Florian I was going for groceries. I needed proof of having been somewhere acceptable. I spent as long as I reasonably could at the market, but soon enough I needed to go back.

Florian wasn't there when I returned; he was at the Chirurgeonate. Killing, maybe, I thought distantly. And each new murder a death I could have prevented, if only I were less stupid. If only I weren't weak. I left the groceries in the kitchen and went to lie down. The blue beads from Malise's broken angel eye bracelet were still scattered around my bedroom. I left them there.

∼

I was growing very tired of showing up to work injured. I told anyone who asked that I'd been in a fight, and that answer surprised them all deeply enough to forestall any further questions.

I spent my free hours the next day trying to repair my magic. Florian hadn't tried to cast on me again; he would soon, I had to assume, but not yet. I had some time to try to untangle his silver.

I found an empty lab in one of the buildings, one with plenty of space and nothing flammable, and set about trying to call some lightning. I knew now that I could disregard Florian's advice not to push myself while his "treatment" was in progress; that could only be a lie. Still, I was nervous as I tried.

And with good reason. It hurt. It hurt worse than before, and there was a sickening edge to the pain now. As I stood in the lab trying to conjure, every spark of lightning I managed to summon burned. While I had recently been able to summon it instinctively, involuntarily, a conscious application was more difficult. To my immense unease, I felt danger from it—if I wasn't careful, I might shock myself. That had never happened before, except for when I'd given myself my fractal scars. For the sake of my pride, I was determined to keep it from happening again.

I concentrated. A thin bolt of lightning appeared in my hand, and I twirled it between my fingers happily—then it vanished, leaving behind it a pulse of agony. I doubled over with a muffled yelp. My most successful effort yet, and the most painful. Such a display wouldn't be nearly enough to do anything but anger Florian, even if I could find it in me to hurt another person with my magic.

Still, it felt wonderful to even see the lightning again beyond errant sparks drawn from moments of fear or pain. It was nice to have proof that my magic still lived. I braved the hurt awhile longer to keep conjuring, to keep clearing the dust away.

But there was no marked improvement as I kept practicing; I wasn't doing anything to make myself better. Without actual treatment, I hadn't progressed, and throwing myself at the problem wasn't helping.

I went to sit at one of the tables in the room and rested my aching head on the wood. Once I wasn't concentrating on anything, all the pain from Florian's discipline returned in exquisite form. I felt a swell of tears start and crushed it mercilessly. He would not make me cry. I wouldn't allow myself that luxury until I was sure he'd seen the sun for the last time, one way or another.

I tried for another half an hour, filling the room with flashes of lightning here and there, until I was exhausted and something inside me felt ready to give way. It was enough, I decided; if I kept going, there was the real possibility of breaking something. I was going to need to talk to Gailhardt.

It took fifteen minutes of sitting alone in that lab before I trusted myself to go find Gailhardt without telling her everything I knew. The temptation to give all my troubles over to someone else, no matter the risk, was nearly irresistible—but if I wasn't ready to involve Gennady yet, Gailhardt was out of the question. She was formidable, but if I told her about Florian's murders, he would come out on top before I could blink.

She was in her office. I knocked; she called me in. When she saw me, her hand flew to her mouth. "Desfourneaux, what happened?"

"What," I said bitterly, "is something the matter with my face? Everyone keeps asking."

She got up and sat me down in the second available chair. "Tell me."

I debated over how much I could reveal. Was there some degree of truth I could be allowed? Eventually, I said, "My keeper hit me."

She hissed. "More than once, it looks like. You fired him, I assume?"

I was silent.

"You need to. And you need to report him."

"I just need to get some things in order, and then I will."

She drew another breath, and I held up a hand. "I know," I said. "I will. I just need some time." To soften it, I tried to smile. "I appreciate your concern."

"Can you go to the Chirurgeonate to be healed, at least?" she asked.

"It was swarming with inquisitors," I said. "They took Malise. I'm afraid to go back."

"They took *her*?" Gailhardt said sharply. "The gall—the foolishness—"

"We'll fix it," I said.

"The Chirurgeonate will revolt. There must be a dozen other innocents too, then."

"We'll fix it." My voice grated.

She winced, understanding that I was only barely containing myself, and subsided for some time before saying, "A hedge healer, then. You could go to a church and see if one of them will fix you up."

The thought hadn't occurred to me, even though Malise was a hedge healer. "Maybe," I said woodenly. Then I realized how Florian would react if I came home healed, and I shook my head. "He'd be angry. I'll have to wait until I'm free of him."

She crossed her arms. "And when do you think that'll be?"

My hands were unsteady. I clasped them tightly. "I don't know. It's complicated."

"You're afraid he'll come after you if you leave."

"It's *complicated*."

She gentled, giving up the argument for lost. I was grateful. Surely she'd come at it again later, but at least I'd have a reprieve for now. "Why did you come to see me? Did you need something?"

"My magic," I said. "He was . . . treating it, but it wasn't working. It's still broken. I still need help." *So I can defend myself*, I nearly added, before catching it.

"Was he treating it *properly*?" she asked grimly.

To my horror, I laughed.

"The others and I are having a meeting tonight," she said. "You should come. I can't give you an immediate fix, but we can resume working on it."

Oliver would be there. Oliver would see me injured again; if Florian found out, he would cut my leash short. "I can't."

"Why—"

I said, "Please, Gailhardt—please. I just can't. I know it's a great deal to ask, but if you could find the time to see me alone, in private, I'd appreciate it more than I can say."

She reached out to touch me on the shoulder. I shied away; she let her hand drop. "I can try to treat you right now," she offered. "We'll forgo the preparatory stage we were in before, if this is urgent. I don't think any students are planning to drop by. We can figure out a schedule for more appointments later."

I exhaled carefully. "Thank you," I said.

She got up and came to stand in front of me. "I'll need to touch you, of course."

I set my jaw and nodded. There was no reason to be afraid of that. Still, it was hard not to move away when she put one hand on my forehead and began to cast, seeking inside me to find my magic.

She hadn't been looking for very long at all when she gasped and jerked back from me. "What?" I asked. "What's wrong?"

"You're all tangled up," she said, with sick marvel. "The fracture from before—something's holding it open. Someone's magic."

Malise hadn't seen it so clearly; she was a healer, not an expert in identifying different magical signatures. She could only sense vaguely that there was something wrong, something foreign. Of course Gailhardt would understand with far more precision. I cursed myself.

The discovery had frightened her; she withdrew from me and began to pace. "That's witchcraft. Who's the witch, Desfourneaux? Your keeper? You need to tell the witchfinders—the inquisitors, maybe—"

"I will," I said. "When I'm ready. When I have the evidence I need, when I'm sure I'm safe. For now, it's a secret."

She shook her head.

"It's a secret," I repeated. "It needs to be. For my safety."

"Stars and saints," she whispered. But she didn't argue.

The guilt of presenting her with this and then swearing her to secrecy ate at me, but I told myself I had no choice. Either I'd soon find a solution and be able to reassure her in good time, or I'd die, in which case I would no longer be her problem.

"Is there any hope of repairing it?" I asked.

"With time and great care, yes. If you keep seeing me, I can help with the untangling. Then you'll be able to heal the original rift on your own time, I think."

So Florian hadn't ruined me. I would one day be whole without him. I slumped in my chair, dizzy with relief and gratitude.

"I'm sorry I didn't let you help me earlier," I said. "It was just that he didn't want me to."

"And you trusted him to do what was best."

I'd barely known Florian, but yes, I'd trusted. "He has a certain force of personality," I said weakly, by way of excuse.

She looked me over with poorly concealed pity. I could imagine what she was thinking—was I truly so desperate for attention and acceptance that I hadn't seen what he was from the start? And I had no answer for her.

"Well," she said, with the faintest hint of her usual archness. "You're letting me help you now, and I will do my best."

She cast on me for a while longer, trying to pick at the knots she'd found, trying to clear Florian away. With each dive, my head hurt more, until I had to give in and beg her to stop. "I'm sorry. I don't think I can take any more."

"I think I felt some improvement," she told me generously. "Next time we'll try for longer. Try casting again. See what you can manage."

I took a deep breath and summoned a small thread of lightning between my thumb and index finger, slowly growing it until I could hold it properly in my hand. The pain came, but I ignored it until I'd kept the lightning for ten full seconds. When I let it go, I was smiling.

"Thank you," I said. "That's wonderful."

"You need to be careful with it. A mistake could undo all your progress." She rubbed her eyes. "And if you let him cast on you again . . ."

I expected that it would do nothing less than destroy me; I nodded. "I'll try."

She checked her watch reluctantly. "I have a class soon. I hate to leave you in these kinds of straits—if you need, I'll—"

"I have a class too; I'll go," I said. "Don't worry."

"I'll worry if I so please."

"I suppose I mean *have faith*."

"Easier," she said, with quiet unhappiness.

I left her to her schedule, returning to the bloodstained chessboard I'd made of my life.

Chapter 16

I wasn't prepared at all to see Oliver. I was, in fact, barely prepared to see anyone, and the man I was falling in love with was near the pinnacle of the list. Unfortunately, he took the choice away when he came to see me at the Pharmakeia that same day.

He was waiting for me outside my office when I came to pick up a folder before my last class; he saw me and swore. "What happened this time? Your face—"

That hurt badly, the *this time*, as though I'd developed some kind of unfortunate habit he was chastising me for. I knew he didn't mean it that way, but I looked away from him nevertheless. I couldn't answer.

"The inquisitors again?"

I gently moved him aside so I could go into my office. He hovered outside the door, looking lost and horrified, until I took pity and motioned for him to sit. "Go on," I murmured, and set myself down gingerly behind the desk.

He perched on the chair as if ready to spring up at any time. "Adrien? What happened?"

Unlike Gailhardt, I didn't think I could trust that Oliver wouldn't go to Florian if I told him that it had been my keeper. I'd need to lie. "The inquisitors," I said, with a nod.

His face darkened with fury. "I thought they'd already ruled you out."

"The Clementia is cruel," I said carefully.

It was good enough. He believed me. "I'm sorry." He got up to stand next to me and examine my bruises. The brightness of his clothing—purple and yellow this time—hurt my eyes, but I refused to look away. "They really did a number on you."

"I'm sorry I haven't been to see you," I said, suddenly remembering that I'd agreed to visit his apartment sometime. "It's just—I've been—"

"I came to see why that was," he admitted. "I didn't expect . . ."

"I wanted to. I would have. It's been impossible lately."

He let me go, but he didn't step back. "I've been worried."

I thought of what I'd almost let Florian do, and suddenly I was standing and reaching for Oliver.

Without hesitation, he opened his arms. "It's all right," he said, squeezing me.

So much affection, so freely given—it was a foreign thing to me. I rested my head on his shoulder and weathered the wave of enervation that followed. "It's really been . . ."

"I heard they think they got the angel," he said. "When they were at the Chirurgeonate. They figure one of those doctors was the right one. It's over now. You won't have any more problems with the inquisitors; they finished their job."

I imagined Malise shivering in the Umbra. Did the chains bite terribly? Did the wards ache? Was she hungry? "Finished their job," I repeated distantly, and moved back a little. He let me go, which I regretted at once.

"Well—yes. They did what they were meant to do," he said.

I reached for Malise's angel eye bracelet. When I realized its absence, my heart jolted as though I'd missed a step on a staircase. "Maybe."

"Listen, let me take you to lunch," he said. "Let's just spend some time together. You could use it."

I paused. The number of people taking me to lunch lately was climbing perilously. We were all caught between the jaws of disaster, and now I was considering a date.

"You know," Oliver said, "if we're meant to be anything more than friends, we need to actually see each other." He was trying to be funny, I could tell, but instead there was only a fragile hesitance.

"I want that," I said.

"It doesn't have to be today. You're hurt; we can—"

"Please kiss me," I said.

"Oh," he said uncertainly.

"Oliver. I don't want to beg." I was aware that it was going to hurt, given the cut on my lower lip. That wasn't important. *This* was what I needed to give me the strength to work against Florian. If I had this, I could act.

He folded one of his hands around mine, brushed the other across my cheek. Unlike our first, this kiss wasn't brief. It was supremely gentle, as though he were afraid of breaking me, but not brief. He lingered on me. When it was over, I felt the loss like a blade.

"Thank you," I said.

He gave me a weak smile. "Excellent, wonderful. That was good. Now let me feed you."

Florian would not find out, I told myself. Florian could not find out. "Of course," I said. "Just let me put a sign on the lecture hall door." I'd need to tell my students that class was canceled. I regretted it—but for once, something was more important than work.

I scribbled *class canceled* on a sheet of scrap paper and went to the hall of St. Osiander to pin it outside. Oliver followed me; after I was done, I turned to him. "Let's go."

He guided me off the Pharmakeia's campus, staying solicitously close to me. I abandoned my caution and reached for his hand, and he gave it to me, and we walked like that for some time. I stopped paying attention to where we were going and let myself drift, aware of only Oliver and the vaguest shapes of the streets.

We ended up at a quaint little Saebar place, dark inside, with staff who smiled as they took our orders. Oliver and I sat side by side. A single stick of incense burned at the back of the restaurant, and I was in no shape to withstand even a trace of smoke; I started to nod off even before the food arrived, listing against Oliver's side. He shook me gently back into the world when it was time to eat.

He finished his noodles long before I finished my duck, and he took to watching me eat, fiddling with his utensils. Every so often I'd look up, and he'd avert his eyes with a smile, acknowledging that he'd been caught. I didn't mind—it was nothing like the gaze of a prying stranger.

"I'll pay for this," he said once I was done. I began to sleepily protest, and he held up a hand. "It paid well to be Haruspex Ambrose," he said. "Come on. Let me celebrate my good fortune. It would make me happy."

I would do most anything to make him happy. I nodded.

He paid; we left. I'd started to flag by then, and he supported me gallantly for the last stretch of the walk back to the Pharmakeia. "Well," he said, once we were back on campus. "Can we do this again sometime?"

"My keeper—"

"Damn your keeper," he said. "He isn't your master."

The desire to make him understand burned, acid under my skin.

"Does he *act* like your master?" he asked.

"I know he isn't," I said, evading the question. "I just don't like to fight with him."

"I'll wait a long time," he said. "I'll wait a long time for you. But . . ."

I had to tell him. I had to tell him. I had to tell him.

I couldn't tell him.

"I know," I murmured, and forced myself to look at him again. "It's too complicated right now. But it won't last forever."

He looked so relieved that I immediately felt as though I'd misled him. Florian had been right about one thing, at least, one thing I could never deny. In that beautiful koi garden, he'd reminded me that even in the best of all possible worlds, I would make Oliver suffer.

I scratched at my wrist. "You need to know that it won't be easy. I'm not an easy person to be around. You have to understand the—the reality of that. Please."

"Even if you're right, won't there be good times too?" He was trying to keep his voice steady, but I could hear the bewilderment.

What could I give him?

I'll bleed myself on the altar for you every day, I thought. *I'll do anything you want, anything you could ever ask. No one else will need you so much. No one else's debt will be so steep.*

He spoke again. "I can reach for you. I need you to reach back, though."

Gently, gradually, the veil of despair parted. The world slid back into view. He wasn't asking for a grand sacrifice. He wasn't asking for my soul. He was asking me to reach back. *Love is not an ancient shrine, and Oliver is not a knife.*

"There will be good times," I said, and took his hand. "Soon. I swear it."

He sighed in relief and gifted me with a weak smile, absolving me. "Then I'll be patient."

It was difficult to withstand the perfect grace of his motions, the careless turn of a wrist, his easy self-possession. I shivered.

He brushed my hair back. "Are you cold?"

I entertained the brief, disorienting fantasy of having him bend me over my office desk before deciding my ribs hurt far too much for it. "Only tired," I said.

"I should let you go, then."

I wanted to protest, but if I stayed much longer, I wasn't sure I'd get back to Florian in time. "For now."

He showed me his crooked smile again, rueful this time, and dipped his head. "All right. Another time, then? I'll see you soon?"

"God," I said, "I hope so."

~

When I got home, Florian asked me where I'd been, and I told him that I had only been working late. I cringed from him. I begged him to believe me; I told him I would never disobey. All the while, I mentally categorized the items around the house I might murder him with. The display satisfied him; Oliver's acting skills were rubbing off on me.

I took out the Astragestum tarot deck that night, shuffling through, begging the universe for any sign of what I was meant to do.

Szerena's Crown. The Crypt. The Rache. The Heresiarch. Every card I drew was from the Court of Monsters. Every single one. I stopped before the theme could continue and shuffled them all back in.

~

I knew now that I could no longer delay telling Gennady. Involving him might send everything crashing down if he wouldn't heed a plan, but he was the only member of the Clementia who would listen to me. I'd run out of options; caution was now out of the question. Oliver was right. I had choices to make.

The next evening I could slip away from home, I went to Gennady's apartment, agonizingly aware of how I'd sent him away the last time we'd spoken. I knocked on his door, praying he'd be home.

He was there, although he took his sweet time answering, as he always did. He squinted balefully when he saw me, registering my injuries, trying to read me. Behind him, Lady's tail switched back and forth uneasily.

"You were right," I said.

His face darkened. "Ha. Knew it. Knew I wasn't being crazy. Knew I shouldn't have listened to you." There was a vicious satisfaction in his voice that cut me, although I knew it was well deserved. Gennady's instinct had been the only one sharp enough, and I'd made him doubt himself.

"May I come inside?" I asked.

He gave me a curt nod. I stepped past him inside with Lady trailing behind me.

"So?" he said. "Talk."

"I can't get away from Florian by myself."

Lady began to circle me protectively.

Gennady sat down on his couch and put his feet up on a small, stained table with a thud. "So I'll come kill him. In and out. Easy. Better late than never."

I stayed standing. "He's the angel," I said softly, and then I couldn't stop talking. "He's been enchanting me. He told the inquisitors Malise is the killer. They took her to the Umbra. I don't know what to do."

Gennady took a breath to respond.

My words spilled over. "We need to get the inquisitors to convict him, or the witchfinders, or the Vigil, maybe—*someone*, something. We need to find some sort of evidence beyond just my word—he's ready to give me over to the inquisitors too."

Gennady was silent for a moment. When he spoke again, it was with genuine bafflement. "Are you fucking kidding me? You picked a serial killer as your keeper? You sent me away so you could play nice with a *serial killer*?"

"Yes," I said.

"The Vigil won't take the case," he said once he had digested most of his outrage. "It's witchy stuff. Not our business. I bet the witchfinders won't want to get involved either. It'll piss off the inquisitors. That's Clementia politics."

"Maybe Theo and Silvestra will listen," I said desperately. "They believed that I didn't have anything to do with it, that I didn't know. They thought it was Malise, but maybe if I go to them, they'll at least *consider* what I'm saying—"

"The inquisitors that tortured you?" he said, and barked a scornful laugh. "Broke your fingers? Yeah. That's a great idea. Another Desfourneaux original."

"There might be no other option."

He gave me a withering look. "There's a pretty fucking obvious option. I go to your house and kill the guy. Like I keep saying."

"No," I said. "You don't understand how powerful he is, and that won't do anything to help Malise. We need him convicted, not dead, or she'll never leave the Umbra."

"Ugh." But he didn't argue; I remembered with great relief that he respected Malise.

Lady meowed quietly, and he looked at her. "Yeah," he said. "I know."

I raised my eyebrows.

"We're not exactly great detectives."

"I can't do it on my own."

"Obviously," he said. "I'm just saying it's going to be hard. We can't do it with just the three of us, probably."

"Which is why I think we should ask Theo and Silvestra."

There was a blankness in his gaze now, a look familiar to me from our earlier days. "If you want to go to them, that's your business. They'll torture you again for the hell of it, but I can't stop you."

"Mostly," I said, as my voice cracked, "I just wanted to tell someone."

He didn't soften, exactly. He would never soften. But his gaze lost some of its faraway quality. "Well, now you have. Congratulations."

"I need you to be careful. Florian is powerful. If you attack him, there's every chance he might kill you first. He would only have to touch you, and you could be gone in an instant."

Gennady thought he was immortal, although I'd once held him dying in my arms. I knew that. Any warning to him about the possibility of death would be a momentary distraction at most. "Sure," he said. "Whatever."

"This is important."

"I said sure."

At a certain point, I needed to trust him. I'd told him; all I could do was hope he wouldn't turn me into the instrument of his demise. "Thank you."

"I only stayed away because you made me," he said, not meeting my eyes. "I didn't want to. But I was trying to listen. And now look."

I had to swallow to clear a tremor from my voice. "I'm sorry I didn't believe you."

To my incalculable relief, he accepted my answer. "Yeah. So, what should I do if *you* die?" he said blithely. To betray his lack of care, Lady whined.

"Do everything you can to help Malise." She had other friends, but none who knew the truth. "Promise me that."

"I bet your ghost would haunt me if I didn't."

"Absolutely," I said. "I'd never rest."

"Well." He scratched his nose awkwardly. "Maybe you just shouldn't die."

A harried laugh escaped me. "That's the plan, my dear."

We talked strategy for a while longer, but nothing came of it. Eventually, I realized with a start that I once again needed to get back to Florian. Every day, every night, that leash dragged me back and forth. "Be well," I said to Gennady, biting back the nagging feeling that this might be the very last time I saw him, and I should make it count. With that feeling came the urge to make a scene, and there would be nothing he would hate more.

"Bye," he told me, without the slightest evidence of complication. "See you.

If you don't talk to the inquisitors yourself *really* soon, I'm going to start do-ing stuff for you."

"I will."

"And if you die tonight because you went home to that guy without me there, I'll spit on your grave every day forever."

"Noted."

Only Lady showed some ceremony, graciously tipping her muzzle at me as I got my coat and walked to the front door. I leaned to run a hand across her glossy fur, and then that was that. I was back out in the world—I was alone.

I missed Oliver terribly by the time I got home.

There was no need to, because he was there. He was waiting. He was wait-ing inside, in fact, waiting with Florian. I stepped inside the house, and I saw him sitting by the coffee table facing my keeper, and I felt every molecule of mine freeze.

I had never actually told him that he shouldn't come. I'd been so afraid of turning him against Florian and spurring him into action that I'd neglected to tell him *not to come.*

The door shut behind me. Florian said, tonelessly, "Welcome home, Adrien."

Oliver waved, then hesitated when he saw my expression. "What's wrong? Is something wrong?"

"No," I said softly, standing there looking between the two of them. There was still a chance that Florian didn't know I'd been to see Oliver. He could think that this was only an unexpected visit I had nothing to do with.

Then Oliver said, "I've been thinking about what we said this afternoon. I came to tell your keeper that it's very nice how concerned he is about the company you keep, but he doesn't need to worry."

I set my coat down over the back of one of the chairs at the dining room table and went into the kitchen to get a knife.

I came back; Oliver jumped up once he saw what I was holding. "Hold on, now," he said, blanching. "What's that for?"

"Yes," Florian said opaquely, "what *is* that for? Are you going to hurt us?"

The cards were all laid out now, revealed to both of us. Florian saw that I was not obedient, had not been obedient, did not intend to be obedient. I saw that he was going to make me pay. I turned to him with the kitchen knife held out a bare inch or so. "You need to leave now," I whispered.

While Oliver wasn't looking at him, a brief, slick smile drifted across his face and then vanished. He put his hands up. "Don't," he said, with stunningly credible apprehension. He turned to Oliver. "You've set him off. I was afraid of this."

Oliver shook his head mutely, eyes wide with fundamental disbelief.

"He's the angel," Florian said, and in that moment, even I nearly believed his display of terror. "He's been keeping me hostage here. He told me that if I turn him in, he'll kill me. Now we're both going to die." I saw that he'd been planning this, setting this up even before I'd walked in the door.

"No," I said, fighting to speak through a vast, howling void. "He's lying—"

"Help me stop him," Florian said to Oliver pleadingly. "He needs to be stopped. He's killing people. He'll probably kill *us*, but if we work together . . ."

Oliver wasn't looking at him. He was looking at me, at where I stood holding my weapon.

I begged him, silently, to *think*. To put together all the facts. To understand. But I couldn't read him; I couldn't read his eyes.

Neither could Florian, evidently. "Or if you're not going to help me," he said, "then at least run and get yourself out of danger. I'll fight him alone." I admired the finishing touches he put on his words, the brave self-sacrifice, the heroic resignation.

I was grateful to Florian, for once—his suggestion that Oliver leave was a godsend. "Go," I told Oliver. "Please go home."

He hesitated. "Adrien—"

I felt myself swaying where I stood, the tip of the knife dipping in desperation. "Go!"

"Find someone to warn," Florian said. "Tell the witchfinders, or the Vigil—someone. I won't be complicit in this any longer."

Oliver looked back to me. I nodded. "I promise. He's lying. But you should leave."

He turned cautiously and crept away from us. Neither Florian nor I moved until he'd reached the front door and slipped outside, and we heard his running footsteps leading away from my little house. I remembered that he'd said running was difficult for him since his accident; I hoped it didn't hurt.

After he was well and truly gone, Florian straightened up, looked at me, and smiled. "Are you *sure* you're not going through some daimoniacal troubles, Adrien? Because you seem to have believed you'd get away with this, which certainly qualifies as a delusion."

I brought the knife up again silently.

He walked toward me confidently, freely, and without further thought, I swung the blade. I missed by an inch—and then he grabbed me by the arm, and I realized that I'd had no idea just how powerful he was, because my body was moving without my say. My fingers uncurled against my will. I dropped the knife.

"I hate to do this," he said. "I really do. I would have preferred not to resort to this, but you've forced me."

"What are you doing to me?" It was rhetorical; I knew exactly what he was doing. If he could stop a heart with his magic, why wouldn't he be able to manipulate limbs as well? Once he touched me, I was doomed. He'd been *merciful* with me until now.

He didn't answer. "Now," he said, "you know what needs to happen. If I can't trust you, it's time to pay the inquisitors a visit."

"By all means," I snarled. "They're just as likely to believe me as you." I thought no such thing.

"Oh," he said. "Absolutely, they're going to believe *you*. You're going to confess."

"Why would I—"

"For my convenience," he said. "If you confess to being the one and only angel, that'll save me some time cleaning up the mess you've made with the actor. In return, I will tell the inquisitors that I was mistaken about Tyrrhena. She'll go free, although I'm afraid you won't. If you don't confess, I'll just . . . kill you. And she'll still rot."

"They'd know it was a murder."

"They wouldn't," he said patiently. "I'd put you to sleep, Adrien, and while you were out, I would get nepenthe. I'd come back and fill you with enough to kill you ten times over. No one would think twice about it."

In that moment, I'll admit, it seemed a tempting end. "When the deaths continue, they'll know it wasn't really Malise or me."

"I'll find a way around that. I'll change my methods. I've done it once; I'll do it again." He ceased to be human for me. I was dizzy; his bright gray eyes seemed to multiply. I imagined I could hear the beating of many wings.

Florian cleared his throat politely. "Give me your attention when I'm speaking to you."

I focused until I could see him clearly again. I would find a way out of this, if not for myself, if not for Malise, if not for Florian's victims, then at least to repair the godforsaken embarrassment of having bent to this man.

"I've told you your options. Make your choice," he said.

"I'll confess," I said, although the words were copper in my mouth. I had never told him that Malise suspected him. The threat she posed was unknown. For that alone, even the slimmest chance my confession might free her was worth it.

"Perfect." He patted my arm. "There are still inquisitors stationed at the Pharmakeia, correct?"

I couldn't nod; his magic wouldn't let me. "Yes," I said. "They've made it permanent."

"So they'd be there now?"

I didn't answer.

With a flick of his wrist, he moved something inside me just enough to send a white lance of pain searing through my entire body. I shrieked.

Florian sighed. "Would they?"

"Yes," I said, panting. "There are night classes. As long as there are students on campus, there will probably be inquisitors."

"Well, then. Let's be on our way."

Chapter 17

Florian hailed a caleche to take us to the Pharmakeia, although it was only a short walk from my house. I suppose he didn't want to risk any sort of interference on the way there. He kept me silent during the entire ride; I tried to say something to the driver, tried to beg her for help, but my mouth wouldn't open. Florian took my arm, and that alone was enough to shackle my every faculty as though his touch held the weight of chains.

I tried to savor the sight of the Pharmakeia as he walked me onto campus. There was every probability that this was my last chance to take it in. Whatever might be next, whether death or the rot of the Umbra, could ensure that. I couldn't cry out to the people we passed that Florian was holding me by force. I couldn't look at them. He controlled even that, and what repulsed me most was the way he had me walk at his side, arm in arm, as though we were friends taking a leisurely stroll.

He took me inside the first building we came across, the same building that housed my office and the hall of St. Osiander. "We're bound to find some inquisitors somewhere," he murmured to me conspiratorially. The ambric lights and witchlight sconces illuminating the hallways cast strange shadows across his face. He let me go and took a step back from me, severing our connection. Now only fear kept me from running—but the fear was just as powerful as his magic.

It could only be fate that the first inquisitors we saw were Theo and Silvestra. Of all the options, of course it would be them, my torturers—and now, possibly, my saviors. I dared to hope.

They hadn't seen us yet. When Florian noticed them, he smiled. "Up you go," he said, and slipped away. I knew he'd be watching me, that he would know if I lost my nerve, but I felt the vise of his presence ease from around my ribs by a degree. I still held my one advantage—Florian's self-confidence, his hubris. He had a single, enormous blind spot; that was the reason he was bringing me anywhere near the inquisitors. He couldn't conceive of the idea that any living soul might believe a junkie daimoniac.

With my vision tunneling, I forced myself to walk up to the inquisitors. It was good to move under my own power, for once, no matter what I was moving toward.

"Ah," said Theo. "Desfourneaux."

"Are you all right?" Silvestra said doubtfully. For a moment, I almost believed that she cared. She motioned to my face. "You haven't had any run-ins with the other inquisitors, have you?"

I shook my head.

They both waited awkwardly for me to speak. The gleam coming from the hilts of their swords hurt my eyes. "I have a confession to make," I said.

Instantly, the two of them stiffened up, watching me on high alert. They went from people to instruments of the Clementia in the blink of an eye. "Go on," Theo said.

If I failed, if I couldn't convince the inquisitors once they'd taken me away from Florian, I was going to miss the sunlight. "I'm the angel," I said. "It's me. I know you've taken Malise Tyrrhena for it, but that was a mistake. That was— part of my plan. I've been going to the Chirurgeonate and killing patients."

There was a very long, very dead silence.

"Why are you confessing now?" Silvestra said finally. She drew her sword, completely without relish.

I hadn't prepared for any questions. "Guilt?"

"Why did you do it?"

"I don't know," I said. My throat closed up; I fought past it.

The two of them exchanged a bewildered stare. "Listen," Theo said. "Why are you really saying this?"

"You need to believe me," I told him. I was begging; I didn't dare look over my shoulder to see if Florian was pleased, if this was sufficient. What would he do if they refused to take me? "Believe me. Arrest me—take me to be tried, or whatever it is you do."

Cautiously, as if looking for a trick, Silvestra retrieved her pair of handcuffs from her belt and approached me with them. She circled around behind me as Theo kept watch in front.

I became aware, then, that people were *seeing* this. No matter that only night classes were in session—there were enough students and staff left inside the academy that the hallway hadn't remained vacant. First a few people had collected, and then a group, and then, as Silvestra handcuffed me and word spread through the immediate classrooms, a crowd.

I looked around. Florian was gone. I was tempted for a moment to recant immediately, but if I was planning to do so at all, there were better times. I might be safer at the inquisitors' headquarters than walking free in the world.

Silvestra wasn't gentle when she cuffed me, but she wasn't rough. There was no malice, only a businesslike efficiency. Immediately, the panic rose in me—I couldn't move my hands; I was bound; it was just like Florian—and I devoted all my attention to not struggling. The antimagic in the handcuffs sickened me, weakened me, a spiritual nausea.

I barely heard Xantha's voice saying, "Professor?"

She was one of the students watching, ashen and wide-eyed. This was the *second* time she was seeing me taken away by the inquisitors, I realized. What were the odds? As my gaze flickered over the gathered crowd, I discovered that I recognized more than a handful of the students and most of the faculty. A hollowness set upon me: the hollowness of a community lost. My reputation would not survive this particular blow.

Or so I believed, until Gailhardt, pushing her way up from the back of the crowd, said, "Absolutely not."

Theo lifted a hand in exasperation. "What? You're going to stop us? He just confessed to being the angel. We don't have any choice in the matter."

"He confessed under duress, clearly," Gailhardt hissed. "We know how you people work. You tortured him before—of course he'd say what you want."

The crowd rumbled in agreement, a resentful wave of sound. Xantha lifted her chin bravely. "I thought the angel had already been caught," she said. "Why are you arresting people now? Why are you even *here* still?"

"The Clementia needs to monitor the Pharmakeia and the Chirurgeonate more closely for a while," Silvestra said darkly. "It's been trouble after trouble. You lot just can't seem to keep it together."

"But the angel—"

"According to the professor here, we have the wrong person."

"You've taken more than enough of us away," said another voice I recognized. Cosima Rabena, chair of the Department of Mekhanical Studies. She faced Theo and Silvestra with crossed arms and a narrow glare.

"Because—" Theo began.

"And you won't be taking any more," Rabena said.

I was frozen silent by the possibility of the inquisitors deciding they had a genuine rebellion on their hands. People would die.

"If you choose to obstruct the Clementia," Silvestra said, "you'll be charged and tried for it. There will be consequences. Are you sure you want to risk that for one man who's *just confessed*?"

"It's not just about Desfourneaux," Gailhardt snapped. "He isn't the only academy magician you've kidnapped—and what about the innocent healers? Everyone knows not all of them were guilty. You can't terrorize the Pharmakeia and the Chirurgeonate at the same time and expect us both to just take it."

"It's the law," Theo said. He drew his sword too, but it carried the air of a defense rather than a threat. "Will you follow it, or will you make the Clementia come down on this place like a hammer?"

Xantha and the students surrounding us looked at each other, and then she looked at me. She said to the inquisitors, "There are only two of you."

Theo hefted his sword; I came back to my senses. It wasn't about me, not really, as Gailhardt had said—but I could stop it. "Don't," I said. "I'll go."

The Pharmakeia at large protested, a furious torrent of voices united. Xantha shook her head. "No—"

I sought Gailhardt in the crowd and locked eyes with her. "You have a responsibility to allow this," I said. "Or they'll start killing students."

Beside me, Theo murmured an uncomfortable protest—but I knew his heart. I knew the two of them were capable of it if pushed.

I continued. "Even if they're subdued here, there are other inquisitors in the academy right now. They'll come. Just let me go with them."

Gailhardt was fighting back tears. Xantha failed to do so. Rabena simply stared.

"You're not a martyr," Gailhardt said. "This isn't a sainting. You don't have to do this." But I could see that I'd won. Wordlessly, Rabena turned and began to shepherd the angry, frightened students away. The other faculty slowly followed suit, until the crowd had begun to thin dramatically. I felt its loss badly; the fear was worse now.

Gailhardt and Xantha were soon the only ones left. I smiled weakly at them.

"For God's sake," Theo said. "Get out of the way. We're not going to murder him. It's just that we have no choice."

"Whatever people begin to say about me," I started to say, and broke off when Silvestra shook me irritably and began to walk me toward the nearest exit. The antimagic in the handcuffs pulsed—I followed her lead as well as I could.

The last thing I saw of the Pharmakeia was Gailhardt guiding Xantha off. I was proud, at least, of that.

～

My second time being held in the inquisitors' headquarters was less frightening than the first, somehow. I already knew the worst that could happen, and I knew that my greatest threat was not in the building with me.

They sat me down in a different interrogation room. I wasn't released from the handcuffs. Silvestra paced; Theo went outside again and was gone for a long while. When he came back, it was with a group of three other inquisitors, all more finely dressed than he was. From the way they all stood, it was clear they were superiors. The overcrowded room felt stuffy and claustrophobic now.

Theo sat and stared at me. The others all stayed standing. Eventually, he said, "You know I don't believe your confession."

"Why not?"

"Because we saw who you are," he said. "When we tortured you. We broke you. We saw your nature." He sounded far away.

I resisted the urge to point out that that's not how torture works at all. "I was forced to confess," I said, fighting to sound calm, to sound rational— above all, to *avoid* sounding like someone desperately concocting a lie.

One of the inquisitors Theo had brought back with him spoke up. "Now look what you've done, Theophile. You've given him an out, and he's taking it."

Silvestra cocked her head, slowing her pacing. "Go on."

"The angel's name is Florian Albrecht. He's a healer with the Chirurgeonate. He framed Malise Tyrrhena and now he's trying to frame me. He threatened to murder me if I didn't confess." I delivered it all in a measured, reasonable tone. I didn't dare look at any of them to see if I was believed.

There was no need to look. A series of dismissive snorts from the senior inquisitors told me all I needed to know. "Or how about this," one of them said, a silver-haired man with a heavy brow. "You changed your mind at the last second after confessing, and now you're trying to squirm out of it like a coward by telling us that our informant is actually the criminal."

"We know Florian Albrecht," another said. "He's been a valuable source. We've arrested a great many witches in the Chirurgeonate with his help. Are you Malise Tyrrhena's accomplice? Did she instruct you to say it was Albrecht?"

"No," I said quickly. "I told you—he framed her. He told me that if I confessed, he'd withdraw his accusations against her. He's my keeper; she's my alienist—I'm her friend—"

Keeper, alienist. The words produced an instant reaction. "So you've just brought us a madman," the silver-haired inquisitor said to Silvestra, incredulity writ large.

"That part's not relevant," she said.

He pinched the bridge of his nose.

"If I may," Silvestra said to her superiors, "I wouldn't be surprised if he's telling the truth. I don't think he's capable of being the angel."

There was a silence. She took it as an indication to go on. "He may have a dubious record, but he's not violent—"

"Explain what you mean by *dubious record*," said the silver-haired inquisitor.

I closed my eyes.

"Well, sir, it's true he's been through two witchcraft trials—"

"Unbelievable," I muttered.

"My God," the inquisitor said, as Theo and Silvestra both winced repentantly. "*Two* witchcraft trials?"

"The Philidor solarium and something to do with the Mulcaster affair," Silvestra said. She had to disclose; I understood that. My resentment was in no way curtailed.

"In that case, he isn't getting a third chance. Take him to the Umbra now," the inquisitor said.

"Sir," Theo said. "No trial?"

"What is the point of an inquisition otherwise? What are we here for, if not to cull the threat faster than the attorneys allow?"

Theo shook his head. "I really think we should consider what he's saying. It is possible that Albrecht—?"

"Florian Albrecht is a well-respected healer who has been nothing but an asset to the inquisition, and this man . . ."

He looked at me. "Desfourneaux," I provided.

"This man, Desfourneaux, will not escape justice another time. He confessed. A later retraction, made out of cowardice, means nothing."

Of course I'd been an idiot to think the inquisitors could be allies. Even Theo and Silvestra's testimony wouldn't be enough.

"The deaths will continue after I'm put away," I said. "They may no longer be heart attacks; Florian may change his method. But he'll keep killing patients. You'll see." I didn't think Florian was capable of restraining himself for very long. His hunting grounds might change, but he would never stop.

For a singular moment, I saw my conviction sway the silver-haired inquisitor. But after the instant passed, no one rushed to unchain me. "The Umbra," he said. "Are we all agreed?"

Slowly, one by one, the other inquisitors all voiced their consent—all except Theo and Silvestra. As one being, the gathering stared at them.

Theo was fiddling with his silver badge. "What about Malise Tyrrhena, then? They can't both be guilty."

"Of course they can. All this means is that he's either her thrall or her accomplice, and it makes no difference which," one of the superior inquisitors snapped. "It certainly seems as though there's more going on here than we thought, but those are details to hash out after justice is done."

Theo opened his mouth to say something, clearly a protest, but Silvestra nudged him before he could speak. "We'll take him there," she said. "Right away." I couldn't read her tone.

With a series of grim, satisfied nods, having borne witness to my makeshift conviction, the other inquisitors all filed out of the interrogation room to get back to their various terrible duties. Only one of them even looked at me as he went, and when he did, it was with fascinated revulsion. I was the city's newest monster.

When I was alone in the room with Theo and Silvestra, I said, "Will you really take me to the Umbra?"

"Oh, absolutely," Theo said.

"You are the most incompetent people I have ever met."

He continued. "We'll take you, but that doesn't mean we can't do anything for you. Maybe a note will find its way into the hands of that Vigil boy you asked us to spring. Deme Nymphes commissariat, right? Maybe he can do something to return the favor to you."

"He's only a lieutenant," I said. "How is he supposed to defy the inquisition?"

Silvestra scoffed. "As if you really think he'll have any trouble defying *any-thing*. No, he stands a chance of getting you out. The Vigil guards those cells, not us. Then you'll just have to stay put until we catch this Florian of yours."

"He's not *mine*," I said, but I had started to hope again. "He's powerful, you know. If you're going to go after him, you'll need to be very careful. Never let him touch you."

"We know how to handle a witch," Silvestra said impatiently. "Aren't you going to thank us, by the way?"

I stared her down. Even terrified and heartsick, I knew that the look I gave her was withering. "You tortured me. Helping me catch Florian is the least you can do—and, incidentally, your job. No, I won't thank you for doing the bare minimum, and doing it *late*."

She was the first to look away.

Theo hauled himself up and motioned me up as well. "All right," he said. "Let's not quibble over who did what."

I prepared myself to fly into a fury until I saw the look in his eyes, a rueful apology. "If you insist," I said, and stood.

Chapter 18

I counted the seconds on the journey to the Umbra. It wasn't long, but I counted anyway; I needed to value every single moment spent outside the depths. At first, it was as though we were only going to the Penumbra, a place I'd been enough times now to develop some sort of defense against—but soon we took a turn into the underprison. The inquisitors found a staircase, one of many that descended into the Umbra, and walked me down it, Theo ahead of me and Silvestra behind.

The cell blocks were noticeably smaller, lit with searing ambric lights that flickered and pulsed. There were no bars, no windows, only a solid, crushing sense of abandonment. It was, above all, lonely. Even the Vigil guards and raches standing outside every cell, two per prisoner, couldn't lessen the impression of the Umbra as a land of the lost.

Then there were the wards. I cannot overstate the depth of unease I felt as they descended upon me and began to settle in. They clung to me, they cloyed; their presence was a brand. It didn't hurt, not exactly, but they brought a peculiar bereavement.

Silvestra saw me shudder and placed a hand on my shoulder. "Steady," she said reluctantly. I shrugged her off.

In place of conventional cell doors, the Umbra had stone slabs laid in front of the opening to each cell. There had to be some sort of mekhanism in place for moving them aside, I thought absently. I knew which cell they were going to put me in even before they stopped in front of it and motioned for the stationed Vigil to draw aside the slab of stone. I knew because it was calling to me. It wanted me.

The Vigil officers drew a lever carefully from the wall next to the cell door. Together, they pulled it with all their strength, and the grinding of mekhania sounded throughout the narrow hallway. Somewhere, wheels were turning. The slab began to move aside. Once it was hanging to the left, I could see a metal door waiting. One of the Vigil officers produced a set of keys and began to release each of the many locks on the door in turn.

When the metal door swung open, I realized that the inside of the room wasn't nearly as interesting as I'd imagined. It was a basic stone cell soaked in wards, with chains attached to one wall, and nothing else of note. Still horrifying, but there were no evil contraptions waiting for me. I could survive it until Gennady came to get me, I thought. That was all I needed to do. He wouldn't be more than a day.

I told myself this so I wouldn't snap.

Theo and Silvestra guided me inside. I knew better than to press them on the issue of my release in front of the Umbra guards, although it wasn't easy to bite my tongue. "There you go, Professor," Theo said, and nodded for the guards to close the cell again.

Before they shut me in, the guards confiscated everything from my pockets, removed my handcuffs, and chained me to the wall. Their touch as they restrained me was freezing. "We'll bring you the clothes to change into later," one of them said, and then the metal door was closed. I felt the stone slab roll back into place with a heavy thud. As the final sounds of the door shutting faded out, it was as though I'd been struck; my breath left me.

The lurking possibility that I would spend the entirety of the rest of my life in the Umbra floated somewhere in the depths of my mind, waiting for me to acknowledge it. I refused it; it wouldn't do to make myself a mess of nerves for when Gennady came. He'd tease me.

I wondered if the guards would allow me paper and a pen to occupy myself before realizing that it was a ridiculous notion, and I had no earthly way of asking for it. The resulting surge of my distress would have broken the ambric lights overhead if it were not for the wards. I found an oddly sterile corner to sit in, just about as far as the chains would allow me to move, and waited.

Normally, I find the quiet buzz of ambrics soothing. It's a familiar sound, safe, nearly homey. In the cold of the Umbra, it began to grate. I was cut off from it; I was foreign to it now. It was nothing more than a reminder of the magic I'd lost—the magic that, even if not for the wards, was still broken.

One of the things I loathe most is wasted time, time not spent in the pursuit of usefulness. After the Philidor solarium disaster, I devised one rule for myself: *Be useful, Adrien Desfourneaux, or be nothing.* So to be in the Umbra, where time could *only* be wasted, was a torment, but I had no choice. I scratched myself, drawing blood from my wrist. Over the past few weeks, I'd acquired a starfield of little scars across the skin there, papering over the faded ones from times past.

I forced myself not to think of Oliver, not to wonder if he'd believed Florian's deception. I forced myself not to think of what the future held at all; instead, by habit, I wandered the past. I have always kept in my head a comprehensive archive of every sin, every humiliation, and I spend my idle moments ensuring that it remains pristine. Once I caught myself retracing the record of my first dose of nepenthe, I'd had enough. In desperation, I scrambled to conjure some distraction. There was nothing to read, nothing to write, nowhere to go, no one to talk to—

I'd composed a lecture recently about the impact of the Torrine magocracy on their technological development. Haltingly, I tried to recite it to myself, but without class participation, its conclusion came rapidly. I fell back into rumination.

The knowledge that Malise was captive somewhere nearby didn't help at all. Occasionally I fantasized about finding some way to break out and free her, but the impossibility of the idea made me feel ashamed every time. She was here, right here, and I could do nothing for her.

Let me be briefer: I was in the Umbra for only about ten hours before the cell was opened again in the earlier hours of the morning. I slept not a moment. I never moved. They never did bring me the white witch's robe. When the metal door rolled aside once more, hope leapt inside me, and I forced it down mercilessly; I would not survive a disappointment.

I didn't have to. It was Gennady. He and Lady strolled inside the cell, and he surveyed me critically while Lady came over to push her head against my side. "Wow," Gennady said, and offered me a hand up. When I didn't take it immediately, he hauled me up bodily and let me stagger as the blood came rushing back into my legs.

"Aren't you happy?" he said curiously, while the guards outside peered into the cell with uncertainty.

"More happy than you will ever know," I told him with careful control, so I wouldn't burst into tears. "Please take me out of here now."

"Get the chains off," he told the guards. They moved to obey. Once the metal dropped away from my skin, I began to hope that we would get away with this.

As Gennady led me out of the cell, one of the guards said, "Whose orders did you say you're releasing him on, again?"

"Prefect Velleia's," Gennady said, as breezily as if he were telling the truth. "Don't you recognize me? I know her personally. Inquisitors Silvestra and Wycliffe will back me up." I felt myself pale. I wasn't aware that he was capable of lying so well, and the fear that this newfound ability would suddenly desert him was very real.

The guards murmured in unease, and their raches' tails twitched. "This isn't really standard . . ."

Gennady sighed. "I'm Vigil. Like you. You really think I'd be helping a witch escape?"

They were silent.

"Would *you* risk your hide for some magician?" he asked. "For love or money?"

"No," one of them admitted.

"Yeah. Velleia wants the guy out, so I'm following orders. Don't know why. It's not my job to ask her questions."

"Still," one of the guards said.

"If you want me to go bother her about this, I'll need your names. She'll want to know who's holding things up," Gennady said. Lady chittered impatiently.

I had dealt with Tessaly Velleia before, and so I sympathized with the guards as they both winced. "No," one said. "Just take him."

Gennady kept it together until we had walked out of sight of the two guards, up the stairs again, away from the glaring white ambric sterility of the underprison. We emerged back into the Penumbra, and even the sight of the regular cell blocks with their legions of helpless incarcerated couldn't crush my relief. I was free, and they were not, and I deeply regret to say that in the moment, I barely cared.

Gennady and I made good time on our way out into the open air, afraid that someone would question us again. Once we were back on the city streets—the wonderful, chaotic, living city streets, back in the very first gloried rays of morning sunshine—I stopped him. "Velleia?" I said. "A smaller lie wouldn't suffice?" To take Tessaly Velleia's name in vain was a risky, risky thing. She was a Prefect; Gennady couldn't have gone higher without claiming one of the empresses.

He shrugged. "Well, who's going to ask her? Who has the guts to check? I told the warden Velleia wanted you free, and that she's pissed at everyone.

Said she's thinking about demotions. *He* won't ask her about it, and if those guards ask *him*, he'll tell them the same thing."

I stared at him.

"What? You didn't think I could plan one step ahead?"

"I'm just very impressed."

He lit up at that, giving me a big grin.

"Thank you for coming to get me," I said. "Thank you very much. Theo and Silvestra told you where I was?"

"Sure," he said. "I almost cut them up when they told me what happened, but I figured then I wouldn't be able to get you out."

"They did what they could." The city air was sweeter than I'd ever imagined it could be. It wasn't fully light out yet, but it was getting there.

"You'll have to hide out until they get your keeper," Gennady said. "Since, you know, I was lying. Someone will figure it out eventually. Not today, but sometime."

I hoped that Gennady would be able to explain himself to his superiors when the time came. It was possible that even if I was proven innocent, they would still prosecute him for my escape. If they did, I could only imagine that he would see the demi-lune.

We would have to deal with that later. I realized that I hadn't been paying attention to where we were walking. Gennady stopped us on the side of Via Tarasio and called over a caleche. Lady hopped inside first, and the two of us followed her. "Florian might still be at my house," I said once we'd sat down. The thought jolted me—maybe he hadn't left. Maybe his infestation was still casting its shadow over my space, eating my food, paging through my books. I'd assumed that once he thought I was gone for good, he'd go back to wherever he'd been living before, but it was no time for assumptions.

"Doesn't matter," Gennady said. "We're not going there."

"Then where—"

He growled. "My place."

"Stars," I said, "you are going to hate that."

"Yeah, I am. But what else are we going to do?"

I couldn't think of a single alternative.

Soon enough, Gennady interrupted the sound of the horse's hooves going over the cobblestones with a sigh. On the floor, Lady echoed him. "So, how bad was it in there? Were you going crazy?"

"The wards are stifling." I called a small spark of lightning into my hand

and watched it, just relishing my magic. It wasn't repaired, but I could at least manage that. "I would rather die than stay there."

He didn't seem to know quite what to say to that, and we didn't speak again until we arrived at his apartment. I tried to take my time getting out of the caleche, wary of my various aches, but he hurried me in. "C'mon, before anyone sees."

"I don't think I'm as famous as you're imagining."

He glared at me as we crossed the threshold. "You really want to take chances?"

The fact that he was now the one suggesting caution was too much. I shook my head.

Once inside, I went to go sit down in his kitchen. He came to hover nearby, and we both stared grimly at each other until I began to find his gaze unsettling and looked away.

"Clock's ticking," he said.

But my mind was on other things. "Did you see Malise while you were there?" I asked, although I already knew the answer. "Do you think you'd be able to get her out too? Is there anything we can do?"

Gennady shrugged. "I could only choose one of you. Two would have tipped them off. So."

I wished that he'd chosen her. She deserved the sunlight. If there was a choice to be made between the two of us, it was no choice at all—it must always be her.

"Sorry," Gennady added.

It was one of the very tiny handful of apologies he'd ever made to me, and I treated it with the respect it deserved. "It's all right. You did well. We'll get her out soon enough."

He began to pace. "So what are we supposed to do now?"

"We need to have Florian investigated and convicted. We need to help Theo and Silvestra convince the other inquisitors that he's a suspect, and we need to secure some undeniable evidence."

"Those two should be over here soon," he said. "I told them to come this afternoon. They'll help us figure it out."

"You're really all right with so many people being in your apartment?"

"Hell, no."

I smiled. "I'm proud of you."

He narrowed his eyes. "You stop that right now or I'll take you back. I'll do it."

I knew he was joking, but the thought still sent a sick chill through me. "My apologies," I said with false archness.

All of a sudden, I was starving—I hadn't eaten in a very long time. I sagged in my chair, uncomfortably faint.

He noticed it and made a face, clearly bewildered as to what could be bothering me. I found myself reluctant to tell him. Here I was, already imposing on his hospitality, such as it was, and I was considering asking for more. It seemed unthinkable.

But the lack of sleep combined with the hunger until I feared I might pass out, and I had a feeling he'd mock me mercilessly for that. "Some rice," I said. "Or some bread, maybe. Do you have anything to eat? I'm a little hungry."

His expression cleared. "Yeah, yeah. Sure. There's some bread in one of the cabinets and some butter in the icebox. You can make yourself something." He went to rummage in the icebox himself and came up with a container of raw meat, which he fed Lady out of his own hand.

I looked away. "Just the bread is fine."

It was cheap, coarse stuff, and I was infinitely grateful for a few bites. Eating made me feel, for a moment, more grounded, less like the earth was falling away under me. It made me feel something like a person again, a sensibility that had begun to erode lately.

"You really need a stronger stomach," Gennady said once Lady was done wolfing down her food.

I looked up at him quizzically with my mouth full.

He grinned blackly. "We could've stopped this whole mess at the beginning. That's your problem. Sometimes someone just needs a good killing, and you can't see it."

I thought of Florian's hands at my temples, at the buttons of my clothing. I felt nothing. I thought of Malise's face as the inquisitors had taken her away, and I felt *something* unnamable. "I've been thinking about that," I admitted.

Gennady considered me with uncharacteristic sobriety, chewing something over.

"Yes?" I asked.

I saw a glimpse of the creature within him for a moment. "I hope *you* don't have to kill anyone," he said. "I hope I can always do it for you."

I had nothing to say to that.

He gave me a mockery of yet another rictus grin and clapped me on the shoulder. "Go nap or something until the inquisitors get here. You can take the couch."

I wanted to tell him that I couldn't possibly sleep, that I couldn't let my guard down like that. Before I was halfway through the protest, I discovered that I was already listing to one side on his couch, and things were getting fuzzy, and then Gennady's apartment had fallen away into the void of space.

~

No one bothered to wake me up until the inquisitors were both standing directly in front of me, staring at me and chatting with Gennady.

"Bit of a conundrum," Theo was saying as the world tore me back into consciousness.

I sat bolt upright with a sharp gasp. My glasses had fallen off; I reached around for them. "Good God."

Silvestra rolled her eyes.

"Wakey-wakey," Gennady said helpfully. "Let's talk options."

"Options," I repeated. "Options?"

He held up an index finger. "First option: you know this one already. It's the one where we just kill the guy. We've been over it a couple times. Way too many times."

After taking a pause to reorient myself in the conversation, I nodded my acknowledgment.

"Option two," Theo said, "we actually plan something, stick to that plan, and don't get any of *us* killed."

The small amount of sleep I'd managed to steal had done me well. I searched the corners of my mind and discovered that there was something new there. "We need to—" My voice was thready. I tried again. "For Malise, for the others, we need to get him to incriminate himself. He has to be the one to provide proof. A murder attempt with witnesses. I don't think your superiors will accept anything less; he has them under his sway."

The inquisitors looked at me with pity. "It would really be something if he decided to do that, but let's not count on it," Theo said gently. "A little foolhardy, wouldn't it be?"

There was another piece of the puzzle I was missing, something my sleeping self had gotten hold of that I couldn't remember. I sat and worried my wrist with my nails, feeling it just out of reach. "There will be a way," I said. "We can slot that in later."

Silvestra tapped the hilt of her sword impatiently. "There's no way to predict exactly which patient he'll go after next. The Chirurgeonate is too big; he has plenty of targets."

"So we'll nudge him in a particular direction," I said slowly. "We'll take away the unpredictability."

Gennady sat down next to me and put Lady on his lap. "How?"

I stood to pace. "Just let me think."

Generously, they all allowed me a few minutes of silence. To my dismay, I couldn't make use of any of it, not with their gazes heavy upon my back.

"Well," Theo said, "maybe—"

The instant everyone's attention was off me, I had it. I interrupted him without hesitation or regret. "We'll get someone Florian doesn't suspect to tell him that the inquisitors have decided to let me go free. That they're still suspicious of me, but they didn't have enough to convict, so they had to release me."

"Not how that works at all," Silvestra said.

"He's not Clementia. He doesn't know that."

Theo seemed miffed. "And then what?"

"And then he'll need to take action to frame me more securely. He won't ever have planned that I could be released, and he'll infer that I might have named him; he won't know how to account for the loose end. It'll derail him. He'll need to kill someone connected to me, someone I'd be a suspect in the murder of."

"Who would you have motive to murder?"

"In reality? No one at all. In his mind? I can think of two options."

I admit it: I savored their frustration when I didn't elaborate. I enjoyed their urging to go on. "Enlighten us, Desfourneaux," Silvestra snapped.

"He knows two enemies of mine who have no connection to anyone else involved: Phaedra Keynes and Henri Thirkeld. A professor and a doctor. He knows I hate them. He knows that *other people* know I hate them. Without other information, that's who he'll go after. He'll break his pattern to implicate me."

Silvestra shook her head. "You can't guarantee he'll behave that way. It's too far a leap."

It was a fair point, a solid point. Of course I could make no guarantees. Of course Florian *could* decide differently.

But he wouldn't. He had disassembled me; he'd seen the workings of my mind perfectly, but in return, I'd seen *him*. I understood Florian. I knew what he was. I knew that he would now consider me unworthy of the mercy of death. If he thought the Clementia doubted his judgment that I belonged in chains, the outrage would blind him to all else. He would need to see me in the Umbra. And, without question, I knew that he was so as one with murder that his first resort would be to pile up more bodies. If he were me, he'd kill his enemies; the plan would come naturally to him.

"Nothing is certain," I said, taking great pains not to allow my voice to become too loud. "But it's a start."

Theo hummed. "You'll need to enlist those people's help. They'll need to cooperate. Agree to risk themselves. Why would they do that for you?"

"They won't. They'll do it for you, because you'll arrest them otherwise." I felt, immediately, how wrong it was—and didn't back down.

Theo raised his eyebrows. "Now that's an assumption."

"By all means. Choose now to become squeamish about what you do. Choose Keynes and Thirkeld to extend your tender professional sensibilities to. Sabotage the only plan we have because of a concern you never showed to me, or anyone else."

Gennady snorted in approval. He liked when I was difficult.

The inquisitors watched me with startlement. "Mouthy," Silvestra said.

"Thank you *so* much."

"Three things," Gennady interrupted, with an attitude of deep concentration. "Who's going to tell him all this stuff? How are we going to get the other inquisitors to listen to us? And how are we going to get him to try to kill someone right in front of the inquisitors? You still haven't answered that one."

"Theo and Silvestra are responsible for the second issue. As for the rest, there is a solution," I said lamely. "Just let me think."

The plain fact of the matter was that Florian would never make an attempt while anyone was watching. Never, never, never. As long as he knew he was being observed, he wouldn't. Could the other inquisitors watch him from a distance? No. What distance would there be? Thirkeld and Keynes wouldn't be out in an open field.

The problem was an impassible tangle. I began to doubt—

Then I had it, and despite everything, I smiled. "*No one* will watch him."

Silvestra snarled in frustration. "Wh—"

"He won't *see* anyone watching him."

"Oh," said Theo, and turned pink with the embarrassment of not having thought of it before. "Oh, damn it."

I held out my hand. "The device. Give it here."

From a pocket, he took out the small mekhania sphere he'd shown me on the first day we met. The invisibility generator, the secret piece of Clementia mind magic they'd been so proud of.

Silently, Silvestra gave hers over as well. I inspected them, ensured that their mekhanisms were still intact, felt their solid promise in my hand, and returned them. They would do.

Of course the inquisitors hadn't thought of using the spheres to any real effect. They didn't need stealth or subtlety; they needed only their badges and swords to do their awful work. Once they had deployed their new toys a few times here and there, they'd realized that force got them more results than eavesdropping. After all, a false confession is a result.

"Uh," Gennady said. "Anyone want to clue me in?"

"These will allow the other inquisitors to follow the two potential victims and remain invisible to Florian. They alter the perception of everyone around the user. It's a form of enchantment. They'll be there the whole time, but he'll never know."

Gennady's gaze sharpened. "Enchantment. That's witchy. Some Clementia you are."

"Needs must," Theo muttered guiltily.

"We don't use them that often," Silvestra said.

"Barely at all," Theo added. "The witchfinders breathe down our necks about it. Now their experts are claiming the things will have side effects in the long term. I doubt they'll stay approved through the end of this month."

In retrospect, that seemed almost certain to be true. "Side effects for the user or the observers?" I asked.

"You know, it's been rather unclear," he said.

I decided I didn't care. "You could have used these to *investigate*. To clear people's names."

We all knew that the purpose of an inquisition isn't to clear anyone's name. Theo crossed his arms. "Why don't we just use these to follow Albrecht *now*? Isn't that simpler? Less risky?"

It was much simpler, yes, but Florian would notice a prolonged deception.

Even if the observers were cloaked, given time, he'd sense that something was wrong. We'd need to depend upon brief moments of opportunity while he was distracted. "No. If you follow him constantly, he'll catch you. I have no doubt," I said.

"All right, then," Silvestra said mulishly. "Let's focus up. Who are we going to use to relay the lie about your release to Albrecht? It can't be Theo or me. He saw you with us, and he might suspect we've made a deal." For the first time, she sounded as though she truly expected me to have the answer.

And I did. It came to me like lightning. Usually, I would have taken pleasure in that, would have preened in the glow of my solution. Not now. Not now, because I hated the answer I had. I hated it passionately. "Oh," I said. "No."

Chapter 19

Of course it was Oliver.

Who else could I trust? Who else was, by trade, an *actor*? We needed someone utterly convincing—there would be no second chance. And Oliver would have a built-in reason to be talking to Florian: me. He would go to Florian, pretend to have been convinced by his ruse, tell him he was terrified that I was now on the loose. He would plant the seed in Florian's mind that something must be done.

"Oliver," I said to Gennady's apartment at large.

Everyone considered the suggestion, some with more confusion than others.

"Who the hell is Oliver, again?" Silvestra said.

"One of the people from Gailhardt's group. You interviewed him. He's a friend."

"A civilian," she said.

"*I'm* a civilian," I said tiredly, "and that has never stopped anyone. Listen. He's an actor; he'll perform the role well. I trust him implicitly. Florian won't question his involvement. He's a good choice."

Gennady shrugged. "Sure. I don't have a problem."

"I don't like it," Theo said. "I really don't."

"You think I do? I *hate* it."

"We'll leave it up to him," Silvestra said. "Get him over here. Lay it all out for him. Tell him what the danger is, and the stakes, and ask him to make the decision."

I nodded firmly. "Of course—" Then I remembered what Florian had told Oliver, and the prospect that Oliver had believed him loomed large. If he had, then there was nothing to be gained in this corner except for further complications, and the quiet death of another little piece of me.

No, I decided. He wouldn't believe Florian. I had faith that Oliver had seen me clearly. I had faith in the looks we'd exchanged and the way he'd held my hand. It wouldn't be a problem. "Gennady," I said, "would you get him? But make it very clear that he isn't under arrest? I can't overstate the importance of that."

Gennady made a face. "Sure. I'll look for him."

"Do you have paper and a pen? I'll write the addresses of his home and theater for you."

It took a ridiculously long time for Gennady to find anything to write on or with. When he finally came up with a pen and a torn-off corner of some unidentifiable paper, I jotted down the relevant addresses and gave them to him. There was no guarantee that Oliver would be at either of those places, but I had no other addresses to give.

"Want me to go right now?" Gennady said, put-upon, pocketing the addresses.

"If you would."

Lady yawned. Gennady retrieved his saber from where he'd left it propped up near the front door and shook himself out, settling back into his soldier's shell in preparation for facing the outside world. "Okay."

"Thank you," I said. "Again, please don't frighten him."

He looked a bit hunted. "I'll try, but no promises."

I made my choice to trust him, as I had done over and over again before, and watched him leave without further comment.

The inquisitors imposed an oppressive silence. I didn't turn to face them. "If this goes wrong, it's on your head," Theo said.

I closed my eyes.

When Gennady came back with Oliver in tow, I noted with relief that Oliver didn't look terrified out of his mind. Gennady had done well. Then a second wave of relief hit me: he was *here*. He'd agreed to come; he believed me. I sprang up and went to him, and within an instant his arms were around me.

"I'm sorry I couldn't help," he said immediately. "I didn't know what to do—I've been trying to figure something out, but I figured—"

I hushed him, unmindful of the other people around who were looking at us. "You're here now."

"I was useless."

"He would have killed you if you hadn't left," I said. There was a world other than this one where Oliver had believed Florian, I knew, and I was separated from that world only by the thinnest layer of grace.

"I know a poor actor when I see one," he said.

I refrained from saying that Florian had fooled me, at least, fooled me very badly, and gave him a last squeeze before letting him go.

When he stepped back from me, I noticed that he was moving a little gingerly. "Are you all right?" I asked.

"It's nothing. My back is acting up."

He'd had to run from the house. Of course the ancient injury would be bothering him again. My ire toward Florian grew, impossibly, brighter.

"He says—" Oliver nodded at Gennady— "that there's a way I can help now."

"It's dangerous," I said. "I want you to know that."

He was wide-eyed, but he set his jaw. "What is it?"

"We need you to go to Florian and talk to him. Lie to him."

"Why? About what?"

"We need him to try to kill someone," Gennady said cheerfully.

Oliver blanched; I hurried to clarify, and once I began to explain in earnest, I found that I couldn't stop the words. I outlined the plan, and then some—I detailed every minutia that occurred to me, and when I was through with that, I simply begged him to understand.

"I hate it," I said, pacing. "I hate that this plan puts you in danger, I hate to use you this way, but it's the best thing I can think of, and otherwise no one will listen, and I *need* to help Malise, and—"

He said my name. I stopped talking.

"I'll do it," he said. "Of course I'll do it. Just don't wear yourself out."

"You'll do it even though he'll probably kill you if you flub your lines?" Silvestra said.

I saw that her question chilled him; I saw him tense. But he made a great show of blinking at her disapprovingly. "I don't flub."

She threw up her hands. "I see I'm outnumbered. Fine. Risk yourself if you want."

It did not feel good in the slightest that between the inquisitors and me, I was the one putting Oliver in more danger. I was worse than the torturers. "You need to think about it," I said softly. "Florian might hurt you. Think about it." *For the benefit of a man you've never done more than kiss*, I thought.

"He's a monster," Oliver said grimly. "Warn me all you like, but I know the right thing to do."

I loved him. I admitted it to myself.

The guilty relief of finally having confirmed a workable plan nearly bowled me over, and I went to sit down on Gennady's couch again. "We should get it done as soon as possible," I said.

"No time to rehearse?" Oliver said, a gentle tease. "Ah, well. An improvisational role. I can do that."

"The lie is short, at least. I've been released, and unless I'm connected more directly to the murders, the inquisitors have nothing against me. You're terrified that I'm free; you say something must be done."

"Easy," Oliver said.

"I don't understand," I said, absently scratching my wrist. "Malise barely ever spoke to him, and she figured him out before I did. How did I miss it?"

Oliver frowned. "He's a powerful magician."

I crossed my arms pettily. "*I'm* a powerful magician."

"You know what I mean."

"He fucked up your brain," Gennady said impatiently, breaking the individual reverie Oliver and I had fallen into. "You were dumb to let him cast on you, but that's why you didn't see it. It's not a mystery."

Oliver came over to me and took my hand, stopping me as I reached to scratch again. "Please don't do that to yourself," he said.

"It's worse lately," I said, with exhaustion.

"This will be over soon. It'll get better then." He gave no sign of disgust with my unfortunate habits.

Theo cleared his throat, tired of playing a background role. "We need to hurry up with recruiting those two people you mentioned, if this 'plan' of yours is going to have a chance."

I ignored the doubtful spin he applied to *plan*. "Keynes and Thirkeld. You'll have to loan me one of those spheres for me to use if I'm going to walk around the city without the risk of being caught."

Both inquisitors made uncomfortable noises. "Those things aren't for civilian use," Silvestra said.

I drew a breath to give her a piece of my mind, but Theo held up a hand to stop me. I bit my tongue and glared at him. "Please," I said, "tell me how else we'll manage it. If I'm seen and recognized, you won't be able to bluff your way out of it a second time."

"You don't know that," Theo said.

"You can't really be so jealous of a piece of mekhania that you'd risk us all just to keep it to yourselves."

It was an effective phrasing; I saw them both waver. "No," Silvestra admitted eventually, "I suppose not."

I felt something resembling satisfaction. If nothing else, at least I'd be able to take a look at some interesting magical technology. "Good. Teach me how to use it."

Silvestra raised her eyebrows judgmentally. "You just press the button. It's not that hard."

I smiled. "It must have taken a great deal of work on the part of the Clementia's mekhanics to make it so *accessible*."

Was I relishing the fact that the inquisitors were no longer able to terrorize me, and I could vent my feelings toward them as I liked? Was I overcompensating, trying to claw back some pride after Florian's gutting? Maybe. I watched Silvestra work her jaw, and for a moment, I could relate to Gennady— to the perverse joy he often seemed to take in frustrating people.

"I think I should be the one to go with you," Theo said ruefully. "Less trouble for everyone."

I had no objections, and I had no desire to wait any longer. I held my hand out to Silvestra, and she slapped the invisibility sphere into it with great resentment.

"So," said Oliver, "shall the rest of us just wait here until you've talked to your two potential targets?"

"If you wouldn't mind," I said. "If it isn't too much trouble?"

He nodded easily. "As long as your friend Gennady will let us use the kitchen."

"Whatever," Gennady said.

I looked over the small crowd of people gathered in Gennady's small apartment and sighed. Oliver, Gennady, and Silvestra were going to be cooped up with each other for some time, and I wasn't sure all of them would survive it.

"Be kind to each other," I told them, very hypocritically. I looked at Gennady as I said it.

With that, Theo instructed, "Use the sphere before we go outside."

I found the button and pressed it. I felt absolutely no different, but everyone except Theo, holding his own unused sphere, blinked in disorientation—they couldn't see me. I turned the sphere over in my hand, examining it carefully, but my fascination was cut short when Theo grabbed me by the arm and guided me outside into the street without another word.

"You're only going to be using that thing until we set foot inside the Pharmakeia," he said to me. "Hand it over after we get there. I'll give it back when it's time to go to the solarium."

"Absolutely not. That complicates things unnecessarily. I'm keeping it on me."

He was shaking his head before I was even done speaking, conceding. "Fine. No more talking once we get in the vehicle."

"I know that. I'm not an idiot."

"You're not an idiot, but you *do* like to talk. The sphere is supposed to protect against sound, too, but you'll strain the enchantment—it might slip."

The caleche came; the driver acknowledged only Theo. I got in alongside him and stayed quiet. It was a strange thing to have a wall of void sensation between myself and another person. I've often felt either invisible or excruciatingly obvious, but the choice had never been taken away from me so decisively. It was for the best that the witchfinders wanted these devices buried, unnamed side effects or no.

Once at the Pharmakeia, we stepped out of the caleche. "Do you know where Keynes is teaching right now?" Theo asked.

"We're not going to drag her away from her students," I said flatly.

He rolled his eyes. "All right." I wasted no time showing him where Keynes's office would be. I took us to Thanatology's offices, and we wandered until we came upon her name on a plaque—I'd never had a reason to find her office before.

I wondered if anyone would find it odd that Theo was without Silvestra, but no one who passed looked twice at him, apart from the usual nervous glances. Inquisitors weren't like witchfinders, I supposed, who came in pairs no matter what. We made our way to Keynes's door without issue.

I deactivated the invisibility sphere and knocked. There was no answer. "Well, let's just stand here uselessly for however many hours it'll be until she's back," I said.

Theo tried the door. It opened. He motioned me in gallantly. "She doesn't lock it. You people are so trusting."

"It seems wrong to take advantage of that," I muttered.

"Don't you hate this woman? Wouldn't you like to give her a bit of a scare?"

"No!" I said. It was a flagrant lie, although I felt ashamed.

"Well," he said, "*I'm* going inside. You may as well follow." He strolled into the office and settled down in a chair by the window.

After a few moments of agonized fidgeting outside, I came inside—and sat behind the desk.

Theo laughed. "Going for the greatest dramatic effect there?"

"Not at all," I said delicately. "It's just more comfortable."

Keynes's office wasn't what I'd expected from a thanatology professor. The previous department chair, Marsilio Kirchoff, had kept a nightmare of an office, filled with skeletons and various macabre trinkets. There had been tanks of murky water with unknown shapes floating within. The task of reinhabiting Kirchoff's office had fallen to a music and biology professor, Dmitry Dietz, when no faculty from the thanatology department were willing—not even their new chair. Dietz had volunteered to clean and repurpose Kirchoff's awful tanks, and so the space was now his. The tanks held tiny stingrays instead now; by all accounts, the rays were happy, and Dietz was far less upsetting to encounter in the hallway than Kirchoff.

While Kirchoff had tried his best to live up to the aesthetic of his discipline, Keynes made few concessions to the traditional look. She had a small mouse skeleton arranged in an attitude of play sitting on her desk, and the texts were on the subjects you'd expect, but other than that, it was an orderly space.

I pulled a book off her shelf, something about skin sloughage, and skimmed. We sat quietly for maybe ten minutes before Theo said, "I'm sorry about what happened."

"What happened?" I wanted to make him say it.

"The interrogation."

"Oh? Was that in some way unpleasant for me?"

"It's the job."

"That's no excuse."

"I like you, you know—you seem like good people. We don't need to be friends, but—"

"Good," I said. "We won't be friends. I don't know how many times I need to say that you *tortured* me."

"It's an inquisition."

Like a mimic bird, I thought. *He only knows a few sentences.* "Please don't say that like it means anything. The Vigil, the witchfinders—if nothing else, at least we're all *used* to them. Meanwhile, the inquisitors are mayflies. You've all of their cruelty with nothing to back it up."

Theo lifted a hand incredulously.

I smiled. "No hounds, no eyes. Just noble blood and tin badges."

"Empress Illyria herself called for our formation," he said, once he had controlled a visible flare of anger.

I made an expansive gesture of apathy. Empress Illyria was as real to me as any god or saint, which was to say not very.

He sighed. "We're on the same side here."

"To my extraordinary displeasure."

I'd edged over the line. "Don't push it," he said softly. "I'm trying here, but don't push it."

Unbidden, I remembered how I'd cowered before Florian. I snapped the book I was staring unseeingly at shut and replaced it on the shelf. "Or what? You'll break more of my fingers?"

He massaged his temples. "You've gotten braver," he said.

"You're not used to people being brave around you."

There was a meditative pause. "No, I suppose not. I'll try to adjust."

Finally, I gave an inch of ground. "Best of luck with that," I said, and actually meant it.

Content with that tiniest piece of mutual agreement, we stayed quiet until Keynes's footsteps sounded outside the door. I sat up straight.

She opened the door and saw me in her chair. I waved pleasantly. Immediately, she opened her mouth to say something, but Theo cleared his throat. "Let's be civil," he said.

She didn't scream. "Witch," she said to me, in a strangled whisper. "Witch. What are you doing out of the Umbra—they said you were sentenced—?"

"Not at all. Hello, Phaedra." I tried not to seem too pleased with her surprise and decided to have mercy on her quickly. "I hate to banish the mystery of the moment so soon, but no, you're not about to be murdered or arrested."

She narrowed her eyes, trying very hard to seem as though she hadn't been worried. "Then what? And get out of my chair."

"No, thank you." My refusal wasn't out of spite; it just hurt less to sit than stand. She didn't have to know that.

Theo got up and made her a sweeping bow. "Theophile Wycliffe," he said. "Call me Theo."

"What are you doing here with Desfourneaux? Did you help him escape? Why would you do that?"

"He isn't guilty."

Keynes began to scoff.

"I truly am not," I said. "But I know who is. In point of fact, we're here because we're hoping you can help convict him."

Her disbelieving laugh could have shattered glass. "Explain. You're not making any sense. I've half a mind to go looking for a different inquisitor— see how smug you stay."

It was good to know that some things never change. "Would you mind?" I said to Theo. She might receive it better from him than from me.

He hummed thoughtfully. "Well, give me a moment to put it all together."

"It had better be good," Keynes said.

We waited in tense, unrelenting silence. I was about to take on task myself when Theo spoke again. "The angel is a doctor named Florian Albrecht. He forced the good professor here to confess on pain of death. He's been framing other doctors he doesn't like to get them out of the way. We need to catch him in the act of killing someone, so we're going to convince him that he needs to murder one of Desfourneaux's enemies in order to get him properly convicted."

"So you're *sacrificing* me?" she hissed. "You'll convict him over my corpse? Assuming I believe any of this, even, that's—"

I grimaced. "For God's sake. No, we're not sacrificing you. You're going to have inquisitors following you around, and they'll stop him before he manages anything."

"You don't *know* that for sure."

No, we didn't. We really didn't. But it was the best plan we had available to us. It was Malise's life versus Keynes's safety, and there could be no doubt as to which I valued more. "Of course we know for sure," I said, and I looked her right in the eyes while I did. It was craven, and I had no regret.

"Do I have a choice?" she asked. To her credit, her voice was steady.

"No," Theo said.

My stomach turned, but this had been exactly what I wanted. This was what I'd told Theo to say. I couldn't turn away now. "I would venture to say that you have a responsibility to your city that demands you help us," I said, very gently. "There's a serial killer loose."

"It's not my business—"

"You seemed to think it was," I said, "when you were busy accusing *me* of all manner of things. You seemed to consider yourself a true defender of the people."

She threw up her hands in frustration. "Why do you have to do this at all? Why can't this inquisitor just go arrest him?"

I remembered something she'd said to me not long ago at all. "Who do you think the rest of the Clementia will believe?" I asked quietly. "A healer, or a mad witch? They have to catch him red-handed to even the scales."

Keynes bared her teeth.

"All you have to do is go about your daily business for a while with a few inquisitors following you around for your safety," Theo said. "We'll be using invisibility spheres. Eventually he'll come to find you when you're 'alone,' and then we'll grab him."

"I don't *want* to live my life being followed by inquisitors," she said. I couldn't blame her.

Theo crossed his arms. "It won't take more than a few days at most. You might even be done the same day we give him our false information, if he gets impatient."

"You'll arrest me if I don't agree."

"Yes," Theo said. He sounded deeply tired.

"I'll do it," Keynes said bitterly.

I exhaled in relief. "Thank you."

Theo stretched. "Wonderful. If all goes well, we'll have a team of inquisitors to guard you ready by the end of today."

"And if it doesn't go well?" she asked. "What then?" I got up from behind the desk, and she pushed past me to take my place, collapsing into the chair with a deep sigh. It was strange to see her in anything other than an attitude of spite.

"Then good luck to us all," I said.

"We'll be in touch," Theo said, regaining his cheer. I had no idea how he could maintain such a bearing, even if it was a front. With no time to waste, he turned toward the door and swept his way out, leaving me alone with Keynes.

"Desfourneaux, you bastard," Keynes said.

I didn't object. I only said, "The inquisitors will do their best to keep you safe," and then I was gone as well.

Theo and I stared at each other once the door had shut behind us, neither of us particularly heartened. Eventually, he shrugged. "One down, one to go. Let's go to Westbrook to find that doctor you hate. Use the sphere again, and pray we don't run into Albrecht when we pass through the Chirurgeonate on our way."

I startled; I'd grown so used to the specter of Florian in my house that I hadn't realized he would likely be at the Chirurgeonate now, at this time of day. My subconscious had placed him at the heart of my home. But no, of course he would be at work. In his element.

I used the sphere again to render myself invisible, and we cut through the Chirurgeonate with a wary eye. Every blue doctor's coat we passed made my heart seize for a moment—but, as it turned out, we didn't run into Florian at all, and soon we were at Westbrook's gates. Seeing the place again was like stepping into another world. Somewhere sterile but safe, remote from the rest of the city, a prison and a haven.

Well. Not quite. Nothing would ever be comparable to a prison for me again, not after the Umbra.

We went into Westbrook, and I deactivated the invisibility sphere. At least there were no inquisitors in the solarium. We asked the nearest orderly where Dr. Thirkeld could be found; the young woman surveyed us doubtfully. "He isn't being arrested," I said. "We just need to talk to him about something. If you could show us in his direction . . ."

"Have I seen you before?" she asked.

"Yes. Where is Thirkeld?"

"He's treating a patient," she said, scratching her nose. "After that, he usually takes a break around this time."

"Which room?" Theo asked.

"We won't interrupt him," I said, with a sharp look for Theo. "We'll just wait for him outside. I promise."

The orderly seemed to decide that obstructing an inquisitor was more trouble than it was worth; she gave us the room number without any further questioning. We thanked her and went to wait outside.

"So," Theo said quietly, as we stood there. "How is it here, when you're a patient?"

For some reason, I didn't mind that he put it in the present tense rather than the past. It was perfectly likely that I'd return to Westbrook someday. Those were the basic facts. "It is what it is," I said. There were far lesser institutions. Maybe Thirkeld had a heavy touch with the laudanum sometimes; maybe not all of the orderlies were gracious—but Westbrook was well funded, held to a high standard.

"You're lucky you're an Astrine," Theo said.

"Mm," I said without enthusiasm. "Thirkeld once told me the same thing."

"You know, you're not what I expected of an akratic."

I knew that I should feel insulted. Instead, I felt mostly bewilderment that I could possibly be mistaken for anything else. "What *did* you expect?"

He reconsidered. "If I tell you, you'll only glare."

Smart. I let him stay quiet on the subject.

Before too long, Thirkeld came out of the patient's room. He walked right into Theo and jumped back, retreating with his hands up. The obvious fear in his eyes jarred my conscience uncomfortably, and I stepped forward.

"Don't worry," I said. "It's all right. Let's go somewhere quiet, shall we?"

"What on earth are you doing here with an inquisitor?" he barked. "Bringing one into a *solarium*—I thought you'd been arrested, and good riddance—"

"No need to worry," Theo said mildly. "We're not here to bother any of the patients. Just you."

I took the initiative to find us an empty space, an unoccupied patient's room, and brought us all inside before closing the door.

"Explain," Thirkeld said to me. I was finding that I liked him rather more in this state—angry, off his balance, and most importantly, without condescension. The humiliation of our last encounter at the Chirurgeonate was still acute.

Wearily, for the third time of the day, I explained the situation.

"Absolutely not," Thirkeld said. "I don't trust the inquisitors to stop him in time if he comes for me."

"They're very competent," I lied. "You have nothing to fear. And this is the right thing to do."

To my exceptional surprise, that seemed to give him pause. *The right thing to do.* Where Keynes had required coercion, Thirkeld might have something of a conscience. I hoped that he wouldn't ask if he had a choice. That was entirely for my own benefit, not for his, but I hoped nevertheless.

The wish was not rewarded. "Do I have a choice?" he said.

"Desfourneaux here says I'm to arrest you if you don't agree," Theo said brightly.

I lifted my chin. I'd chosen to play the part of the villain, and I owed it to everyone around me to at least play it with grace. "We need this done."

"I underestimated you," Thirkeld said to me. There was a nasty edge to his voice. "You're a menace."

For a terrible moment, I balanced on the edge of despair. He was right, and it stung; I have never wanted to be a menace. A force, maybe, but not a menace.

The moment passed. "Well," I said, "try not to underestimate me again."

Theo smiled. "There's no effort required on your part, Dr. Thirkeld."

"Except for the effort of patience," Thirkeld said.

Theo's smile grew a mite sharper. "Patience is required of us all these days. When the inquisitors come to you—sometime today or tomorrow—be civil, won't you?"

Thirkeld said nothing.

"Wonderful." Theo turned to me. "Well, that's both of your potential victims accounted for. I hope there's no one else you're not thinking of."

"I don't have that many enemies," I said.

"Feel special," Theo said to Thirkeld, and moved to leave the room.

"Thank you for agreeing," I said to Thirkeld, very stiffly. He scowled; I followed Theo. I was eager to leave the solarium. I could hear someone crying nearby, crying like a child, and I wondered if it was anyone I knew. The absurd fear that someone might stop me to take my shoelaces was difficult to shake. Dimly, far removed, I wished I had any nepenthe.

"What next?" I asked Theo. I was hoping he would have some idea of how to proceed so I could stop thinking.

Thankfully, he didn't hesitate. "Now we go to the other inquisitors and try to convince them to go along with this. We can move ahead even without them—have Valary follow one target and me the other—but it'll be riskier, and I'd rather have them all right there to witness the proof. They could throw it all out, otherwise."

"Maybe we should have done this part first," I said. "That would have made everything easier."

"Oh, we absolutely should have. But we were putting it off. Trying to keep up the momentum for as long as possible. Leave the worst for last."

I nodded queasily.

"So," he said. "We'll swing back by your friend's place to get Valary, and then it's off to Deme Alidor."

I readied the invisibility sphere. We left the Westbrook solarium to its business.

Chapter 20

When we stepped back inside Gennady's apartment, I was glad to discover that no fights had broken out. My instant proof was that Silvestra opened the door, and I had no doubt she would be the loser of any fights in which Gennady was also involved.

"So you weren't caught," she said.

"No 'happy to see you' for us?" Theo said.

She pursed her lips and pulled him inside. I followed, wondering if the two of them liked each other at all. Not all inquisitors made the choice to be part of a duo. They had to have *something* in common.

It was a mystery to be left for a later date. We went inside, and I saw with delight that Gennady and Oliver were sitting across from each other in the small living room, actually *talking* without any signs of animosity. I dared to hope that they might get along.

They both looked up at Theo and me. Oliver sprang up, clearly delighted, and Gennady rolled his eyes—but I saw a tiny release of tension in his shoulders. He was relieved. At his feet, Lady yipped happily.

"You're back," Oliver said.

Theo sniffed. "Of course. It was just a quick jaunt."

"Did Kearns and Thorton agree?"

"Keynes and Thirkeld are both cooperating," I said, suppressing a laugh.

Theo went to go rummage through Gennady's kitchen cabinets, saying over his shoulder, "Now we need to get the other inquisitors on our side. Get ready to go, Valary. Time to go begging HQ to understand."

"I don't beg," Silvestra called to him coldly.

"Time to go politely request, then, if you like."

Gennady and Lady got up and rushed to supervise Theo's rummaging. He shouldered past me on his way over, sending me stumbling. It was the kind of shove he might give a fellow soldier. I wasn't built to take it, but I didn't protest.

I went to sit down next to Oliver. He put his arm around me, and I couldn't stop myself from leaning into him. I hadn't meant to, but I was huddled against his side almost instantly. *Isn't this all a little fast?* a part of me asked. *A little quick for you to be sprawling all over him like that?* But it was Oliver making the gestures, Oliver taking the initiative, and I could only be grateful.

"You can rest for a while now, at least," he said. "While the inquisitors go talk to their friends."

"Oh, no," Silvestra said. I remembered her presence and sat up again, guiltily. "This is *his* plan. He's at the center of this; he's coming with us."

I put my head in my hands and said something not perfectly civilized. "I'm tired of that place," I said. "Nothing good happens there. If I never had to step inside another Clementia building again . . ."

I expected Silvestra to scoff, but she looked away. "They could stand to pretty the place up." That was the closest she was going to get to acknowledging that I had good reason to hate Deme Alidor, I gathered.

Theo came out into the living room with two sandwiches and handed one plate to Silvestra. She tore into it immediately, and the two of them ate like wolves. They didn't bother to sit down. They were done quickly, and Theo fed the remnants of his food to Lady, who took them daintily.

Silvestra dusted her hands together and set her plate down on the coffee table. "All right," she said. "No time to lose. Day's wasting. Let's go."

I hated to leave Oliver's warmth; I lingered for a few precious moments before hauling myself up to join the two inquisitors at the door. I fished Silvestra's invisibility sphere out of my pocket again and readied it. She gave it a covetous look but didn't ask for it back.

"Everyone feel free to just keep treating my apartment like a goddamn hotel," Gennady called from the back. "Go on! In and out all the time—see if it bothers Lady and me. I should make you all pay by the hour!"

Oliver began to dig through his pockets for change. I smiled, memorizing the scene, and we left.

When we reached the inquisitors' complex, I wordlessly handed Silvestra her invisibility sphere back—either we'd succeed in convincing the inquisitors that I deserved to be free, and I wouldn't need it anymore, or we'd fail, and it would do me very little good.

The three of us all took a deep breath before crossing the threshold. I was struck by sympathy for them; it was their heads too if we failed. "It'll be fine," I said.

They both made dismissive sounds and strode onward, taking us deeper into the headquarters than I had ever been. As we passed different inquisitors, they looked at us quizzically—but no one questioned Theo and Silvestra.

We finally came to a large oak door, and they stopped in front of it. I was half surprised that there were offices at all, before I thought about it. Of course there would be offices for the senior inquisitors. It didn't matter if there were interrogation rooms in the building too; the Clementia always requires bureaucracy. The place wasn't a dungeon, no matter how much it felt like one.

"The Head Inquisitor's here," Silvestra said unhappily. "Elemire Driesan."

Theo closed his eyes and knocked.

"What?" a voice from within called. Theo opened the door and peeked inside before letting Silvestra and me see as well. At a polished mahogany desk sat a man in his sixties wearing inquisitors' garb, looking at us with raised eyebrows. I recognized him from my impromptu sentencing.

When he realized who we were, his gaze took on a killing quality. He stood, clearly poised to draw his sword. "Explain," he said to Theo and Silvestra.

"We're aware that we've disobeyed orders," Theo said quickly, both hands raised slightly as if to ward off a blow. "However, we had excellent reason. We know that Desfourneaux was innocent, and we know who the real angel is. We know how to prove it."

"I should run him through right here. All of you," Driesan said.

Silvestra coughed. "We'd prefer that you didn't, sir."

Theo edged in front of me. "The inquisitors were originally established to help weed out dangerous magicians from the Pharmakeia and Chirurgeonate, yes? Shouldn't we pursue every possible uncertainty to the fullest extent we can?"

Driesan said nothing, which Theo took as encouragement. "If we're wrong, you can just execute Desfourneaux and discipline us however you want."

"If you're wrong, you'll have aided a witch in escaping the Umbra, and then you'll be beyond discipline."

Theo and Silvestra stood ashen and silent.

"Will you at least stand to be presented with the truth?" I asked quietly.

I saw an undefinable shift in his attitude; perhaps he was swayed by my phrasing, or maybe it was Theo and Silvestra's earnestness—whatever it was, he bent. "Talk," he snapped.

I drew a weary breath and related the plan and all salient information to Driesan.

He grew steadily more annoyed the longer I spoke. By the time I was done, he was tapping his fingers on his desk. "A good try," he said, "but—"

Logic fled from me in a single deft leap. "Please," I breathed, and took a step forward. "Please? Would you just . . . please . . . send a few inquisitors to observe? I know it would be dangerous, I know it's a matter of faith, and you have no reason to trust us, but please—"

There was an uncomfortable silence. I hated the way I was becoming more and more accustomed to begging.

"You can torture me again, if you insist," I said. "Whatever it takes. The city needs Florian put away. The Chirurgeonate needs the angel gone."

"Take the chance," Silvestra said.

"Two inquisitors," Driesan said, eventually, as if it were the most difficult thing in the world. "If any volunteer for it. One for the professor and one for the doctor. They'll accompany you both." He nodded to Theo and Silvestra.

One extra inquisitor for each potential target wasn't much assurance at all, but that wasn't the important part. The important part was that he'd given his blessing to the plan at all. He hadn't demanded that I be sent immediately to the demi-lune or back to the Umbra. I wished dearly for somewhere to sit down in relief.

"Thank you, sir," Theo said. "Will you tell the other seniors, or should we?"

"I will, so none of them decide to kill you anyway in a fit of pique."

"That seems wise."

Driesan shook his head, clearly tempted for a moment to retract his blessing, but he didn't. "Where should we send the volunteers for this?" he asked.

I spoke up to give him Gennady's address, which he took down on a notepad on his desk. His pen left vicious indentations in the paper.

"I can't believe myself," he muttered. "I must be mad."

Theo was clearly fighting back a smile. I prayed he'd succeed. "Please tell them to bring invisibility spheres. We'll move out to observe the targets once Albrecht has been primed with the false information."

Driesan grunted his reluctant assent. "It would be best for you to leave now," he said, looking me over with clear distrust still. "And best for you to be very smart about this. Very cautious. The Silvestra and Wycliffe family names won't take you an inch further here."

I found the nerve to say, "A few more things."

The inquisitors all stared at me in varying attitudes of disbelief.

I couldn't help but laugh nervously. "The matter of my standing with the Pharmakeia. If we can prove this, would you send word to the Archmagister that I've been cleared?"

"We'll hardly need to," Driesan said dourly. "They nearly rioted. They think you're a martyr."

That was some measure of comfort. Now I had to muster the courage to ask what *really* interested me, no matter how terrified I was of the answer. "More important," I said, "Malise Tyrrhena."

"What about her?" Driesan said.

"Well, if you believe us, you must also believe that she's innocent."

I thought I saw a shadow of guilt flit across his face. "We were beginning to have that suspicion without you," he muttered. "We couldn't get her to crack."

I devoted all my attention to not flying across the room to strangle him.

"You're asking if you have permission to go get her from the Umbra," Driesan continued.

"You *just* said you're not sure if she's guilty."

He waved a hand. "We can't go around—"

I leaned forward, feeling myself shed bits of lightning as I moved. "It would be ever so good of you to agree."

"That wasn't a *threat*," Theo said hastily.

"Of course it wasn't," I said. "Releasing Malise is the right thing to do. I suggest you do it."

Driesan's eyes narrowed in controlled fury. "It's daring of you to ask for that kind of special treatment before you've proven your case," he told me.

Good. It was refreshing to be daring. "Can you look at me and tell me you really think Malise Tyrrhena is the angel?" I tried not to wonder if she'd cried when they'd tortured her.

He turned his gaze away. "I'll send word to the Umbra," he said. "Wait until tomorrow, and then you can go get her as you please."

I drew a breath to thank him.

"Go now," he said immediately to Theo and Silvestra and me.

The three of us nodded and filed out, each of us trying to be the first one through the door. We didn't speak as we made our way out of the inquisitors' headquarters, not until we were back in the sunlight away from the stone-chilled air.

"That went better than I expected," Theo said weakly.

Silvestra shrugged. "We're not dead."

I said, "I need to sit down."

Theo graciously indicated the filthy street curb, but I declined the invitation. It could wait after all.

He heaved a weary sigh. "Back to Richter's apartment, then?"

I had rarely crisscrossed the city so many times in a single day. The speed of travel was becoming dizzying. "He'll be so glad to have us back," I said, and waited for someone else to take care of the ride. Silvestra stepped to the side of the street and raised a hand.

We knocked. Gennady opened the door with a growl. "Kind of wish you'd spend more time away. It's crowded in here."

Lady led him out of the doorway with a soft meow, and we filled the apartment once again. I felt keenly for Gennady: if I'd had so many people in my own space, I'd have cracked almost immediately.

Feeling for him didn't stop me from following him and saying, "Do you mind if I make some tea? If I could use the kitchen for a moment . . ."

He stared at me. "I don't have tea. Who drinks *tea*?"

"Me," I said, injured. "If you don't have any, that's all right."

"Coffee?" he said.

"Not advisable."

"Suit yourself."

So I wandered back into the living room and folded myself up next to Oliver again. I was quickly running out of reasons to keep pretending that our relationship, such as it was, followed any rules of decorum. He patted my leg absently, and I jumped in surprise. Neither of us acknowledged it.

Theo cleared his throat. "I hate to interrupt, but do we know where Albrecht will be today? Can we get this done now?"

I suspected he didn't hate to interrupt at all. "He'll be at the Chirurgeonate," I said. "Where else? He's *such* a dedicated healer." I couldn't help the venom that crept into my voice.

"Well, then, get ready for your show," Silvestra said to Oliver.

"Will you be with me?" Oliver asked the inquisitors. "Using your little devices to shadow us."

"Yes," Silvestra said. She smiled blackly, humorlessly. "With any luck, he'll try to kill you right there and we can expedite this whole process."

"Valary," Theo said.

"Just a joke."

Only Gennady laughed.

"It'll be best if Oliver goes back home after he gives Florian the information," Theo said. "He won't be able to tell you how it goes; you won't know if things are on track until we actually catch Albrecht."

"Give me one of the devices," I said, on impulse. "I'll go with one of you." I don't know why I offered, other than the unfounded belief that my mere presence and intention would be enough to protect Oliver. It wasn't as though I could have fought.

"No," the inquisitors said in unison. I understood from their tone that there would be no argument and looked away.

Oliver straightened the collar of his blindingly purple jacket and lifted his chin.

"Thank you," I said to him uselessly. "I'm sorry."

He stood. "It's all right. Let's go before I lose my nerve."

I got up as well and went to press a kiss to his cheek.

"Once more for good luck?" he said.

I kissed his other cheek.

"Try again."

I kissed him on the mouth, just briefly. It all felt very teenage; I wasn't sure I *liked* that, but there was something to be said for the novelty.

Oliver tousled my hair and turned decisively toward the door. "Off to the show."

I wanted to tell him to wait, to spend more time in the warmth of safety— but speed was of the essence.

"Good man," Theo said. Silvestra only nodded. The two of them took out their invisibility spheres; the mekhania whirled into motion, and they were gone. There was no evidence of their presence as they followed Oliver out of the house—not even footsteps.

Once the house was empty but for Gennady and Lady and me, I went into the kitchen to see if there was anything that needed cleaning up. He followed me automatically to hover over me as I started putting things that had been displaced back into cabinets. Occasionally, he made a small sound of disapproval and returned whatever I'd put away to a different place. I'd never figured him for a tidy person, but it seemed he at least had a system.

Eventually, he went to sit down at the kitchen table and stare at me. I joined him and focused on an oddly shaped stain in the rough wood.

"Oliver's not horrible," he said brusquely.

"Really? You don't dislike him?"

"Not that much. He's fine."

I had no idea what to do with that kind of good fortune. Gennady wasn't fine with anyone. All I could do was smile hopefully at him.

"Quit grinning," he said, as Lady jumped up into his lap. "Just because I don't want to kill your stupid boyfriend doesn't mean you should be smiling."

Obligingly, I forced myself into an attitude of neutrality.

"And just so you know," he said, "I hate having you in my apartment."

"I know," I murmured. "You've mentioned. I'm sorry."

"But the Clementia isn't after you anymore, so you can go home now, right?"

"Not really. We still don't know if Florian ever left my house. It would be bizarre of him to stay, but it's not out of the question."

"Well, a hotel, then."

"Tomorrow morning, I'll be able to get Malise out of the Umbra. Maybe she'll want me to stay with her for a little while."

"I sure hope so," he said.

I sighed. "I'm sorry, but I need another favor—will you come with me to the Umbra to get Malise out?"

"You need me for that?"

"You're Vigil. Your presence will help."

"Yeah, but do you *need* me? I mean, really think about it."

"I don't want to go back there alone," I said quietly. "I don't."

He dragged his hands across his face and nodded. "Fine."

"Thank you."

I wanted to leave then. Waiting until tomorrow seemed like an almost impossible task; every moment I waited was another moment Malise spent under the lights and wards of the Umbra. But Driesan had said what he said, and there was no way to speed up the process. I needed to pass the time until the next morning somehow.

"You should probably sleep," Gennady said. "I bet you'll be out for a long time."

"There's no way."

He and Lady both scoffed. "Yeah, there is. You just close your eyes and see what happens. It's easy. Go sit on the couch and try it out."

"I need a change of clothes," I said.

"You are so *picky*," he said.

I waited.

"Wear something of mine, and you can wash yours in the sink." The idea seemed to pain him. I didn't like it either, but there wasn't much alternative.

He went to find some of his simple black civilian's clothes for me; once changed, I did what I could for my own outfit with soap and water and hung it in Gennady's kitchen. With that done, I dragged myself up and retreated to the couch, deeply uncomfortable in Gennady's wrongly sized clothes but not stupid enough to express it. At least he'd had more than a uniform available.

Gennady had been right. As soon as I stopped moving, exhaustion overtook me again, and I slept until very nearly the next morning. He woke me up with a few hours' notice; I changed again and neatened up. It was time, finally, to get Malise.

"I bet they make it so cold on purpose," Gennady commented as we cleared the last staircase down into the Umbra and were bathed by the harsh ambric lights. He rubbed his hands together. "I bet it's some sort of tactic, you know?"

The nearest pair of Umbra guards stared at us, taking in his Vigil uniform and everything about me. "You're the guy who's here for Malise Tyrrhena," one of them said to me, as his rache circled Lady. I was made aware, not for the first time, that Lady was much smaller than most other raches. "You're the one who got released just earlier."

"That's him," Gennady said.

"That never happens."

"Please show us to her," I said tightly. I tried not to look down the hallway at the cell I'd occupied only recently, tried not to feel the chill of the wards settling down on me.

"Cell twenty-seven," he said. "Larissa and Vosco will get the door open for you. Go on. It's just around the corner there. We can't leave our post to show you, so you'll have to find it yourself."

Gennady and I rounded the corner slowly, peering hard at the faded numbers painted near the ceiling in front of each cell. I would have hurried for Malise's sake, but I was willing to bet none of the guards would have liked that.

When we found cell twenty-seven, I took a deep breath and addressed the soldiers in front of it. "Head Inquisitor Driesan issued permission for Malise Tyrrhena's release," I said, hating the way my voice echoed in the sterile silence. "Would you please open the door?"

"They told us someone was coming to get her. That's you?" one of the guards asked, a woman with a grim set to her mouth. Larissa, I assumed. I saw her recognize me from my captivity; I saw her curiosity sharpen. I hoped it wouldn't become *too* sharp.

"That's me." *Very, very obviously, almost too obviously to conceive of,* I prevented myself from adding.

"I remember you," she said to Gennady. "You were the one who came to get *him*." She nodded at me.

"I'm Gennady," he said brightly, and didn't clarify. I couldn't know if there were any consequences waiting for him regarding my escape, but that was a worry for a different day.

"So glad we've all affirmed our acquaintance," I said thinly, "so that we can now proceed."

I waited for the two guards to go through the arduous motions of unlocking the multiple doors. The process seemed to take even longer this time than it had when I was put inside one of the cells: I had no idea what state we'd find Malise in, but I knew it wouldn't be good.

"You know," the second guard said to me conversationally, "looks like the inquisitors really messed up their investigation."

Gennady barked a laugh. "Yeah, they really did."

I ignored them as the second door swung unlocked.

Malise sat cross-legged in the center of the room, watching us calmly. Outwardly calm, at least—she may have been quiet and still, but her spirit was raving. I knew it by the tilt of her head and the way she didn't blink.

"Malise," I said, and stepped forward. I feared she might flinch from me, but she didn't move away. She wasn't in her own clothing anymore; she'd been given the Umbra witch's uniform to wear, a heavy white robe. Her chains lay still on the floor like overfed snakes.

"Adrien," she replied. Her voice was raw. From disuse, I hoped, and not from screaming.

"Unchain her," I said to the guards, tonelessly. They moved to obey. I watched their every move, ready to intervene if they jostled her at all, but they were steady. Once the chains were off, she rubbed her wrists, hands shaking finely.

I went to her and helped her stand. I could have picked her up entirely to spare her the effort. I didn't, trying to preserve her dignity.

"Is it over?" she asked. She seemed to be holding herself together through force of will alone.

I wanted nothing more than to tell her that everything was done, but it would have been a lie. "Not quite," I said. "Florian is still free. But the Head Inquisitor approved your release. We convinced him of that much, at least."

She blinked when I mentioned Florian and met my gaze directly for the first time. "Florian . . ."

"You were right," I said. "I'll tell you about it later."

"You're hurt," she said dazedly.

I remembered with distant surprise that I was, indeed, still hurt. Florian's work had faded into the background of my consciousness until she reminded me. "Keeper's efforts," I said, shamefaced.

"I recommended him to you in the first place," she whispered. "It took me so long to realize."

That was too much to bear—that now, of all times, she felt *guilty*. That she was thinking of me.

"My dear," I said. "It doesn't matter."

She leaned heavily on me, and I helped her walk out of the cell with very small steps. Gennady hovered uncertainly outside with Lady pacing back and forth around him.

"Where are we going?" Malise said. To my horror, I heard the hollow ring of tears in her voice. She wasn't crying yet, but it was a close thing.

I squeezed her shoulder. "Do you want to go home?"

She nodded jerkily.

"Then we'll take you home."

Silently, I dared either of the Umbra guards watching us to say anything, but they were both wise. They stayed quiet, barely looking at Malise as they closed the cell back up behind her. The sound of the doors sealing up again drew a gasp from her; I took her hand, and Gennady stepped around us to walk on her other side.

Gennady and I supported Malise through the rest of the hallway until we reached the first set of stairs back up. "Oh," she said, staring blankly up at the staircase ahead of her.

"I could carry you," I offered.

"You'll drop her," Gennady said. "I'll do it."

Malise quelled us both with a weary stare of disapproval. "I'll walk."

It was miserable to watch her struggle up every set of stairs until we emerged into the Penumbra, but I knew that she'd never forgive me if I took the choice away from her. She was horribly out of breath by the time we reached the prison proper.

I wondered if anyone would see Malise's clothing and stop us as we left the Penumbra. Some of them would have been informed of Driesan's permission, but perhaps not all. One Vigil guard approached us, mouth open and hand at the hilt of his saber, but Gennady snarled. "Don't even think about wasting my time," he said, as Lady hissed softly.

That was enough to guarantee us a quiet passage out into the open air. The power of perceived confidence is truly astonishing. "It's better without so many wards," Malise murmured, looking down at the ground as she walked.

I took her hand again, and we didn't stop until we were at the side of a major street in Deme Eudora. Then I swept her up gently, slowly, into a hug. She dropped to her knees, pulling me down with her, and we knelt there on the dirty pavement, inconveniencing passersby. Gennady watched and fidgeted.

"The sun feels good," Malise said, her head bowed against my chest. We stayed that way until she had gathered her strength enough to stand again.

Our journey to Deme Palenne and Malise's house was deathly silent, all of us either too exhausted or empty or uncomfortable to speak.

Chapter 21

As we stood in front of her house, Malise finally began to cry. Frustration, more than anything else, was what did it. "I don't have my keys," she said indistinctly, wiping her face. "They took my keys."

I felt exceptionally stupid. Of course she wouldn't still have her personal effects. "We can get a locksmith, and—"

Gennady dug through his uniform's pockets, coming up with a set of lock picks.

"A man of hidden talents," I said wearily.

He nodded his acknowledgment and began to work on the door.

Malise gave a broken laugh, recovering from the momentary slip.

The door swung open in record time. I had no idea why I hadn't expected sooner that Gennady would carry lock picks. Why not? Once we were inside, I helped Malise into her bedroom.

"Give me a little while alone," she said. "I need some time to think. I need to change into something—something different. I need a shower. I might sleep."

"All right. I'll try to make you something to eat in the meantime."

She offered me a weak smile, and I went into the kitchen to see if there was anything left in the place that was still good to eat. There wasn't; everything had gone stale or rotted, and there wasn't enough in the icebox to make much out of. We'd have to go out for something later.

Gennady had been following me uncertainly everywhere I went through the house, as if afraid to touch anything. I turned to him. "It means something to me that you're kind to Malise."

Lady sneezed. Gennady made a face and went into the living room. I should have known better than to try any sincerity. While he was gone, though, I could be alone with my own thoughts. I kept semi-alert in case Malise came out and needed me, but otherwise, I sat down in the nearest chair, closed my eyes, and drifted.

I could still feel the traces of Florian's magic inside me, as though a parasite had taken up residence. I knew that he was still swaying me, whispering to me—I wasn't free of him. I might have broken the primal hold, but a part of me would belong to him for some time yet. If I ever had to face him again, I wasn't sure I'd enjoy discovering exactly how much power he had over me still.

That was an *if* problem, however. *If* I had to face him. Assuming all went well, I might never see him again. I tried to put it out of my mind and waited for Malise to come out.

She did, eventually, dressed in her usual casual clothes instead of the witch's robe and looking magnitudes less dreadful.

"We'll burn that robe later," I said to her.

She nodded and came over, gesturing for me to stand. I obliged, and she guided me to her couch in the living room. Gennady was there—he saw us and silently headed into the kitchen with Lady instead, trading places. Malise and I sat down together.

"I'm sorry," I said. "I'm truly sorry. I would have had you out sooner, but—"

"It isn't your fault. You were enchanted," she murmured.

That meant nothing. I'd let him do it because I was weak.

"This looks nasty," she said, brushing a hand very lightly across a bruise on my cheek.

"It isn't, really."

"May I heal it?"

"Please."

Even after having been confined under the influence of so many wards, her power flowed out strong and true. Florian's remaining marks were swept away like so many particles of dust.

The relief made me shiver. "Thank you, my dear." I looked her over carefully. "What about you?"

"I was healed before they put me in the Umbra," she said with a twisted smile. I had never seen that kind of smile from her before; I had never seen that bitterness. I waited to see if she wanted to elaborate, if she wanted to tell me. She didn't. I would coax it from her bit by bit over the following months, I decided, but now was not the time to push.

"I wanted to kill the inquisitors, you know," I said.

She closed her eyes. "I held out against confessing. I knew there would be no taking it back. At least I can pride myself on that."

"You have so much you can pride yourself on," I said.

She fought back another wave of sniffles.

"Would you tell me everything that's happened?" she said. "Catch me up to speed?"

"I can do my best."

She patted my arm. "Your best is fine."

So I told her. By the end of the explanation, she had her head in her hands. I couldn't see her expression. I wasn't sure I wanted to.

"That's it," I said lamely.

I had skirted around some specifics; I'd told her, for instance, that Florian had tried to strengthen the enchantment, but I'd been vague on how. I'd left a generous void around the kiss, around his utter dissection of me in the Vesperide koi gardens. Once she straightened up again, I could tell distinctly that she knew what sort of details I'd avoided. I was too familiar with guilt to misinterpret the look in her eyes: *I will never forgive myself for this.* She was still thinking of recommending Florian to me.

"Stars and saints," she said.

I hummed. "We can wait until this is over with for a full postmortem." I'd tell her more in time; I'd try to show her she was blameless.

She exhaled slowly. "Any time you like, my dear."

"I won't ever take another keeper," I said.

Her pause was both grim and brief. "Then we'll find another way."

"Easier said than done."

She was looking into my eyes, straight past me, searching for the sleeping daimon—sizing up her foe. When she refocused, seeing me once more, her voice was steady with determination. "We will find a way."

Before I could answer, I saw Gennady and Lady peeking around the kitchen door frame.

"Yes?" Malise and I both said at the same time.

"I want to leave," Gennady said mulishly. "I'm bored just sitting around. Are you two good now?"

I blinked, surprised he'd lasted so long. "Of course. You don't have to stay if you don't want to. Thank you for helping."

"Really?" he said cautiously.

"Really," Malise said. She offered him a faint smile.

"Great. See you sometime, then." With that touching farewell, he crossed to the door and let himself out.

Malise and I contemplated the space where he'd been for a few moments. "Odd," Malise said.

"He's done so well."

"I know. I'm proud of him."

I ran through the list of things she could possibly need.

"Are you hungry?" I asked her. "I couldn't find anything in your kitchen that was still good."

"Starving," she admitted.

I disentangled myself from her and stood to offer her a hand up as well; she took it and hauled herself to her feet. I tried not to notice how unsteady she was. "Do you want to go somewhere now?"

"Just let me fetch the change on the dresser," she said, and went into her room.

When she came back, we went outside. Once we were in the fresh air, Malise seemed happier. It's wonderful how a little wind and sunlight can do that for a person—smooth the corners off the uncertainties of a crisis, soothe myriad hurts that seem otherwise permanent.

We stepped off the front porch. "Hello," Florian said, and took Malise gently by the arm.

〜

Malise screamed. I did not. I'd been wondering how much sway Florian had over me, yes, had been wondering what I'd find out when I saw him again— and now I had my answer. He had enough influence to stop me from killing him immediately, and with that, we were lost.

Florian looked otherworldly. There were dark shadows beneath his eyes; his head hung loosely from his neck. He'd always carried himself with precise control, even during his wilder moments, and it was unnatural to see him unraveled. "So you're *both* here. Let's go back inside, shall we?" he said. There was an odd, buzzing timbre to his voice.

Malise tried to jerk her arm away from him, and he narrowed his piercing gray eyes. She doubled over with a shriek; I could almost feel the agony of his punishment myself, overflowing from her secondhand. He walked her back inside her house, and I followed.

"Shut the door behind us," he told me. I obeyed. Soon we were all standing in the living room looking at each other, Malise panting with pain and fury, Florian smiling very slightly, and me—

I don't know. I can't recall what I felt for those first few moments. It must have been a special fear indeed to leave me blank. I could sense Florian's magic, the clinging threads that hadn't been torn yet, snaring me as I breathed and blinked. Every automatic process was subject to his will.

"It's a shame your Vigil boy isn't here," Florian said conversationally. "It was hard to avoid him on his way out. Do you think he'd be able to save you if he were here?"

"Let her go," I said.

He squeezed Malise's arm until she whimpered. I knew his silver rings must be digging into her skin. "I don't think I will."

"Monster," Malise said.

Florian caught me looking at him speculatively. I was trying to determine if I had the speed and skill to strike him with lightning before he could do anything to Malise. He understood what I was wondering; he shook his head. "I'd burst her heart before you could cast," he said. I believed him.

"You must know you can't kill us and get away with it," I said. "The inquisitors already know it's you. You'd just be giving them proof."

"Oh, I know." He patted Malise's head fondly. "I know they're looking for me. Your actor friend is quite a talent. He almost had me fooled. It was a good plan, Adrien; I'll give you that."

I laughed. It was not a sound a sane person would have made. "Not good enough."

"No. They say the stars can see everything. So can I. I knew something was wrong as soon as he came to me. I could *sense* them there with him. Their heartbeats in the air—I could feel them."

I wondered if Florian could feel even the minuscule firings of lightning inside my brain as I fought an atavistic spike of terror. "Is Oliver dead?"

"I'm sure you'd like to know," he said.

That meant he hadn't touched Oliver at all. Florian would never have missed the chance to taunt me outright if he'd been hurt.

"How did you know I'd be here?" Malise asked.

"Adrien's little trap made it obvious. I knew he wouldn't leave you there. You have him very well trained, Dr. Tyrrhena."

"What do you get out of this?" I said distantly. "Out of killing us. What do you gain? You're still going to spend the rest of your life in the Umbra, if they don't execute you as soon as they find you. Why?"

"I told you. I told you that I could be the one to help you take responsibility for yourself. To bow to the consequences you earn. And I will."

Even now, at this latest of hours, he wouldn't speak to me as an equal.

I made eye contact with Malise—she was touching Florian. Was she faster than me? Could *she* put him down before he could kill her? I had no doubt that her power as a healer rivaled even his.

"No," Florian said. "I wouldn't advise it." It was as if he were inside me, watching me from inside my own skull.

I drew a shuddering breath. "You can't—"

He reached out and brushed my cheek, a curious motion, wondering where my bruises had gone. I tried to move away before he could touch me, but the traces of his enchantment crowded my mind, and I was too slow. "Down," he said brutally. I felt a fundamental pressure in my veins, drawing me to collapse in front of him.

He stared down at me with disgust. "Maybe I should make you kill her instead," he said.

The reality of the situation hit me then, a little late. I'd been comforting myself with fantasies of rescue, but there was nothing there. There was no one to help us. We had been finished as soon as we'd both hesitated to end him on sight.

"Well?" he said. "How about that? Would you like that?"

"What?" I mumbled.

"Why shouldn't I have you kill her, Adrien?"

He was angry I'd chosen Malise over him. I'd meant something to him after all.

"Don't you think that would be amusing?" he asked.

I struggled to stand again and said, "I'll do it."

Because I could make it painless. I had healing magic too, just like Florian. I had never before imagined using it that way, but I could bring death just the same. Florian would make it agonizing when he killed her. I would not. With my help, she could slip away easily, easily.

Malise shook her head. "No."

"It won't hurt," I said. I expected that I would cry—could never have resisted—but I was seized with a sudden feeling of responsibility. Here at the end of things, I had agreed to be the one to shepherd Malise out of the world, and that would be the last thing that ever happened before Florian snuffed me out, and I was going to need to do it *well*.

"It won't hurt," I said again, after a dreadful pause. It was all I could think to say.

"That isn't the point," Malise said, with great poise. "I won't make you do it."

"Then you want to suffer," Florian said. At least he had finally abandoned his worthless talk of mercy.

Malise said nothing.

"She should at least be able to lie down first," I said. Most people hope for that—being able to die in their own bed. It was a gesture toward Malise on my part, and it was a gesture toward myself: I could not bear the sight or sound of her crumpling to the ground when I killed her.

Florian shrugged. "If you truly think that matters."

I took Malise's free hand and walked with her to her bedroom.

And Florian was so assured of his victory, so certain of our weakness, that he let go of her. I felt something in the air change. Arrogance. We always could count on Florian's arrogance. He was strong, and he was wily, but he would overestimate himself every time. A pulse of hope, of *spite*, guttered back to life inside me.

Malise and I stared at each other once we reached her bed. He'd made a mistake; we'd both seen it, and there was a chance now that we could capitalize on it.

I had to try, of course. There was no doubt of that. There was no excuse for simply giving Florian his way without resistance. Not again. It was a matter of principle now.

"Do you want to lie down?" I asked Malise.

"I'll sit," she said evenly, and did so.

Florian could detect heartbeats. We knew this now. If I simply put her into a deep sleep, he'd be able to tell. I could slow her systems down to nearly nothing, and that might work for a little while longer, but not *very* long. Still, a small amount of time was better than nothing. I could put her under, carefully, and then let her wake up while Florian was busy with me. With any luck, she'd be able to end this, even if it wasn't before I was dead.

As long as Malise agreed to it all. I sat down next to her and framed her face with my hands. "Trust me," I said, and only that. I could think of nothing else.

As I was trying to invent other clever codes, she nodded at me. That was all I really needed, I reflected. She trusted me. Either she understood, or she would figure it out.

I put Malise to sleep one slow degree at a time. There was every chance Florian would catch on and force me to kill her in actuality; I wanted to give her as many moments of light as I could. Her breathing, her heartbeat, all of it—I slowed everything down to a dreamlike crawl. She slumped against my shoulder, and I eased her onto her side before standing up.

I remembered again what Oliver had said about the art of acting. *True for you. It's true for you.* To fool Florian, Malise needed to be dead. And what would that be like?

All would be hollow.

"It's done," I said to Florian, gazing down at Malise, imagining my world without her in it—a hostile place, no better than the barren surface of a distant planet.

Florian felt Malise's wrist, searching for a pulse. I took great pains not to hold my breath. If my work wasn't perfect, if I hadn't slowed her down enough to mock death . . .

He drew back, satisfied. "Thank me," he said.

"What?"

"For not torturing her to death."

"Thank you," I said faintly.

"So," he said. "Now it's just the two of us."

"Why did you choose me? When did you decide to use me like this?"

"I already knew I needed contingencies," he said, shrugging. "I chose *you* because I had to."

"You had to?"

"When I read your solarium records, I thought, *It's got to be that one.*"

It was too similar to what Oliver had told me inside the Copper Arch Theater for me to withstand; a single mote of frail lightning drifted from my mouth on an exhale.

"We've always known the cure for akrasia," he told me. "It's not magical. It's not chemical."

He was focused on me entirely, missing the slow, slow beats of Malise's heart. It was working. "And what's the cure?" I asked, although I knew his answer.

"Euthanasia."

Quick as a snake, he brought one hand to my throat. "Kneel."

His magic forced me down before him. The other hand rose, and he encircled my neck—not squeezing quite yet.

I realized that he wasn't going to use his magic to kill me at all. No, he needed something visceral. Of course this was how I'd go; in fact, it seemed inevitable. Before the angel, I'd been choked in the Penumbra's bloody dirt by a witch who'd wanted me silent, and the inquisitors had done it so I'd say what they wanted, and Florian would asphyxiate me with his bare hands now because I'd dared to speak against him. If I had no voice, I reflected, it could have been different.

But slow was good. This would give us time.

I looked up at him, feeding him my terror, trying to entrance him further. My spell had been a short one; it was fading from Malise now. My magic unwound from her lungs, her heart, fled her veins—she would wake up soon.

Then my willpower flickered, drowned for a moment in the silver sea; my control slipped. I felt the urge to warn Florian. When I spoke, I wasn't sure what I'd say.

What came out was, "Higher."

He blinked. "Higher?"

"Your . . . grip. Needs to be an inch higher."

He adjusted his hands and began to cut off my air.

The pressure of his fingers around my airway was nothing like when Theo had choked me—that had been business. This was more immediate, more intimate.

He'd turned away from Malise on the bed. I couldn't see her either; I couldn't see anything but him. If she managed to catch him off guard when she woke, he and I would both discover it at the same time. I realized very quickly, as the raw desperation began to set in, that we were cutting it close.

"Look at me," Florian said. I heard him only as though from far away. I didn't obey, and he shook me violently until I did.

The room tilted. I lost my balance and tipped forward into him, and somewhere in the back of my dimly lit mind, a switch flipped: *Here it is.* I was going to die. Not in the next few minutes, but *now*. Any plans were useless, were for nothing—I was going to die. Malise was not going to wake up in time.

I'd wanted the element of surprise, but I'd forgotten that patience is only a virtue when you don't have someone's hands around your neck. I managed to raise an arm to shove at him, to send a bolt of lightning out into him—

He saw me coming. He squeezed harder, and my arm dropped against my will as his magic bound me. The lightning never made it out.

That was it, then. That was all.

But just before my vision failed, I saw a shadow rise behind Florian. Malise's shadow, like a resurrection. She'd made it back into consciousness after all. Florian sensed her at nearly the same instant. He let me go—he struck her a savage blow across the face, sending her reeling backward.

Immediately, she grabbed his wrist before he could withdraw, and a brilliant explosion of blue frost and silver filled the room. The two of them stood frozen for a single moment; I could feel the primal discord of dueling magics, a terrible split in the air as they fought their instantaneous war.

Malise was the better healer. I knew this without doubt. She would win, I thought; she would put him down. He'd be asleep within moments—there was no way she could bring herself to kill. Once Florian was caught off guard, once the playing field was even, she'd exceed him.

Except, naturally, I'd forgotten something. Malise had no practice with *forcing* her spells on anyone. She would have no experience with breaking down the barriers. Florian, on the other hand, had made it into an art. He was a genius of violation, and when push came to shove, he would not be outdone.

The blue light and frost were sucked into oblivion as silver blinded me, and Malise fell to the ground at the same time as I managed to stand. Florian's back was turned; I gathered a storm and leveled it at him. I couldn't rush—if I gave it anything less than my complete concentration, my battered magic would rebound, and I'd only knock myself over. I closed my eyes. Calm. Calm.

Build the spell. Layer by layer. Craft it. A thing of beauty. No instinct, no rush, nothing for my unhealed imperfections to corrupt. I nearly had it.

Then I heard a sound I'd heard only once before in my life: a wet, grating thump.

It was, of course, the sound of a blade punching through a rib cage. My eyes opened in time to see Florian looking down at his chest in consternation, down at the end of the saber sheathed securely in him. A red gleam caught the light.

He fell slowly, without dramatics. His limbs splayed awkwardly. Gennady placed a boot on his back and heaved him forward, drawing the saber back with a lazy flourish. Once the metal was out, I could move again; I scrambled back as Lady came strolling into the room, licking her mouth in animal anticipation.

Malise dragged herself up off the floor. We all stayed perfectly still—the rest of us standing and staring, Florian dying.

"Wow," Gennady said. "I'm gone for two seconds and look what happens."

I was too slow to look away as Lady bent her head daintily over Florian and tore out his throat in a neat, blooming bite. I locked eyes with him; I saw the spasm when Lady swallowed. I saw him start to fade faster.

A singular desire seized me then, a hunger I'd never once felt before. It wasn't enough that he was looking at me as he died. I needed him to feel the lightning before he fled beyond my reach; I needed him to understand. I moved toward him, and the air around me began to hum in eerie disturbance, a seething shriek. I had no earthly idea what the bolt I was gathering would do to him—I had no idea what it might do to me.

But Malise scrambled to his side and breathed, "No."

My grim hypnosis, my desperation to hold Florian's gaze, vanished. There was pain in Malise's voice; I looked to her instead, and the scream of ravening lightning guttered away. At her cue alone, I knelt in the blood.

Florian was at the precipice of the void now, poised to enter the dark. We could wrench him back.

"Don't touch him," Malise said, gasping. "Not while he's still awake."

She was right. As long as Florian still clung to consciousness, touching him would mean risking death. I had no doubt that even now, he was capable of it. He had nothing to lose, and precious little to gain by living—he would kill us rather than be healed.

Gennady whistled lowly. "You're really this stupid?"

I glanced up at him.

He bared his teeth. "He has to die," he said. "You need to understand that."

I had given the world so much grief. It was possible that what I owed it now was simple: Florian's end.

Malise spoke again. "I can't, Adrien. I'm so sorry."

That decided it. This was no longer about me. It was no longer about Florian. It was about her healer's oath. I would keep her hands clean at any cost.

She came to kneel next to me. We watched Florian struggle against his blossoming death. "Only just before it's too late," she murmured.

"You two are the dumbest people on earth, and I'm going to kill him again immediately," Gennady said.

Florian made a final choking sound. "Now, I think," I said: Florian looked more or less dead.

Malise didn't move. "One more moment."

We waited another heartbeat before each of us took one of his hands and began to heal. His silver rings were cold; his influence on me waned—my battered, broken magic worked, although the effort and pain were great. The wound in Florian's throat closed enough to save him. Blood no longer poured from his chest. Blue light flooded the room again; he breathed; small sparks of lightning and flakes of frost showed with every exhale—it was working.

His eyes fluttered open. The moment I knew he wouldn't die, I was seized by a depthless hatred. I felt the turn in Malise's magic, felt her switch, and followed suit.

His power fought us. I growled lowly, a savage sound I'd never expected to make, and turned out the lights.

The realization would come only later that Malise and I had made angels of ourselves anyway, in the end. We'd done as Florian had done. We hadn't killed, but we'd be stained nevertheless.

The three of us watched him sleeping. I'd never seen his face in repose, absent of calculation. He could almost have been the man I'd believed him to be. "He won't wake up for days," Malise said into the silence.

I looked up at Gennady. He had his saber ready still; he'd gone wild-eyed. "I said I'd kill him again. I meant it."

"I know," I said. "You don't have to approve. You don't have to understand. I know I was wrong the last time I asked you to listen—but give me another chance."

He snarled and advanced a step. "You've got to let me do it for you. I told you I always would. If you wanted *him* to live, you never should have saved *me*."

Malise so rarely raised her voice, but now it rang out with anguish. "Gennady!"

He stood with his mouth open, blank. Lady twined around his legs and chirped softly. After I had failed him so categorically the first time, after he'd seen the consequences of heeding me, how could I ask him to try again?

Tongue-tied, still shivering with the pain of pressing through the wound in my magic, I tried to think of something else to sway Gennady—but I failed. All I could think was how wretched it was, how essentially unfair, to have given myself this headache for *Florian*.

"I made promises," Malise whispered.

Gennady lowered his saber.

I stood carefully to touch him on the shoulder. "Thank you, my dear." I had never imagined Gennady as a miracle before, but now I had no other word.

. "Lady smelled him," he said, eyes fixed on Florian. "Caught him on the wind when we were walking away. Had to sneak back in the house—we weren't too close."

Lady paused in grooming herself to bark in acknowledgment. If they'd been an instant earlier or later, I reflected, Florian wouldn't have been distracted enough to miss them. His last fit of vicious ecstasy had rendered him mortal.

"I'll go find the inquisitors," I said. "I'll bring them here, and they can take custody of him."

"We'll watch in case he wakes up," Gennady said.

I looked at Malise. "Do you want to stay or come with me?"

"I can't walk. I'll stay here." She hadn't stood yet; dazedly, she examined her bloody hands. "Oh, it's going to take such a long time to clean all of this."

"I'll help," I promised, and hurried out. The sooner I informed the inquisitors, the sooner I could find Oliver again.

Chapter 22

I checked Westbrook first. Thirkeld would be there; if the inquisitors assigned to him had made any concessions whatsoever toward doing their job, they would be with him. If I couldn't find Thirkeld, I'd check the Pharmakeia for Keynes and *her* team of observers.

I realized only after I stepped inside that I had Florian's blood all over my clothes. I stopped walking, overcome with nausea, and caught the horrified eye of the nearest alienist.

"Don't worry," I said. "It isn't mine."

He seemed worried nevertheless. "Whose is it?" he asked. I recognized his tone—the patient, earnest, inquisitive, and utterly opaque voice of a professional questioning a maniac. An orderly had noticed me as well, and the two of them were exchanging furtive glances.

I *knew* the orderly. We'd interacted during my latest two stays.

I sighed deeply. "Could you get Dr. Thirkeld for me?"

Neither moved.

"Xavier," I said to the orderly. "Please go get Thirkeld. Thank you."

The alienist spoke again. "Why exactly is it that you want to see him?"

To be doubted *now* was beginning to make me feel vaguely rabid. "I need to speak with the invisible inquisitors that are following him around."

"Oh?"

"We were pursuing a serial killer, you see."

"Really?"

"I did find the killer, in point of fact. You'll note the blood."

"Yes."

"And either I'm being very serious, in which case you should get him, or something is terribly wrong with me, in which case—by God, don't you think I should be assessed?"

Xavier went to get Thirkeld while the alienist watched me.

Within minutes, Thirkeld came inching cautiously around the corner, and two inquisitors materialized ahead of him, striding toward me. It was Theo and a stocky blonde woman I didn't recognize. I managed to avoid flinching at their sudden appearance, but the observing alienist let out a startled yelp. "Dismissed," I said to him. He left to avoid the inquisitors as quickly as he could.

"Whose blood?" Theo asked tightly.

"Florian's."

"Is he dead?"

"In a coma."

He shook his head. "Is anyone *else* dead?"

"No."

"He came to find you? Not Keynes or Thirkeld—you?"

I shrugged. "He sensed you and Silvestra with Oliver from the start—he figured out something was wrong. He went to find Malise to punish me. I just happened to be there."

Theo swore under his breath.

Thirkeld caught up to us, wide-eyed with alarm. "What's going on?"

"It's over," I said shortly. "You won't be followed anymore. Florian's about to be taken into custody."

He looked at the inquisitors for confirmation.

"He's at Malise's house waiting for you," I told Theo.

Theo nodded at Thirkeld. "Well, thanks for your cooperation. That's it. Let's not keep in touch, shall we?"

Thirkeld surveyed me for a few moments, looking at all the blood. I smiled politely. "You must be relieved, Henri."

"Let's not keep in touch," he agreed, and turned on his heel.

Theo sighed and looked at the other inquisitor. "You find Keynes's team and give them the news. I'll go get Albrecht."

She nodded and hurried away without another word.

Theo began to move for the solarium exit, and I was happy to follow. "Damn fine work," he said, "if you'll allow me to comment."

"I'll allow it," I said.

"How did you manage it, when it sounds like he got the jump on you?"

"Oh. Gennady impaled him."

He raised his eyebrows. "Gennady was there?"

"Raches have an excellent sense of smell." I didn't feel much like explaining in detail, and Theo didn't question me any further.

On the trip back to Malise's house, I began to worry that I'd miscalculated. Maybe Theo and I would open the door to find Malise and Gennady dead. He could have been faking; we could have been too gentle. It wasn't impossible that he could worm his way out of this too—that the nightmare wasn't over.

Theo saw me fidgeting at the doorstep and nudged me with his shoulder. "Calm down. I'm sure it's fine."

I didn't want to hear it from him, but I granted him a weak smile. "Probably."

Still, I hovered for a moment before opening the door. Until I went inside, nothing was certain; I could put off any horrible discoveries by dithering. Knowing for sure would solidify it all. I wasn't ready to do that.

Theo was. He moved past me and let us into the house. Malise and Gennady were there in the living room, watching over Florian in his lonely pool of blood, a patch of red night on the wood floor. It was all right after all.

Malise's posture relaxed once she saw Theo. I imagined it was one of the few times anyone had ever relaxed because of an inquisitor. "Stars," she said. "Finally."

Theo stood above Florian with his hands on his hips, looking down at him speculatively. "Looks like you did quite a number on him."

"That had better not be a criticism," I said. "And there had better not be a witchcraft trial waiting for us somewhere along the line—or a court-martial for Gennady."

"Well, you used your magic to put him to sleep, didn't you? Against his will?"

Malise and I were silent. At Gennady's side, Lady's pupils thinned.

"I'm not going back to one of those cells," Gennady said casually. "I'd die first. You better keep that in mind."

Theo shook his head and concealed a grin. "We'll have it all taken care of. I'm only playing. You won't even need to worry about your names being in the papers."

"What a wonderful joke," I muttered. Malise covered her face.

He raised his hands. "Now, now. Everything's fine. We've won. Take a moment to bask in it."

"What's next?" I asked. "Does *Florian* go to trial? What?"

Gennady made a derisive sound, but he didn't speak up.

"That's up to Valary and me," Theo said. "And I suppose it's only right that we defer to *you*. I'll tell you, though, there's not much point. He's going underground one way or another, trial or no."

I looked at Malise.

"Yes," she said, of course. "A trial."

I wish I could say that I agreed out of some sort of commitment to justice. I wish I could say that I believed so fiercely in anything. Mostly, I wanted to see Florian's face when he realized he'd met his better. My peace of mind depended on it—my *ego* depended on it. "Absolutely," I said.

Theo nodded. "Well, then. We can arrange that."

"We won't have to testify?" I asked.

"Valary and I will take official statements from you and present them."

"I'll still go." It would be harrowing to hear the inquisitors present whatever statement I could make myself give, but I'd endure that.

Gennady had been watching me carefully. As soon as I answered, he spoke up. "I'll go too. You know, just in case you decide he has to be executed right there."

"Unlikely that we'll contract that job out," Theo said dryly. "But very well."

"Great."

I picked a clean patch of floor to pace. "Is the Clementia going to investigate the matter of all the people who were imprisoned on Florian's bad information? Malise and I are free, but what about them?"

"They'll be cleared if there was no evidence against them other than his word," Theo said gently. "We'll see to that."

"You really must come up with a better way of doing all this."

"I don't think the inquisitors will be doing much handling of anything at all going forward," he said. "It's been a disaster. We'll have to see what our future is."

I didn't disagree.

After an awkward hesitation, Theo nudged Florian with his boot. "All right. Time to get him to HQ. I don't suppose anyone is going to help me put him into a caleche?"

No one volunteered. He looked at Gennady. "Not even you, soldier boy?"

Gennady rolled his eyes. "If you really can't do it by yourself. Weakling."

Theo ignored the jab.

"Please get him out of here," Malise said. I could tell she was keeping her anxiety under tight watch, but she couldn't hide it entirely.

"Immediately, if possible," I added.

"I can get close to it." Theo motioned to Gennady. "Come on. Let's drag him to the street. I'll just flash my badge if the driver balks."

And between the two of them, they hauled Florian up out of the congealing blood and began to carry him toward the door. I went to open it for them. They took him outside the house, making good progress toward the nearest main street; the few nearby pedestrians made absolutely no effort to interfere. I watched until they rounded a corner.

Malise came to stand next to me; I turned to her. "He hit you," I said, remembering. There was no bruising yet, only a redness on her cheek, but it was visible.

"It was glancing," she said.

"Liar. Let me heal it."

She nodded. It wasn't lost on me that we had played this scene already today; we were only switching roles.

I guided her to her desk in the corner, and she sat down. There was a great silence as we both unraveled, considering what had almost happened, what everything had almost cost.

"Would you have done it?" she asked.

"Killed you?"

"Yes."

"To save you from Florian, I would have," I said.

She considered me seriously. "Thank you."

I could speak of it no more. All the terror and venom had left me; above all, I felt empty.

Malise anchored me back. "Do you still have it in you to go get food? After I change my clothes *again*."

I looked at her askance. "You have an appetite?"

"No, but I'll faint if I don't eat. Or if I can't get away from the smell of the blood."

"We could go get Oliver," I said. Florian had given away that he wasn't hurt, but I had no idea how he was otherwise. Had he been frightened? Was he worried?

"I'd like that," Malise said. We laid some towels haphazardly over Florian's mess and abandoned the problem for later. In returning to my house so I could shed my own share of the bloodstains, we discovered that Florian had left the door unlocked, which irritated me despite the convenience. It was only with Malise's company to bolster me that I could stand to venture inside; we hurried on to find Oliver without lingering.

~

Oliver was at the Copper Arch Theater, the second place we checked. He was alive, undamaged. He was perfect. There was no show going on; they were in rehearsals for another play, something I didn't recognize with a pair of imperial astrologers who fall in love. Oliver played one; I found that I was unaccountably jealous of the other actor after hearing only a few lines and tried to be reasonable.

Malise and I were noticed shortly after coming inside. "Excuse me," one of actresses called, breaking off in the middle of a word. "You can't be in here."

The others turned to look at us; Oliver's face lit up when he saw me. "No, they're fine."

"You know them?"

"He's my boyfriend," he said candidly.

This couldn't be *new* information to me, not exactly, but the word startled me anyway. I raised one hand in an awkward wave.

"Ooh," said the actress. "In that case."

"Go on without me," Oliver said, and hopped off the stage to greet Malise and me, although his fellow players groaned in protest. The three of us went outside.

"If you're here, does that mean it's all over?" Oliver said. "After I talked to him, Florian just . . . left. Did he go to try to kill one of those people?" He was wearing blue robes, spotted liberally with stars, and touches of faint, glittering makeup.

I found myself smiling without meaning to. That he hadn't been left in fear was a deep relief. "Not exactly. I'll tell you all about it in a moment, but Florian was taken back to the inquisitors' headquarters." Saying it made it true; I felt a vise unclench from around my rib cage.

He shook his head, stunned by our reversal of fortune. "Thank God."

"Thank *you*," I said.

He grinned. "I don't believe we've met," he said to Malise.

"Malise Tyrrhena," she said, and bowed. It was a tired motion, but sincere. "I'm Adrien's friend."

"My best friend," I added. It was important that he know this.

Oliver bowed as well, a graceful sweep. "Oliver Harcourt. It's a pleasure." He gave her his lovely smile, and she smiled back.

"This is all because of your plan," he said admiringly.

"Oh," I said. "Oh, no. The plan failed spectacularly."

Oliver's smile flickered. "Did it?"

I nodded.

"How?"

Although I explained it in the gentlest terms possible, by the time I was finished, Oliver had a hand to his mouth.

"You—you healed him?" he asked slowly.

"Please don't call us stupid for it," I said. I projected some weak humor into my voice, but the request was deadly sincere. I didn't think I could handle it. "I know it was risky, but . . ."

He shook his head. "No. It's not stupid. I wouldn't have done it, but it's not stupid."

"In any case, he's dealt with."

"We can get back on schedule now," he said slyly, having made the wise decision to steer us away from solemnity. "See about getting to know each other better."

I had no idea how he felt so comfortable saying something like that in front of another person, but I knew I was going to have to get used to forthrightness with him. "We can," I said. "I was hoping you'd come have lunch with Malise and me."

"Do you want to go to that little Saebar place again? Or is it bad of me to take you to the same place twice? I want to be classy, of course."

"I like Saebar food," Malise said. She was looking between Oliver and me with some hopefulness.

"Then it's set," Oliver announced. "We'll go right now." I sensed that he was trying to do his part to distance us from Florian's specter as quickly as possible. If any of us took a moment to breathe, we risked falling back into the silver drowning pool. He steered us eagerly through the streets of Deme Lettia, taking my hand.

We found our seats at the restaurant and waited to order, all looking around at each other with blatant curiosity. If I was lucky, Oliver was thinking about the future with me. He and Malise were wondering about each other's presence in my life, wondering how the other fit into the recent nightmare. We were a table of fascinations. I had no fog of pain hanging over me any longer; I could see Oliver with clear eyes, and I liked what I saw.

"So, you're a healer. That's very respectable," Oliver said.

"And you're an actor," Malise replied, not quite flattered but appreciative. "It must be fun."

"*Such* fun. I love the stage."

"He's good. I saw him perform," I said.

"You'll have to come see me some time," Oliver said to Malise, feigning a subtle preen. "I'd compensate your tickets."

She brightened. "When's your next show?"

They talked theater for a while; Malise knew more about it than I did. She'd seen *Starcrossed*, the Copper Arch's upcoming play, and the two of them discussed its themes and merits while I drifted, happy to let them chat.

Eventually, when we were all done eating and talking, and Oliver had insisted once again on paying for all of us, Malise said, "I need to get home and clean."

We walked outside the restaurant into the din of the city. "Gennady probably knows some of the Clementia crime scene cleaners," I said. "I'll ask him if he can get one of them to come to your house and take care of it. In the meantime, just . . . try to step around it?"

Oliver clapped his hands together softly. "Sounds like a plan."

Malise gave my arm a squeeze. "We can talk more later."

I saw that she had reached her limit. She'd helped Oliver and I drag ourselves back into the sunlight, and now she needed to cry. "Goodbye, my dear," I said.

The both of us paused for a moment too long, each weathering a flash of anxiety—this goodbye was temporary, yes, but it was difficult to be confident.

"Tomorrow," I said.

She bowed and was gone. I watched as she disappeared down the street, trying to decide if she would recover.

Oliver could read me. "She's going to be fine," he said.

I made sure my tone was gentle. "You weren't there. He terrorized her. He wanted to make me kill her. And she was in the Umbra for far longer than I was; she was tortured."

He winced, but he didn't back down. "She'll mend. I can see it."

I could only hope he was right.

"What about you?" he asked carefully. "Are *you* going to be all right?"

I was not. Not for some time. "With work."

"You don't seem to be afraid of work. Gailhardt will help."

"Have you made progress with her? Has she helped you much?"

He nodded emphatically. "It used to hurt me to try to cast as well. I could never move so much as a single drop of rain. Now I can manage a few simple things on good days."

"I suppose I have no choice but to trust in her."

He weighed his words before speaking. "You know, I've worried before that you might think less of me. My magic is nothing now. But you—you have something special. I can tell, even when you're struggling."

"No," I said, frankly horrified.

He smiled. "Even if I can never cast well again, you won't feel like you're slumming it?"

It was all backward.

"Never," I said. I tried to think of something more reassuring, but all I could muster was, "Don't think that."

He sobered. "You know, I've been thinking about what you told me before. That it's a bit of a risk to be with you."

I nodded with my heart in my throat.

"You're taking a risk too."

"What?"

"Anyone could be terrible," he said. "We'll both wait and see."

His easy romanticism had charmed me, yes, but this bleak pronouncement undid me completely. I hugged him. My glasses misted; I pulled back and took them off to clean them, embarrassed beyond compare.

He smothered a laugh. "You must be exhausted if you think *that* was worth a hug."

Anyone could be terrible. It was the single sweetest thing a man had said to me. I knew I couldn't explain why; I only nodded. "I really am."

"Go rest," he said gently. "I'll visit you tomorrow—are you going to work? *Can* you?"

I'd lose my mind if I didn't try, I thought. At the very least, I needed to make explanations. "Yes, I hope so."

"Then I'll come by." He blinked at me, all innocence. "Say, how thick are the walls of your office?"

"Not thick enough," I said severely.

"Too bad. We'll figure something out."

Leaving him again brought me almost physical pain, but I managed it. I went home, finally, and stood outside my door, transfixed for some time with paranoia before I let myself inside.

Florian had left some belongings in my guest room. A watch, a pen, one shirt—nothing much, but enough to contaminate the entire space. I inched into the room, almost expecting to see him there. I fancied that the shadows seemed thicker somehow. I gathered his leftover items and carried them, ceremonially, to the trash, and then I stripped his bed and set the linens to wash. I would spend hours in the following days scrubbing every inch of the room clean, falling into a reverie of anxiety each time. I'd flinch at every sound; I'd creep through my own house like a burglar, afraid to disturb Florian's lingering shade. It would be weeks before I picked up the scattered blue angel eye beads from my broken bracelet.

I might heal, but it wouldn't be quickly.

Chapter 23

Florian's trial was held in one of the larger interrogation rooms in the inquisitors' headquarters. Apart from Theo, Silvestra, the two inquisitors who had helped monitor Keynes and Thirkeld, and Head Inquisitor Driesan, a panel of four witchfinders was in attendance. Gennady and I sat far in the back with Lady pacing at our feet. A single attorney, who looked nervous beyond belief, had been appointed to give Florian a bare facsimile of a fair trial.

Florian sat heavily chained to a chair in a manner strongly suggestive of the Umbra's restraints, the metal gleaming and writhing with antimagic. The witchfinders surrounded him, at the ready with weapons drawn—the light of the antimagic shone off their blades and mekhania eyes. Florian stared out at the audience with supernatural calm, taking in each person one at a time, his expression never shifting. He seemed at peace with the world, apart from the slightest hint of tension in the way he sat beneath the chains.

Theo caught my eye and winked at me. I looked away.

"Let the trial commence," Driesan said.

Florian's attorney laid out the most threadbare defense anyone could have possibly imagined. It wasn't that he was intentionally failing; there was simply no solid case to be made. Still, he made his efforts—he questioned my reliability, my sanity, my morality. He questioned my complicity. All of that was his right, and I closed my eyes throughout, trying not to feel it.

When he fell silent, the gathered Clementia all seemed to shrug.

Florian tested his chains idly after the defense was complete, measuring the scant millimeter of give.

Theo and Silvestra stood up.

"Inquisitors Wycliffe and Silvestra," Driesan said. "Go ahead and present."

Paradoxically, it was more difficult to sit through their recitation of the victim statements. My ears rang; for the most part, I watched Florian. Every so often, I would hear a direct quote I'd given, and I'd burn in shame. When they finished and it was time for questions, I focused again.

Driesan went first. "You never actually saw the accused commit any crimes," he said.

"No," said Silvestra, "but that's only because he slipped away from us when he went to murder Malise Tyrrhena and Adrien Desfourneaux. They can confirm that. Gennady Richter, a Vigil officer, was also there."

"I was there," Gennady crowed. "I was more than there. We opened him up like a rabbit on an altar. I'd do it again. I'll do it again right here."

Although the gathering ignored him utterly, I saw Florian blink, and Lady's mocking, hungry cackle made me lean down to pet her. She and Gennady had kept close to me, unwilling to let anyone else within striking distance.

"The two magicians in question have both been imprisoned in the Umbra," Driesan said. He looked at me, and with difficulty, I gave him no reaction.

"Falsely," Theo said. "Because of Albrecht, who provided inaccurate information. Rather—who *lied*. We've since confirmed that Desfourneaux was teaching during some of the heart attack deaths, and Tyrrhena was with other patients. Regrettably, the inquisition considered Albrecht's testimony and forged documents sufficient. No one checked."

I savored the wince of acute discomfort Driesan failed to conceal.

"Meanwhile, Albrecht has no alibi for any of them," Theo said.

Driesan turned to Florian. "Do you wish to confess?"

"Naturally," Florian breathed. I shuddered. Now that he had nothing left, all the artifice was stripped away; nothing remained of the man I'd known as my keeper except for a discarded mask. There was a febrile quality to the way he tilted his head, the way his silver gaze flickered to me.

I froze under it, fixed like a prey animal—

And widened my eyes at him innocently, giving him a prim wave.

He lunged at his chains. The witchfinders' mekhania all sparked in unison, cantrips popping in the air. He fell back, stunned.

"Naturally," he continued as if there had been no interruption, panting now. "The work was important."

Driesan raised his hands slightly—*See?*—and addressed the room at large. "I trust no one will require any extra debate, considering our . . . delay in handling this."

"You mentioned that Desfourneaux also confessed," one of the witchfinders said.

Theo turned to Florian. "You forced him to do so, didn't you?"

"He was easy to force," Florian said, drawing grimaces of distaste from the room. Lady let out a horrendous yowl.

Theo said, "There you have it. And it was a flimsy confession."

With that quibble satisfied, the officials stared around, coming to an unspoken consensus: case closed.

"It's a good thing," Driesan said tiredly. "To have this over with. The Chirurgeonate will be pleased to hear the news."

"And to no longer have an untested faction of the Clementia haunting its grounds," I said. "I hope the Pharmakeia will enjoy the same privilege."

I couldn't help myself.

Every person in the room, save Florian, looked at me with roughly the same expression—one of disappointment, but not surprise. I shrugged. They weren't going to retroactively convict me. I'd earned my tongue.

"Yes," Driesan said, after he'd reined in his visible temper. "We'll be leaving the magicians to their own devices, for the time being. The inquisition has been . . ."

"An experiment," Theo said hopefully.

The witchfinders looked at each other, but they let it pass.

I stood up and gave the group a bow—shallow, but sincere. I was grateful, but I'd given Florian and the inquisition quite enough of my time. "Thank you," I said, and made my way to the door. Gennady and Lady followed.

Florian turned his head minutely to track my progress. "Adrien."

Despite my better sense, I stopped. My breath caught.

"You will always be exactly what you are."

The words had the weight of divine condemnation. There was no greater insult. It was also the highest compliment Florian was capable of giving. "I know that," I said.

Gennady spat on the floor.

Florian closed his silver eyes, and we left.

"You're going to need to leave this nest of vipers," I said to Gennady as we walked together. I had grown too sick of the Clementia's ever-grinding gears to keep quiet. The thought of Florian in prison brought me little comfort now that I had felt the coldness of those cells.

Gennady shook his head. "There's nowhere else for me, and there are always going to be soldiers," he said. "Soldiers and witches in chains."

I knew I had no choice, for both our sakes, but to refuse to cede that ground.

〜

Returning to work was a surreal experience. Driesan had already told me that the Pharmakeia had never considered me guilty, that they'd nearly rioted over my imprisonment, but it was hard to believe. Part of me expected doubtful stares and whispers as soon as I set foot back on campus. Maybe some of my students and peers would be calling for the inquisitors to come take me again. It was all startlingly reminiscent of the aftermath of the Mulcaster conspiracy, when I had no idea who approved of me and who did not.

But I was greeted, in large part, with solicitous curiosity and admiration. Many of the details of the ordeal had spread. People were avid to know how the Umbra had been, how we'd managed to defeat the angel. Was the Umbra very cold inside? Were the chains very cruel? What was Florian like? Where was he now? My ego enjoyed a brief celebrity, and my self-consciousness painfully endured the same.

When I went to teach my classes again, the students were all supernaturally attentive, even though the material had nothing to do with what had happened. It was a nice change from usual, when attentions wandered often enough. *My* attention, for once, was constant as well—there was nothing to distract me, no sword hanging over my head. Chalk and ink and lead and paper have always done me an enormous amount of good, and so it was then.

I'd worried privately that the pain of the entire affair would send me spiraling after all, that Florian's lie would now become true. That, at least, I was spared, and my gratitude was keen.

After my last class one day, Xantha stayed behind to talk. She lingered near the lectern, hugging her books to her chest, waiting for me to speak first.

"I'm sorry I ended up going with the inquisitors," I said. "Even if it was necessary, I know you risked a great deal to try to stop it."

She shook her head. "I was just worried."

"Your faith in me was very heartening," I said hesitantly.

She seemed happy, set at ease. "Good. That's good. Everyone else had faith too, you know. Well—almost everyone else."

There would always be exceptions.

I turned to put away the chalk and erase the board. "The Pharmakeia's confidence means more than I can say."

"Listen," she said, "I was wondering."

I turned back to look at her.

"Would you take me on as a quadriviate?"

I don't usually help students with their postgraduate programs. After they finish their triviate courses, some might choose to stay with the Pharmakeia longer to pursue the quadrivium—but I hadn't been an adviser in years.

"Ah," I said.

"Please? I wouldn't need much help, and your specialties are everything I'm interested in. I'm graduating soon. I think you'd be a good choice."

"You have to consider—"

"Yes, yes," she said animatedly. "I know. You don't have to agree, but I'd appreciate it."

I couldn't deny her. "Of course." I reached for my bag and smiled at her. "We can talk more about it later. I'll help you put together a plan."

She beamed, and I felt like a fraud. Still, I waved the doubt away—as long as she was putting her trust in me, I might as well try to deserve it.

"I can't wait," she said, and bounded away. The pleasure of seeing her excited about the future nearly overwhelmed the terror of being a part of it.

I scheduled a private appointment with Gailhardt as soon as both of us could manage. It was a few hours before one of the group meetings; I hoped to get a double dose of treatment that day.

The first half of our time was spent on explanations of what had happened. I was, as I had often been recently, tired of explaining, but she deserved to know. I tried to keep any unnecessarily lurid details to a minimum. When I was finished, she sat in her chair looking at me with a mixture of horror and approval.

"Good," she said. "It's what he deserves."

Her righteous satisfaction warmed me. "You've been a good friend," I said. "Thank you for your defense when I confessed. I'm sorry I had to reject it."

She crossed her arms. "I thought I was going to lose control. The idea of those bastards taking you away again."

"Things will go back to normal now," I said, more a prayer than an assertion. "I'll just need help with my magic. And with—with the enchantment that's left."

She eyed me carefully, critically, trying to determine what sort of shape I was in. Evidently, she was satisfied. "We should focus mostly on the latter."

"I can't tell you how grateful I am—"

She clicked her tongue. "Hush. Magicians must stick together in these times. You don't need to thank me."

I quieted obediently, but I smiled at her, my very best smile.

She got up. "Ready?"

"Ready." Her touch when she put a hand to my temple was gentle, if businesslike. I didn't flinch.

The procedure this time wasn't cut short by the terrible shock of realization; she knew the tangle was there now, and she took her time beginning to unravel it. "It's already getting better, it seems," she said, after she had been casting for a while. "Time will play a part in healing."

"That always seems to be the case," I said. The effect was subtle, but I felt as though my thoughts were freer, lighter. Florian's grip was slipping the final few degrees.

We lapsed into silence while she finished up. When she let go of me, I felt a small trickle of power like a single speck of blood at an injection site, but the pain was even fainter than that. "That should do you well enough until the meeting," she said.

"Thank you."

"Speaking of," she said archly.

I found myself grinning.

"I'm glad about Oliver. The two of you seemed to be getting along very well during those early meetings."

"Were we that obvious?"

"Of course you were," she said. "You're welcome."

"I suppose you did introduce us," I said, happy enough to give her the credit.

There was an awkward pause while she decided whether or not to say what was on her mind. She did. "It was about time you stopped pining after Leynault."

Casmir. I hadn't thought of him at all, I realized, with some amount of guilt. "Was everyone at the Pharmakeia aware of that?"

"Not everyone. Just those among us with even the barest powers of observation."

"Well. I'm sure when Casmir comes back, he'll be relieved to find that I'm no longer such a nuisance."

She reached over to give me a bracing nudge and sat back down at her desk, neatening a stack of paper. "One thing at a time."

"I think I have more friends than I realized before," I said.

"Good of you to notice."

"That hasn't always been the case. Give me some time to adjust."

Her demeanor softened. It was strange on her. "You'll have all the time you need now."

Not *all* the time. All the time until the next disaster, more likely—but that caveat was nothing new. I nodded my agreement anyway and stood up.

"I'll see you later tonight," Gailhardt said, checking her watch in response. "I think we have a full roster for this group meeting. They'll be glad; people asked after you when you stopped coming."

"I'll try not to take up too much of everyone else's treatment time," I said.

She waved me out the door. "As if I'd let you. Go on."

I went, eager to get home and rest before I had to return to the Pharmakeia for the meeting.

Gailhardt's gathering started off quite well. The others were, as Gailhardt predicted, happy to see me. They were all kind about not demanding too many details of the incident from me; it was nice to slip back into the routine of the meeting unchallenged. Shortly, it was time for us all to demonstrate our progress.

Oliver stood in the middle of the circle of chairs, holding out the glass of water in front of himself and squinting at it. Slowly but surely, by infinitely small degrees, the surface of the water began to rise up on one side, lopsided, defying gravity. "There," he said with satisfaction, and dropped the spell. He seemed winded nearly immediately, but his smile didn't fade.

The rest of us applauded, Gailhardt and me with the most enthusiasm. "I don't see what's so special about that," Mary muttered under her breath as she clapped. Alain nudged her disapprovingly.

It was marvelous to see Oliver improve. It pleased me nearly as much as my own progress did. He came to sit back down next to me, and I beamed at him.

"Your turn," he said. "Go on."

I hadn't used any significant power since healing Florian—since bending him to my will. Part of me was afraid that I'd suddenly discover that the ability had left me entirely. I'd ventured where I shouldn't have; maybe the universe would see fit to punish me for it.

But Gailhardt had done good work. I raised a hand and called my lightning; even after I waited for a heavy moment, there was no tangled recoil. It hurt, but not badly. I twirled the bolt and let it dissipate into lovely sparks.

The subsequent applause did make me feel vaguely condescended to—it was nothing as impressive as what I *should* have been capable of—but I forced myself into the group spirit and bowed briefly before taking my chair again. "So striking," Oliver said, watching me with uncomplicated fondness.

"Flattery will get you everywhere," I said dryly. "Just don't abuse the strategy, for my sake."

"No promises."

I'd been the last person to show off my progress. Gailhardt stood in the middle of the circle holding an ether meter; she put the instrument down on the nearest table and dusted her hands together with satisfaction. "A very productive meeting today," she said. "Good work from all of you. This study is more successful than I'd dared to hope."

"You'll let us read any papers you write about it, I hope," I said. "It seems only fair."

She laughed. "You'll be the first to see them. In the meantime, it's getting late. I'll see you all next time."

"So," Oliver said, as the meeting dispersed. Everyone murmured *goodbyes* to each other, filing out into the dim Pharmakeia hallways one by one.

"So?" I echoed.

"Will you come back to my apartment tonight?"

Up ahead, Mary heard him and snickered before speeding up to give us some privacy. I passed a hand over my eyes.

Although it was a clear effort, Oliver valiantly resisted saying anything further.

"Come back to do what?" I said, just to stall—to prolong the moment.

He rearranged his expression into one of absolute neutrality, utterly innocent. "Oh, we'll see."

I stopped walking. "That's fine," I murmured, once I'd recovered my ability to speak. "Of course."

He tilted his head. "Just fine?"

There was a terrible pause while I fought my paralysis. "I mean I'm happy," I said meekly.

"You're not so used to this, are you?" he said.

I pulled my hair a little. "I'm not."

We walked again. "You don't *have* to come with me," he said. "You do know that?"

My urge toward self-sabotage has limits. "I can't tell you how much I want it," I said, "but I can show you. Take me home, and I'll show you."

He went quiet, grinning, watching me sidelong. Eventually, he revealed the sum total of what he'd been thinking about: "You do look nice tonight."

We rounded the last corner out of the Pharmakeia, and Oliver set our course for Deme Lettia. I assumed he lived near the theater. "You know just what to say," I told him. "If I didn't know better, I'd think it was all calculated."

He shook his head. "No calculation. I'm just that good."

Inanely, I regretted never having eaten the baklava he'd brought me before. We enjoyed a companionable lull until we reached his apartment. He lived on the first floor, and it was a nice building—clean, not dangerously tall, with plenty of windows and a well-maintained coat of green paint. He led me into his unit with an ironic, dramatic sweep of one hand. "My kingdom," he said. "I know it's not much."

It was cozy more than small—whatever he made as a lead actor was enough to keep things comfortable. In truth, the decor was hideous; every piece of furniture was a different garish, searing color. There were more than a few chintzes. But he had bookshelves lining the walls, and this repaired a great deal of the offense. Mostly plays, I noticed, when I went over to inspect the spines.

"I thought you might like those," Oliver said, watching me happily.

"I do. You'll have to point me toward some of your favorites one day."

"We can make that our pillow talk."

A small gray cat stalked out of the bedroom and came up to me, rubbing against my shins. I bent down to scratch its head.

"Colette," Oliver said, sounding almost anxious. "Isn't she pretty? Do you like cats?"

I decided that I did. "Of course."

"Oh, thank goodness."

I had to laugh. "Were you really worried about that?"

He scooped the cat up for a moment to kiss her head before letting her down again. "My ex-girlfriend hated her. Always tried to convince me to get rid of her."

"How terrible," I said, more than a little amused.

Colette waved her tail and went into the kitchen as soon as she was done with being admired. Oliver followed—and shut her inside.

As soon as there was nothing to distract me from Oliver, I remembered why he'd brought me to his apartment. It hadn't been to meet his cat. We stood there, neither of us quite looking at the other, until I cleared my throat. "So—"

"Do you still want . . ."

The hesitance gave him a wonderful glow. "Stars and saints," I said. "I'm not going to change my mind *that* quickly."

He reached for me, drawing me a step closer. I weathered the unwelcome echo that sounded in my mind: Florian's voice, patient, benevolent, so unsuited to the lethal magnetism of his touch. I went still.

Oliver brushed a hand over my cheek, pausing. "Hmm?"

"I thought of you," I said. "When I could. To try to drown him out."

Before he could respond, before I could allow Florian to ruin this for us even now, I took him by the collar. "Don't stop."

His lips were at my throat before I finished speaking. I made a tiny sound, remembering for the moment my recent strangulations—but the hesitation passed instantly.

It was torture to keep myself still while he gifted me with two small love bites. By the time he paused to examine his work, I'd run out of patience.

"Quickly," I demanded, taking his hand and pulling him toward his bedroom.

He laughed and hurried along.

I fell into single-minded concentration, until I realized that my shoes were off, my glasses were on the nightstand, Oliver was tossing my jacket away—it had happened in what felt like an instant.

Once my jacket was discarded on the floor, my deck of Astragestum cards slipped out of one of the pockets, bound by string.

"Oh," Oliver said. "You kept those."

"Of course."

He leaned over and plucked a single card from the middle of the deck.

The Grand Clepsydra in the Court of Wonders, upright. Certainty. Constancy. Commitment.

"A good draw?" Oliver asked.

I nodded. "Put those away," I said. "Superstition. Pay attention to me."

So he tucked away the deck and took off my shirt.

He traced a lightning fractal across my chest. I squirmed. "Does it hurt?" he said.

"Often."

"Will you be annoyed if I say they suit you?"

"Not at all," I said. "I do cultivate an aesthetic."

He found that hysterical; he buried a laugh in my shoulder. "I know you do," he said, as I helped work on his buttons. "Your cufflinks are shaped like lightning bolts."

"I'm happy," I said quietly.

He stopped undressing, but that was more out of respect than hesitance. "So am I."

The instinct to try to fold our clothes vanished. I slung an arm over my face to hide my flush, shot through with desire.

When I glanced back up, he was looking me over admiringly. "You and I are going to have so much fun," he said. And he was right.

∼

Oliver was very good, and it had been some time for me, so I kept nothing whatsoever of my dignity, and I minded not in the least.

∼

I wanted to talk with him too much to fall asleep afterward, although the temptation was real. "Can you go get one of those plays from the living room?" I said after we'd cleaned up, stifling a yawn and nestling back in the tangled sheets.

He groaned. "Really? I have to get up again?"

I batted my lashes comically, hoping to amuse. "Please?"

He hauled himself up and went to get the book, settling down heavily next to me with it once he returned. "Here. Are you satisfied?"

"Incredibly. Read to me."

"Bossy!"

I hesitated, dropping my playful imperiousness. "Do you mind?"

In response, he opened the book and flipped to a dog-eared page. "We can start with *Starcrossed*," he said. "I won't even have to look at the words."

He read to me, putting on different voices for each character, waving his hands dramatically whenever a scene called for some emphasis. I watched him, my attention flickering in and out; for the most part, I followed the story, but there was a significant part of me that was dedicated simply to looking at him.

We fell asleep like that, eventually, with the book discarded to one side and my head on his chest. I hadn't slept so soundly in years.

Biographical Note

Madeleine Nakamura is a writer, editor, and lifelong fantasy devotee. She began writing her first book the day she realized a computer science degree wasn't happening. Her debut novel, *Cursebreakers*, was awarded a Kirkus Star. She is based in Los Angeles, California.